I0523337

Praise for the Caught Up in Love Series

Caught Up in RAINE

"O'Connor's contemporary romance is very realistic and will tug on the heartstrings of probably more readers than she expected...Jillian and Raine have faced a lifetime's worth of secrets and heartbreaks...you'll want to cheer them on until the very end." *~RT Book Reviews*

"The plot is driven by a May-December premise that is blown away in the sexy love scenes." *~Library Journal*

"For all the contemporary romance fans out there, this book is for you." *~Night Owl Reviews*

"Urban fantasy author O'Connor (*Trinity Stones*) branches out into romantic women's fiction with a sexy tale of angst, guilt, love, and hate." *~Publishers Weekly*

"LG O'Connor had me at "hello" with this plot. Phenomenal writing skills at work is what has made Caught Up in Raine a hard to beat Romance for 2016..." *~HEA Romances with a Little Kick Blog*

"This story is both beautiful and haunting...I loved every second of this sexy, sweet and romantic book!!!" *~The Romance Reviews, Top Pick, 5 stars*

"O'Connor delivers a unique women's fiction story packed with emotion, humor and sexiness. I could not turn the pages quickly enough…" ~**Caridad Pineiro,** *NY Times & USA Today* **Bestselling Romance Author**

"WOW! What an absolutely fantastic story! I absolutely fell in love with Raine, and wanted Jillian for a girlfriend! Well written and very relevant as a contemporary romance with two amazing, memorable characters." ~*Carla Susan Smith, Author of A Vampire's Promise*

Rediscovering Raine

"The writing is gorgeous; it's a beautifully touching story that warms the heart and gives you hope. I am truly in awe of Ms. O'Connor who could make me feel so much in just a few pages."~ ***Book Obsessed Chicks Book Club***

"Proving herself a force to be reckoned with in the world of contemporary romance, L.G. O'Connor does not disappoint with this addition to her series." ~*Amazon Review*

Caught Up in Rachel

"If *Caught Up In Raine* is the cake, and *Rediscovering Raine* the frosting, then *Caught Up In Rachel* is the decoration on top. L.G. O'Connor has once again proved herself an exceptional story-teller, able to capture all the fear and wonderment of becoming a new parent with this welcome addition to her series. A remarkable gift for inviting her readers to experience all the joys and heartache of her characters, I can hardly wait to see what she has in store for future novels." ~ *Amazon Review*

"A beautiful and inspiring story full of tender moments." ~*Love at 1st Read*

Caught Up in Love

Three Women. One Story.

A unique blend of contemporary romance and romantic women's fiction, the multi-award-winning *Caught Up in Love* series centers around three New Jersey women: romance writer Jillian Grant, her sister, Kitty, and Kitty's daughter, Jenny. All part of a family that is plagued by loss, each woman harbors her own guilty secret and must confront her past to find redemption and surrender her heart for a second chance to get caught up in love.

Jillian & Raine's Story
Caught Up in RAINE (Book #1)
Rediscovering Raine (Book #1.1)
Caught Up in Rachel (Book #1.2)
Caught Up in Raine Collection (All of the above)

Jenny & Devon's Story
Shelter My Heart (Book #2)
One Summer Day (Prequel Novelette)

Kitty & John's Story
Surrender My Heart (Book #3)

COMING SOON
Caught Up in Christmas (A novella)
Join Jillian, Kitty, Jenny, and their families for one last tale, and the bittersweet conclusion to the Caught Up in Love series.

Sign up for my newsletter at www.lgoconnor.com for release updates and extras!

Shelter My HEART

Caught Up in Love
Book 2

LG O'CONNOR

COLLINS-YOUNG PUBLISHING

Dedication

To all my readers and fans ~ you are the ones who make this all worthwhile. Thank you for sharing my stories and for letting them into your lives!

Chapter 1

Jenny

"WHAT'S THE MATTER, Jen?" Russ asks, his voice all early-morning gravel. My fiancé studies me from under a half-lidded gaze from the other side of our mussed bed, his cheek still resting on the pillow.

I glance over as I stuff my suitcase for a two-week visit home to New Jersey and prepare myself for the inevitable. "What do you mean?" I ask, trying but failing to sound natural.

He half sniffs, half chuckles. "Did you just hear yourself? You're wearing that frown you get when we fight. What did I do? Tell me."

The downside of being with someone for six years: they know you too well. But this time, it isn't about something he did; it's about something I did.

He gives me a sleepy smile and slithers across the bed toward me. The covers fall away from his bronzed shoulders, and a shaft of light from the rising sun casts a shimmering halo of deep red over his unruly mop of dark-brown curls. There was a time when this vignette would've sent my heart fluttering and had me reaching for my camera to capture that shot.

But not lately.

"Come on, Jen," he cajoles. "Tell me." I stare down into his swoon-worthy green eyes on the other side of my suitcase, happy for the barrier between us. Double-edged sword, that, being with someone for six years. I take a deep breath and release the hounds. "I quit Gustav yesterday."

As I anticipated, it takes only half a second for Russ's eyes to widen with a look that's a mixture of panic and horror. He scrambles into a sitting position on top of the rumpled sheets. "What do you mean, you quit your job?" he shouts. A flush creeps up his neck. He crawls away to sit on the opposite edge of the bed. "Why would you do that without asking me first?"

I cringe and pluck seven days of clean underwear from our secondhand bureau and press them into my suitcase. "I'm sorry, I didn't want to upset you," I whisper and drag the suitcase to the foot of the bed. How can I explain to my fiancé the lack of oxygen in my lungs when I wake up in the morning to go to work or the painful gasp that passes through my lips whenever I look at the small diamond on my finger? Or how the high-windowed walls of the sleek San Francisco apartment we're arguing in—funded in part by his parents— are choking the life out of me?

I grab the last of my clothes and glance at him out of the corner of my eye from behind a curtain of hair, afraid to say anything else for fear of blurting out things I can't take back.

"Yeah, well," he snaps, "I love the way you waited until right before you hop on a plane to Jersey to tell me you quit your job. Brilliant, Jen." His shoulders slump like a deflated balloon. "We're a couple. You're supposed to tell me about things like this *before* you do them."

I grind my teeth at the lecture, even though he has a point, and throw up my hands. "Why does it have to be so serious all the time? We're a year out of college. Shouldn't we be enjoying our lives? Going to bars, getting drunk, traveling and seeing the world instead of becoming our parents at twenty-three?"

He twists his body to face me and glares. "What the—
Seeing the world? This coming from someone who's wasting
her two-week vacation to go home and babysit." He smacks
the side of his head and snarls, "Oh, that's right! You don't
have a job, so it's not really a two-week vacation."

My jaw clenches and my neck fills with heat. I curse the
tears that spring to my eyes. Just like Russ to lash out and
belittle me. I swallow hard. "That's not fair. I love my family. I
thought you did, too . . ."

Asshole. I'm not going home to babysit. I'm going home to
help my aunt Jill and uncle Raine with my new baby cousin,
who is expected to enter the world via C-section if she doesn't
arrive by Thursday. Not that my aunt really needs me. She
has my mom, who brings a new intensity to the word
maternal, to dote on her endlessly. But I want to be there. The
truth is, I miss home and need some breathing room to get my
head straight. At least I can be useful at the same time.

Russ has the good sense to look sheepish. "You know I
do," he mumbles and jerks his fingers through his unruly
hair.

I dab at my eyes. "I still have my part-time job at the
gallery," I offer, grabbing my makeup bag.

He gives a derisive sniff and turns away. "That wouldn't
even keep us in groceries."

Again with the belittlement, as if my contribution isn't
worthy. Helplessness and inferiority land like a blow to my
middle. That's always been the crux of our issue, hasn't it? If I
can't live up to his definition of success, he rubs it in my face.

The copywriting position I quit at Gustav Publishing
didn't hold much in the way of a large paycheck like his cool
tech job at Nanotekx, a Silicon Valley start-up promising
Microsoft-level riches when it goes public. But at least Gustav
was a job.

Not that I hadn't needed some help to get it. They

interviewed me thanks to Aunt Jill's best friend and agent, Brigitte. But I'll never know whether it was a favor to her or my own merit that secured me the job. Russ considered my position respectable enough to discuss at parties with our friends, but it wasn't the kind of job that paid large rents in the city.

Now it won't pay for anything at all.

Tears prick my eyelids as I wrestle with the zipper to close my suitcase. I bite my lip so that I won't cry and ignore the unhappiness that gnaws at my insides. A sunbeam catches my diamond, and the reflection bounces off the white walls of the bedroom in a kaleidoscope of happy colors, mocking me with emotions I should feel but don't.

I haul the suitcase off the bed. "I'll find another job when I get back," I say with false calm to his bare back and dipped head, wiping away an escaping tear before he can see it.

"You sure you want to come back?" he whispers, still not looking at me.

I freeze. Do I? Russ is the only guy I've ever loved—my high school and college sweetheart. I still love him, I remind myself, even though the thought leaves me hollow. "Of course I do," I reply finally, hoping I'm not lying.

Abandoning my bag, I round the bed to stand next to Russ on the other side. As a peace offering, I attempt to bridge the gap between us by touching his hair. The curly strands feel good under my palm. He flinches, and I jerk my hand away as if I've been burned.

"I'm sorry. I should've told you last night," I say, trying to sound as if I mean it while hiding my hurt at his retreat, well deserved as it may be. The truth is that I didn't want to hang around for the fallout and be forced to commit to decisions I'm not ready to make. Whatever I decide, I want it to be well thought through.

He meets my eyes and gives me a recriminating look. "We can't get by on just my salary. My parents will wig if I hit them up for any more cash."

My anger flares. "Why would you need to do that? What about that big bonus you said was coming?" God knows he's already spent some of it on new electronics.

"That's still months away," he mutters, avoiding my eyes.

"Then let's move someplace cheaper," I say, a suggestion he's rejected more than once.

He closes his eyes and grinds his teeth. "Let's save it for when you get back, okay?"

My cell phone chimes across the room, signaling that the cab is waiting downstairs.

"I gotta go. I'll call you when I get there." Anxious to leave, I lean in for a hug but turn my mouth away. I can't bear to kiss him when he's angry.

He gives me a half-hearted squeeze, obviously feeling the same way. "Give my congratulations to Jillian and Raine."

I'll call him later and apologize after we both cool down. Leaving Russ angry unsettles me but not enough to interfere with the relief that washes over me when I get into the taxi and relax into the seat.

As the cab pulls away, I take off my ring and draw in the first full breath I've taken in weeks. I close my eyes, and my lungs fill with the luxurious feeling of air.

Chapter 2

Jenny

I RUN THROUGH Denver International airport, pressing the phone to my ear and trying to keep my backpack from flying off my shoulder into a passerby.

"There's been a *complication*," my mother says, an unmistakable tremor in her voice. I recognize the tone. The last time I heard it was ten months ago when my great-aunt Vera died.

Ice water rolls through my veins. Even after all the therapy, I still suffer from extreme anxiety because of the death that has surrounded our family; someone close to me has died every two years since I was sixteen, making four funerals in total. My aunt Jill thinks our family is cursed by the specter of death. Maybe. But what haunts me is the knowledge that, in hindsight, I should've done more for the first one who died. The other deaths just feel like punishment.

Let's hope I'm not due for another dose.

"What kind of complication?" I ask, struggling for breath. "How serious?"

I scan the gate numbers, looking for B46. The incoming flight was so late I missed my first connection. I'm heading to my second. Hopefully, I won't miss that one, too.

"Aunt Jillian's in the emergency room . . . she's bleeding."

My heart drops and my voice climbs an octave. "Is she going to be all right?"

"I hope so, honey. I'm sorry—I didn't mean to burden you," my mom says thickly, her words followed by a pause and a muffled blowing sound. "Just text us the new flight number, and Daddy will meet you in baggage claim when you get here."

"Okay," I choke out over the rising lump in my throat. "Gotta go." Sweat drips down my back as I arrive at the gate and join the end of the line. I shove my dying cell phone into my backpack and wait. The thought of not getting on this flight makes me close to crazy.

My aunt's unexpected pregnancy at age forty-three has been a rough ride for her, especially since it's her first child. My thoughts take a morbid turn. If anything happens to Aunt Jillian or the baby before I get home, I won't be able to live with myself. At this point, I'm not sure I can survive any more funerals.

"How may I help you?" asks the smiling woman behind the airline counter.

I hand over my crumpled itinerary. "I missed my connection to Newark. They told me I could get onto this flight."

The woman's fingers tap-tap-tap over the keyboard. After a moment, she frowns and hands back my flight info. "I'm sorry. All the comparable seats are full."

Panic grips me. "Wait. What? They told me to come down here to get rebooked. I missed my connection because *your* airplane was delayed." My finger jabs the paper. "You need to book me on a flight . . . now." Don't these people talk to each other?

Taking back the itinerary, she resumes her mad finger tapping. She sighs a few minutes later. "Everything is booked for tonight. I can get you into a coach seat first thing tomorrow morning."

"No! You don't understand. I have to leave tonight," I say, unable to rein in my panic.

"I'm sorry. The only thing I have is a first-class seat. I can upgrade you for four hundred dollars."

"I don't have four hundred dollars," I squeak, a moment before I burst into tears. My finances consist of a maxed-out credit card, the $28 in my pocket, and another $234 in my bank account. Nothing has gone right since I woke up this morning. Nothing. And now the aunt I love as much as my own mother is in danger.

"You don't understand," I blubber. "My aunt and her unborn baby are in the hospital and they could die. I have to get there!" I'm beyond feeling pathetic or ashamed. The Vault of Black Doom that holds my deepest fears cracks open, its jaws snapping at my heels.

A look of sympathy passes over the woman's face. "I'm sorry. I wish I could help you. The best I can do is a flight tomorrow."

An arm reaches past me and drops a platinum credit card onto the counter. "I'll pay for her upgrade," says a calm male voice from behind me.

I wipe my eyes and turn. A guy with sandy-colored hair and nice blue eyes stands behind me, wearing a business suit and a shy smile. He couldn't be more than a few years older than me. He's on the tall side — I have to look up to meet his eyes. No small feat since I'm five foot nine and spend a fair bit of time looking over the tops of people's heads, even when wearing flats as I am now.

"I can't," I whisper.

He raises a brow and nods. "You can." He steps up next to me and pushes the card closer to the airline attendant. "Please, take this."

I'm at a loss, stuck between guilt and relief. "Um . . . I'll pay you back," I say. Shrugging my pack off my shoulder, I rummage in the outside compartment to find my journal and a pen. I turn to a blank page and thrust the journal out with a fine-point Sharpie. "Please. Give me your name and number?" I'll ask for an address when I call.

He shakes his head. "That's not necessary."

"Please?" I say again, giving him a wan smile. This time a flush rises in my cheeks. God, I feel both grateful and foolish at the same time.

"Here's your card," the woman says to him as she pushes back his plastic. Then she glances my way and hands me a boarding pass. "And this is yours, Ms. Lynch. Enjoy your flight."

He sighs, then reaches into his suit pocket and pulls out a business card. "Here. It's really not necessary." All of a sudden, he seems older … more mature. Maybe I've misjudged; maybe he's closer to thirty. Behind his warm smile, I see a touch of sadness and recognize the emotion I know so intimately.

I glance at the card.

Devon Soames | Kingsbridge Industries | 973-555-4678

"Thanks, *Devon*." I let his name slide off my tongue.

He gives me a parting smile and a tip of his head before turning his attention back to the airline attendant.

Flipping the creamy card in my hand a couple of times, I hunt for a plug to charge my phone and come up short. Abandoning my search, I squeeze into an open chair in the packed waiting area and say a prayer that my suitcase makes it to Newark with me. Glancing at the business card once more before I tuck it away, I notice the odd sparseness of information. Who doesn't have an e-mail address or a social media presence in this day and age?

Then it hits me. It's a modern-day calling card. Only given as a courtesy to someone he already knows … as a reminder. It isn't an invitation but rather a polite barrier to contact. Chances are that the closest anyone ever gets to him using this

number is a pleasant-sounding administrative assistant.
Chances are he will never take my call.
Intrigued, I wonder, *Who is Devon Soames, anyway?*

Chapter 3

Devon

"HOW DID IT go?" asks my twin sister, Leticia. A thread of anxiety seeps through her calm voice. Holding the cell to my ear, I step away from the boarding lane with my stuff and cup a hand over my other ear to hear her better over the airport din.

"As well as can be expected," I say, wishing I didn't have a six-hour flight ahead of me and wanting nothing more than to curl up with a can of beer and a bowl of chips in front of a game on TV. But that flawed desire wouldn't become reality anytime soon even if I were at home. Beer and chips are off-limits and there is nothing in season right now worth watching. But a guy can dream, even when dreaming remains a dangerous prospect.

"Meaning what?" she asks.

"Meaning I think they were suitably impressed." *Fooled was more like it.* I recount my meeting with the board and the highlights of my trip to one of the biotech companies held by Kingsbridge Industries. Five or six more holdings are left to visit after this, and then my charade will temporarily end.

She releases a sigh of relief on the other end of the phone. "Good. That's good. We only have four months to go."

"Yeah, four months until I sign my future away in the name of family fealty," I mumble. *If I live that long*, I think, reminding myself that I'm doing this for my mom and Leticia. So they have a future. So they'll be taken care of. It doesn't matter how long I make it past that—as long as no one learns my secret before I'm sworn in as CEO.

"Dev, I'm sorry ...," she says softly. "I know there were things you wanted to do."

I pinch the bridge of my nose to ease the throbbing behind my eyes. "It's okay, Lettie."

The overhead speaker announces, "Final boarding, Flight 683 to Newark, New Jersey." I'm the only one left standing at the gate.

"I've got to board. I'll see you when I get home." I hang up and head for the plane.

The stewardess greets me with a warm smile and a look of relief. "Welcome aboard, sir," she says and closes the door behind me.

I spot my open first-class seat. A small smile unexpectedly touches my lips when I notice the dark, flowing hair of my seatmate as she huddles over something in her lap.

Ms. Lynch.

Lettie would've smiled at my impulsive move to pay for Ms. Lynch's upgrade. When we were younger, Lettie always teased me about having the heart of a romantic. She thought I was a sucker for saving damsels in distress and trying to fix girls who were broken ... until I was the broken one.

I blame my quixotic streak on Lettie and all the games of make-believe we played as kids. Lettie dressing up as her favorite Disney character du jour and enlisting me as the knight or the prince—whichever one the story called for. My inducement? The cool toy sword she talked Mom into buying me one year for Christmas. To this day, I still have a fascination with swords and a collection hanging on my bedroom wall—the only place in the house Lettie would let me display them. Apparently I still save damsels in distress—something I haven't done in what feels like an eternity.

Ms. Lynch looks up from the window seat with wide blue eyes—startled—as I squeeze my carry-on into the overhead compartment. After pulling out a thick audit report to review on the flight home, I tuck my briefcase next to my carry-on. The report is equal parts work I have to do and a prop to keep from getting entangled in unwanted conversation.

I slip into the aisle seat next to her, struck by a mixture of discomfort and pleasure at the unanticipated surprise.

A pink tinge spreads across her cheeks, and she removes one of her earbuds. Soft rock music leaks out at the threshold of my hearing. "Um, hi," she says.

My lips tip up in a half smile before I can stop them. "Hi . . . Ms. Lynch," I say, feeling stiff with the formality of it, but it's all I have.

She breaks into a wide grin and sticks out her hand. "Jenny." Then she arches a brow and adds, "Unless you'd prefer I call you Mr. Soames?"

I chuckle and shake my head. "God, no. That would be just plain weird."

The stewardess stops next to us and retrieves Jenny's glass.

"Would it be possible to get a glass of water?" I ask.

"I'm sorry, sir. We're just about to take off. I can bring you something when beverage service resumes once we're in the air."

Jenny reaches down into her pack and hands me a bottle of water. "It's the least I can do," she says before I even realize it's for me.

"Thanks." A feeling of warmth spreads through me at the small kindness. I take a drink to satisfy my parched throat, one of the many symptoms I live with. Suppressing a smile, I place the bottle, capped, into the pocket of the seat in front of me.

The plane taxies and picks up speed. Jenny replaces her

earbud and gives me a quick smile before closing her eyes and relaxing into the leather seat.

My hands rest on top of the heavy report in my lap, and I do the same—close my eyes and relax into the seat as we head nose-up into the air. Drowsiness overtakes me and I drift off, not quite unconscious.

I think of the pretty girl next to me, wishing I had a normal life. Wishing I had the guts to do what normal guys do when they find themselves faced with this kind of opportunity. I feel the sides of my mouth droop. There I go down that wishing path again.

"Normal" and I don't live in the same world, I think just before sleep sweeps me under.

I wake with a start and turn my head toward the aisle to do a quick check for drool before facing front. All clear. Jenny is working on her computer next to me. The weight of the audit report presses into my lap, reminding me I have work to do. I pull down the tray and lay the document on top.

I turn the first sheet and stare at the tiny print.

"Can I get you a drink?" the stewardess asks as she sets down a napkin in front of me.

"What do you have in a red?" I ask, imagining Lucas, my private physician, with a reproving look on his face.

"Pinot Noir and Cabernet Sauvignon."

My jaw sets in silent rebellion. "Pinot, please."

"And you, miss?" she asks Jenny, who continues to type on her computer. I tap her on the shoulder. She looks up, startled, until she sees the expectant look on the stewardess's face.

She removes the music from one ear. "Diet cola, thanks."

The images on her screen catch my eye. Two photographs rest side by side. A couple. Their expressions are riveting. An unexpected feeling of longing overwhelms my senses, taking me aback. Good art does that to me. It's why I love to paint, doing it in the stolen moments when I'm not bound by some other duty. I think of my latest project, a half-finished canvas sitting on an easel in my shared art studio.

"Did you take those?" I ask.

She nods and touches the screen. "Last summer in my aunt's studio."

"They're good. You're a photographer?"

She gives me a small smile. "No. Nothing like that. They were originally shot for a book cover. My aunt Jill is an author." She points to the late-thirties/early-forties woman in the photo. "That's her. She's also a former fashion photographer. She put a camera in my hands when I was ten and taught me everything I know."

"Who's the guy?" I ask.

The side of her mouth quirks up. "My uncle Raine. But he was just her cover model then. They'd only met a day or two before these were taken."

My eyes pop wide. He looks about my age. "How old is he?"

She chuckles. "Yeah. Kind of weird, huh? He's twenty-five and my aunt Jill is forty-three. They're expecting their first child." Her smile fades. "It's been a complicated pregnancy."

I remember her distress at the counter. Her concern over her aunt and the baby got to me. Pain and loss are things I know too well.

"So I heard."

"I'm trying to decide which picture to blow up for their wedding present. I could use another opinion. Want to help?" she asks, her eyes glistening.

"Sure," I say before I have time to think too deeply on it. The Kingsbridge report can wait. "You made it sound like they were already married."

I'm not sure when the glass of wine arrived, but I take a swallow. The crisp notes hit my tongue in a rush on their way to my empty stomach.

She angles her computer so I can see her screen more

clearly. "They are. It's a long story. She wanted to wait until after Rachel was born to have the fancy wedding. But my uncle Raine didn't want the baby born out of wedlock, so they had a quick civil ceremony to make it legal when my aunt was eight months pregnant."

I eye the guy somewhat suspiciously, wondering if her aunt has money. In my world, marriage for financial gain is less the exception and more the rule. "Is he a good guy?"

Her face lights up. "Yeah. The best." Her finger traces them on the screen. "I've never seen two people more in love than they are. I saw it even before they did—in these pictures." A look of sadness settles around her eyes, as if she's suddenly remembered something, and a tear slowly slides down her cheek.

My chest tightens, and my hand twitches at my side. I sit frozen, unsure of what to do, feeling awkward. *She's a stranger*, I remind myself.

The tear falls, splashing onto the back of her hand. A second one follows. She hastily wipes them away, runs her wrist across her eyes, and sniffs.

I take a deep breath and contemplate my options. The worst she can do is shut me down. That's better than my ignoring the obvious and feeling like a coward. Despite my discomfort, I push forward and tentatively touch her shoulder. "Jenny, are you all right?"

"I'm sorry. It's been an awful day," she says as tears cascade down her cheeks.

I pull the napkin from under my drink and hand it to her. Before I can talk myself out of it, my eyes connect with hers, and I utter the words I've said a thousand times to Lettie. "Need a hug?" I hold my breath and wait for a response, hoping I didn't overstep any bounds.

She dabs the napkin under her eyes and nods. I resume breathing and wrap my arm around her; she leans over so her head rests on my shoulder.

Jenny feels far different from my sister in my arms, and she stirs things inside me my sister definitely does not. My lips rest atop her head. The fresh scent of flowers from her soft, silky hair fills my senses. A small feeling of triumph, as if I had passed over a personal hurdle, spreads through me for reaching out. I close my eyes and remain silent.

I can't tell Jenny it will be okay. I don't know if it will. Plus I gave up on happy endings four years ago, when life threw me some nasty curve balls.

Still, I'm happy to know that I haven't lost my appetite for rescuing the occasional damsel in distress.

Chapter 4

Jenny

"I'M SORRY," I say, as I regain my senses and push out of Devon's warm embrace and away from the woodsy male scent of his cologne. I could've rested my cheek on the lapel of his fine suit for the rest of the flight . . . happily.

Still, I feel like such an idiot for blubbering like that in front of him and letting him comfort me. The scene at the airport counter was embarrassing enough. I shift back into my seat and pick up my laptop from where it has slid onto the floor.

"Are you coming or going?" I ask to fill the dead air and to recover from my mortification over the sudden intimacy.

"I'm on my way home," he says softly, catching my eye. "What about you?" He seems a little less distant now that we've touched. I look to see if there's a flash of gold on any of his fingers and come up empty. If he's married, he's not wearing a ring.

"I'm going home, too," I say, putting my laptop away.

"Where's that?"

"Summit," I reply.

His eyebrows shoot up. "Really? Where in Summit?"

I give him a sideways glance "Tulip. Why?"

He shrugs. "I live on Essex."

Now it's my turn to be surprised. "Really? When did you graduate high school?"

He chuckles and presses his head into the headrest. "We definitely never met in high school, unless you went to an all-boys boarding school in England."

I'm not terribly shocked. My town has some stupid wealth. Not to mention he lives on the north side, where the real money is. But England? For the first time, I notice his white, straight teeth and the dimple that shows up when he smiles. "Uh ... no. Nothing so posh. Summit High School. My parents believe in getting the most out of their tax dollars."

"It's a good school," he says matter-of-factly. "I wouldn't have minded going there."

"You didn't answer my question." I give him a direct stare and ask what I really want to know. "So how old are you?"

He glances at me, his lips twitching as if he's fighting to suppress a smile. "That's a different question."

I can't help but grin, my black mood behind me. "Come on. Want me to guess?"

He clasps his hands. "Go for it."

I sit back and narrow my eyes, studying his face and clothes. The clothes are definitely expensive, so he's wealthy—or at least his parents are. *"Hmm."* I examine every detail. A fine head of sandy-blond hair, no receding hairline. Not much in the way of lines around his eyes. Clear eyes, blue. Full lips. Sensuous. Kissable. Shit, I move off his lips. Smooth neck, a nice square jaw. Tiny cleft in the chin. The backs of his hands are masculine and youthful, and his fingers are long and tapered.

He looks at me askew. "What's taking so long? You're making me feel like a lab specimen."

"Just studying you, like I would if I were commissioned to photograph you," I say, still squinting and taking him in. After a few moments, I smile. "Jury is in."

"Should I do a drum roll?" he teases.

"Well, now that I have a clue to your background, you could be younger than I thought. Fine clothes don't necessarily mean you're established in your career. Initially I thought you were closer to thirty—especially after you pulled out that super-serious encyclopedia-size document you have on your tray. No one under the age of thirty would have a job requiring them to read that."

"Thirty?" he gasps, then covers his eyes and groans. "That old?"

I chuckle. "I've since revised my estimate down."

He removes his hand from his eyes. "Thank God. Where'd you land?"

I bite the inside of my mouth, a little nervous to say what I think and why.

"Well?" he asks, raising his eyebrows.

"I was going to say twenty-six because there's this pain you carry right here," I say softly and hover my fingertip over the smooth skin next to his eye. His lips part and he stays silent. My hand falls away without touching him. "But then I think, maybe not. I have the same thing and I'm only twenty-three. So I settled on twenty-four."

A smile creeps onto his lips and then fades. The pain and sadness now sit clearly on the surface of his face, unmasked by my assessment. A twinge of regret hits me for being so honest. His pain is his business, not mine. "Thanks," he says.

"For what?"

He takes my hand and squeezes it briefly. "For seeing me."

AN HOUR LATER, we're well beyond our awkward moment. I coaxed him into talking about his favorite literary works—*The Great Gatsby* and anything by Ernest Hemingway (God knows why)—before we moved into film.

"Oh, come on, really?" I ask, horrified that he considers *Dawn of the Dead* a seminal twentieth-century film.

"It's a classic," he insists. "It scared the piss out me when I was ten. I couldn't sleep for a month. That's the mark of a great horror film."

My face freezes in disgust. "How did you find that movie, anyway? Didn't it come out when our parents were growing up?"

He gives me a sour look. "See? You've heard of it. I bet you've heard of *The Wizard of Oz*, too."

"Of course I have; hasn't everyone?" I ask.

Folding his arms over his chest, he looks smug and says, "Yeah, well, that came out even before your parents were born. That's the point of a classic — everyone's heard of it."

I crack a smile. "You win."

He grins and punches the air. "Yes. Victory."

I lean back on the headrest and gaze at him. Once he relaxed, his handsome face melted into boyish youth. I wonder what he looks like dressed in jeans and a T-shirt, and if the hairs on his arms are the same sandy color as the hair on his head.

He turns and catches me staring. "What?"

"Nothing." I smile and ask, "If I call the number on your card, will you answer? I'm serious about paying you back."

A flicker of surprise passes over his face, and then he puts his hand out palm-up. "Do you still have it?"

I dig it out of the front pocket of my pack and give it to him.

He takes a pen from inside his jacket, flips over the card, and scribbles a number on the back. "To answer your question, no. That one's answered by my service. This one's answered by me. Text or call."

I take it back and stare at the handwritten number.

"Jenny?"

"Hmm?"

"Look at me," Devon says. His eyes are big and blue. They remind me a little of my uncle Raine's. "I don't want your money."

"I know, and I don't care," I say. "A debt is a debt." I don't mention that I may need to borrow the money from my parents. If he knew that, he definitely wouldn't take it. I have to say I really like that about him.

I tuck the card in my backpack, and one thing is clear now that I've spent time in his company: my issues with Russ are deeper than I thought.

Chapter 5

Devon

BY THE TIME the driver loads my bags into the limo and I climb into the back seat, it's nearly ten-thirty. I'm bone weary. The fifteen-minute ride to Summit passes in a blur as I doze on and off in the darkness, thinking about the plane ride home.

I'll admit I felt a pang as Jenny and I parted ways at the entrance to baggage claim. Given that she's hell-bent on paying me back for the upgrade, I figure chances are good I'll hear from her within the next two weeks, while she's home.

Not that it should matter. But suddenly it does, even if she gets in touch just as a friend. That's the best course of action for me anyway.

Lettie opens the front door wearing yoga clothes before I can pull out my key. Her pale-blonde hair is pulled back in a ponytail. Without makeup she looks about fifteen. At least to me.

"I saw the car drop you off," she says.

I give her a peck on the cheek. "How's Mom tonight?" I ask as I wheel in my bag and set it inside the door, dropping my briefcase next to it.

"Good. The night shift nurse came on at ten," she says.

"Mom's still a little upset that Sadie isn't Gladys." Her former nurse retired last month.

I shrug. "Nothing we can do about that."

She squeezes my arm. "Her bath should be done by now. Why don't you go see her and then meet me in the kitchen for a snack? We can catch up."

My stomach rumbles at the thought of food. I slept through the meal on the plane. Later, when the flight attendant offered me the special low-sodium meal, I waved it off.

"Sounds good," I lie. Honestly, I'd rather go straight to bed hungry after visiting my mom than rehash any more of my visit to Denver. I want to savor the memory of those hours on the plane when I actually enjoyed myself in someone else's company without the weight of my responsibilities perched like an anvil on my shoulder.

I head to the west wing and my mom's suite. We moved her here after the nursing home owned by Kingsbridge went bankrupt over two years ago. Millions of dollars were embezzled and never found. They could never prove which member of the executive team had done it. My father's will didn't provide anything beyond a stipend to augment the full coverage of her care at the Kingsbridge-owned facility. That left the burden on Lettie and me. We pay for her round-the-clock care with a portion of the modest annual stipends we get from our trust funds. Luckily, the expenses for the house and all my father's properties are taken care of out of an estate fund . . . control of which goes to the eldest male heir when he turns twenty-five.

Right now that's me, much to the chagrin of my illegitimate half brother, Phillip. A bastard in more ways than one.

After a quick knuckle-rap on the door, I crack it open.

Sadie, an elderly black woman, sits beside my mother's bed with an open romance novel facedown on the table next to her. The hospital bed is tilted up. My mom's long steel-gray hair fans out on the pillow. Her eyes light up when she sees me, but only half her face lifts in a smile. The right side of her body lies slack and withered. Her right hand, an atrophied, curled claw, sits frozen in numb oblivion. She beckons me with her left.

She lost her ability to speak with the stroke, but that doesn't mean she can't communicate. One blink means yes and two mean no, and then there is the pointing and hand squeezing. Between us, we've figured out our own language.

"Can you give us a few moments?" I ask Sadie, not wanting to speak freely in front of staff.

Sadie takes her book and smiles. "I'll be in the sittin' room out front in case you need me."

The door closes with a soft click.

I return my mom's smile and sit on the edge of the bed next to her. Taking her good hand between mine, I lean in and kiss her forehead. "I just got home."

She squeezes my hand and wrinkles her left brow.

"It went well," I say. "Lettie did a great job of prepping me." I shake my head. "She should've been born a boy. She's better at this than I am—and she enjoys it." Lettie is three minutes older. If she were male or if my father hadn't been such a patriarchal sot when he was alive, she would be the one taking over as CEO.

Mom dips her head and squeezes my hand again.

"I know you don't like when I say things like that, but it doesn't make it less true."

She takes her hand from mine and circles her finger in the air in front of my abdomen. Leave it to my mom to remind me of things I'd like to forget.

"My follow-up with Lucas is tomorrow." If I never saw the inside of a hospital or a doctor's office again, I'd be a happy man.

My mom's fingers wave in a flutter of motion, then trickle

downward. My eyebrows head into a frown, but I do my best to freeze them in place. "The gala?"

Our family foundation holds an annual fund raiser for the hospital. At least that's what it is on the surface. It's really a society check-in with a modern version of Mrs. Astor's Four Hundred. This year, the board members of Kingsbridge will be there to see for themselves if I'm still alive and kicking and in good enough condition to take on the mantle of the family business.

She blinks once. Yes. The gala.

"I think that's what Lettie wants to talk about downstairs when we're done," I say.

With a smile she points to my heart and raises her left brow in question.

"No," I say softly. "No one special to bring this year." As I say it, I think for a second of Jenny and then discard the idea as ridiculous. I don't even know if she has a boyfriend.

Mom caresses the side of my head. "I just can't right now. I can't." She pinches my ear.

"Ow!" I brush her hand away and bark at her. "Stop. You know why . . ."

She blinks twice; she doesn't agree. Lettie says I inherited the romantic streak I used to have from Mom. Mom still has hers. I wish I could say the same.

She kisses my hand, pats it, and then closes her eyes.

"Night, Mom. Sleep well."

"HEY, HAVE A seat. These will be ready in a second," Lettie says as she pulls a tray of piping-hot blueberry muffins from the oven. The fresh-baked smell assaults my senses, making my mouth water.

"So, I've been thinking about the gala," she says.

I sit on a bar stool at the kitchen island and groan. "Do we have to talk about this now? Can't it wait?"

She gives me a hard look and drops the pan on the stove top. "I could really use some help here, Devon."

"What kind of help? I thought we had an event planner. We're paying for one, that much I know," I snap, in no mood to take any more crap. I'm looking forward to escaping to the city and locking myself in my art studio after my doctor's appointment tomorrow. It's my one free day this week.

"I'm talking about getting you a proper date," she snaps back. "With October just around the corner, you should be setting a tone of stability. That you're looking to settle down."

"Oh, really?" I say, my hands clenching into fists as anger bubbles up in my chest. "Says who?"

"Says anyone and everyone associated with the board of this company!"

I pop off the stool and pace to work off my agitation. "Isn't it enough that I'm out there parading around as some kind of business savant capable of taking over our father's multi-billion-dollar company?" I ask, my voice rising. "That I had dreams, too, Lettie? That I left them behind so that I could make sure we aren't turned out on the street with nothing but annual trust funds that barely cover Mom's expenses because our father was a narcissistic prig? That even if I make it to twenty-five, I might not make it to twenty-six? Isn't that fucking enough?" Pacing didn't help. I'm seething by the time I finish. I pass a shaky hand through my hair as I grind my teeth.

Tears well in Lettie's eyes on the other side of the island. "I'm sorry."

Seeing her on the verge of tears takes the wind out of my sails. I sometimes forget this is as hard on her as it is on me. She has her own set of obligations to uphold. All we have is each other and Mom. I can't stand when we fight. Weariness hits me with the force of a sledgehammer.

"I'm going to bed," I say, turning to leave.

She bolts over and grabs my arm. "Wait, don't go. Have a

muffin."

"I need sleep," I say.

"When have you ever turned down one of my muffins?" she teases, brushing her tears away.

The aroma grabs me in a chokehold, and my stomach sends a painful reminder that I promised it food and haven't delivered. "Fine."

Defeated, I return to my seat. She plucks a muffin from the pan, puts it on a plate, and then pours a large glass of milk from the fridge.

"Here," she says, pushing it all toward me.

The spongy, warm goodness hits my tongue and I moan in delight. A second muffin replaces the first.

She wiggles her eyebrows. "Better than sex, eh?"

I give her a dirty look. "I wouldn't know."

"Whose fault is that? The ball that's left still works, doesn't it?" she asks, raising her brows.

Why in hell would she bring that up? My nostrils flare and my face heats. I drop what's left of the muffin onto my plate. "You wanna talk about my dick next?"

"No, because as far as I know there's nothing wrong with that, either. For Pete's sake, will you go get laid already? It can't be healthy to live on masturbation alone."

My jaw clenches and my voice goes low and cold. "For fuck's sake, Lettie. Why are we having this conversation? Isn't there anything you consider too personal?"

She releases a breath, and her voice softens. "I just want you to be happy again."

"And that's going to do it? Getting laid?"

"Maybe," she says. "Because living like a monk sure isn't helping."

I press the heels of my hands into my eye sockets and rub. Polishing off the last bite of muffin in silence, I drain the glass of milk and get up to leave.

"Dev?"

I huff. "What?"

"You need a date for the gala."

I stare her down. "I have one," I say, leaving the kitchen before she has time to respond.

I kick myself all the way to my room. Why didn't I ask for Jenny's number? Then again, she lives on Tulip. How hard can it be to find Jenny Lynch?

Chapter 6

Jenny

"IT'S GOOD TO have you home, Pumpkin," my dad says as he squeezes me into a hug. Before I left Devon at the bottom of the escalator a few minutes ago, I considered dragging him with me to the baggage carousel, thinking Dad might want to thank him for bailing me out. But then I reconsidered, after every scenario that raced through my head ended awkwardly.

"How's Aunt Jill?" I ask, slipping out of his arms. I spot my suitcase on the baggage carousel. "That's it." I point and Dad hoists it off.

"Better." He lets out a breath, his face flushing red. "Sweetie, what have you got in here, an engine block?"

I laugh, and my shoulders relax. "It's not that heavy. You need to work out more." My dad stands a hair under six feet tall, is paunchy, wears glasses, and looks like the director of finance he is. He's also a major classic car buff, hence the reference to car parts.

"So is Aunt Jill out of danger?" I ask as we head to the exit.

"Mother and child are both fine as of now. They stopped the bleeding and contractions but Lucas admitted her. She's staying in the hospital until the baby comes."

"Next Thursday?"

"No, her water broke. If she doesn't go into labor by early Sunday morning, they'll induce." Today's Friday.

"How's Raine doing?" I ask.

"He's an anxious wreck, like all first-time fathers," Dad says, and he pulls me to his side as we walk. "I remember the day you were born. I was the same as Raine."

"Mom okay?"

"Fine. She's already taking over. I wouldn't be surprised if she steps on Raine's toes as they battle it out for supremacy."

I crack a smile. Normally I'd place my bets on Mom, but knowing Raine the way I do, I'd say the odds are even.

"Can I see Aunt Jill?"

"Lucas booted everyone out but Raine about thirty minutes ago. Your mother's bound to be home by now. She'll take you to see Aunt Jill in the morning."

Disappointment washes over me as we walk out into the warm night air. I'd really hoped to see her, if for nothing else than to convince myself she was all right. If my flight to Denver hadn't been so delayed, I would've made it. Then again, had I made it, I never would've met Devon.

"Oh, Dad?"

"Yeah, honey?"

"I kind of borrowed four hundred dollars from this guy to get a seat on the plane," I say sheepishly, bracing myself.

"What?"

I explain with a nervous gesticulation of my hands. "The only way I could get on the flight was to buy an upgrade for a first-class seat. I kind of burst into tears, and this nice guy took pity on me and paid for it. I want to pay him back."

My father pulls me to a stop in the parking lot. "Jenny! Why didn't you call me or your mother? We could've given them our credit card over the phone."

"I didn't think of that." I shrug. "I was slightly distraught. Mom had just told me Aunt Jill was in danger. I wasn't thinking straight." My sometimes therapist, Dr. Graham, would've been disappointed. My coping mechanisms are sorely lacking today.

His voice softens. "It's okay, honey. Did you take the man's contact information?"

"I'm not an idiot, Dad. I have his card in my backpack."

We reach the car. "I never said you were an idiot, Jenny. I've never thought it, either." He squeezes my arm, and his voice softens. "I'll write a check in the morning."

I take out my phone, wondering if Russ called or texted. I'm relieved to find out my cell is dead and put it away. I'm still mad about this morning. Then I remember my ring. I twist my fingers into the pocket of my jeans and fish it out. Rather than putting it on, I drop it into the change compartment of my wallet. I can't bear the feel of it on my finger.

"How's Russ?" Dad asks, as if he's read my mind. "Have you two decided on a date yet?"

"No … He's fine. He's sorry he couldn't come, but he didn't have enough vacation time to do this and attend Aunt Jill's wedding in August."

He looks at me suspiciously from the driver's side. "And you did?"

"Let's just say I'm between jobs."

Dad sighs. "Do you need money, sweetheart?"

"Thanks. No. I'll be fine." Well, maybe I won't, but that's something I'd rather take up with my mom. That, and how I might be calling off our engagement …

AS I FINISH drying my hair the next morning, Mom shouts from the front door, "Jenny! There's a delivery for you."

Hair done, I bounce down the carpeted stairs. Mom's standing at the bottom, holding a large houseplant in a basket.

"Is it from Russ?" my mom asks.

God, I hope not. He was more than a little pissy on the phone last night, but this wouldn't do much by way of an apology. This is something you give to your English teacher, not your fiancée.

I pluck the card out of the long-stemmed plastic holder and wonder who would send me a plant.

Hope everything turned out okay with your aunt.

Call me? I have a request. Devon

Ignoring the flutter in my middle, I smile at Devon's resourcefulness. All right, from him, this is the perfect choice—thoughtful without being presumptuous.

"Who's Devon?" my mom asks, looking over my shoulder at the card.

"The guy who lent me money for my upgrade," I murmur, staring at the card. I head upstairs to get his business card from my backpack.

"*Jen-knee*," she says with slow, disyllabic emphasis at the bottom of the stairs. "Why did he send you a plant?"

"To be nice," I say and disappear into my room.

My fingers shake as I retrieve the card and flip it over to the handwritten number on the back. I punch the numbers into my phone.

"Devon Soames."

My mouth quirks up at his greeting. "Jenny Lynch," I reply.

His voice warms. "Oh, hey. You got the delivery?"

I chuckle. "Yeah. You piqued my Mom's curiosity. She wonders why a guy I just met would send me a plant."

"Because I couldn't think of a faster way to get in touch with you without being creepy and showing up on your doorstep. By the way, it took me over an hour to figure out what to send. I didn't want you to get the wrong impression."

This time I laugh at his candor. "Thanks, it was creative and hit the right tone. Oh, and I have your money."

"That's not why I asked you to call me," he says evenly.

"I figured that," I say.

"Do you have time to meet for coffee later? Starbucks, maybe, after lunch?"

"Ah, sure. I'm going to the hospital now. I should be able to meet you . . . say one o'clock?"

He blows out a breath. "Perfect."

"Do you want to tell me what this is about?" For the life of me, nothing springs to mind. Based on his claim of not wanting to give me the wrong impression, this doesn't sound like a date.

"No, I'd rather wait until I can see you in person."

"See you later then," I say.

"Jenny?"

"Hmm?"

"Thanks."

"You're welcome . . . I think." Even though it's clearly not a date, I can't get the goofy grin off my face after I hang up.

Chapter 7

Devon

"SHOULDN'T YOU BUY me dinner first?" I ask Dr. Lucas Wilson, wearing a sarcastic grin as I stand half-naked with my khakis down around my ankles. His hand massages my remaining testicle, examining it for a recurrence of disease.

He chuckles despite himself. "I'm sure you could get a better offer from someone prettier." He pulls his hand away and motions for me to get dressed. "Everything appears normal. Any issue with erectile function?"

I shake my head and sit back on the table, white paper crunching under me. "No."

Lucas picks up his clipboard and checks off a couple of things.

"What about your sex drive?

You'd think I'd be used to these questions by now, but heat warms my cheeks anyway. "Normal."

Lucas glances up with a raised brow. "What's your definition of normal?"

"You know, *normal*. I want sex and can have it. Is that normal enough?" I say with a huff, unable to meet his eyes.

"So you're sexually active right now?"

I glare at him and cross my arms over my chest. "Define

sexually active."

Lucas lets out an exasperated sigh and lowers his pencil. "Devon, I'm not asking you these questions to pry. The answers give me an indication if your issues are advancing. Just because you want sex doesn't mean you're actually having it."

My jaw tightens. "Does masturbation count?"

He suppresses a smile. "That counts."

"Fine. Then let's leave it at that."

Lucas checks off another box. "Let's finish this in my office. I have your test results back." He leads the way and I follow.

It's Saturday. We have the place to ourselves. He always meets me alone for the sake of discretion. Mine. It pays to have a concierge doctor who's a general practitioner and surgeon on a private retainer. Lucas was a close friend of my father and still sits on the board of my family's foundation supporting Memorial Hospital. He's also the only person besides Lettie and Mom who knows my secret, and he willingly keeps my medical records under an assumed name. If the Kingsbridge board ever found out, my place as heir would be at risk thanks to my father's placing a condition on the inheritance when I was twenty-one and fighting testicular cancer. I need to be healthy—as in alive and not terminal— and able to reproduce in order to inherit, or my half brother Phillip can take my place. My sperm count is lower than normal but still high enough to get someone pregnant.

Lucas settles into the chair and lifts my folder off his desk. Glasses perched on the end of his nose, he stares down at his notes and then at me.

"Devon, I'm not going to mince words. Diet, meds, and exercise will only go so far. The initial damage to your kidneys from the chemo seems to be progressing. Your creatinine levels are elevated, higher than they were six months ago. You're heading to stage five. At some point soon, we need to talk about dialysis if we can't find you a suitable organ donor."

A shiver slides down my spine even though he's not telling me anything I don't already know. The complicating factors are my tissue type and rejection markers. Of all the ways to be special, this isn't one I'd choose.

"How long?"

He shakes his head and releases a breath. "Three months, six months, a year? I can't be sure."

"No dialysis." After the torture of chemo, I can't live like that again—in a state of misery, dependent on a machine to live.

"Don't be foolish, Devon. You're a young man. Without at least one healthy kidney, you'll die of renal failure."

"I don't care," I whisper and press my lips together.

"I've put you on the list, but our best chance is to find you a live donor," Lucas says.

"Then I guess I'm screwed," I say. Lettie, even though she's my twin, isn't a match, and neither is my mom.

"We'll wait. It's not dire yet."

Humph. I look away. It's not his life that's at risk.

Lucas pulls out a bunch of plastic bottles filled with the pills I'll need to keep my kidneys functioning, places them in a bag, and hands them to me. "For this quarter. You're sticking to your diet, exercising?"

I take the bag. "Yeah."

"Don't give up hope. I'll do the best I can to keep this at bay until we find an alternative," Lucas says kindly. "It's far from over."

"Thanks." Much easier for him to say. Me? I feel like a dead man walking.

Chapter 8

Jenny

"HI," I SAY, beaming as I enter Aunt Jill's hospital room. Mom went to get a cup of coffee to give me some time to visit on my own.

"Hey, Pumpkin." Smiling, she opens her arms wide to receive me. For some reason, she and Dad are the only ones in the world who still call me that. It makes me feel five again.

Her thick chestnut hair is twisted in a pile on top of her head, and her skin is pale against the drab blue of the hospital gown. I'm hit by a subtle antiseptic smell as I get closer. Monitoring equipment surrounds her bed and gives off a blend of blinking and blipping beeps and whooshes. She's tethered to a bag of fluid by an IV tube embedded in the back of her hand.

I let her take me in her arms, but her huge belly won't let us get too close. "How's Rachel doing in there?" I ask, caressing the hard mound.

Her hand covers mine and her smile crinkles the skin around her amber-colored eyes. "Much better."

"Where's Raine?" I ask, surprised my aunt Jill's alone.

"I made John take him down to the cafeteria to get something to eat. They're like a pair of doting hens," she says affectionately.

"John's here?"

She gives a nod coupled with a warm smile.

Detective John Henshaw is a friend of the family. Well, to everyone except my dad. John and Mom were high school sweethearts, and if you look closely, you can see the tenderness they still harbor toward each other. None of us know the whole story about why they broke up all those years ago—Mom won't talk about it. All we know is they broke up when Mom was in her twenties. The "pretty" story is that she met my dad and decided she loved him more. But based on the look in Mom's and John's eyes whenever they're together, I'm not sure I believe that.

"I'm sorry, I tried to get here yesterday but I missed my flight," I say, taking a seat in the chair next to the bed, relieved to finally see her in person.

She shakes her head. "Yesterday was awful. It's probably better you missed it."

"Yeah. My day sucked, too, not that it even remotely compared to yours." I give her the synopsis. When I finish, she stares back at me, sadness creasing her brow.

"Don't settle, Jenny. If Russ isn't the one, break it off." She takes my hand and squeezes it. "Don't make my mistakes. Please. Live your best life—whatever that means for you." Her mistakes. She's referring to the years she spent before Uncle Robert died, living in an eighteen-year marriage that was safe but never measured up to the love she'd lost at eighteen. Happily, she found that again with Raine.

Living my best life. If only I could be so lucky.

My vision blurs until tears spill down my cheeks. "I know you're right, but I feel like such a failure," I say, making a half-hearted attempt to wipe away the wet trails.

"You're not a failure, honey. Failing is making the wrong decision and fooling yourself into believing it's the right one." She hands me a tissue from the box next to the bed.

I blow my nose. "But what if it's just me?"

She shakes her head. "You're the only one who counts in that equation. Remember the test? The question I asked you the day you told me Russ was moving to California?"

"Can I breathe without him?" I ask.

She nods.

"These days, the only time I can breathe is when I'm not with him." It wasn't always this way. But if I'm honest with myself, it started not long after I moved to San Francisco, and it progressively grew worse.

She reaches for my hand and says, "Then you have your answer, my love."

The door swings open a second later as I'm dabbing my eyes and in walks Raine, dressed in what looks like yesterday's suit. Dusty circles from lack of sleep lie under his blue eyes, making them sink into his face and look overly bright, but that doesn't do much to detract from his blond Viking good looks. I'm still getting used to seeing him with short hair—well, short for him. He used to wear it long, down around his shoulders. Then he cut it all off when he thought he'd lost my aunt Jill last winter, though it looks as if he's growing it out. It's getting floppy on top.

Devon's hair is only a shade or two lighter, I think unexpectedly.

"Hey, Jen," he says, enfolding me in a warm hug. He's tall enough to tuck me into his shoulder and make me feel small. "You okay?"

"Yeah, fine. Glad to be home." I squeeze him a little tighter and then let go. I miss talking to him, but unloading on Aunt Jill is enough for now. To repeat my story again would make me feel like a total loser. Besides, he's got more important things to worry about than my wreck of a love life.

"Do you need me or Mom to bring you something else to wear?" I ask, eyeing his rumpled apparel.

"No, I'm heading home in a few minutes to shower and

change," he says, giving me a wry grin. "Besides, I don't want you or Kitty rummaging around in my underwear drawer."

I laugh and give him a small shove. "I didn't think of that. Trust me, the feeling's mutual."

Raine and I had a rocky start when we first met. It wasn't until after my great-aunt Vera died last summer that we became friends. Even though we're only a couple of years apart, he's had to overcome adversity to get to where he is. It's made him stronger and more mature. I admire his unwavering sense of family and honor. Not to mention his wicked sense of humor.

"Where's John?" Aunt Jill asks.

"He'll be back later," Raine says as he walks over. He kisses her tenderly on the lips and then rubs her belly. "She's good?"

She beams up at him. "Not even a cramp."

"'Kay, I'm going to go, baby. Be back in a little while," he says and heads to the door. "See ya later, Jen. We'll catch up."

"Sounds good," I say to his departing back. My mom pokes her head through the door in his place. "May I come in?"

"More the merrier," Aunt Jill replies, massaging her protruding stomach.

I glance at my watch. "Mom, can I borrow the car? I need to drop that money off at one."

"Sure, sweetie," she says and fishes around in her oversize bag for the keys. The bag has seen better days. My mom will never be a candidate for the cover of *Vogue*. Her sense of style is in desperate need of help. Chances are, if it's from the eighties, it's still in her closet. But she refuses to listen to either me or Aunt Jill. We've all but given up outside of Christmas and birthday presents that she'd be too mortified to ever return for fear of our finding out. She even wears what we give her at least once—just to prove she kept the gift.

"I'll pick you up later. I shouldn't be long," I say. At least I don't think I will be.

I LUCK OUT and find a parking spot near the Summit train station. The Starbucks is across the street on the corner of Beechwood. Tables with umbrellas line the sidewalk.

Devon is waiting outside, wearing the standard uniform of khakis and a polo shirt. God, this town is so predictable.

Me? White shorts, a clingy J. McLaughlin V-neck shirt in a blue-and-white stripe, and my favorite pair of strappy sandals. I can't lie. I'm a product of this town just as much as he is.

I take off my sunglasses as I get closer and smile. "Hi."

His eyes light up. He's got good cheekbones on top of that nice smile. "Thanks for coming."

He opens the door for me, and we're hit with a wave of cool air. A flutter tickles my midsection. And I have an answer to my question. Light-blond hair covers his well-defined forearms. Not the coarse, curly kind but the soft, refined kind.

The place is crowded, but we manage to procure our drinks quickly—an iced coffee for me and an iced herbal green tea for him. We find an empty table outside. For some reason, he picks the one farthest from the door. We angle our chairs under the shade of the umbrella, away from the hot summer sun.

"Oh, before I forget." I reach into my purse and hand him an envelope containing $400 in cash. After some coaxing, Dad wrote the check out to me, and I cashed it on the way over. I convinced him that handing Devon a check from my parents' bank account would make me seem lame and leave him with the wrong impression.

He gives me a sour look. "Seriously?"

I meet his gaze head on. "Seriously."

He runs his fingers through his sandy hair. "Fine," he says, but he leaves the envelope in the middle of the table. He clasps his hands and stares. His mouth opens as if he's about to say something and then shuts.

I take a sip of iced coffee through the straw to give him a moment.

He sighs and shifts uncomfortably in his chair. "I . . . um. . . would you be willing to do me a favor?"

"What kind of favor?" I ask, arching a brow.

"This is awkward." He gazes down at his hands, looking tortured.

"Just ask me," I say in hopes of putting him out of his misery.

"My family sponsors an annual gala to benefit Memorial Hospital—"

"You want a donation?" I blurt.

A horrified look passes over his face, and he flames an indignant red. "No! Of course not."

"Well?" I suppress a smile, then chuckle. "Come on, Devon. I don't bite. Just ask me."

After some hesitation, the tension in his shoulders eases. "Will you go as my date? As a friend?" he asks, still as red as a boiled lobster.

The flush of warmth filling my chest has nothing to do with the weather. I lean back in my seat and cross my arms over my chest. "Only if you tell me why you're asking." Not that I'm trying to make this harder on him, but his request raises my radar. "What aren't you telling me, Devon? I'm not saying I won't go, but I want to know what I'm really agreeing to."

He shifts forward and presses his hand to his forehead. "Can I trust you?"

"I'm a stranger," I remind him.

He repeats the question more slowly, locking his gaze on mine. "Can. I. Trust. You?"

"Yes," I say softly. The truth is he can. Once I decide to

take someone on as a friend, I'm about as loyal as they come. "You have my word."

His expression shifts to worry. "This is an important event for me, and if I don't want to end up going with one of my sister's vapid friends, I need you to come with me. Having someone fun to hang out with during what promises to be a very stressful event for me personally will make it easier." There's no mistaking his honesty or his earnestness.

One look in those incredible blue eyes of his and I'm done. How could I refuse?

"As a friend?" I ask, wanting to confirm his intentions.

His mouth tips up in a smile as his skin regains its normal color. "Yeah, as a friend. Just don't tell anyone that."

Now I'm convinced I'm right. There is a story.

"When is it?"

"It's in two weeks. Saturday, June twenty-eighth."

My heart drops and I slump in my chair. "I fly back to San Francisco that day."

His mouth sets in a determined line. "What if I fly you back on Sunday instead?"

"What do you mean, 'fly me back'?"

"I'm scheduled to visit a company owned by Kingsbridge in Silicon Valley next month. I could arrange to be there that Monday." He shrugs as if it's a no-brainer. "We'll take the corporate jet on Sunday."

My ears prick up. "Corporate jet? Then why did you fly commercial yesterday?"

He shakes his head. "The jet was already booked by a board member. Let me check on it today. Would that work?"

I chew my lip. "It could." Then I slump again. "Wait a second. Is this a black-tie event?"

"Seriously? That's a problem?" he asks, looking at me like I've sprouted a second head.

Men, I think with a flash of annoyance. "Yes, seriously. I don't have a dress with me." I drop my head in my hands.

God knows that buying one with my limited finances is out of the question. Borrowing one doesn't seem too feasible, either. There's no one I know who is even remotely my size. I tower over all my friends who still live in town. Add to that small boobs supplemented by the miracle of Victoria's Secret push-up technology and curvy hips. Nope. Not one among my silicone-enhanced, size-four munchkin friends. Forget my stuck-in-the-eighties mom and my petite aunt Jill.

"What's your afternoon look like?" he asks calmly over his folded hands.

"Huh? What's that got to do with anything?"

"Answer my question," he says more firmly.

I eye him warily. "I have to go back to the hospital to drop off my mom's car."

"Then what?"

"Nothing until my aunt goes into labor, which might not happen until tomorrow."

He slaps the table. "Great! You're free."

"Free for what?"

He rolls his eyes. "To go shopping and let me buy you a dress, Cinderella. Lucky for us, we have a world-class mall five minutes away," he says, getting up to leave. "Come on. I'll follow you to the hospital and then we'll go from there."

"You can't buy me a dress!"

"Sure I can. You're doing me the favor, remember?" He takes the envelope from the table and shakes it at me. "If it makes you feel better, you'll be paying for part of it."

My eyes widen. Part of it? How much does he plan on spending?

He takes my hand to pull me to my feet. I'm startled by the smooth warmth of it. His fingers are long and elegant compared to Russ's thick stubby ones, not that there's anything wrong with Russ's fingers, mind you.

"Some stubborn woman once told me, 'A debt is a debt.' Oh yeah! That was you," he jokes, wearing a silly look, then adds, "Has anyone ever told you you're cute when you're indignant?"

I nudge him with my purse and laugh. "You're a piece of work."

He gives me a crooked smile. "So I've been told. Where's your car?"

I point across the street at my mom's Volvo. "Where's yours?"

"There." He points two spaces down, to a Bentley.

I smirk. "I wouldn't have picked you as the Bentley type."

He snorts. "I'm not. It was my father's and happened to be the only car in the garage with any gas in it, thanks to my sister."

We dump our trash and meander toward the crosswalk.

"You don't have a car?"

"I do. But I'm waiting for double Q plates so that it's street legal."

My brows shoot up. "You have a classic car? What kind?"

He smiles shyly and there's a look of pride in his eyes. "A 1970 Aston Martin. I had it shipped from the UK after university. I just haven't gotten around to dealing with the paperwork."

"Don't tell my father," I say.

"Why?"

"He might want to marry you. He's a huge classic car buff. He shows his cars every year at the Summit Classic Car Show downtown."

A look of delight fills his features. "Really? What does he have?" Gosh, he really does have a great smile . . . and that dimple.

"I'm not sure I want to ruin the surprise. I'd rather let him show you his stable — as he calls it — if you're interested."

"Come on, tell me at least one," he says as we cross the street.

"Fine. A 1975 Mustang GT," I say.

He lifts an appreciative brow and purses his lips. "Not bad."

"See you there," I say as I unlock the Volvo and he walks past me toward the Bentley. Then it hits me—he talked about his father in the past tense. I wonder how intimately he knows the inside of a funeral home and hope his level of experience isn't anywhere close to mine. Granted, I still have both my parents, for which I'm grateful. It's others I was close to whom I've lost.

No sooner do I start the car than my phone rings. It's Russ. My stomach quivers ... and not in a good way. I can't tell whether it's from guilt, dread, or both. Whichever it is, I don't want to deal with it right now, so I let the call go to voice mail.

As I pull up to a light, my phone chimes—a text. I glance at the small screen:

Hey, babe. Hope U R having a good day. I'm sorry I've been such a dick. Call me when you're free. Love you.

Dread. Definitely dread.

Chapter 9

Devon

WHY DID I agree to come in? I wonder, feeling self-conscious as I follow Jenny down the hall toward her aunt's hospital room.

"My mom's a little overprotective and old-fashioned. She's not going to let me run off with a total stranger for the afternoon without meeting him first," she said, pulling me reluctantly from behind the wheel of my car. "Otherwise, you can meet her here in the parking lot—and that would be weird."

"I'm not a stranger. I sent you a plant," I said, grinning despite myself. The truth is that I understand; my mom is the same way. Chances are good it would make her happy to see me with someone like Jenny . . . if I planned on being with anyone.

Visitors and nurses buzz by us in the corridor as we come to a stop midway down the hall. Jenny pushes open the door and crashes into a doctor on his way out.

"Whoa there, Jenny!" he says, catching her by the arm to steady her.

I inhale sharply.

Lucas's eyes snap up and widen in surprise. My stomach

clenches, waiting for what happens next.

"Sorry, Lucas. I didn't mean to mow you down," Jenny says and then glances back at me. The breath stays frozen in my lungs. "Is my mom in there? I need to give her the car keys and introduce her to my friend Devon."

After a pregnant pause, I make the decision for us. "Dr. Wilson," I say, extending my hand. "Good to see you."

"I didn't realize you knew Jenny," Lucas says, a smile slowly creeping onto his lips.

"We just met." I think back to Lucas's grilling earlier this morning and guess at the source of his smile. Maybe he thinks my options have improved.

"Well, aren't you full of surprises," Jenny says, turning to me.

Lucas nonchalantly picks up the ball. "Devon's father was a dear friend of mine. I still sit on the board of his family's foundation."

Her lips part, and she gets a look that tells me she's gathered some useful intelligence. "Good to know."

"To answer your question," Lucas says, pointing behind him, "yes, your mom's inside. Good to see you both." I catch him winking at me as he turns to head down the hall.

"Wait here a sec," Jenny says before slipping inside.

A few moments later, an older woman with graying hair and kind dark eyes follows Jenny out the door. Her mother wears a wide, welcoming grin. In stark contrast to Jenny's fresh-faced beauty, she's plainly dressed without makeup, giving the impression that she's older than she probably is.

"Hi, you must be Devon. So lovely to meet you! Thank you for helping Jenny out of her pickle yesterday," she says, clasping my hand firmly. Her skin is warm and slightly rough to the touch. "And what a lovely plant."

A flush rises in my cheeks. "It was nothing, really. I was glad to help."

She releases my hand. "Jenny tells me she's going to the

mall with you to consult on some purchases for the upcoming hospital gala." With a pointed look, she assesses me from behind her friendly tone.

A glance at Jenny reveals a look of wide-blue-eyed innocence. Clearly she spun the message to hide the true intent of our shopping trip.

I clear my throat and reply politely. "That is, if you don't mind, Mrs. Lynch."

"Oh, please, call me Kitty," she says and waves her hand. "Not at all. Dinner's at six thirty if you'd like to join us ... unless of course my sister goes into labor."

I tip my head. "That's very kind." Rather than turning her down directly, I choose to stay noncommittal.

Jenny kisses her mom on the cheek. "I'll see you later."

We walk silently down the hall.

"Consulting on some purchases?" I snicker as the elevator door closes.

She shrugs. "You *are* making a purchase, correct? I assuming that I'll have a vote on which dress we pick — so I'm consulting. It's the truth."

"Yeah, in a twisted sort of way."

She gives me a dirty look. "I couldn't exactly tell her you were buying me a dress without another twenty questions, creating the wrong impression, and getting a flat-out refusal. I did it for you, so be grateful."

"For me? You're over eighteen and legally allowed to make your own decisions," I say.

"Yeah, well, while I'm staying under my parents' roof within earshot of my mom's very vocal opinions, I'll do it my way."

I give her a half smile. "Just as long as it's not because you're embarrassed to tell her you're coming as my date."

An odd look passes over her face. "Embarrassed? Of course not. Why would I be embarrassed?"

I hide my inward cringe with a dazzling smile. "You seem

like the kind of girl who can pick and choose her dates. Guess I'm just feeling lucky."

One side of her mouth quirks up. "Smooth."

Despite the nice recovery, I still want to kick myself for the irrational flash of insecurity. Then again, I'm not exactly issue-free.

Chapter 10

Jenny

"RIGHT THIS WAY, Mr. Soames," says Naomi, the Neiman Marcus saleswoman, who wears a form-fitting emerald-green suit. She leads us to a private dressing area through the high-end designer section. The one used by the personal shoppers.

My mouth goes dry; $400 won't go far in this department. I glance at Devon and whisper, "How did she know we were coming?"

"I called her on the way to the hospital to drop off your car."

"You shop here ... *often?*" I ask, gawking as we pass dresses from designer labels I could never hope to afford unless I hit the lottery.

He shakes his head. "Nope. First time. My sister Lettie usually shops here for black-tie events."

We arrive at the private room. I gently pull him to a stop outside and say, low enough that only he can hear me, "I'm sure there are less expensive places we can go to get a dress."

He squeezes my arm and says quietly, "Stop worrying about money. I've got this."

I can't decide if he's stupid rich or just plain stupid as he propels me through the door and into the plush room. A velvet settee is parked in front of a dais, behind which lies a door leading to what I can only imagine is the actual dressing room.

"Have a seat, Mr. Soames." Naomi points to the settee. Then she smiles at me and takes the measuring tape from around her neck. "Let's get you measured, and then I'll bring in some selections."

Giving Devon one last woeful look, I follow Naomi into the dressing room.

After I strip down to my underwear and stand with my arms in various positions at my sides, she finally announces, "You're closest to a size eight, but we may need to alter the top if the style doesn't allow for a push-up bra."

Humph. Like I need a reminder about my lack of endowment.

She stares at my feet for a few seconds. "Nine?"

I nod, impressed that she got it right on the first guess.

"Wait here. I'll be back," Naomi says, leaving me alone, swathed in a downy white robe.

"How're you doing in there?" Devon asks softly on the other side of the door.

"Fine," I say, pacing in my bare feet, feeling painfully out of place, and wanting to find an explanation for the butterflies in my stomach. Granted, I've shopped here before, but never on this floor. Who knew it even existed?

No sooner do I sit down than the door opens and in waltzes Naomi, laden with several boxes of shoes and at least eight hangers holding full-length dresses—all costing somewhere in the range of two weeks' gross salary, based on the designer labels I recognize from years of reading *Vogue*.

"Here, take these." She hands me the shoeboxes, then hangs the dresses on the nearest hook. They blind me with a kaleidoscope of color.

Naomi plucks the first hanger and holds it out—a jeweled green number with a high Empire waist and a halter top in silk chiffon. Silver beading circles the top under the bustline.

"Do you have anything to help keep your hair up?" she asks, assessing me with a practiced eye. Good point. I'll probably wear it up for the gala.

She's in luck. I have clips in the makeup bag inside my purse. I twist my hair into a quick chignon and secure it on top of my head. A few tendrils fall loose along the sides of my face. Not bad, if I do say so myself.

"That work?" I ask in the mirror.

Naomi smiles. "That will do nicely."

I slip into the green Valentino dress; the hem pools on the ground.

"Here, try these." Naomi hands me a pair of matching green satin Valentino heels. I step into them.

She motions with her finger for me to turn in a slow circle. Satisfied, she points to the door. "Show him."

Some looks are priceless . . . like the one on Devon's face when I walk into the room.

His jaw drops a full inch, and he blinks a few times before he regains control of his face. His gaze caresses me from head to toe before resting just below my jaw. "Wow. You look amazing."

I flush with pleasure and smile demurely. I can't remember the last time Russ looked at me this way. This is only the first dress. Suddenly I look forward to trying on the next one.

I spin in a slow 360, the dress flaring out at the hem as I twirl. "So, I've been thinking . . ."

"About what?" His eyes drift from somewhere near the base of my neck to my face.

"I don't know much about you. Being that I'm your date for the gala . . . and you don't want people thinking you're there with some random girl you picked up on an airplane," I say, making googly eyes at him. "Maybe we should tell each other enough to survive a cocktail conversation without surprising the bejesus out of anyone."

He chuckles deeply. "For the record, I didn't pick you up." Leaning forward on the settee, he rests his elbows on his thighs. "You already know my taste in books and movies. What else do you want to know?"

"That won't get me very far. Let's start with the basics," I say, heading back to change. "Where did you go to college?"

"Oxford. You?"

"NYU. What did you study?"

"Economics and fine arts," he answers.

My brows pop up. "Really? What medium do you prefer?"

A smile touches his lips. "Oil on canvas."

"Ah. A painter." I duck into the dressing room. "I'm impressed. I would've never guessed."

"What about you?" he asks through the door.

"Business and art history," I say to the white wooden slats separating us as I shimmy out of the Valentino. "With an emphasis in photography."

Naomi takes my castoff and hands me a deep-royal-blue dress with a square neck and spaghetti straps in a glossy satin. It's Armani. I slip it over my head, the silky length traveling along my body until it hits the floor. I put on the pair of Christian Louboutin heels she has waiting. Surreptitiously I read the price tag on the dress and gasp. $5,450. Before I can think more deeply on it, Naomi has me tottering back out in front of Devon.

Devon lets out a low whistle when he sees me. "Very nice."

"Just to recap what I know about your education. You went to high school and college in England. Prior to that, were you educated in the United States?" His years abroad explain his slight British accent when annunciating certain words.

"Yes. I grew up in Summit but went to private schools."

"Why did your parents ship you off to England? Seems far."

"My father was born and educated there. He wanted me to follow in his footsteps."

"Your parents are English?"

"No, just my father," he says, an amused twinkle in his eye. "I feel like I'm being interviewed."

"You are." I circle back into the dressing room and try on dress number three. A clingy black column that fits like a second skin. Nope. I look as if I've been dipped naked in black paint. Sorry, Devon. You're getting a pass on this one.

Naomi opens her mouth to speak and I freeze her with a glance. She hands me the next dress after I shimmy out of that one and hand it back to her.

Number four is black, too, but much more appropriate for being seen in public. A nice Calvin Klein with a plunging neckline that pools between my breasts, making them appear larger than they are. I walk outside, pleased with this selection.

Devon's eyebrows quirk up. "Hmm."

As I'm twirling, I ask quietly, "When did your father die?"

"Three and a half years ago," he replies evenly. "At sixty-five."

I do the math. His father had him at almost forty-five. "How old is your mom?"

"She's sixty-five now." I'm a little surprised at his parents' ages.

"How many brothers and sisters?"

"One sister, my twin, Leticia, and a younger half brother." His voice wavers with distaste when he mentions his unnamed half sibling. "You?"

"Only child," I say and hesitate before asking my next question. "Can I ask you something personal?"

"More personal than this?"

I give him a tight smile. "Yeah."

His shoulders tighten and he grows wary as if bracing himself. "Sure."

"Do you prefer women or men?" I ask, thinking I know the answer but wanting to know if I'm reading him wrong.

He narrows his eyes, looking slightly offended. "Do I seem gay to you?"

I shrug. "Not at all. But what does gay 'seem' like these days? It's not a stereotype that cleanly captures everyone."

He huffs. "No. My preferences run strictly to women."

"Then why don't you have a girlfriend?" I blurt. "I mean, you're obviously smart, interesting, attractive, funny ..." I trail off, almost, but not quite, sorry I asked. Something doesn't add up. There's this underlying reluctance and the sadness that lurks around his eyes. What's he hiding? The weight of it sits like a ghostly mantle on his shoulders.

"No real reason," he says, blushing and avoiding my gaze. "I don't really have time, I guess."

"I don't believe you." I'm not sure why I call him out, other than that I want to know. It seems like such a waste.

"Why's that?" he asks with practiced ease. "Did you ever think that maybe I just haven't found the right woman?"

I shake my head. "It's just that I think you're a good guy. And I think you have a lot to offer someone lucky enough to be with you."

His sadness unmasks itself right before my eyes. "I'm glad you think so. I wish that were true." He swallows and clears his throat. "What's the next dress look like?"

Something melts inside my chest, and I have the overwhelming desire to take him in my arms and not let go. I return to the dressing room to satisfy his curiosity but also with a mission. I'm determined to find out what has a stranglehold on his happiness, and then I want to do whatever is within my power to release it ... as impossible as that may turn out to be.

Chapter 11

Devon

I CLASP MY hands so tightly together that my knuckles turn white as Jenny disappears inside the dressing room. It's the only thing that keeps them from shaking as they rest in my lap. Not much seems to escape her vigilance. One of the hazards, I guess, of spending time with someone smart and observant.

More than that, she seems to care.

Part of me wants to open up and tell her about my situation, and maybe someday it would've come to that. But she lives in San Francisco and she's only home for two weeks. I think I can survive her prodding that long. Outside of that, I haven't enjoyed a woman's company this much since before I was diagnosed.

The best part? There's no pressure. Though . . . seeing her in those dresses sends me straight down the wishing path. Wishing I could touch the delicate curve of her neck . . . maybe lay my lips at her nape. Most men go for breasts and ass. But it's the curve of a woman's neck that does it for me. Not that I'd turn down a nice set of boobs or a shapely bum, but my inner artist craves the long neck of a Degas ballerina. Jenny's is enough to send a tingle through my groin, waking it from its apathetic state.

I think of my unfinished canvas in the city and want to scrap it in favor of Jenny's portrait. I wonder if she'd sit for me just for an afternoon. That's all I'd need.

"Do you like this one?"

Startled out of my contemplation, I look up to see her coming back into the room.

"I'm not sure this is my favorite," she says, wrinkling her nose. "What do you think?"

Purple with no straps, the dress clings to her curves but isn't as nice as the last few.

"It's bloody awful," I hear from behind me as I'm about to agree with Jenny. "Naomi must have something better for you than that."

Jenny's eyes widen, and I whip around in my seat.

"Lettie? What are you doing here?" I say, barely suppressing a snarl.

"Just wanted to stop by and say hi," she says as she sweeps in, dressed in a short-skirted designer suit as if she just stepped out of the office. Impossible since it's Saturday. She comes over to kiss me on the cheek and whisper in my ear. "Are you kidding me, Dev? Miss a chance to meet your new girlfriend?"

I bite my tongue as she straightens up and heads straight for Jenny. "Hi, I'm Devon's sister, Leticia Soames," she says, wearing a wide smile and offering her hand.

Jenny glances at me and winks. "Hi. Jenny Lynch." Jenny stands a good seven inches taller than Lettie in the heels she's wearing, making her my height. *Maybe she'll consider a lower heel*, I think, with a flash of vanity.

Naomi walks out of the dressing room. "Leticia, so good to see you." *Yeah, right.* No doubt she gave Lettie a heads-up the second I hung up with her.

"Please tell me you have something more suitable than this for Jenny," Lettie says and gives a disapproving glance.

"We've had better luck with the earlier selections," Naomi says, eyeing the offensive purple dress.

"Devon, which of the dresses do you like best?" Jenny asks, ignoring them. "In order of preference?"

"Honestly? The first three—the green, blue, and black ones are all nice. I'd be happy with any of them. What about you?" All of the designs are flattering and expose Jenny's neck, which is all I care about.

Lettie's ears prick up. "Can I see them?"

I give her a warning look. "Lettie, don't you have someplace to be?"

She smiles smugly. "Not for another hour."

Jenny shrugs and takes her into the dressing room, followed by Naomi.

I scrub a hand over my face as the women chatter away behind the closed door. A few minutes later, they come out. Lettie and Naomi both look deeply satisfied, carrying the blue dress and a shoebox while Jenny emerges behind them, looking shell shocked in her street clothes.

"I'll package this up. Meet me at the register when you're ready," Naomi says, leaving the personal shopping lounge.

"Jenny has agreed to come over to our place for dinner this week." Lettie winks at me and then turns to hug Jenny. "So good to meet you. Gotta run." A moment later, she's out the door, hot on Naomi's trail.

As soon as we're alone, I sigh. "I'm really sorry about that. Are you all right?"

Jenny looks pale and gives me a wan smile. "Do you realize how much you just spent?"

"Hey," I say softly, placing my hands on her shoulders. "I'm sure it's south of ten grand. Don't worry."

"Ten grand is like five months' salary for me," she says, looking somewhere between horrified and forlorn.

"It's not for me."

"Devon, this isn't how I live," she says softly, avoiding my eyes and locking her arms across her chest.

"Would it make a difference if I told you that this wouldn't be how I lived either if I had a choice?" *Or a future.*

Her eyes meet mine. "How would you choose to live?"

"Simpler . . . much simpler," I whisper and brush a silky tendril behind her ear, glad her hair is still up. Before I overthink it, I trail my fingertips lightly down the warm, delicate skin of her neck. Her eyes close and she shivers under my fingers. There's a tightening and filling below my waistline that I can't control as I cling to this moment where nothing exists except Jenny's skin under my fingertips.

"I want to paint you," I murmur, breathless, afraid to move away and break this spell. Equally afraid of the overwhelming desire to feel her lips on mine. Instead I lean in and place a kiss on her forehead. "Come to my studio, and I'll show you how I'd live."

She swallows next to me. "I'd like that."

Our breath hangs in the air, neither of us making a move to push away. Heat fills the space between us in the air-conditioned room. Her nearness leaves me wishing I could close the gap.

But a blaring tune from Jenny's purse jolts us apart. I thank the universe and step away to regain my composure as she digs in her bag next to me and pulls out the offending device.

"Hello?" Jenny walks off, then freezes in midstride. "I'll be right there." She turns to me wide eyed. "Devon, my aunt just went into labor. I need to go!"

$$\mathscr{Chapter\ 12}$$

Jenny

THE DRESS IS safely ensconced inside a garment bag, hanging in back of the Bentley, and the shopping bag containing the shoes is on the back seat. Devon will keep it all until the night of the gala, thus saving me from an interrogation by my mom.

We drive in companionable silence as I contemplate the contrast between Russ and Devon. Given the choice, Russ would take Devon's apparent wealth in a heartbeat while Devon—if what he said in the dressing room is true—would choose a simpler life. Why is it that so often we want the opposite of what we have? Maybe I'm naive, but I think I'd be happy living marginally better than paycheck to paycheck as long as I was doing something that I loved. Possessions are nice, but they don't mean that much to me. Love and meaning in life far outweigh them.

My brows knit together in a frown as I stare out the window. I'm almost sure that's the root of my issue with Russ. It wasn't until we graduated from college and had to take on adult responsibilities that I really saw the blindly ambitious side of him. I wish I could say that I miss him right now. But I don't. Sad as it sounds, being with Devon, even as a friend, more than fills the void left by Russ. I'm more convinced than ever that my relationship with Russ is beyond hope.

With a final sigh, I let go of the heaviness of my situation and turn to the man beside me. Having met Leticia, I can see their uncanny likeness. With the exception of the masculine and feminine features they carry, there's no mistaking they're siblings. She's a slightly paler shade of blonde than Devon, yet she shares the same fine bones, which make him handsome and her pretty.

"When do you want to take me to your studio?" I ask, thinking back to the moment in the dressing room when his finger sizzled a sensuous path down my neck, raising a delicious shiver over my skin. I don't want to question it too deeply or think about the mixture of guilt and longing that consumed me in that second.

He still doesn't know about Russ, and I'm torn about what to tell him. But if we're just friends, should it really matter?

"How's next Saturday?"

"Sounds good." I'm sure I can make that work.

We pull up in front of Memorial Hospital.

He gives me a wry smile. "Thanks. I had fun today."

"Yeah, me too." I lean in and kiss him on the cheek. "I'll be in touch."

I RACE TO the maternity floor's lounge. Mom, Dad, and Aunt Jillian's best-friend-slash-agent, Brigitte, stand chatting in a cluster while John Henshaw watches the scene safely from a distance. I'm surprised to spot Raine. Dressed in a pair of worn jeans and a King Metaljam T-shirt, he's pacing like a caged tiger hopped up on Red Bull.

I hug Brigitte and turn to my mom. "Isn't Raine supposed to be helping Aunt Jill breathe or something in the delivery room?"

"They decided it's too risky to deliver naturally, so they're moving ahead with the C-section," she says and then covers her mouth and whispers, "They were afraid of complications, so they wouldn't allow nonmedical personnel inside. Lucas scrubbed in since Raine wasn't allowed in the operating room."

"Is Raine all right?" I ask, knowing how crappy that must've made him feel.

Mom pats my shoulder. "Why don't you go over and talk to him, sweetie?"

No need to ask twice. I excuse myself and approach Raine. Light reflects off his simple gold wedding band as he runs his fingers through his tousled hair.

"Hey," I say.

He freezes in midpace. "Hey."

"Want to go for a walk before you wear a hole in the floor?" I ask, hoping to provide a distraction.

He shakes his head. "I need to stay here. In case Jillian needs me."

I eye the row of seats. "Want to sit, then?"

One side of his mouth tips up in a half smile. "Sure."

I sink into one of the seats, and he perches on the edge of the one next to me, ready to spring to his feet at a moment's notice.

"So Kitty said you went to the mall with a guy? What's up with that?" Raine asks.

I shrug and glance away. "He's just a friend."

"*Uh-huh.*" He squints and runs an appraising eye over my face until his gaze settles on my hands. "How's Russ?"

Based on his tone I'm guessing he noticed my ring-less finger. My lips press together, and I shake my head. "It's not good."

He sighs, and his expression softens. "Sorry to hear that, Jen." He throws an arm around my shoulder. "You want to come home?"

"Maybe." *More than you know.*

"Listen, I can hook you up with Conrad if you decide to move back. My last company was interested in hiring you before you left. I think Conrad would be, too." *Conrad Designs is the firm in New York City where Raine works.*

Raine's offer warms me, but I have to know. "Was that because I'm your niece?"

He squeezes me into his side. "No, Jen. It's because they thought you were good."

"Thanks," I say, grateful, then crinkle my nose and feel bad asking the next question. "Do you think Declan might need a waitress over at the Grasshopper while I'm home? I'm desperate for some cash."

He kisses my forehead and pulls out his phone. "I'll give him a call and find out." Before I know it, he's on his feet. After trading a few good-natured Scottish and Irish insults, Raine hangs up. "Call him Monday to work out a schedule. He can put you on for a few shifts."

"Thanks," I say, enfolding him in a hug. "I've missed you and Aunt Jill."

His forehead creases in a pained expression at the mention of my aunt. "We've missed you, too. Thanks for coming home to help with the baby."

The chatter stops and a throat clears behind us.

It's Lucas. His hands are stuffed in the pockets of his scrubs.

I let Raine go. He takes a tentative step toward Lucas and asks in a strained voice, "Is everything all right?"

Lucas breaks into a wide grin. "Dr. Pressman sent me out to get you. Let's go see your new daughter."

Tears of happiness well in Raine's eyes. He smiles at me and squeezes my shoulder before following Lucas back to see my aunt and my new cousin.

Raine and Aunt Jill's relationship never ceases to amaze me. I envy the love they have for each other without begrudging them any of it. I can only hope to find that someday, too, knowing it's not what awaits me back in San Francisco.

Speaking of … I take out my cell and decide on a preemptive strike. I've ignored Russ's calls and texts all day. With an inward groan, I dial his number.

He picks up on the third ring. "Hi. I was wondering when I'd finally hear from you."

"Sorry, it's been a crazy day. The baby was just born."

His voice perks up. "Wow, that's great. Give my best to everyone."

"I will."

An uncomfortable silence follows.

"I'm sorry for the way I acted yesterday morning," he says finally. "I was shocked, that's all. You'll find another job when you get back."

"I know," I say.

"My mom's bugging me for a date, Jen. Have you talked to your mom yet?"

I press my eyes closed and think of my engagement ring tucked in my wallet. "Not yet. Soon." *Never.*

I can't wait much longer to tell him I'm ending our engagement, but this isn't the time or the place. In fairness to Russ, this isn't something I should do over the phone. Not after a six-year relationship. But given how things are shaping up, I don't think I'll have a choice. Though there's someone else I want to tell first—my mother. Once I work up the nerve. Her approval means more to me than avoiding Russ's wrath and the possibility that he'll toss everything I own over our fifth floor balcony when he finds out.

"I love you."

"Love you, too," I mumble, conscious that the words no longer hold tingly warmth or the same meaning. "Call you later."

"I'm heading out tonight. Call you tomorrow?"

After we hang up, I wonder where he's going on a Saturday night without me.

Chapter 13

Devon

"ARGH." I DROP my head into my hands and rest my elbows on the mound of paper littering my side of my father's partner desk. "Couldn't they have sent electronic files? What do they think this is, the Stone Age? A freakin' Silicon Valley start-up and they send paper. We should divest them as soon as we get the chance."

Boy, do I hate Mondays, especially when I have to stuff my brain with operational crap in preparation for another Kingsbridge company visit. It's been like this for the last two years. Nonstop work ever since I went into remission and left the hospital with a clean-enough bill of health. And I wonder why I don't have a life.

"Oh, for Pete's sake, stop whining!" Lettie says, sitting opposite me, shuffling through the other half of the reports. "It was your brilliant idea, Einstein, to move up this meeting. If you'd waited another two weeks, we would've had their quarterly closing documents. But no ... you have to do everything the hard way. It's going to take us from now until then just to wade through all of this shit."

"I'm sorry, but weren't you the one pushing me to get a date for the gala? Flying Jenny back to San Francisco was part of the deal. Two birds with one stone and all that bollocks," I snap, exasperated. "I wouldn't have had a date otherwise."

Lettie stops shuffling. "What are you talking about? You could've asked Veronica."

I scowl at her. "That anorexic social climber? No way. One date with her was more than enough."

"At least you'd know who you're dealing with," she retorts.

"Weren't you also the one who said I needed to convince the board that I'm settling down by taking a suitable date? One look at Veronica and they'd know it was a sham."

Lettie narrows her eyes at me. "What do you even know about this girl? What's her name again?"

"Jenny Lynch," I say and grit my teeth.

"Have you even looked her up on Google?"

One look at the blank stare on my face and Lettie rolls her eyes. "You're so pathetic sometimes." She shoves the reports aside and drags her laptop over.

Her fingers tap the keyboard in a rapid-fire staccato beat.

"For fuck's sake, Devon!" Turning the laptop to face me, she points at the screen. "Did you even know that she has a boyfriend? It's right here on Facebook, doofus. See where it says, 'In a relationship'?"

A crushing weight descends on my chest. No, of course I didn't know because I never asked. It shouldn't matter, I remind myself. I asked her to go to the gala as a friend. My jaw tightens anyway, and I want to hurt someone.

She turns her laptop back around and squints at the display. "Some guy named Russell Montieth. Looks like they both went to Summit High School." Her fingers get busy again.

"It doesn't matter, Lettie. I'm not going to marry her, we're just going to hang out," I say more calmly than I feel.

Lettie looks at me with wide eyes. "So you weren't planning on getting laid, then?"

My fists clench at my sides. "No! I wasn't!" Well, maybe I was in my dreams.

She shakes her head. "Sometimes I wonder how we sprang from the same loins. Why in hell not? Oh yeah, because she has a boyfriend!"

I lean halfway across the desk. "Why are you so damn obsessed with my sex life? Isn't Howard keeping you satisfied?" I lob back at her.

Howard Cato III, heir to some shipping company. They've been dating—rather, hooking up—for the last year when he's stateside and not traveling internationally on business. Unlike me, Lettie likes to have sex with few to no strings. She definitely would've made a better guy. Lord knows she's got a big-enough set of bollocks.

"As a matter of fact, he is. He's rearranged his schedule to make sure he's home a week before the gala. I should be well satisfied before, during, and after unlike someone else I know," she says, giving me a snide look.

I circle back to Jenny's having a boyfriend, and a small bubble of anger and betrayal wells up inside me. Intellectually I know I don't have the right to feel it, but emotionally I can't help myself. How selfish is that? I offer her nothing, yet I want to have her to myself. Maybe it's because if I were healthy I'd want a chance. Maybe. Who am I kidding? Of course I would. But I'm not healthy, and that's what matters.

"And . . . they live together in San Francisco," she says, her fingers continuing their tap dance across the keyboard.

My heart drops again.

"Oh. My. God." She stops typing and squeals with devilish delight.

"What?" I bark in a gruff tone that I don't recognize as my own.

Lettie's eyes connect with mine as a wide smile splits her face. She picks up one of the random reports on the desk and makes it dance in her hands as she sings in a juvenile voice,

"He works for Nanotekx."

My spirits unexpectedly lift as if I might have some control over my own destiny, though I'm not sure how.

My cell phone rings. Lettie lunges for it, but I get there first. "Will you freakin' back off?" I say, glaring.

It's Jenny.

"Hey, hold on a sec."

I glare at Lettie and step into the hall. My heart thumps. I can't decide if I'm happy to hear from her or totally pissed off that she didn't tell me about her boyfriend. Either way, I'm not ready to discuss it.

"What's up?" I ask.

"I know it's totally last minute, but I was wondering . . . would you like to come to the city with me? My friend Crystal's show opens tonight on the Lower East Side. She's a painter, like you."

I'm totally taken aback. My mouth hangs open for a full second. "Yeah . . . what time?"

"Pick you up in an hour?"

I glance at my watch. It's almost five. "Sure."

"Where do you live on Essex?"

"Number nine."

"See you then."

Lettie looks up, slack-jawed, when I walk back into the library.

"What's the matter?"

"I found out something else while you were gone," she whispers.

Alarm bells trip inside me. "About Jenny?"

She shakes her head. "Nope. Her boyfriend."

"What about him?" I ask as I approach her. She shows me her screen. More Facebook. A couple caught in a lip-lock in a picture posted last night. The guy's hand is squeezing the girl's ass. An ass that clearly doesn't belong to Jenny. The guy tagged is Russ Montieth. He's with some girl whose name I don't recognize.

Lettie gives me a tight smile. "Looks likes Russ is having an affair with his boss at Nanotekx."

My heart suddenly aches for Jenny in more ways than one. One part of me wants to shelter her from finding out, a second part wants her to know the truth, and a third hungers for something else entirely.

I have an idea and bargain with myself until I settle on something that I can live with. I decide, screw it. Boyfriend or not, I'm going to make her mine, within reason, for the next two weeks . . . if she's willing. At least I won't feel guilty about it.

Game on.

Chapter 14

Jenny

"I'LL DRIVE HOME," Devon says, white faced, from the passenger seat as I squeeze between two cars into a spot on Forsyth Street that I found thanks to my uncanny parking karma. Though I'll admit, finding a parking spot on Manhattan's Lower East Side isn't nearly as challenging on a Monday night as it is on a weekend.

"What? Why?" I ask, turning the wheel with my eyes glued to the rearview mirror.

He doesn't release his death grip on the inside door handle until we're at a dead stop and parallel to the curb. "Because you shaved at least a couple of cats' lives off me, and I don't have any to spare."

"Don't be ridiculous. That was stellar New York City driving," I say.

He glares at me. "This isn't Italy. There are such things as traffic laws, you know."

"Oh, *puh-lease*. Besides, I've never been to Italy." I turn off the ignition and bat my eyelashes at him. "We're here."

He can't keep a straight face and breaks into a grin. "Maybe I'll take the train home."

I poke him in the ribs. "Will you stop already?"

He flinches and starts to laugh. "Don't. That tickles."

"Good to know. Ammo for later." I wink. Despite his complaints about my driving, I'm really glad he came. After a day and half hanging around the hospital, visiting with my family and the new baby, I had an undeniable craving to spend more time with Devon. To get to know him better before the gala, I told myself. Not a lie, just a stretching of the truth. Either way, I can't deny that I enjoy his company. He makes me feel alive in a way I haven't for a while. True, I could've come to see Crystal's show alone, but that seemed so . . . lonely. Especially on a perfect warm summer night in the city.

The gallery is only two blocks south on Forsyth. I lock the car, and we stroll down at a leisurely pace.

"How's the baby?" Devon asks.

I beam whenever Rachel is mentioned. "She's so cute. Big. She and my aunt go home tonight. My mom and I will rotate and give them relief for the rest of this week."

We walk close together without touching until my sandal catches on the uneven sidewalk and I stumble. Devon lunges for my upper arm to prevent my fall, and the momentum swings me on a collision course straight into him.

"You okay?" he asks as I lean against the firm planes of his chest. He's close enough that the warmth of his breath touches my cheek and the subtle scent of sandalwood from his cologne fills my senses. A new energy crackles between us. Something shifted after he ran his fingers down my neck in the dressing room on Saturday. Maybe I'm just crazy or imagining things. But he doesn't move and neither do I.

"Yeah . . . thanks," I say, suddenly self-conscious. I'm close enough to stare directly into his eyes. The color isn't a solid blue. Flecks of gold and brown dot the centers of his irises.

A smile tugs at the corner of his mouth. "You won't fall if I let you go?"

I take a deep breath. "No. I'm fine. Stupid sidewalk."

He releases me and chuckles. Rather than moving away, he offers me his elbow. "Here. To prevent any accidental wipeouts."

Flashing a sheepish grin, I loop my arm through his and feel a blush spread across my cheeks. "Thanks."

The gallery is small and crowded. I don't think twice before grabbing a flute of champagne as the waiter passes. I'm hoping to chase away the flutter in my midsection, but I'll have to cap it at two if I expect to drive home. "None for you?" I ask Devon.

He shakes his head and frowns.

I raise my glass. "You don't mind if I have one, do you?"

He shakes his head again. "No. It's just me. I can't."

I arch a brow. "Why?"

He gives me a tight smile and looks away. "Where's your friend?"

I narrow my eyes at his deflection but let it pass. Instead I rise on tiptoe and surf my gaze over the top of the crowd. I spot Crystal's blue-streaked hair at ten o'clock and point. "This way."

The white walls are covered with her canvases. The theme is a juxtaposition of nudes over abstract backgrounds. The blend of the genres looks like da Vinci overlaid on an explosion of Kandinsky, Miró, and Pollock. The intensity of colors is nearly blinding, in a pleasing way.

Crystal sees me as I approach and breaks into a peal of delighted squeals a moment before she hurls her five-foot-two-inch frame into my open arms. I'm amazed the champagne is still safely in the glass after impact.

"Holy crap! I can't believe you're here!" she says.

"The show is amazing!" I say, glancing around. Crystal and I were good friends in high school. Voted "Most Outrageous" senior year, she hung out with the Bohemian crowd. More often than not, we would team up and lead the set design for all our school plays.

"So who's your friend?" she asks, giving Devon an appreciative once-over.

"This is Devon," I say warmly, meeting his eyes.

Devon steps forward with his hand extended.

"Screw that." Crystal throws herself into his arms. Ignoring the startled look on his face, she plants a big kiss on his cheek. "If you're with Jenster, that's good enough for me."

Devon gives me a look of utter helplessness as Crystal clings to him like a barnacle on a boat bottom.

"You're so totally hot," Crystal finally says and lets him go. "How long have you guys been dating?"

An endearing blush spreads across Devon's cheeks and his lips flap open, then shut . . . like a guppy's. I cover my mouth with the back of my hand to stifle a laugh. Oops, I should've warned him about her. In all fairness to Crystal, the last time we spoke was last summer after Russ and I "took a break," as he likes to call it. So seeing me with Devon isn't strange to her. I wouldn't even have known about tonight's event if a postcard hadn't arrived in my parents' mailbox.

"We're just friends," I say to save him before sipping my champagne.

"What a shame," she mumbles and shifts her gaze to Devon. "You should do something about that."

He clears his throat and points to the nearest painting. "What inspired you?"

I start to appreciate Devon's talent for diversion.

Crystal and Devon spend the next fifteen minutes engaged in a deep discussion of pigments and abstract expressionism until the gallery owner gives Crystal a tap on the shoulder and whispers something in her ear.

"Gotta go. I have a live one over there. Don't leave without saying goodbye!" she says and disappears into the crowd.

"Sorry about that," I say, slipping my arm back through his. "She's a little intense."

"No problem, *Jenster*." He grins.

"Very funny," I say as we mill around.

"I want to show you something," Devon says suddenly and drags me toward one of the paintings on the other side of the gallery. It's a female nude over a psychedelic background. Her back is to the viewer and her head turned to the side, showing her face in profile.

We stand in front of the canvas. "See that?" His finger traces a path down the back of her neck and then curves around to skim along her shoulder.

"See what exactly?" I ask, at a loss.

"That curve, right there? It's the most sensual part of a woman's body," he says, giving me a wry smile.

"Really? Is this scientific fact or opinion?" I ask.

He sweeps the hair back off my shoulder and eyes my neck. "Opinion. Mine."

I clear my throat and amble over toward the next painting. "So when do you find time to paint?" I ask, hoping he doesn't notice the slight tremor in my hand. Without thinking twice, I throw back the rest of the champagne and discard the glass on the nearest passing tray.

He clasps his hands behind his back as he walks. "Kingsbridge's been a time suck lately. I don't really find it, I just take it. Usually Saturday or Sunday afternoons."

"*Hmm.* When I met you on the plane, I would've never guessed you had a creative side. It's a nice surprise."

His eyebrows draw together. "Should I be offended?"

"No. It's only that looks can be deceiving," I say. "Do you show your work at all?"

"I used to. I had a couple of small shows in university before ..." His voice trails off, and he nods at the next painting. "What do you think of that one?"

I pull him to a stop. He tenses under my touch. "Not so fast. Before what?"

He shakes his head and sighs. "There's a lot you don't know about me, Jenny. And just as much that I can't tell you."

"Can't or won't?"

"Both," he says, meeting my gaze.

Frustration bubbles up inside me, and I have the sudden urge to stamp my foot. "Why? What's so terrible? Are you being chased by drug dealers? On the Most Wanted list? About to be arrested for white-collar crime? What?"

He gives me a bleak smile. "Nothing like that. All I can tell you is that I'm trying to protect my family." That look of sadness he carries at the corners of his eyes glares at me like a neon sign.

"Lettie and your half brother?"

He snorts. "No. Lettie and my mom. My half brother ..." He shakes his head. "Let's not go there."

"Ah. Family politics. Got it ... I think." I cock my head.

"Close enough," he says. This time he reaches out and takes my hand. "Be patient with me. I'll tell you more. Just give me some time, okay?" His lips brush my knuckles, and then he releases my hand. A tingle of awareness travels through me from scalp to toe, triggering a traitorous rush of warmth in my core.

I nod and gather my wits, switching back to my original line of questioning. "Where's your studio?"

"Am I being interviewed again?" he asks, amused.

"Kind of. Doing my prep work for the gala," I say. The truth is, I want to learn more than the basics about his life, but if he's not ready to share I won't push. That said, I'm seriously starting to doubt my own intentions. So much so that I reach for another glass of bubbly confidence from the passing waiter and take a sip. The effervescence tickles my nose, and I get a tiny head rush.

"Is that all?" he asks. "Just prepping for the gala?"

I shake my head and answer honestly. "No."

He squeezes my arm. "Good ..."

A little thrill shoots through me.

"To answer your original question, my studio is uptown."

"Here? In the city? Why so far from home?" I ask, continuing to sip and letting the rush of alcohol course through my veins.

He shrugs. "It's more convenient than you think. Plus I share the studio with some other artists to keep expenses low."

"Expenses? You're concerned about expenses? After spending almost seven thousand dollars on my outfit?" I say, barely able to suppress a smirk.

"Listen, if it makes you feel any better, I'm taking that from the clothing allowance Lettie and I get for family foundation- and Kingsbridge-related events. It wasn't straight from my pocket."

I stare at him, agape. Clothing allowance? Who gets a clothing allowance? Another reminder that maybe I should ignore this crazy reaction I'm having to him. Despite the perks, I'm not sure how close I want to get to his world.

"Getting back to the shared studio, what are you working on right now?" We resume our stroll around the gallery.

"I'm in the middle of a few projects. Nothing too inspiring." He leans down and whispers in my ear. "Which is why I want to paint you."

A shiver traverses my spine at the sensual tone of his voice. There's no way I can be imagining this. What's more, I hope I'm not.

I finish the champagne and ditch the glass on a table.

My heart skips a beat. Is it suddenly warm in here, or is it me? I look him in the eye and feel as if I'm seeing him for the first time. God, he's attractive. Why does he have to be so damn attractive? And those lips? Shit. Stop looking at his lips! He's a friend. Yeah, but it's not like you want to kiss any of your other male friends. My lungs convulse and I hyperventilate. "I need to go outside."

The look on his face turns to panic. "Are you all right?"

"Air . . . Need air." I turn on my heel and dash for the door.

Devon races after me. "Was it something I said?"

"No." *Yeah, but not in the way you think.*

Outside he grasps my arm and points to one of the benches in the park across the street. "Let's go sit down."

"Can we walk instead?" I ask, pulling from his grasp and crossing my arms over my chest.

A worried frown is pasted to his brow. "Sure, whatever you want. You're not going to faint, are you?"

"No. I'll be fine. Really." I'm struck by his concern, but how do I explain my sudden urge to taste his kiss, to feel his lips on mine? Didn't he make it clear he just wants to be friends? Or is he backpedaling, too? Either way, I have no right to step over that line, and the last thing I want to do is put us in an uncomfortable position and leave him without a date for the gala.

And then there's the small matter of ending my engagement. Damn it. How did I end up here?

I stalk away into the dusky night to find the nearest tree. It's the closest I'll come to finding a place to hide . . . from myself . . . from Devon. Stupid, I know. But I just don't know what's come over me.

Devon seizes my arm and pulls me to a stop. There's an unmistakable look of confusion in his eyes. "What's the matter? What did I do?"

"I'm sorry," I say over my pounding heart. "It's not you."

"I don't understand," he says softly, stepping closer. "Talk to me."

I press my eyes shut. "I know we're just friends but I can't control this overwhelming desire to . . ."

"Shhh," he says and slowly draws me into his arms. My eyes pop open until I'm staring straight at those sexy gold and brown flecks in his eyes. "Jenny . . ."

Then I know I'm not imagining it. I know we're both thinking the same thing.

His lips hover close to mine, their gravitational pull

stealing what's left of my breath. I'm sure of it now. He's waiting for me to bridge the gap. Just when I think I can do it, I turn away.

"I have a boyfriend," I blurt, hanging my head and feeling hope drain out of me. I refuse to start something with Devon based on deception. Regardless of how I feel about Russ, I owe him some acknowledgment.

"I don't care," he whispers. "It doesn't matter to me. I know it should, but it doesn't."

My heads snaps up. "What?"

He casts his eyes downward. "Jenny . . . I. . ." Letting out a breath, he shakes his head and meets my gaze. "There are a million reasons why I can't think of life past the gala. Can I make you a proposal?"

I give him a sideways glance. "What kind of proposal?"

"If all I could offer you was the next two weeks . . ." Pain replaces the worry etched into his brow, and hope shines from his eyes. He cups my cheek in his hand and asks softly, "Would you take them?"

A lump rises in my throat as I experience a combination of relief, desire, and the knowledge that wherever things may take us, our time together is finite. Given my situation, it's for the best. Still, his proposal wraps me in a veil of sadness, because I get the distinct feeling that it's not his preference.

"Is there someone else for you, too? Is that why?" I ask.

"No. Nothing like that," he says, letting his hand slip from my cheek and twining his fingers through mine. "If we start something knowing it all had to end between us after the gala when I drop you off in San Francisco, would you do it?"

My mouth opens, but the answer gets stuck in my throat. Being with him for the next two weeks isn't where my hesitation lies. Rather, it's the thought of saying goodbye that worries me. What if I get attached to him and find I can't let go? Then there's my situation with Russ. God help me.

"I've never cheated on him," I whisper, feeling compelled

to make Devon understand that if I say yes, it's not because I've done this before. Sadly, I can't say the same about my fiancé. He had a slip during college that almost tore us apart. Regardless, the truth is, if I still planned to marry Russ, I wouldn't be standing here.

The hopeful glimmer in Devon's eyes wavers. He releases my hand and steps away. "I realize it's an unfair request. We could just keep our distance and stay friends. It's your choice," he says quietly.

His withdrawal leaves me unexpectedly bereft. "I don't want you to think less of me," I say over the lump still resting in my throat.

A look of earnestness creases his sandy brow as he gently brushes a lock of hair from my face. "That would never happen."

A spark reignites in my chest, but before I can speak he rests a finger on my lips and says, "Before you say anything, there's something else."

"What's that?"

"The more I think about what my sister said to me, the more I think she's right. We'll have to be convincing enough at the gala so that the board thinks I'm considering marriage. Can you do that?"

One thing is clear. His offer doesn't come without consequences or a price ... for both of us. I'm just not sure whose price will be higher. But whatever I choose, I have to commit to it one hundred percent.

I remind myself of something Raine once told me: "There are no guarantees. There are gambles, chances, and hope. You'll have to place your bets in life, there's no getting around it. For what it's worth, the best advice I can give you is to follow your heart."

But what if my heart can't be trusted? *Gambles, chances, and hope.*

I step into Devon on an inhale, and against every shred of

good sense I ever thought I possessed, I accept the odds and whisper my answer, "Yes."

His face lights up and his strong arms enfold me inside their warmth. Taking his face in my hands, I melt my lips onto his . . . and remember what it feels like to breathe.

Chapter 15

Devon

THE MOMENT JENNY'S lips touch mine I almost come undone. I've wanted to kiss her since she picked me up at the house.

Something cracked inside me the moment I saw that her boyfriend was cheating on her, making her fair game. For now I'll blame the decision to compromise my principles on white knight syndrome, and the belief that I may never get another chance to be with someone like Jenny while I'm alive. Maybe—just for two weeks—we could accomplish two things at once: letting whatever happens happen and delivering a convincing performance to the board.

I couldn't be sure she was interested until she stumbled on the sidewalk, and even then it took me until she ran out of the gallery to confirm it. Either way, it had to be up to her, and I was fully prepared to respect her wishes if she declined my offer. But I needed to know whether she would be honest with me first—if she'd admit to being in a relationship. For all my bravado earlier this evening, I don't think I would've followed through on my intentions if she hadn't. Honesty is important to me, too. Granted, there's a lot I don't want her to know, but I've been honest about that. I'm not hiding that I have secrets … I'll even tell her some of them. There's no escaping it if I plan to take this further.

I pull her closer until her breasts press into my chest. My tongue gently parts her lips and slips into her mouth, locking us into a heady dance of exploration against the backdrop of cool, dry champagne. The feel of her against me is better than I could've imagined. My groin tightens and fills so fast I'm almost embarrassed by my lack of control.

No erectile issues here. I shift my pelvis back so that Mr. Happy isn't anywhere close to knocking on heaven's door.

As I end the kiss, she pulls me back in for another. Her nails glide up and down the back of my shirt, raising gooseflesh on my arms. My chest heaves as we break apart, and I hope the mild dizziness I'm feeling is from exertion and not an abnormal lack of oxygen from my condition.

"I've wanted to do that all night," I whisper. "But I've wanted to do this even more." Hugging her close, I bury my nose at the juncture of her neck and inhale the sweet, warm scent of her skin before leaving a kiss there. She shudders under my touch.

"Let's say goodbye to Crystal and head back?" she says softly.

"Sounds good."

"Devon?"

"Yeah?"

She extracts the car keys from her purse and gives them a jingle. "Will you drive us back? That last glass of champagne did me in."

I take the keys and give her a wry grin. "No need to ask twice. You're not going to have any drunken regrets tomorrow, are you?"

She dips in and leaves a featherlight kiss on my lips. "Not a chance."

A flutter of hope echoes in my chest. I beat it down and remind myself this arrangement has an expiration date.

WE PULL INTO the Broadway Diner parking lot in Summit during one of my childhood stories growing up with Lettie.

"She did *what*?" Jenny giggles.

I kill the engine. "She would steal the heart-shaped marshmallows out of my cereal bowl. I'd come back from whatever silly errand she sent me on—'Devvie, can you get my American Girl doll?'—and they'd be gone. No pink hearts. To be fair, she'd drop a few green shamrocks in to lessen the blow." I'm laughing with her by the time I finish although I still feel the sting of betrayal in my young heart at the retelling.

"What a nice brother . . . ," Jenny coos next to me, running her fingers down my arm.

"More like my first lesson in female manipulation," I say in my own defense. "You know what she'd do when I called her on it?"

"What?"

"She'd blink her big blue eyes at me and say, 'You would've given them to me anyway if I'd asked.'" I shake my head. "I couldn't win for losing. Between her and my mom, they brainwashed chivalry into me early."

"That's not such a bad thing," she says. "It sounds like it was fun being a twin."

I smile and take her hand as we walk into the diner. "It was and it still is. As much as Lettie can be a nosy, overbearing pain in the butt, she's incredibly loyal. She's always there for me when I need her."

"And you for her?" Jenny asks.

"Yeah, and me for her."

The waitress seats us at a table near the window.

"I'm starving," Jenny says, scanning the menu.

I give it a half-hearted glance, looking for low-sodium options and settling on egg whites and plain toast. I'm thirty minutes late taking the meds in my pocket. Food will help.

"What are you having?" I ask Jenny.

"Pancakes."

"Pancakes?" I imagine that sick feeling from the weight of them in my stomach. "This late? Better you than me." I take Jenny's hand in mine. "So what else do you want to know about my childhood?"

She leans closer. "You mention Lettie and your mom a lot, but not your dad. Why?"

I shrug. "He traveled a lot and wasn't around much when we were young. He always worked when he was home. Don't get me wrong. He treated us well enough. I'm not sure how to describe him beyond blaming his attitude on a cold, upper-crust British upbringing. Traditional ideals like freaking boarding school." I shake my head and finger a packet of sugar as I remember. "It was one of the biggest fights my parents ever had. My dad arranged for me and Lettie to go to boarding school—apart, mind you—without telling my mother. She went ballistic when she found out."

"Sounds like you weren't very close."

"Yeah, you could say that. How about you? Are you close to your parents?"

Her face lights up and she nods. "My mom and I are close but in a different way than I am with my dad. Mom's kindhearted and very supportive but a little old-fashioned, and my dad is more relaxed and easy to talk to." She looks at me shyly and smiles. "He taught me how fix cars. I spent hours helping him in the stable, getting his babies restored and just talking. That was before I discovered boys. But even now, I still help him sometimes."

My respect for and awe of Jenny escalates a few notches. "Cars, huh? Aren't you full of surprises?" I say, turning the phrase back on her that she used on me about painting. I make a mental note to visit Motor Vehicles this week and see about some plates for the Aston Martin.

The waitress returns and takes our order. No sooner does she snap her pad shut than the decibel level rises as a group of rowdy teenagers enters the diner.

"Jenny!" a voice exclaims from the crowd that just walked in.

The color drains from Jenny's face and she jerks her hand away, hiding it in her lap.

"I thought I saw you through the window," says a young girl with dark, curly hair. "When are you going to call Mom?"

"Ronny," Jenny says, trying to regain her composure and failing.

Ronny eyes me suspiciously. "Hi, who are you?"

I smile politely. "I'm Devon, a friend of Jenny."

"*Huh,*" she grunts and promptly ignores me. "So my vote's for a June wedding next year after graduation."

Jenny and I lock eyes. I'm not sure which of us is whiter. All I know is that my stomach just dropped to somewhere around my knees.

I clear my throat and rest my napkin on the table. "Excuse me for moment. Here, sit." I motion Ronny toward a chair.

Jenny pastes on a smile. "I'm still working dates out with my mom. I'll be sure to call her in a day or two." Her words fade behind me as I head to the men's room to take my meds and kick myself in the ass but not before I hear Ronny ask, "Where's your engagement ring?"

Great. Just great.

I down my pills and splash some water on my face before returning to the table. Jenny's there alone when I return, looking distraught, while Ronny and her friends are stationed on the other side of the diner, out of view and earshot.

I slip into my chair and reposition the napkin on my lap, afraid to speak for fear of what will come out of my mouth. Is a fiancé so different from a long-term, live-in boyfriend? Sadly, to me, the answer is yes.

"Say something," she hisses from across the table.

"Like what?" I ask, passing a hand across my chin.

"I'm sorry. I should've been more specific."

"You think?" I snap, and then I immediately regret it. "It's not your fault. It's mine."

Our meals come, but I've lost my appetite.

She slumps in her chair. "It's not . . ." Letting out a breath, she stops and wrings her hands. Then she looks into my eyes. "I'm not wearing a ring because I decided to give it back."

Something reignites near my heart. "Why?"

Jenny folds her hands in front of her. "We've been together since I was sixteen. He's all I've ever known. My first love. When he got a job out west after he graduated, he didn't ask me to go with him, so I broke up with him. I should've left it at that. I should've recognized that we'd changed." Her eyes fill with tears. "He came home for Thanksgiving and talked me into going back with him. I gave him an ultimatum . . . by Christmas I had a ring."

I stay silent as she crushes a napkin in her hand.

"It didn't take me long to realize that I'd made a mistake." She shakes her head. "Nothing I did measured up. I didn't have a flashy job, and I wasn't making the kind of salary he was. Money became an issue fast. He wanted a lifestyle we couldn't afford, and before I knew it, his parents were sending us money every month. Then he started picking at me about every little thing. Not cleaning the apartment well enough or not making what he wanted for dinner. The walls started closing in on me . . . until I couldn't breathe."

My shoulders relax as I listen to Jenny's story, and my anger at her evaporates although I want to smack some sense into her idiot fiancé. What's the matter with the guy? Obviously he doesn't deserve her.

"We had a big fight the morning I met you. It's one of the reasons that I was so psycho at the airline counter. Between that fight and the thought of something happening to my aunt Jill and the baby? I was a total mess."

"So you're breaking off your engagement?" I ask.

She nods. "He just doesn't know it yet."

I take her hand. "Thanks for telling me." Rather than thinking I made the wrong decision, I'm convinced that I made the right one.

Chapter 16

Jenny

"JENNY, DARLING, TELL me what's going on," my mom says the moment I walk in from the garage, her hands planted on her generous hips.

A chill ripples through me. "What do you mean?" I ask, avoiding her eyes and fumbling with my purse. After watching Rachel for part of the morning and then waitressing at the Grasshopper, all I want to do is take a shower before I head to Devon's for dinner.

"The wedding, Jenny! I just hung up with Russ's mother," she says. "Not only are you here to help with Rachel, but we're supposed to pick a date and do some planning. All you've done is avoid the topic since you've gotten home. So I'll ask you again, what's going on?"

"We have time," I mumble and toss my purse onto the counter. She's right. I've been pushing off the inevitable, afraid of her reaction, and I'm not sure I want talk about it now and ruin my night.

Mom blows out a breath and asks quietly. "Is it that boy Devon?"

"No! He has nothing to do with it," I say. "And he's not a boy."

"Man, boy, whatever," Mom retorts. "If he has nothing to do with it, then why did Ronny Montieth see him holding your hand Monday night at the diner?"

My mouth drops open, and what feels like ice water races through my veins. I wonder if that's why I've had a welcome reprieve from Russ's calls and texts for the last few days. I hadn't noticed how much time had slipped by; it's already Thursday.

Mom's eyes soften, and she comes over to take my hand between hers. "Sweetie, do you love him?"

"Huh?" I'm confused about which one she means. I barely know Devon, but my heart is definitely fonder of him right now than of Russ.

"Russ? Do you love Russ?" she asks softly.

Funny, it's easier talking to Aunt Jillian and Raine about Russ than my own mother. I guess because I feel they have less of a bias. Mom would love to see me paired off so I can supply her with grandkids. Maybe now that Rachel is here, that will satisfy her for a while.

"Sit with me, Jenny." Her warm brown eyes plead.

I collapse onto a chair by the kitchen table.

"You're having second thoughts, aren't you?"

It takes me a few breaths to respond as I prepare for Mom's reaction. I rest a palm over my eyes and nod. "It's not like I thought it would be. We've changed, or maybe I just never knew him this way before." No longer able to avoid the truth, I drop my hand and force the words through my lips. "I don't think I can marry him."

She covers my hand, her eyes glistening. "Then don't, baby. Don't marry him," she says earnestly and shakes her head. "Marriage is one of the most important decisions you'll ever make. Take your time and make the right one, no matter what."

It takes me a moment to realize the confrontation I've been dreading isn't coming. Relief washes over me like a giant tidal wave, unleashing a whole host of pent-up emotions.

My vision blurs and I bite my lip. "So you're not upset that I want to break off the engagement?"

She sighs. "No, honey. I would've been upset if you married him because you were too afraid not to."

The burden lifts from my shoulders and I feel a whole lot lighter. For some reason, she and her high school sweetheart, John Henshaw, spring to mind.

"Mom?"

"*Mmm?*"

"Is that why you didn't marry John? Did you find out he wasn't the person you thought he was after you both grew up?"

A tear suddenly slips down her cheek, and she brushes it away. "No, honey. He's always been tried and true. It was me who turned out to be the disappointment." She leans over and kisses me on the cheek. "Always be true to yourself, Jenny."

I sit stunned and unmoving at the table as she leaves the room, and I realize she's just handed me a small piece of her and John's puzzle. Another thing is clear: she still loves him, and I'd bet all the tips in my purse that he feels the same way.

Tomorrow . . . I'll tell Russ tomorrow.

I GIVE THE bouquet in my hand one last glance and ring the bell at a few minutes to seven. Between my tips from last night and this afternoon, I have cash in my wallet, less the cost of flowers.

My heart picks up a beat as I wait for someone to answer.

Then the door swings wide, and Lettie beams at me from the doorway. "Jenny! How beautiful. Come in." She takes the flowers. "Let me put these in water."

"Thank you for the dinner invitation," I say, following in Lettie's wake. She sure travels swiftly for a woman a whole head shorter than I am. Her pale-blonde ponytail bobs as she walks down the hall. Based on Lettie's attire, I'm glad I didn't overdress. Barefoot with no makeup, she's wearing jeans and a clingy top that confirms what she lacks in height she makes up for in boob. I note the inequity with a pang of envy.

"Where's Devon?" I ask after her. We turn left into the kitchen, which is large, modern, and expensive. Everything you'd expect in a $5 million Summit home. Sad to think our little Colonial on the other side of town would now go for more than a million. It wouldn't be worth half that if Summit weren't so close to Manhattan.

"He just went up to see my mom. He'll be down shortly," she says and finishes arranging the flowers in a vase. Without missing a beat, she picks up the wooden spoon lying next to the stove and stirs. The savory smell in the kitchen makes my mouth water.

"Do you need any help?" I ask, not knowing what to do with my hands and finally settling on crossing my arms over my chest.

"Nope, I have it covered," she says.

"It smells great. What are you making?"

"Brisket." She picks up the timer. "It's got another ten minutes. Have a seat. I'll be done with the gravy in a minute."

I pull out a bar stool at the kitchen island and sit.

Lettie taps the spoon on the rim of the pot, sets it down, and then removes the gravy from the flame. After wiping her hands on a dish towel, she comes to sit next to me.

"So," she says, giving me a tight smile and a hard, appraising look. "What are your intentions toward my brother?"

My eyes widen. "Excuse me?"

"What do you want from him?" she asks calmly.

I bristle. "What do you mean, what do I want from him? Nothing . . . I don't want anything from him."

"Let's speak candidly, shall we?" Lettie clasps her hands in front of her as if she's preparing for a business meeting. "My brother is about to inherit our family's empire, making him a very wealthy man. That also makes him a pretty good catch. So I want to know what a girl with a fiancé and less than three hundred dollars in her bank account wants with my brother."

My jaw unhinges and I stare at her for a full five seconds, until my Irish wells up into my chest and I slap the counter. Better than her face, I reason. "First of all, I'm not even going to ask how you know the balance of my bank account—nor do I care—but I will tell you that I don't want his money, and I think he'd back me up on that. Second, I agreed to his request—as a friend—to get to know him and accompany him to the gala. Third, Devon knows about my situation, and he doesn't care. And last? Our arrangement ends in two weeks after he drops me off in San Francisco. Does that sufficiently answer your fucking question?"

I stand up and glare at her, my hands clenched. I'm not sure if I'm more intent on defending my honor or Devon's.

Lettie nods, her smile turning impish. "It does." She giggles, pops up off her stool, and throws her arms around me in a hug. "I knew I liked you for a reason."

I stand dumbstruck as she releases me and heads to the oven. "I wouldn't have asked if he didn't like you so much and the two of you didn't look so damn cute together." She turns back, wearing an oven mitt. "Are you sure about the just-friends and two-week thing?"

"Uh ..." My brain short-circuits, still frozen on the defensive.

She pulls the roast out, shuts off the timer, and comes back to sit down. "Listen." She leans in toward me and speaks quietly. "I love my brother, and I don't want to see him get hurt. I don't know how much he's told you yet, but he hasn't looked at anybody like he's looked at you since ... university," she says, her word selection hinting at the same British education as Devon.

"*University?* Is that what you meant to say?" I eye her

warily.

She smiles, checks her watch, and slips back off the stool. "Devon used to believe in happy endings . . . I still do. What about you?"

"You and Devon have a knack for avoiding direct questions."

She crinkles her nose. "It's a twin thing. So do you?"

I frown. "Why do you ask?"

"Because Devon's problem is Devon. He's the most loyal person I know, and he's spent the last couple of years sacrificing everything for our family. I'd like him to take a little slice of happiness for himself," she says as sadness settles in the corners of her eyes.

I'm struck in that moment at how similar they look and how they both must be shouldering the same sad burden . . . whatever it is.

"He says the same about you," I say softly.

"That I've sacrificed everything?" she says, her brows lifting in surprise.

"No, that you're loyal." I smile, and the tension drains from my spine.

She glances over my shoulder and breaks into a wide smile. "Hey, Dev."

"Hi." Devon's arms encircle me from behind, and he kisses my neck. A shiver runs over my arms. "You're early."

"I am?" I lean back into him. "Your text said seven."

"What—" He stops and sighs. "Lettie?"

She doesn't answer but rather bats her eyelashes at him. "Grab the plates, Dev."

"Please tell me you're not going to run away screaming at anything she's said," he whispers in my ear.

I chuckle and whisper back, "We're all good."

"Thank God." He gives me one last squeeze and then lets me go to search for plates.

Lettie swings by as he rummages around in one of the

cabinets, and she says low enough that only I can hear, "Just friends, huh? By the way, have you been on Facebook lately?"

Honestly, I hadn't. Ever since I removed all the data-sucking apps from my phone to save on my data plan, my social media usage has suffered.

I haven't decided yet how I feel about Lettie. Her erratic behavior keeps me on guard, but I can't help wondering what else she knows that I don't. One thing I'm sure of: nothing she says seems to be without motive.

Note to self: check Facebook when I get home.

Chapter 17

Devon

"SO WHY DID Lettie drag you over early?" I ask Jenny the moment I close my bedroom door. "I assume she wanted to get you alone for one devious reason or another."

Dinner was civil and filled with polite conversation. I get the feeling that Lettie has taken a liking to Jenny, but I'm not sure the feeling is mutual.

Rather than answering, Jenny widens her eyes at the display on my wall.

"Devon, are those real swords?" She walks past me to get a closer look.

"Yeah. Some are reproductions, but most are antiques."

"How many are there?"

I scratch my head, squint at the wall, and do a quick count. "Thirty-five."

She turns back to me, wide eyed. "Do you just collect them or do you . . . fence?"

I chuckle. "There's not much up there suitable for fencing. For fun, I've taken some sword-fighting lessons."

"What's that big one there?" Jenny points to a Scottish broadsword.

"It's called a claymore, a two-handed sword used by

Scottish Highlanders from the fifteenth through the seventeenth centuries. Most people know it because of William Wallace." I walk up behind her and rest my chin on her shoulder. She relaxes back against me until our bodies are flush. "This section here"—I point to the left side of the display—"are all Scottish and English examples. The section in the center is Spanish and Italian, and on the right side are swords from East Asia—mostly China and Japan."

"Impressive," she says.

I've missed touching her. The feel of her against me kicks up my heart rate. I'm already planning for Saturday. In my head I've started mixing the pigments for her portrait.

She twists in my arms to face me, and I settle my clasped hands at the small of her back. Her warmth and softness press into my chest.

"What sparked your interest in sword collecting?" she asks.

I shrug. "Too many games of make-believe as a kid with Lettie, I guess. Somewhere along the way she convinced me that a guy with a sword could always save the day."

"*Hmm.* Is that so? She said you used to believe in happy endings ... and that you don't anymore. Why's that?" She stares at me with big, blue, inquisitive eyes.

Damn it, Lettie.

"What else did she tell you?" I tense, loosening my hold on her.

She runs her finger over the crease in my forehead. "Stop frowning. She didn't tell me much. As a matter of fact, she's as good as you are at avoiding a direct answer."

"I'm sorry about that," I say.

Her eyes harden. "Then maybe you should start by explaining why your mother didn't join us for dinner."

I blink, and then it hits me. I'm so used to my mother's disability that it didn't even occur to me how odd it would seem to Jenny.

Breaking into a half smile, I twine my fingers through hers and lead her to the sitting area in my room. "Let's sit down, and I'll explain."

She lets me tow her along, casting a dubious glance in my direction. We settle comfortably on the couch. I take a deep breath and begin. "My mom is more or less immobile. She slipped and fell down the stairs when Lettie and I were twelve. The fall paralyzed her from the waist down."

Jenny gasps. "Oh, I'm so sorry."

I squeeze her hand and hold it between mine. "There's more. When we found out that my dad had another child and a mistress in England, my mom had a stroke. It almost finished the job, paralyzing her whole right side and taking her speech. That was a year later, right before we left for boarding school. She lives in the west wing of the house with twenty-four-hour nursing care." I give her a shy smile. "I wanted to visit her before you got here since I didn't know how late you'd be staying."

"So it's not because she didn't want to meet me?" Jenny asks, her shoulders slumping in what I hope is relief.

My heart squeezes. "Are you kidding me? She'd love to meet you. It's just . . ."

"Just what?"

I shake my head. "It's just . . . that I don't want her to get the wrong idea."

"Oh," Jenny says and pulls her hand away.

"Don't do that, okay?" I plead, combing my fingers through my hair. "I can't let my mom think she's on her way to becoming a grandmother. 'Cause God knows that's what she'll want to believe if I take you up there."

"Why? Is she trying to marry you off?" Jenny asks, folding her legs underneath her.

I snort. "She would if she had the chance."

Jenny frowns. "You may be surprised. I thought my mom wanted that, too, until I told her I'm ending my engagement."

My eyebrows shoot up. "Really? What did she say?" I ask. Not because I don't believe she wants to cancel her wedding; rather because she stepped over the line and told someone who mattered.

"She said not to marry him if I wasn't sure. That she would've only been upset if I'd been too afraid to cancel the wedding and married him anyway." She touches my cheek. "I think our parents just want us to be happy, whatever that means."

"Your mother is a wise woman," I say.

"I'm sure yours is, too."

"How about this? I'll introduce you on the night of the gala. She'd appreciate seeing us dressed up," I say, knowing it would give my mom a thrill without giving her too much lead time to wear me down.

Her lips tip up in a smile. "It's a deal."

I narrow my eyes at her and pick up the remote. "Which horror classic are you in the mood for tonight?" Jenny and I declared tonight movie night following dinner. We made a deal to watch a few of our favorite films. I won the coin toss, so we start with mine.

She throws her head back onto the cushion. "Oh boy, what are my choices? No *Dawn of the Dead*, or I might not sleep."

I name my top five, and we settle on *Bram Stoker's Dracula* with Gary Oldman. I cue it up on my entertainment system and dim the lights.

"You want popcorn?" I ask. Lucas would have a shit fit if he knew I'm even considering it.

"No, thanks. Food and horror don't mix for me." She snuggles in next to me, and my arm automatically drapes itself around her shoulder.

"Have it your way," I say, pulling her closer.

"Fair warning, I'm picking the sappiest, most romantic movies I can think of when it's my turn."

"Yeah, yeah. Take your best shot."

What I don't tell her is that I'll probably enjoy whatever she picks as much as any of my horror films as long as she's next to me.

Chapter 18

Jenny

MY HEAD RESTS on Devon's shoulder as the closing credits roll. I crane my neck to peer up into his face. "That was pretty good."

Devon smiles, his eyes sparkling with the reflection of the television in the dim light. "You want to watch another one?"

I spot the time on the cable box, stifle a yawn with the back of my hand, and straighten up. "It's almost eleven. I don't think I can stay awake for another one."

"Wimp," Devon says softly and leans in to kiss the tip of my nose.

"Who are you calling a wimp?" I tease and dance my fingers over his midsection.

Devon bursts into laughter and folds in half, trying to escape my sudden attack. He should've never admitted he was ticklish. He squirms and falls over onto the cushion, and then I'm on him, laughing, my body covering his.

"Jenny ... please," he gasps between peals of laughter. "Stop!"

My fingers freeze, and I stare into his boyish, beautiful face. The laughter stops, and he shifts underneath me until I feel every peak and valley of his anatomy pressed against me.

It sets me aflame. His eyes lock on mine as his arms encircle me, and his hands settle into the hollow at my lower back. Liquid desire spreads through my veins, and my lips seize his. He pulls me tighter to his chest, meeting me with equal fervor. Within seconds he stirs against me, and I don't mind. The chemistry between us is electric, crackling over my skin and making me want something I shouldn't.

His hands travel over me in passionate exploration, caressing, kneading, stroking . . . Between that, the taste of his lips, and the harmony of our kiss, I can't get enough. Devon fills my lungs with oxygen while Russ only takes it away.

I lose myself awhile longer until guilt overcomes me. All I can think of is that until I officially break off my engagement, I'm cheating.

Breathless, I pull back. "I should go . . . ," I whisper. Because Lord knows what will happen if I stay, and I'm not ready to throw all my values out the window in one night.

He gives me a wry smile. "You sure?"

I nod. "Yeah," I say and press a chaste kiss to his lips, then lift myself off him.

He sits upright and turns up the lights. It's only then that I notice that in addition to his collection of mounted blades, large canvases hang on the opposing walls. Not that I didn't see them before; it's more that the weight of our conversation before the movie distracted me from making the connection that they could be Devon's.

"Is this your work?" I ask, pointing to a large expressionist painting. The colors are reminiscent of Crystal's work.

Devon nods. "Yeah, that one's from my Edvard Munch phase. I found the way he set his inner emotional turmoil to canvas inspiring."

There are four works in total, done in various styles. I'm impressed by Devon's versatility. I wander over to get a closer look at a figure drawing done in charcoal. "This is really good."

"Thanks," Devon says.

It's the only one that features a person.

"Have you done many portraits?" I ask, suddenly excited to see Devon's talent in action and applied to me.

"One or two," he says noncommittally, his fingers gently squeezing my shoulders from behind. He presses up against me and nibbles my neck through my hair.

"You sure I can't talk you into staying for another movie?" he asks in a husky whisper. Based on what's pressed into the small of my back, he's got more than movie watching on his mind.

I can't prevent my lips from turning up into a smile. Clearing my throat, I twist in his arms to face him. My hips press overtly into his hard and blatant desire, the size and shape of which is supremely impressive from what I can tell through the fabric separating us. He's always tried to hide it before—but not tonight.

"Tempting . . . truly," I say, meaning it.

He lets out a low growl and dips back into my neck. "You're driving me crazy, you know that?"

Based on the heat burning a path to my core, he's not alone.

"I'll take that as a compliment, but I have to go . . . really," I say softly, and I gently untangle myself from his embrace. If we stayed like that any longer, I might cave.

He gives me a half-sexy, half-disappointed smile and raises a brow, his hand still clinging to mine. "I'll walk you down."

Lettie must've gone to bed, because the house is dark when we leave his room.

"Thanks," I say when we get to the front door, meeting him for one last kiss and cupping his ass with both hands in flirty promise. Once I break up with Russ, all bets are off.

He clucks his tongue at me. "Tease."

I wink. "See you Saturday."

RATHER THAN GOING straight to bed, I take Lettie's advice and turn on my laptop. First stop: my Facebook page. I check out my wall; nothing has been posted since the last time I looked. I tap my nails on the desk in my old bedroom, thinking.

Then it hits me. I pull up Russ's page. He's been going to Facebook less and less in favor of Instagram and Snapchat.

Hmm. His relationship status hasn't changed. Then I see it. I don't have to get beyond the first entry. A picture from Saturday night shared on his wall by someone I don't know.

My mouth drops open. *Who the hell ...?* Then I see the person tagged with Russ in the photo ... his boss, Shauna. Correction, his *married* boss, Shauna. Well, that explains where the little bastard went after we talked on Saturday. You'd think they'd be more careful. Idiots.

My heart hammers as I pick up my cell phone. It's only nine o'clock in San Francisco, and there's at least one person I know who might be able to tell me what's going on. I dial my friend Kelsey, a fellow East Coaster who works at Nanotekx in Russ's group.

"Hey, Jen! What's up? I thought you were on vacation in Jersey," Kelsey says.

I gulp a breath. "I am. Can you do me a favor and log into Facebook?"

"Uh, yeah. Why?" she asks. "You okay?"

"You'll see in a minute," I say. "Go to Russ's page when you get there."

I hear Kelsey tapping on her tablet in the background.

"I'm there."

"Look at the first entry."

A gasp filters over the line. "Oh, Jen! I'm so sorry."

"What do you know about it?" I ask. "Please, just tell me the truth. I'm thinking about calling off the engagement anyway. So just tell me ... everything."

She sighs deeply.

I grip the phone until it cuts into my palm and keep my voice steady. "Spill. What do you know about Russ and Shauna?"

"Listen, Jen, I've only heard rumors. I don't know anything for sure, which is why I never said anything," she says. "So please don't be mad at me for not telling you, okay?"

"Fine, just tell me what you know," I grit out.

"Only if you promise that anything I tell you didn't come from me. I don't want to jeopardize my job," she says.

"Fine. Done," I say.

She lets out a breath. "I started hearing speculation a couple of months ago ... when Russ and Shauna would disappear at lunch, sometimes not coming back for a couple of hours. They were never seen coming or going together, but they would be gone at the same time. The only time I've ever seen them together was at a happy hour on a Friday night after work before the lunch things started. They looked a little too cozy, but I couldn't be sure."

My blood boils as I listen and connect the dots on the timing: the late Fridays, the decline in our sex life that couldn't just be attributed to my waning desire, Russ's erratic and snarky attitude.

What was the point of marrying me, anyway? Like father, like son? It wasn't the best-kept secret that his father dabbled on the side from time to time. It had caused enough strife in his parents' marriage during the years we dated. So much for his swearing he'd never be like his dad after I forgave him for his transgression in college.

Bastard!

"Are you still there?" Kelsey asks.

"Yeah. Thanks, Kels. I appreciate it," I say.

"I'm really sorry. I'd hoped it wasn't true. You deserve better," she says softly.

"Thanks, I think so, too."

"What are you going to do?" she asks.

"I'm not sure yet," I say.

To hell with Russ. I'll deal with him on my terms when I happen to get around to it. At least one thing's been decided: I'm not going to stop myself the next time Devon comes on to me . . . if I don't come on to him first.

Chapter 19

Jenny

"LOOK AT YOU," I say, taking Devon in as he passes through the front door. I'm so used to seeing him in business attire or dressier casual clothes that I'm almost shocked at what he's wearing. *Sexy* doesn't even begin to describe the way his old jeans hug his posterior's contours or the way that T-shirt clings to the carved planes of his chest. Add to that the blond stubble on his chin, and he looks downright bad boy—for him.

He smiles. "I promised to show you what I'd do with my life if I had a choice, didn't I?"

I eye the car at the curb before closing the door. "*Uh-huh.* Somehow I have trouble picturing a starving artist owning a Range Rover."

His sandy brows draw together. "Who said anything about starving? I have enough talent for some level of success, you know."

I chuckle and grab my camera bag.

He tips his head. "What's that?"

"Camera. Fair's fair, Picasso." I grin.

"Well, hello, Devon!" Mom trills from behind me, carrying a dish towel from her breakfast cleanup.

He gives her a warm smile. "Nice to see you, Mrs. Lynch."

"Kitty, please," she says and turns to me. "You'll be home in time for dinner, Jenny?"

I give Devon a questioning look. He answers for us. "Absolutely."

"You're welcome to join us, Devon. Please stay if you can," Mom says.

"I appreciate that," he says, giving her one of his maddening nonanswers.

I kiss Mom goodbye, and we head out.

It takes us less than forty-five minutes to get into the city. We find a parking spot on the Upper East Side in the low Nineties, somewhere midway between Central Park and Devon's studio.

Devon grabs the picnic hamper filled with our brunch, and we head to the Great Lawn. It's only midmorning, but it's already heating up for the day, and there's not a cloud in the crystal blue sky.

We pick a spot half in and half out of the shade and spread out our picnic blanket.

"So what's in the basket?" I ask, my stomach reminding me that my morning coffee wasn't nearly enough.

Devon gives me a crooked smile and wiggles his eyebrows. "Lots of good things." He opens the lid to unpack it. "I used an artist theme with a touch of British influence for inspiration ..." He pulls out a baguette and a few cheeses with labels from the Summit Wine Shop, a bag of red grapes, a bottle of Shiraz, a bag of scones, a pot of jam, and some finger sandwiches sealed in plastic.

"I'm impressed. You even made sandwiches," I say.

"Lettie made the sandwiches, but I'm responsible for the rest," he says.

I glance at the Shiraz. "It's a little early for wine, no?"

He gives me a wicked grin. "Not if you're in France."

"Oh, is that how we're going to play it?" I kid. "I was

under the impression you weren't big into alcohol. Other than that glass of red you drank on the plane, I haven't seen you drink." Even at dinner the other night, Lettie and I shared a bottle but Devon passed.

He shrugs. "Today's special. I'm going to paint your portrait." Then he sheepishly pulls out a thermos. "And I also brought some tea."

"Oh, now I see what you're trying to do. Ply me with alcohol while you drink tea. Planning to take advantage of me, are you?" I grin.

He puts down the thermos and crawls across the blanket with a sexy glint in his eye. I fall backward onto my elbows and he sidles up to me until his face is next to mine and I'm close enough to see the gold and chocolate flecks in his eyes. He draws his finger over my bottom lip. "That night on the plane? I needed the glass of wine . . . so that I wouldn't be too nervous to talk to you."

His admission makes me smile.

I bridge the gap for a quick kiss and then grab my camera bag. "Hold that thought," I say and extract my digital camera.

"Hey, come back here. What thought?" he asks, giving me a look that sends a shiver of anticipation down my spine.

"That one," I say, flipping the camera on and lining him up in my lens.

He blushes and looks away.

"Come on, Dev. Look at me and tell me what you were thinking a second ago."

He turns back, lowers his head, and looks up at me. The effect is sensual and hungry. "You want me to say it out loud?"

"No. Just think it . . ."

Snap. Snap. Snap.

My heart accelerates as he seductively stares me down through the camera's lens. "You're actually pretty good at this," I say.

The corner of his mouth tugs up in a smile. "I'm an artist, too, remember?"

Snap. Snap. Snap.

"Can you give me a profile shot?" I ask.

He does as I ask, graciously putting up with ten solid minutes of my positioning him for my shooting pleasure. Then he takes the camera from my hands and sets it aside.

"That's more than enough lustful thoughts captured on digital film."

He dips in, and his lips touch mine. I roll back and pull him onto my chest. His fingers tangle in my hair as I part his lips and explore his mouth. Then he takes control, deepening the kiss with an intensity that makes my body tighten and tingle. My chest heaves as we share breath, our tongues tied in a delectable dance. I run my fingers through the softness of his hair and down the hollow at the center of his back as our pelvises meet and I feel his rock-hard excitement pressed against me.

After having only been with Russ—that cheating bastard— I wonder what Devon would feel like inside me. A rush of moisture hits the juncture of my thighs. I'm certain now that I want to find out. How he moves, how he tastes, what he sounds like when he comes. I want those beautiful tapered fingers of his to explore every inch of my skin until I scream out his name.

He moans and breaks the kiss. "Jenny ..." His voice is deep and throaty, but it's his eyes that tell me everything I want to know.

"I want you, too," I whisper.

Devon's chest rises and falls in rhythm with my beating heart as he steadies himself on his elbows above me. He lets his head fall down next to my neck.

"There's something I need to tell you," he whispers and rolls onto his back next to me, leaving me bereft and uncovered.

I turn onto my side and stare down at him. "What is it?" Lines of worry are etched into his forehead, stirring the nerves in my belly.

"My studio, the people I share it with?" he says. "It's part of an outpatient support program at Mount Sinai Hospital."

My eyes widen, and suddenly I think I understand why he doesn't drink. "A rehab program? Are you a recovering addict?" I ask.

He sniffs and meets my eyes. "No, Jenny. Cancer. I'm a cancer survivor."

That triggers alarm inside me. I'm suddenly struck by the thought of Devon dying, and tears spring to my eyes before I can stop them. *Damn it.* "You're okay now, right?" I ask, trying to still my quivering lip.

His expression shifts, and he's wearing a different look of worry. He's wearing it for me. "I'm fine. I'm sorry. I didn't mean to upset you." He pulls me into his chest and wraps me in a hug.

I wipe away an escaping tear. "It's not you. I just get super freaked out whenever I think about someone close to me dying. Long story," I say softly, not wanting to discuss the root of my PTSD-like issues.

Devon's breath warms my hair, and he kisses the top of my head. "It was a localized type of cancer, and turns out we caught it before it spread. I'm fine now. Really." He squeezes me tighter and asks gently, "Will you tell me your story sometime?"

I think for a second and surprise myself by nodding a yes against his chest. But I won't tell him now. "What kind of cancer did you have?" I ask.

"Testicular. They had to remove one of them, and then I had a round of radiation and some chemo."

"How long ago?"

"They discovered it during my last year at Oxford. I came home for treatment and finished my degree remotely while I recovered. I've been cancer-free for over two years now."

My worry turns to relief that he escaped death, and my admiration for him—which was already high—jumps up a couple of levels for his bravery. It helps explain the heaviness he seems to carry. I curl my arm around his waist and squeeze him to me. "I'm glad you're okay."

Devon clears his throat. "I wanted to tell you ... you know, in case anything happens between us later. I'm a little lopsided down there."

I crane my neck up and look at him. "You seriously didn't think that would matter to me, did you?"

He shakes his head. "I didn't think so, but I didn't want to take you by surprise and have to explain it in the heat of passion, either."

"Thanks for being so considerate." I chuckle and, with a wicked look, run my hand down the front of his jeans and enjoy the feel of his penis under my palm.

"Hey! No copping cheap feels." He bats my hand away and laughs.

"Just checking out the merchandise for later," I say.

His eyebrows pop up. "Wait. What about me? Don't I get to check out any merchandise?"

I take his hand and boldly place it on my Victoria's Secret-enhanced breast. "Satisfied?"

He smiles and gently kneads me, awakening my nipple enough for it to stand at attention. "For now." His hand drops away.

I sit and pull him up by the arms. "Now that that's all settled, let's eat. I'm starved."

Chapter 20

Devon

"LIKE THIS?" JENNY asks, sweeping her hair up and securing it in a twisted bun on her head.

"Yeah," I say with an appreciative glance. I position the chair in front of the window and set up my easel in a spot where I can catch the light without its interfering as I paint. I'll start with a rudimentary line drawing as a frame and then switch to oils as soon as I'm confident that I've captured what I need to finish without her. Just in case, I'll take a photograph with my phone to have on hand.

"Where do you keep your work?" Jenny asks, moving into the next station to check out my friend James's still life. A large open space, the studio has a total of six stations, a kitchen, and a living room area with a couch and some chairs. That's where we hang out when we're here together.

"The storage room and the bathroom are behind that door," I say, pointing it out. "My finished stuff is back there."

"Is anyone else coming here today?" she asks.

"Nope. We have the place to ourselves." I had the foresight to check and to offer necessary bribes as needed.

A couple more minutes and my palette is prepared.

"Are you ready?" I ask.

She points to the chair. "There?"

I nod.

She takes the shawl I asked her to bring from her bag, and I meet her at the window. Handing it to me, she slips her shirt up over her head and stands in front of me in a lacy black bra.

My eyes travel over her delicious curves. She has strong shoulders like a swimmer's, and her waist curves in above her hips. I love the fact that under the push-up bra she's wearing there's a moderate-size bust that's real. The feel of her breasts against me earlier in the park nearly sent me over the edge. I can't wait to run my fingertips over her nipples and watch them tighten under my touch.

She sits with her back to me, and I drape the shawl low around her shoulders. She clasps it together in front and artfully slips the straps down to remove her bra.

"I could've helped with that," I say next to her ear.

"Not if you're serious about painting me," she says.

"True." I position her in the chair and then go back to my easel to check the angles in the midday light.

One more adjustment and then I'm ready to start. I snap a photo first.

For the next twenty minutes, I sketch until Jenny emerges from the canvas. I force my eyes away from the lines of her neck until absolutely necessary.

And then . . . it takes no more than a minute and a half for my dick to throb uncomfortably inside my briefs. My breath comes in shallow pants as I obsess over her sensuous curves. I channel my raw desire into the portrait and switch to oils.

"How's it going?" Jenny asks softly.

I swallow. "Really well," I say, leaving it at that while my thoughts take a lustier route. My one ball clenches beneath me as my brush meets the canvas in artistic creation.

Shit. I can't go on. "Let's take a break. Stay put for a sec?" I take off the surgical gloves I slid on right before I switched from pencil to oil.

I walk up behind her and rest my hands on her shoulders. My lips gravitate to the base of her neck. She shivers in front of me and leans back. "You're so beautiful, Jen," I whisper. "I want you so much."

She drops the shawl, and my hands move around to cup her breasts as I kiss her neck. Her nipples harden under my fingertips.

Her breath hitches. "I want ... you, too." She stands up and turns into me. A second later, we're a tangle of arms and legs as I lift and carry her toward the sofa. Our mouths are sealed together, and her legs are locked around my hips.

By all that's holy, we make it there without wiping out on any furniture or falling into a heap on the floor. I put her down, and she claws at my shirt until it's up and over my head. Then, in one deft movement, she's at my waistband unbuttoning my jeans and tugging at my zipper. She slides her hands down my hips, taking my clothing with them and springing me free — hard and ready for the taking.

Her lips part and her gaze meets mine a moment before her tongue connects with my shaft.

My hands find her shoulders and my eyes slide shut. Her hot mouth swallows me whole as her hand cradles and massages my remaining ball. Every nerve ending in my groin lights up and sends a signal to my brain, knocking it into sensory overload.

"Jenny, no, you're gonna make me come," I growl, not wanting it to end this soon.

It takes every ounce of willpower I have to shift my hips backward and slip myself free of her mouth. I'm torn between plunging in deep and taking the satisfaction and earning my keep by sharing the pleasure.

"Dev, it's okay. Let me finish," she says through lips that are plump and wet. She makes another grab for me but I step back and out of my jeans, kicking them aside. I lunge in and scoop her up, laying her back on the sofa. I return the favor and strip off her jeans and the black lacy underwear underneath until I'm not the only one in the room who's buck-ass naked.

I lean in and kiss her lips. "Hold that thought and don't move."

I return to my station, feeling the burn of Jenny's eyes on my back and everything else she can see, and take out a new cotton drop cloth. I let it unfold enough to cover my erection for my return trip.

Jenny's watching me approach from a reclined position with an amused smile and half-closed eyes.

"Let's put this down. Who knows what's happened on this thing before we got here," I say, holding out the cloth.

She rolls into a sitting position and gets up. I cover the sofa, feeling better knowing we have something clean to lie on.

Her arms encircle my waist from behind, and she kisses my shoulder, raising gooseflesh along the back of my neck. Her hand moves down to surround my length. "Can I finish what I started?"

I can't believe I've denied myself a woman's touch for so long. This feels way better than I remember. Or maybe it's just Jenny?

I turn in her arms and kiss her deeply, reveling in her bare skin next to mine and wanting so much more. "Not until I have a taste of my own." I lift her into my arms and place her onto the clean cotton covering.

Climbing onto the couch, I kneel between her parted thighs and take in her soft white skin and the rosy pink of her taut nipples.

She gives me a seductive smile. "See something you like?"

"All of it. I like all of it," I say and back up, giving myself enough room to dive down and explore her glistening depths with my tongue. Settling my face between her thighs, I wrap one arm around her hip and inhale her musky scent as I probe and tease the sensitive skin at her core.

Jenny moans and digs her fingers into my flesh. To heighten her pleasure, I use my finger to stroke the wet, silky contours inside her. When I'm sure she can handle it, I slip in another.

"Dev!" She lifts off the couch, her body pulsing around my fingers and under my tongue. I suppress a smile as I back off for a moment. I'll dive in one more time for a double play. Nice to know there are some things I haven't forgotten.

After she screams my name a second time, I reach down to my crumpled jeans and retrieve a condom from inside a pocket. I lean back on my knees to find Mr. Happy standing in full military salute. Ripping the foil open with my teeth, I pluck out the lubed circle and roll on the snug latex.

Jenny's eyes connect with mine, and she pulls me down on top of her. Even with a sheath of rubber separating us, I have no problem finding my way inside.

She's hot and tight around me. I let out a small groan with my first thrust. "You feel like heaven," I say in a low growl, moving in a steady rhythm.

"Faster, Dev." She digs her nails into my ass until I pick up the pace to her liking.

She moans and writhes under me, and just when I'm slick with sweat and on the brink of explosion, she lets out a satisfied scream and grips me hard until I join her. I groan as I clench and release all I have to give. My body pulses in tandem with hers until there's nothing left, and I collapse down beside her. Limbs still entangled, we shift onto our sides.

I'm jelly next to her for a full minute, still buried deep and waiting for my breath to return to normal. When it does, my mouth finds hers and I kiss her until I'm starved for oxygen again and have to break away. "You okay?" I ask, pushing a strand of her hair away from her face.

She curls her hand around my neck and pulls me in for another kiss. "More than okay," she says when she's finished with me. "You're really good at this, you know?"

I bite my lip to keep from smiling. "Does that mean you'll do it again?"

She nods and tucks her head under my chin.

I feel myself shrivel inside the condom and deftly pull out. "In the classic words of Arnold Schwarzenegger, 'I'll be back,'" I say.

Jenny chuckles as I extricate myself and head to the bathroom.

When I return, I snuggle in alongside her and pull her into my arms. "It's been a long time for me, Jen."

"How long?" she asks.

"Four years. Since I was diagnosed."

She traces a pattern on my chest with her finger. "Well, you haven't lost your touch."

"I'm glad you think so."

"You're only my second … lover," she says and stops tracing.

I squeeze her tight to me. "And you're mine."

"Second?"

"Yup."

"I'm glad." She burrows down next to me. "How long does it take you to recover?"

I chuckle deep in my throat. "Give me another ten minutes."

She props herself up on one elbow and narrows her eyes at me. "This time you won't escape me." She licks my bottom lip and gives it a nip.

A rush of blood flows south and reignites my groin. "Make it five."

Chapter 21

Jenny

"OH SHIT," I say under my breath as Devon pulls up in front of my house. The driveway is packed with cars. At least one of them belongs to Russ's family. I had every intention of calling Russ to break the news . . . until I found that picture on Facebook. Instead I ignored all his terse texts asking me to call him.

"What?" Devon gives me a puzzled look.

"I can't ask you in." I fix him with a worried stare as my stomach churns like a volcano about to erupt.

"Why?"

I point. "See that car? It belongs to Russ's parents." Leaning in, I give him a quick kiss on the lips. "I'll call you later."

Devon grabs my arm as I reach for the door handle. "You sure you don't want me to come in?" he asks.

"Do you have a death wish or something? It's bad enough that I have to face them. There's no reason for you to get involved in this mess," I say more brusquely than I intend.

He raises his brows. "No reason? After how we spent the afternoon?"

I blow out an exasperated breath. "That's not what I mean,

Devon."

"Jen … he cheated on you," he says softly. A look of vulnerability and yearning shines in his eyes. I'd told him about Russ last night. I had to, anticipating where this afternoon might lead. Rather than soothing me, Devon's look ignites a different kind of anger inside me.

"Two weeks, remember?" No sooner do I snap at him than I see hurt take root fast and deep in his eyes, dimming the light shining there. He shrinks back into himself.

"You're right. Call me later."

Damn it!

I kick myself for pushing him away and grasp his arm. "Why? Why do you want to involve yourself in this?"

He clutches the steering wheel tightly and stares out the windshield. "Maybe because I care," he says in a cool, controlled voice. "Did you ever consider that?"

I swear under my breath as he drives away, and I head toward the house. I brace myself before walking inside, hoping I don't smell like I spent the afternoon having sex.

The din of angry voices reaches me from the living room.

I hear Russ's mother first. "Well, if your slut of a daughter …"

"How dare you speak of Jenny that way!" my father pipes up.

I grind to a halt at the living room entrance. Russ is sitting silently in a wing chair, surrounded by our irate parents, his face an angry mask. His gaze locks on mine.

Heat rises in my cheeks. "What are you doing here?" I snarl as images of his hands on his boss's ass scream through my head.

The room goes silent, and all heads turn in my direction.

"Jenny, you're home," my mom says, looking flustered and pale.

"Who's the guy, Jen?" Russ grits out and rises to his feet. "Is that why you came home? Why you've blown me off all week and avoided making any wedding plans?"

Ice water chills my spine, but I refuse to relinquish my anger and let him throw this on me. I keep my cool and ask, "What guy?"

Russ's mother gives me a look of disgust. "Oh, Jennifer. Stop pretending. The one Ronny saw you with at the diner." I can't claim Russ's mom and I have ever had a close relationship, but her judgment still stings. She's the kind of mother who will defend her child regardless of fault. Why am I only realizing now what a horrible mother-in-law she would've made?

"This guy," Russ snarls back at me and stalks across the room with his phone thrust in front of him.

My jaw drops when he gets within a few feet. I stare at a picture on Instagram that Crystal must have taken at her gallery opening. Devon's lips are touching my knuckles, and there's an unmistakable look of intimacy between us. When he gets closer, I catch the caption. "Jenster with Mr. Right. Dreamy, isn't he?"

The irony smacks me in the face. *Damn social media.*

Russ pockets his phone. His stormy green eyes stray to my naked left hand, and he asks in a low growl, "Where's my ring?"

This isn't exactly how I planned our breakup going, but I'll take it.

My lips press together in an angry pucker as I dig into my purse and open my wallet. If he wants a show, I'll give him one. I fish out the diamond and throw it at him. "So how long have you been fucking your boss?!"

He freezes and the color drains from his face as the ring bounces off his chest and drops to the floor.

Shocked gasps sound around us.

"Maybe you should check Facebook a little more often," I grind out and turn on my heel to leave.

He catches my arm and jerks me back. "Smells like you've

been doing a little fucking of your own," he hisses under his breath and shoves me away.

"Not sure why you'd care … but I'm thinking Shauna's husband would love to see a picture of you grabbing his wife's ass with your tongue down her throat," I whisper through my sneer, and then I glance at his father, who's shifting uncomfortably on his feet under his mother's watchful eye. "Like father, like son."

A little too much color returns to Russ's face, and he clenches his jaw.

I give him a withering glance and walk away. Let him think about that for a while.

"I'll pack your stuff and have it shipped," Russ says to my retreating back.

I turn and glare at him. "No, you won't. I'll pack my own stuff. A week from Monday. Just don't be there when I do." I'll question the sanity of my plan later.

What the hell just happened?

My vision blurs as I head upstairs to the shower. As angry as I am at Russ, I'm also disappointed that our six years together are ending this way. I can't deny that I feel a pinch of guilt sleeping with Devon before officially ending my relationship with Russ, even though our relationship was over the minute he had sex with his boss.

My inner bitch chimes in, "At least now we're even." But I quickly remind her that's not why I slept with Devon.

By the time I'm out of the shower, the cars are gone and the house is quiet.

"Jenny?" Mom pokes her head through the bedroom door, still looking shaken. "Are you all right, honey?"

"Yes. I'm fine."

She steps inside. "I'm so sorry. They arrived unannounced a few minutes before you walked in. I didn't have time to warn you."

"I'm glad it's out in the open. Really, I'm doing fine." It's the truth. I feel a new sense of freedom.

"Would you like some dinner?"

"I'm not hungry. Thanks, though," I say.

She nods. "Let Daddy and me know if you need anything."

The moment she leaves, I'm suddenly overwhelmed with the need to hold my cousin Rachel in my arms and smell her new-baby scent.

That, and I have a fence to mend with Devon. He's the last person on earth I want to hurt, yet I did a spectacular job of it anyway.

I pick up my cell and dial.

Raine answers. "Yo!"

"What would you say if I told you that you could have tonight to do whatever you want while I take care of the baby?"

"*Hmm.* Hang on. Let me check with Jillian."

He comes back a couple of minutes later. "Can you swing by the store to pick up a few things for me first?"

"Sure. One more thing. Can I bring a friend?"

"Mall Guy?"

"Yup," I say.

"Sure. It'll give me a chance to check him out." He snickers.

"Raine?"

"Yeah?"

"It all hit the fan with Russ in a big way." I recount the shit show that happened downstairs.

Raine blows out a breath when I'm done. "What a douche. I knew I didn't like that guy, Jen. You deserve better."

His words bring a smile to my lips. Between him and Kelsey, it's unanimous. "Thanks. See you in a bit."

Talking to Raine always makes me feel better—but only half-better today. I hang up and dial Devon, hoping to make it the rest of the way.

Chapter 22

Devon

I GRIT MY teeth and let the phone ring. I'm pissed enough at Jenny to punch a hole in the wall. The only reason I haven't is that I'd have to fix it.

She couldn't have done a better job of stabbing me in heart than if I'd handed her one of my swords. That definitely couldn't have hurt any less. Did she think I only had sex with her because of my two-week proposal? And is that the only reason she had sex with me? Or was it to get back at her fiancé for cheating on her?

"Two weeks," she'd said, spitting our afternoon back in my face as if it meant nothing. If anything, it meant too much. More than I wanted it to.

I kick myself for being a sensitive idiot and not letting it roll off my back. But I'm smart enough to recognize it's my personal baggage that's to blame. I'm making her pay for someone else's mistakes.

My iPhone beeps with a message. I stare at it, not wanting to acknowledge her voice mail. Instead I pick up the remote and click on the TV, remembering that the last time I sat here, Jenny sat beside me. I last a total of five minutes.

Damn it!

I snatch the phone to retrieve the message, half-afraid to hear what she has to say, and inhale deeply as I press PLAY.

"Dev, I'm really sorry. I didn't mean to hurt your feelings, and I definitely didn't mean anything by what I said in the car. It was just the shock of seeing Russ's parents here. Turns out they weren't alone. Russ flew home from San Francisco for the weekend and was waiting for me in the living room. What a mess. But before that ... today... was amazing. Listen, do you want to come with me somewhere tonight? I promise it'll be fun and low key. I'm pretty wiped out, all things considered. Dev, I want to see you ... kiss you ... touch you again."

My eyes close as I listen to the message, and I slump in relief. The emotions of the day overwhelm me, giving me a head rush. I stay seated, letting the dizziness pass, and listen to the message one more time before hitting CALL BACK.

She answers on the second ring. "Dev?"

"Yeah."

"Did you get my message?" she asks softly.

"Yeah."

"Will you come with me?"

"Yeah."

"Are you still mad at me?"

I pause. "Yeah."

"I'm sorry. Will you let me make it up to you?"

A smile tugs at my pouting lips. "Yeah."

"See you in fifteen minutes?"

"Okay." I hang up and head for the closet to change my clothes, trying not to feel like a loser for giving in so quickly.

I WALK BESIDE Jenny to the front door, carrying a bag of groceries from the Chatham Kings. She smiles at me and rings the bell.

A tall, good-looking blond guy who can't be much older

than me answers the door. He's wearing a T-shirt, jeans, and flip-flops. Even if his biceps weren't the size of my thighs, there's no mistaking this guy is ripped. He looks exactly like his picture—the one Jenny showed me on the plane. Except bigger.

"Hey, Raine," Jenny says, standing on tiptoe to give him a peck on the cheek.

"That's Uncle Raine to you," he kids, and then he shields himself against her poking him in the ribs. "Hey, stop that and introduce me to your friend." Another thing is clear—there's a friendly affection between them. I'm almost jealous of the ease in their relationship.

"Raine, this is Devon," she says, pivoting between us. "Devon, this is Raine. Even though he's technically my uncle, we were practically in diapers at the same time."

Raine gives her a teasing grin and waggles his eyebrows. "Speaking of ... I see some diapers in your immediate future." He glances at the grocery bag in my hand. "Let me take that from you, man." He presses the bag to his chest and reaches out to shake my hand. "Good to meet you. My niece can be a pain in the butt, but she's worth it."

I smile. "Yeah, I seem to attract the pain-in-the-butt variety. Between her and my sister, I'm surrounded."

"Oh, please, you two," Jenny says and waves her hand. "Step aside, *Uncle*, so I can find my sweet baby cousin."

"In the kitchen. Jillian just finished feeding her." Raine motions with a tip of his head for us to come inside. Jenny slides her arm through mine, and we follow Raine's imposing figure down the marble hallway to the kitchen.

"Rachie's got company," Raine says as he disappears through the doorway with the groceries. I hear him coo, "Daddy's got you ..."

"Hey, Aunt Jill," Jenny says as we turn the corner.

Her aunt is attractive, with long, wavy brown hair that lies loose around her shoulders. The most remarkable thing about her is her eyes. They're the color of polished amber. Her face lights up, and she comes over to greet us after Raine relieves her of the small bundle. On top of the eyes, she has a great smile and a warm glow that gives her an inner beauty and magnetism. I understand immediately why Raine fell for her.

"Devon, this is my aunt, Jillian Grant-MacDonald," Jenny says, giving my arm a brief squeeze.

A smile spreads reflexively across my lips in response to Mrs. MacDonald's welcoming vibe. "It's a pleasure to meet you."

"The pleasure's mine. Jenny speaks very highly of you." She takes my hand in both of hers and shakes it firmly. "Welcome, and make yourself comfortable. Excuse me for a moment," she says, glancing at her shoulder. "Rachel left a little present on my shirt."

"Didn't we tell Mommy to use the burp rag?" Raine asks the baby and chuckles, gently bouncing her as he takes the last of the groceries from the Kings bag with his free hand.

A pleasant smell comes from the wispy steam rising off the pot on the stove. Raine gives it a stir and puts the lid back on while Jenny and I settle onto stools on the opposite side of the kitchen island.

"Do you need help?" Jenny asks Raine. "I can take Rachel."

"I'm fine. Hey, before I forget, Jillian pumped. The bottles are lined up in the fridge. You should be good to go. Are both of you guys staying over?"

My lips part, and I give Jenny a questioning glance. She hadn't asked me. Not that I need to be home for any reason. Lettie is spending the night with Howard, and I visited my mom earlier, not knowing how late I'd be back.

Jenny gives me a crooked smile and squeezes my arm. "I'll run Devon home later and take all the feedings until six a.m. so you can both get some sleep."

I stare into her eyes and whisper, "I'll stay if you want me to."

In answer she brushes a kiss across my cheek. "I'll leave it up to you." It pleases me to have the option. True, it feels a little weird to be sucked into Jenny's world and stay somewhere with people I only met a few minutes ago. Then again, staying here would mean another chance to get close to her.

Raine tips his head at me. "It's cool if you want to stay and keep Jenny company."

"Thanks," I say, feeling oddly self-conscious.

"So what are you and Aunt Jill going to do with your night off?" Jenny asks, a teasing glint in her eye.

"First on the agenda? A long soak in the tub until we're so wrinkled we look like a pair of shar-peis. How one small infant can knock you on your ass still amazes me."

"Lack of sleep could also have something to do with it," Jenny adds.

"Yeah. There's that." Raine reaches for a large skillet from the pot rack over the island. "Hope you guys like chicken stir-fry. But I'll warn you in advance, you'll have to salt it to taste. Jillian still has a sodium restriction."

"No problem on my end," I say, glad that I don't have to ask for unsalted food and raise uncomfortable questions. I notice a sign, *Raine's Roost,* perched on the mantel ledge of the hood over the stove. "So the kitchen's your domain?"

Raine smirks and glances at Jenny. "You could say that. I'll let Jenny fill you in on her aunt's cooking."

Jenny checks to make sure the coast is clear and then says in a hushed whisper, "I love her, but she's probably the worst cook on the planet."

"You don't have to whisper, she's pretty open about it," Raine says. Still clutching the baby, he makes a couple of short trips to the refrigerator to pull out a plastic bag filled with raw chicken and some chopped vegetables in a glass bowl. "I tease her that she only married me for my mad cooking skills."

"That might be partially true." Jenny gives him a

mischievous grin.

He shoots her a mock wounded look. "Gee, thanks, Jen. You don't have to agree so quickly."

The baby snuggles into his neck and lets out a loud burp.

"Good one, Rachie!" He opens a tall container of cooking oil and fires up the flame under the pan. "Hey, Jen, come take the baby."

Jenny pops off the stool to get Rachel. The moment the newborn is in her arms, Jenny's face turns radiant. It makes me wonder how much she wants kids, and a hollow feeling hits my gut. I've never had the luxury of thinking that far ahead.

Raine pours oil in the pan. "Devon, you cook?" he asks, picking up the head of broccoli we bought at Kings and a large knife.

"Not well," I admit.

Raine eyes Jenny and smirks as he chops. "You might want to learn."

"Hey! I can cook," Jenny says, throwing him an indignant stare as she rocks the baby against her chest.

"*Mmm-hmm.*" He glances my way, grimaces and shakes his head, then grins back at Jenny.

"You suck," she says, but there's no malice, only affection, in her voice. She casts a glance in my direction. "He's lying. I cook just fine."

I throw up my hands. "I think I'll sit this one out."

A loud wail bursts forth from Rachel.

"I'll take her," her mother says as she sweeps back into the kitchen and relieves Jenny of her small bundle.

Raine glances over from the sizzling skillet. "Jen, you want to tackle setting the table? This'll only take about ten minutes."

I'm amazed at the amount of comfort and ease they have with each other. Although Lettie and I try for something resembling family life, it strikes me that neither of us has had anything like this since before my mom's accident. Even then, it never really included my father. Boarding school and university afterward never felt anything like family ... far from it. Then there were the cancer years, when nothing was normal. So here I sit at a safe distance with my hands tucked in my pockets, equal parts fascinated and separated by the banter going on around me. Drawn in like a moth to a flame, yet plagued by an uncomfortable feeling that I don't belong.

"So Devon, you grew up in Summit?" Jenny's aunt asks as she rocks the baby to sleep. I shift on the stool at the sudden attention.

Jenny waves me over to the table before fetching the silverware, and I leave the safety of the kitchen counter to relocate next to her aunt.

I scoot my chair in. "Yes, but I left for boarding school in England when I was fourteen and didn't return to live here until ... after university."

Before her aunt can form a follow-up question, Jenny chimes in. "Aunt Jill, Devon's an amazing painter." She catches my eye from across the kitchen.

Tension drains from my shoulders. I'm thankful for the conversational shift, but I can't determine if Jenny's providing air cover to protect me from her aunt's line of questioning or if she's making an oblique reference to how we spent our afternoon.

"She's biased," I say, a blush heating my cheeks as much from the compliment as from the memories of Jenny's naked body beneath mine.

Her aunt's eyebrows lift with interest. "Really? What's your medium of choice?"

"Oil mostly, but I venture into acrylics from time to time," I say.

Jenny slips some silverware in front of me. "Water?" she asks. I nod, grateful. I haven't drunk enough today. "Aunt Jill?"

"Yes, please, Jenny."

"My mom was an artist," Raine says as he stirs the sizzling chicken. "I have a bunch of her paintings here if you want to see them."

"I'd like that," I say, sensing how personal his offer is. Jenny mentioned earlier that he lost his mother to cancer.

A half smile tugs at his lips, and he clears his throat. "Great." The jagged edge of his loss is almost palpable. Having danced with death myself, I'm perceptive when it comes to other people's grief.

Raine's offer reminds me of the conversation I had with Jenny in Central Park this morning. I want to understand why she's so terrified of those closest to her dying. Maybe then I'll understand her reaction to finding out I'm a cancer survivor. If she freaks out like that when I'm in no apparent danger, what will she do if she finds out about my failing kidneys?

It doesn't take more than a couple of minutes for Raine to dish out the steaming mass of chicken, rice, and vegetables onto plates and for Jenny to deliver them.

Raine selects a bottle of white from the wine rack and takes the seat across from me. "Dig in, everyone," he says and uncorks the bottle. He pours me a glass before I can stop him. Rather than say anything, I decide a sip or two won't kill me.

I pick up my fork and make an attempt at polite dinner conversation. "Mrs. MacDonald, your niece tells me that you're responsible for putting the first camera in her hands."

"Call me Jillian, please," Jenny's aunt says and then beams at her. "I did, and now she puts me to shame."

"Oh! I should've brought my camera. I took some great shots of Devon today," Jenny says and squeezes my thigh under the table.

My face warms. I'm not sure I want anyone to see those pictures. I did them just for her.

Raine smirks and pokes at his stir-fry. "Dude, you're in trouble now. That's how it all started with me and Jillian.

Jenny and that camera. She saw all our secrets through the lens before we even knew about them ourselves. Right, baby?" They trade knowing smiles. "My advice? Just surrender, it's a lot easier." He gives me a lopsided grin and stuffs a bite of chicken into his mouth.

I think back to the photos of Jillian and Raine that Jenny showed me on the plane. He's right. Even then you could see the chemistry sizzling between them. The heat in my face travels to my ears, and I'm relieved that Jenny forgot her camera. Surrender? Too late for that.

The conversation quiets and we dig into our meals. True to Raine's word, the food is unsalted but flavorful despite the absence. Lettie is a decent cook, but there's no denying Raine knows what he's doing.

"Great meal," I say between bites.

"Thanks, man." He nods and flashes a crooked smile.

I'm amazed Raine's so close to my age. I wish I were half as together as he is.

"HOLD HER LIKE this," Jenny says, placing the baby securely in my arms so her head rests in the crook of my right one. There's some solid weight to her. I lean back on the sofa to get more comfortable.

Jillian and Raine retreated to the master suite upstairs after dinner, leaving us in the family room, armed with diapers, bottles, bassinet, baby monitor, and an unbelievable number of other accoutrements necessary for taking care of one small newborn.

"She's heavier than I thought she'd be," I say, as I stare in awe at the little bundle wrapped tightly in a flannel blanket with only her tiny fists free to make jerky movements. "And she's really cute."

I'm not an expert on babies but I'm not just being polite. She's adorable, with a shock of fine dark hair, little pink lips in the shape of an O, and big eyes in an undecided shade of blue. I understand Jenny's attraction to her.

Jenny leans on my shoulder and offers her finger for Rachel to ponder. "She was over eight pounds when she was born, so she's probably more than nine pounds now. She's long, too. Must take after her dad." Jenny dips in to sniff her cheek. "I love the way she smells. I call it new-baby smell. I can get lost just breathing her in."

I bend in to see what Jenny means and catch a whiff. It's true, there's something fresh and new about her that sparks a strange euphoria and something else.

A dull ache fills my chest as I flash back to my cancer treatment and the days when I feared I'd live my life emasculated, relying on synthetic testosterone if I lived at all. More so, I feared the loss of potential . . . of missing out on all the things I wanted to do, on having a family, on pursuing my dreams. I feared leaving Mom and Lettie behind.

The happiest day of my life was when they saved my remaining testicle. Even though they offered me a silicone replacement for the one I lost, I rejected it for safety reasons. The second-happiest day was when I went into remission and knew I'd live.

The wishing machine buried in my soul fires up and churns out another useless hope that I'll most likely never be able to achieve. My throat constricts and the happiness I feel threatens to evaporate. I close my eyes and breathe the baby in one more time, hoping to absorb some of her goodness into myself.

Jenny runs her fingers through my hair, and my scalp tingles in a good way. "Have I made it up to you yet?" Her breath warms my cheek. I open my eyes and find her inches away.

I nod, afraid to speak, not wanting Jenny to know the dark road I've traveled in my head. The weight of my situation presses down on me in a new and unexpected way, and I'm left with a sweeping reality. There's no future waiting for us. The closer I get to Jenny, the harder it will be to let her go. And there's a good chance I'll someday become the thing she seems to fear most . . . another funeral to attend.

The baby gurgles, her mouth finding her hand.

I bite back my fear by sheer force of will and remind myself to stay in the moment. Would I rather have nothing or give myself what could be some of the best moments I've had in years? I draw strength from the baby in my arms, full of hope and promise.

The answer is I want them. I want these two weeks with Jenny. Grinding my teeth, I shove back the specters that haunt me.

"What's the matter, Dev?" she asks, tracing the furrow in my brow with her finger.

"Nothing's the matter. Kiss me?" I whisper.

She smiles and leans in until her mouth covers mine. I lose myself in the possibilities and pretend for another night that we actually have a future.

Chapter 23

Jenny

I POUR TENDERNESS into my kiss to meet the naked vulnerability in Devon's gleaming eyes and infuse it with the passion I so desperately feel for him. Rachel's warmth, anchored in Devon's strong arms, lies between us like a magical beacon.

My hand cups the back of his head, his hair soft on my palm, as I deepen the kiss. His mouth fits perfectly to mine, our tongues meeting in a now-familiar dance. I hope that when we finish I've erased that look of sadness he carries around his eyes and released the grip of the hidden drama that unfolded inside him earlier.

I brought him here in hopes of restoring us both with the new life lying between us. More than that, I want to be with him. To see the way he looked at me this afternoon, to feel the way his hands touch my body, to touch his, to enjoy his company. Now that we've made love, I fear the limits of our arrangement. I suspect that another week of him won't be enough. At least not for me. Guess I'll have to figure that out when the time comes.

Our lips separate. "Will you stay?"

He nods. "Yeah."

My thumb gravitates to the skin on the outside corner of his eye, and I smooth back the remaining crease until it melts away. "You sure?"

"Yeah," he says, mustering a weak smile.

I check my watch. "We have an hour before Rachel's next feeding. How about we put her in the bassinet and then I show you around?"

"Wait. Before we do that, can you tell me your story? The one you mentioned in the park? I want to know . . ." I note the haunted look in his eyes and sense something beyond curiosity about why he's asking.

Besides my therapist, the only person I've ever talked with about it was Russ . . . because he was there. I chew the inside of my mouth and lean back as I contemplate Devon's request. I get the feeling it might ease him to know he's not the only one who's had struggles. It's just that mine are filled with guilt and self-recrimination. His aren't.

I wring my hands and dip my head. "I'm afraid you'll look at me differently."

"Hey," Devon says softly and tips up my chin. His eyes meet mine, and I stare into their blue depths. "Have a little faith in me."

"All right," I say. Rachel sleeps soundly in Devon's arms. "Let's put her in the cradle first. Want me to take her?"

He shakes his head and gives me a reassuring smile before rising to settle her in. It warms me to watch him. He really has a way with her. The thought strikes me that he'd make a good father. I can't imagine how terrifying it must've been for him to confront the possibility of losing his testicles. Not to mention his life.

I draw my knees up to my chest like an added layer of protection and rest my chin on top. He sits back down next to me.

"You look uncomfortable," he says.

"You sure you really want to hear my story?" I ask to buy

myself time as dread uncoils in my stomach.

Devon opens his arms. "Come here. Relax." Rather than sit facing him, I reposition myself lengthwise on the couch so that he's spooned behind me with my back resting against his chest and his arms circling my waist. It feels good to be cradled in his warmth. But relaxation? Not possible.

God, where do I start?

I clear my throat and swallow. "Aunt Jill says our family's cursed when it comes to death. Sometimes I believe her. Four people have died since I was sixteen. One every two years." I pause, unsure where to go next.

Devon whispers next to my ear. "Go on."

"The most recent was my great-aunt Vera. Last summer. She was my grandmother's twin sister. My grandmother died way before I was born, so Great-Aunt Vee was the closest thing I had to one on my mom's side. Two years before that, my uncle Robert, Jillian's first husband, died suddenly of a heart attack. And before that, my grandfather."

"That's only three," Devon says.

"I know. They all felt like punishment for the first," I whisper. The familiar guilt wells up inside me, slicing an uncomfortable path to my chest. The feeling that I could've done more.

Devon holds me tighter. "What do you mean? Who was it?"

"A friend . . . back in high school . . . my junior year."

"What happened?"

Reluctantly I inhale deeply and take myself back to the night of the camping trip.

"It was Memorial Day weekend. There were ten of us. We planned to do a hike and then camp for the night up by Lake Hopatcong. Russ and I and a bunch of our friends. I invited Brittany. We played field hockey together . . ."

"*Why did you ask her to come?*" *Russ whispers in my ear as I slather on suntan lotion, my pack lying at my feet, while the rest of our friends mill around chatting and preparing for the hike.*

I glare at him. "Because she's my friend, and I had plans with her before this trip came up," I say. "I didn't want to leave her high and dry." There was no way I would let Russ make me feel guilty about inviting her. Just because one of the senior guys thought she was annoying wasn't my problem. Football meathead. Probably had something to do with the fact that she'd turned him down for a date. He'd just have to deal.

Russ walks off in a huff and I join Brittany to help her load up her pack.

"You sure this is all right?" she whispers as I finish up. "Some of Russ's friends are being less than friendly."

"Some? Don't you mean Scott? Screw him. It's totally fine," I say. "Just ignore him. You're my friend, and that's what matters."

"Easy for you to say," she murmurs.

"Have your meds and plenty of water?" I ask. She'd been dealing with some migraines since getting conked on the head with a hockey stick during Thursday's game.

"Yup," she says, staring at our rowdy horde. "If my mom finds out I'm here and not having a sleepover at your house, she'll freak."

I smile. "What she doesn't know won't hurt us." I briefly think about how she's as much my excuse as I am hers.

We leave the cars in the lot and head for the trail with the stuff we'll need for the night. Halfway up the mountain, while we rest, Brittany pulls me aside complaining of a headache.

"Have you taken something for it?" I ask in a hushed whisper.

She takes off her shades and rubs her eyes. "Before we left."

"How bad is it?" I ask, having little appetite to turn around and figure out how to get home without both of us getting grounded. Not to mention that I was looking forward to sharing a sleeping bag with Russ.

"I'm not sure I can make it," she says, a look of worry etched on her brow. "I might need to turn around."

"Hell no," Scott says from behind us. "You're on your own if

you do that."

I give him a withering glance. "Mind your own business."

"What's up, babe?" Russ asks, throwing his arm around me.

Before I know it, we're surrounded, and everyone is talking Brittany into pressing on. Because if we don't, it means one of the seniors will have to take us home. And none want to leave. Brittany bends under the pressure and decides to tough it out.

Later, fireflies twinkle in the waning light, and I inhale the woodsy smell of the crackling campfire, one of my favorite scents in the universe. I snuggle closer to Russ under a blanket, drinking a beer from the contraband in the cooler as our friend Wayne plays guitar and we sing along in a motley chorus of voices.

I lean over to Brittany, who's sitting next to us, huddled under her own blanket. "How're you feeling?"

She nods. "Fine." But one look at the dark patches carved under her eyes tells me that maybe she's putting on a brave face. Even though I hiked next to her the rest of the way up the mountain, and we made it without incident, I can't help but feel slightly guilty that I let the others persuade her to stay.

"You didn't eat much for dinner," I say next to her ear so she can hear me over the music.

"Not hungry," she says and gives me a wan smile.

"Are you having a good time?" I ask, feeling sheepish.

"Good enough," she says, giving me an apologetic look. "I'm tired. I'm going to go to sleep, I think."

I point to the place where Russ and I set up our sleeping bags, knowing she hasn't set up her stuff yet. "Stay by us."

"She was asleep by the time Russ and I went to bed. In the morning I woke up first to go to the bathroom at about six. It was chilly enough to see my breath. On the way back, I stopped to check on Brittany . . ." I bite my lip, and tears fill my eyes as the heart-stopping image that's burned into my memory resurfaces. "I knew she was dead the moment I saw her eyes. They had this weird film covering them. Her skin was totally white. I'm not sure what happened next. I just remember that I couldn't stop screaming. I don't even know how I got home that day ... or much of anything that happened afterward. When I woke up the next morning, my mom took me to see a therapist. I stayed in therapy for the next year and a half ..."

Devon's arms tighten around me. "I can't imagine what that would've been like. I'm so sorry."

I wipe the tears away with the back of my hand. "In my heart, I knew we should've turned back. I should've taken her back ... I shouldn't have let everyone talk her into staying. She died of a blood clot in the brain. It wasn't long after that the dreams started, and the crazy fear consumed me that everyone I loved was going to die. That it was my fault if they did. The therapist said it's like PTSD."

"It wasn't your fault she died, Jen," Devon says.

I nod. "Yeah, it was. If we had only been where we were supposed to be ... she might've been saved."

"I'm not a doctor, but I know a clot is a hard thing to diagnose," he says.

"Maybe, but I've done my own research. They could've stopped it with medication. She could've been saved," I say, the full force of my guilt and shame burning a hole in my insides. "That's why God keeps taking the people I love. Because I could've done more ..."

Devon squeezes my waist. "It's not your fault, Jen. Sometimes life is just tragic and unfair. You didn't cause her to die — it's just an unfortunate coincidence."

"I wish that was true," I say, turning in his arms to face him. "I'm not sure how many more I can take." What I don't say is that if it's ever someone I've fallen in love with, I'm not sure I'll survive. "So that's my story. Now you know ..."

He brushes a piece of hair behind my ear and meets my gaze with a look of sadness. "I'm sorry. If it matters, my opinion of you hasn't changed."

I had hoped telling Devon would lift my burden just a

little. But it didn't, and I've yet to find a way to make restitution.

I run my fingers under my eyes to get rid of whatever tears are left and reach for the tissues among Rachel's things on the coffee table to blow my nose. "How about we take that tour now?" I ask, wanting to cleanse myself of my memories. I do the best I can to repack my mental baggage and shove it back inside the Vault of Black Doom.

He smiles. "I'd like that."

I glance at the baby—she's still sound asleep—and grab the baby monitor. "Let's go."

THE ONLY PART of the house Devon has seen outside of the kitchen and the family room is Raine's office. After dinner, Raine took Devon to see his mother's artwork. It warmed my heart to see Raine share something so personal with Devon. They seem to have developed a mutual admiration.

"I'll show you my favorite floor first." I lead Devon down to the lowest level.

I flip on the lights to my aunt's studio. A large open space, it's separated into three sections: an area up front for photo shoots, an office area with a desk and meeting table in the middle, and a work space with a long table for laying out and organizing work at the far side. Samples of Aunt Jill's photography, some dating back to her fashion days, cover the walls. The newest addition is a poster-size book cover of *Caught Up in Raine*.

Devon's eyes light up. "Wow, what a great space."

"This is where I took the pictures I showed you on the plane," I say, seeing the day I met Raine unfold in my head. "Aunt Jill asked me to come and pose with Raine for her book cover. It's the day I first met him."

"You almost ended up on the cover, too?" he asks with a spark of interest.

I chuckle and shake my head, thinking back to Raine's holding me awkwardly in his arms and wanting nothing more than to trade me for Aunt Jill. He was a goner even on that first day. "Nah, there wasn't much chemistry between us, and in her heart I think Aunt Jill preferred to have only Raine on the cover. Part of me still wonders if she asked me over just to chaperone the shoot."

After checking out a few more photographs, we make what I think will be a quick stop in the weight room.

Devon lets out a low whistle. "I wish I had this at home."

Given the size of Devon's house, I'm surprised he doesn't. He obviously works out. "What gym do you go to?" I ask. Lucky for me, my parents kept the family membership at the Y downtown.

"Life Time Fitness. I work out with a trainer three times a week," he says absently, picking up a free weight and doing a curl, his upper arm flexing under his shirt sleeve. "I need to consider this . . ."

He puts it down and walks over to caress the Bowflex with a dreamy look in his eye.

"Yeah, because everyone who's anyone has a home gym," I tease, eyeing all the equipment that fills the room. It still surprises me how differently we think sometimes.

Devon flashes me a confused look, as if I've pulled him out of deep contemplation. "What?"

Boys and their toys. "Nothing," I say and grab his hand. "I hope you're in the mood for a movie." We should have time between Rachel's feedings.

His fingers lace through mine, and he gives me a crooked smile. "Plan on getting your revenge?"

"Big-time." I grin and drag him toward my favorite room in the house.

I open the door and flick on the lights in the home theater. Draped in red and purple velvet, with lush bucket seats, the room has the intimate feel of an old-time movie theater, complete with popcorn cart and beverage bar.

"Nice," Devon says and pulls me into an embrace. My arms circle his waist, the baby monitor still clutched awkwardly in my hand. "So what are my movie choices?" he asks, his face close enough so that his full, kissable lips are within striking distance.

"You'll have to wait until after the next feeding to find out," I say, grinning.

Devon's face turns serious, and he cups my cheek. "Thanks for inviting me along … and for sharing your family with me." I'm glad. I like having him here.

"You're welcome," I say, covering his hand with mine.

The warmth of his breath brushes my lips as he leans in to bridge the gap between us. Before he gets there, the baby monitor kicks on. Rachel's fitful warning cries filter through the speaker as she wakes, the signal that we have approximately thirty seconds to get upstairs before she breaks into a full-on howl.

"We gotta go," I say, racing toward the stairs with Devon on my heels.

"JEN?" DEVON'S BREATH is hot on my neck as I unzip my overnight bag to get out my pajamas. My body involuntarily clenches and warms in anticipation.

"Mmm?"

Fed, burped, and diapered, Rachel lies sound asleep in the bedroom between ours and the master suite. The baby monitor sits on the bedside table next to me, turned up as high as it can go to alert us at the first signs of fussing.

To Devon's credit he suggested we find a movie on cable rather than going all the way downstairs to the theater and risking a run up two flights of stairs. Our dash back to the living room earlier proved that even one level was too much distance between us and a crying baby. To sweeten the deal, he offered a rain check for a double feature of my choice. I know at least one of them will be *Titanic* with Kate Winslet and Leonardo DiCaprio. It's my mom's favorite, and because of her, it's mine.

"Do you know what you do to me?" he whispers.

I turn to him and stare up into his eyes. They're dark and filled with desire. "Tell me," I say softly.

"You make me want things . . . impossible things," he says and takes my mouth before I can question him. My knees weaken as he presses me close. Memories of our lovemaking in his studio overwhelm me, and I want him again. Was it only this afternoon that we were together? It feels like weeks ago. I run my nails down the back of his shirt, remembering the smooth skin and muscled landscape underneath.

Maybe I want the same impossible things he does.

"I'll lock the door," I say. A little thrill shoots through me, and I give myself a mental pat on the back for packing the box of condoms from Thanksgiving that I found in my nightstand.

As I secure the latch, Devon sits on the edge of the bed and unbuttons his shirtsleeves. Sweatpants and a T-shirt from Raine lie in a pile next to him. He parts his legs as I approach, welcoming me, and I slide in between them until our bodies touch. With a hungry glint in his eye, he slips his hands under my shirt, and together we lift it over my head.

"Come closer," he says in a husky whisper as his hands clutch my waist and draw me in.

Our gaze connects a moment before his hot mouth hits my breast through the lacy cup of my bra, and I eject a breath. A burst of warmth floods my core, and an aching need spreads inside me. I'm desperate to feel his skin on mine, to consume him.

I curl my hand around the back of his neck to steady myself, enjoying the soft hairs under my fingers. He switches sides, brushing a thumb over the nipple he just abandoned. I gasp when his mouth drops away, leaving me on the edge of desperation. I help him the rest of the way out of his shirt and run my fingers through the soft blond curls on his chest. He makes a move to get up, but I have something else in mind. Planting a hand gently on his chest, I push him back onto the bed and straddle him, clutching his hips between my thighs.

"*Mmm.*" A low moan rises from his throat as his fingers slide down my sides. He stirs beneath me, and I seize his belt buckle.

He traps my wrist and says in a heated whisper, "Wait, Jen, I don't have anything with me."

"I have it covered." I flash a wicked smile and resume disrobing him.

My fingertips travel over the skin of his rippled abs, and he relaxes under my touch. I press on, springing him free and wrapping my mouth around him. The taste of his skin mixed with a mild saltiness exhilarates me as the need to please him devours me.

Devon lets out another moan and his eyelids slip shut, his hands gripping my shoulders as he swells in my mouth.

"Jen," he says, breathless, his fingers digging deeper into my skin. "I'm going to come if you keep this up . . ."

My mouth frees him for an instant. "I know." Then I swallow him deeper. He doesn't understand how much I need this right now. How much I need to capture his pleasure in this moment. To have him surrender to me, and to regain some control over my life.

My tongue flicks over him one last time before he grabs a pillow to muffle the sounds of his release. His body clenches under me as his shaft pulses between my lips. I drink him down, wanting this intimate part of him.

Maybe later we can tap into that box of condoms. For now, at least he'll know what he does to *me* . . .

Chapter 24

Devon

"WHAT'S THIS?" I ask, closing the refrigerator door and taking the proffered envelope from Lettie. There's a slice along the top seam from her letter opener.

"Read it," she says, her face solemn.

It's from Kingsbridge. A request—no, a demand—for another physical. "What the . . . ? Again?"

She shrugs. "I wasn't expecting it, either. I'll try to hold them off until you're back from San Francisco."

"Damn it," I say, running my fingers through my hair.

"It'll be fine. It's not like we haven't done this before. I'll get you another urine sample like the last time," she says.

"But I thought the next one wasn't until October, a week before our birthday?"

"I'm sure they're still going to want that one, too," she says.

I scowl at her and grunt. My level of resentment is higher than normal today, mostly because I've been jamming since early morning on software release schedules, marketing launch plans, and venture capital funding requests for Nanotekx, all the while wishing I were in my studio finishing Jenny's portrait. But that doesn't look like it's going to happen until I return from the Nanotekx visit.

I still don't know exactly what Jenny plans to do after we arrive in San Francisco, other than staying with a friend after she packs up her stuff. She vaguely mentioned wrapping up a few loose ends. Honestly, I haven't pressed her since that's outside the window of our agreement.

The agreement. Yeah. Shit. What I'd do for a different life. At this point, I have nothing to offer her until I know whether there's a new kidney in my future. Until then, I'll need every shred of energy I have to stay healthy and pull off this charade to take my rightful position as heir. That said, I imagine she'll come back east sooner rather than later, which will only complicate things and add an element of temptation I wasn't expecting. My mind drifts back to Saturday night, and my chest nearly implodes.

"Dev, did you hear what I just said?" Lettie gives me the evil eye. "I hate when you don't listen."

"Get used to it. It's a guy thing." I scowl. "Just repeat your question."

"No need to get snippy about it," she says.

I rub my hands over my eyes. "Sorry. What did you ask me?"

"Are you going to Jenny's tonight for dinner?" she repeats.

I blow out an aggravated breath and frown. "Yeah." I'm pissed at myself for looking forward to it way too much.

"Are you going to see Mom first?" she asks. The innocent look in her eye makes me wonder why she's asking. She knows my routine. I smell a classic Lettie ulterior motive.

I eye her suspiciously. "Why?"

She shrugs. "No reason."

"*Uh-huh.*" I thrust the letter at her. "Here." After procuring a bottle of water from the fridge, I head up to the west wing to find out what she's plotting with my mother.

The afternoon nurse, Becky, is reading aloud to my mom when I enter the room.

I nod my greeting.

"Hello, darlin'. I'm on the last chapter, do you mind if I finish reading to your mama? We're both anxious to hear how it ends," she asks in a Southern drawl that I find rhythmically soothing.

Mom lifts her good hand and beckons me over to sit next to her on the bed and listen.

I shrug. "Go for it."

Becky's voice is clear and infused with emotion as she reads:

"'Is it really you?' I ask, and fight back my welling tears.

"His blond brows knit together with the same look of concentration he wore when I first opened my front door and found him on my doorstep the day of the photo shoot.

"He presses his lips together to stop them from quivering and nods.

"I rise to my feet, and my belly clears the table.

"Taking a step back, his eyes widen and focus on my abdomen. I step around the table and reach for his hand. A rush of electricity travels through me on contact, and I feel like I've found the other part of me that I've been missing.

"I place his hand on my belly. 'Meet your daughter,' I say as my eyes overflow until I can no longer see him clearly.

"He pulls me into him, but my belly prevents me from getting as close as I used to. 'God, I've missed you,' he says, and he crushes me to his chest.

"'Come home, Raine,' I say, unable to hold back."

My head pops up. "What did you say?"

Becky gives me a quizzical look. "Which part, darlin'?"

"His name. What's his name?"

"Raine, with an *e* at the end," she replies.

I lunge over to peer at the book cover. *Caught Up in Raine* by Jillian Grant. Jenny's uncle, wearing nothing but jeans, stares seductively back at me. It's the same cover on the wall in Jillian's art studio. I'm not much of a fiction reader, but now that I think about it, I connect the dots. I've seen the title on the *New York Times* best-seller list.

A chord vibrates inside me. I sit back down next to my mother. "Read the rest."

Becky continues:

"My fingers dig into his back, and I release my well of love and pain. 'I'm sorry. . . I love you. Please come home.'

"He squeezes me tighter, and his shoulders shake next to me as the crowd looks on. One person claps, and then another, until the bookstore erupts with thunderous applause and whistles.

"He tips my chin up with his finger, and our wet eyes connect. 'I love you, Jillian. Marry me?' His gaze holds mine.

"'Yes,' I whisper, and our lips touch and remain there until the world recedes around us, and once again, I'm caught up in Raine."

"The end," Becky adds, brushing away a tear. She rises from her chair. "I'll leave you be now."

I hate to admit it, but there's a lump in my throat. These aren't strangers, these are people I know. People who have something I wish I could have someday.

Lettie's fingerprints are all over this . . . what's she trying to do to me?

Mom gives my hand a brief squeeze to get my attention.

I meet her gaze, and she fists her hand over her heart.

"Yes, it was very romantic," I murmur begrudgingly.

She points between me and Becky's empty chair and nods.

"Yes, I've met them. They're really nice people. Happy."

Mom positions her arm as if she's cradling a baby.

I try to suppress a smile. "The baby's really cute. Big for a newborn."

She strokes the length of her hair and then circles her finger at my heart with her left brow raised.

"Jenny?"

She blinks once. Yes.

"What about her?" I ask cautiously.

She makes her sign for the gala and then points to herself.

"We'll come and see you before we go, and I'll introduce you. Okay?"

The left side of her mouth turns up in a lopsided smile. She makes the sign for the baby again and points to my heart.

I blow out a breath. "No, Mom. I'm not getting married and having children," I say more roughly than I mean to.

She loses her smile and squeezes my hand. Hard.

Tugging free of her grasp, I rise to my feet. "Will you just stop?"

A guttural grunt rises from her throat, and anger blazes in her good eye. She points at my heart, strokes her hair downward, and places her fist at her heart.

"I'm not in love with her," I say as calmly as possible, trying to regain my composure.

She blinks once and points to my eyes. She disagrees and says I'm lying to myself.

"I barely know her," I say, resisting the urge to grit my teeth, afraid she could be right.

She makes like she's using a paintbrush.

My shoulders slump. "Yes, I'm working on her portrait, but it's not finished yet."

She points between my heart and my groin and blinks once. She knows we've had sex. *How the . . . ?*

My cheeks burn. "Did Lettie tell you that? How is that any of your business or hers?"

She points to herself and an invisible person next to her, fists her heart, and points at my mouth—because they love me and want to see me happy.

"I know that! But you both have to back off, all right?" I pace in long strides next to the bed.

She draws a wide circle meant to encompass my whole body and holds up one finger. Her face holds anger again. She draws her finger across her neck and throws an invisible object to the floor.

Her message is clear: "You have one life, don't throw it away."

I shake my head and shout. "Throw it away? How's that different from sacrificing the future I want for one that I dread? I'm doing everything in my power for our family without complaint. Don't you get it, Mom? That doesn't change the fact that there's no happy ending waiting for me."

The side of her mouth drops open, and she pulls back as if I've struck her. Then she points at me and shakes her head. She thinks I'm wrong.

I turn my back on her. "Stop, all right? There's no such thing as fairy tales!" I stalk out of her room, blinking my vision clear, and whisper, *"For me."*

Chapter 25

Jenny

"YOU SURE YOU don't want my help?" Mom asks, eyeing me skeptically.

"Nope. I'm good," I say as the salmon bakes and I prepare a cake for the second oven. Raine shamed me into proving myself after Saturday night's dinner. I don't want Devon to have any doubts about my skills in the kitchen. Plus, after my issues with Russ in that department, I could use the confidence boost.

"You've been spending a lot of time with Devon. Is it serious now that Russ is out of the picture?" Mom asks, taking a seat at the kitchen table.

I beat eggs into the batter. "We've only known each other a little over a week. How's that serious?" Okay, so we've spent almost every waking moment together since visiting Aunt Jill and Raine this weekend. He even graciously watched *Titanic* with me on Sunday night, and he did nothing to hide that his eyes were as wet as mine when it ended. Instead he held me close and wordlessly stroked my hair. Between that and everything else, I can't get rid of the uneasy feeling in my stomach or get the sound of a ticking time bomb out of my head.

"You're cooking for the boy, Jenny," Mom says. "Food is love, honey, and let's not forget your little overnight excursion at Aunt Jillian's."

I feel a blush creep up and over my cheekbones as I stir the cake batter with my back turned. "We were babysitting Rachel, Mom. That's all."

"*Mmm-hmm.* I was young once, too, you know, honey. All I ask is that you be safe."

"Are we really having this conversation?" I glance at her and pour the mix into the pan.

"Yes, we are," she says, crossing her arms over her chest. She's wearing one of her long 1980s throwback shirts with bat-wing sleeves over a pair of stretch pants. At least it's too hot for leg warmers.

I roll my eyes and groan.

"I see the twinkle in your eye when you look at him. That's more than I've seen between you and Russell in years."

"I'm not denying that I like him," I say. *Yeah, well, maybe more than like . . .*

"Lucas speaks very highly of his family," Mom says.

My head snaps up. "You've spoken to Lucas about Devon?"

Mom gives me a sheepish look and nervously fiddles with her rings, something she does when confessing to poking around in my business. "Not really, honey, he just happened to mention he had a close relationship with Devon's father before he died and that Devon is a fine young man. Which reminds me. Have you scheduled your physical with Lucas yet?"

I grunt, knowing what's coming.

"I'm not nagging, sweetie, but since you quit your job and don't have insurance, you might want to consider it while you're home."

Just what I need—to be reminded of my parental dependency, I think, holding back a snort.

"I'll call him," I say to appease her, knowing I probably won't. On second thought, I'm low on supplements for my anemia, so maybe I will . . . if I have time. Whatever.

I pop the cake in the oven and decide it's time to break the news about my date on Saturday night, since it's only two days away. "Devon asked me to move my flight and go to the Memorial Hospital Gala with him on Saturday night." I hold back the tidbit about taking his corporate jet on Sunday rather than flying commercial.

Mom looks at me with alarm. "Oh, Jenny! Do you have anything to wear? Do I need to take you shopping?"

"No, I have it covered."

"Covered? How is it covered?" she asks with a frown. "Are you recycling one of your old prom dresses?"

"What? No! Devon procured an outfit for me," I say and prepare myself for impact.

"'Procured'? What do you mean, 'procured' you an outfit?" she snaps.

"He bought me an outfit with the clothing allowance he gets for company and family foundation events," I say, digging myself in deeper.

"Well, we'll need to pay him back," she says vehemently.

My stomach drops. "He won't take the money. He says I'm doing him a favor by going with him, and a debt is a debt, so he's paying for the outfit."

"Jenny, we'll pay him back. How much was the outfit?"

I don't want to lie, but if I answer honestly, Mom will no doubt lose her shit on me. So without remorse, I rip a page from Devon's book of deceptive nonanswers and place a bet on his honor. With a look of innocence, I shrug. "You'll have to ask him."

Mom narrows her eyes. "Jennifer Larissa Lynch, why do I get the feeling you're holding back on me?"

"Sorry, Mom. He didn't show me the credit card slip." Not a lie.

Her mouth opens to form a question, but I switch topics and lob one of my own. "Mom, why did you break up with John Henshaw and marry Dad instead?"

Her jaw clamps shut, and a deep frown cuts across her brow. "Why would you ask me that?"

I pull out the salad greens. "I was thinking about our talk ... you know, about not marrying Russ. With everything that happened, and then meeting Devon during this whole mess, I started to wonder about what you said the other day ... about John."

A pained expression covers her face. "Jenny, honey, there's some things that I can't talk about with you or anyone else ... for a lot of reasons. I'm sure it's the same for you. The only thing I can tell you is that sometimes things just don't work out." She moves to leave the way she always does when questions come up about John.

I stop ripping the romaine. "You still love him, don't you?"

"I love your father, Jenny." She answers as if one negates the other.

"I know, but that's not what I asked." I wish she didn't think I was so naive. I know that's not how it works sometimes, especially based on Aunt Jillian's experience.

For some reason, I ache to hear her admit that she still loves John. Her observation about the way I look at Devon and not Russ—I've seen the same in her. The only spark I've ever seen in her eyes comes when she looks at John. I don't doubt she loves my dad, but the passion she feels for John just isn't there with Dad. Sometimes I wonder if that's why she lets herself go. Not to be mean, since that's not my intent, but she could be more attractive—pretty even—if she tried by just keeping her grays covered, wearing some makeup, and upgrading her appalling wardrobe. I can't help but wonder if she locked herself in the eighties and threw away the key on purpose—like a modern-day version of Charles Dickens's Miss Havisham—because those were the years she spent with

John.

She gives me a tight smile and heads for the door.

"Mom?"

She stops at the threshold. "Yes?"

"It's okay if you do," I say softly. "Still love him."

She walks away. It's only when she gets down the hall, close to the bathroom, that I hear the soft, muffled sound of her crying.

Her tears hit the center of my chest, and I feel terrible that I'm responsible. But one thing's for sure, she just confirmed what I already knew.

The doorbell rings before I can think much more about it.

"I'll get it," I yell, mostly for Mom's benefit. Dad's out back in the stable, cleaning the place up in preparation for showing Devon his bevy of classic beauties.

I set aside the greens and head to the front door, my belly fluttering in anticipation.

Devon's standing on the landing with a bouquet of summer flowers.

We both break into smiles, and I lean in to get a taste of those delectable lips of his. On the way my eyes catch a glimpse of the little blue convertible he drove over in, and my jaw unhinges. I miss his mouth in favor of looking over his shoulder.

"Holy crap, Devon! You said you had an Aston Martin. You didn't say you had a 1970 Aston Martin DB6 Volante! My father's going to need a defibrillator when he sees that!"

Chapter 26

Devon

I GET A kick out of Jenny's reaction. Chuckling, I point at my lips. *"Ahem?"*

She pulls back and meets my gaze, her look of awe at the car turning into something with a bit more heat. *"Mmm, where were we?"*

"You were about to plunder my mouth with your tongue," I say and touch my forehead to hers. "Unless you'd rather dump me for my car."

"Tempting," she says, and then her lips meet mine and she finishes what she started before she spotted the Volante. Her arms circle my waist and she pulls me so close that I can feel every swell and curve of her against me. Mr. Happy perks up with an inappropriate display of affection. Jenny reacts by grinding into him. I moan softly and half wonder what the chances are of getting arrested for taking her in the front yard, as I revel in the taste and texture of her kiss.

A masculine throat clears behind us down the hallway. "If you're out there any longer, I might have to sell tickets." I pull away from Jenny and silently recite the Ancient Greek alphabet in an attempt to dampen the overenthusiastic celebration happening below my waist.

Jenny shares a mischievous grin with me as her father approaches from behind her. "Hey, Dad, check out what's in the driveway."

She looks up to catch his reaction as he clears the doorway.

"Devon, good to see . . ." Her dad's mouth freezes open and his eyes bulge as if he's a kid who's been handed a lifetime supply of free video games. "She's yours?"

My mouth quirks up in a proud smile. "Yes, sir."

"Where on God's green earth did you find her?" he asks, pushing past us and heading toward the car like a missile on radar lock.

I wink at Jenny, hand her the flowers, and follow him. "In England. My dad bought her at auction for me as a present for graduating from boarding school."

Without waiting for her father to ask, I pop the hood so he can take a look underneath. "It's a ZF five speed. Only seventeen were made."

Jenny's mom appears at the front door, relieving Jenny of the flowers before disappearing back inside. Freed from her burden, Jenny runs over to join us.

"This model has power-assisted steering, an improvement over the DB5," her dad murmurs to no one in particular. "Weber carburetors . . . How many miles?"

"Fifty-eight thousand and change," I say.

"Nice." Her father studies the engine with an excited glow in his eye. After a couple of minutes, he straightens up and places his hands on his waist. "She's one amazing car, Devon. You're lucky to have her. Just let me know if you ever put her up for sale."

I purse my lips and nod. "Thanks." Then I glance at Jenny. "But I think I'll keep her for the foreseeable future." The car and his daughter. I just wish "foreseeable" were a lot longer when it came to Jenny.

Jenny's brows lift in a questioning stare.

"Jenny, what time's dinner?" her dad asks.

Her expression changes to alarm. "Oh my God! The salmon!" She dashes for the front door.

Chuckling, her father claps me on the back. "Guess that answers my question. How about after dinner I show you my beauties out back?"

I give him a genuine smile as we walk toward the house. "I'd like that. Jenny tells me you have quite an impressive collection."

He lets out a breath. "Ah. So I thought . . . until you pulled up in that little hussy."

I laugh. "Yeah, she's pretty brazen."

Jenny's father leads the way inside. Good thing, I've never been farther than the front hall.

We arrive in the kitchen to a flurry of activity between Jenny and her mother as they buzz around in the last-minute throes of meal preparation. Sweet and savory aromas fill my senses between the fish and the cake Jenny just removed from the oven.

"Hey, Pumpkin, smells like the salmon made it out alive, so to speak." Jenny's dad waves me in front of him toward the set table and chuckles. "I'm glad you didn't need to pull out the fire extinguisher."

Jenny smirks at him. "Not funny, Dad. Mom took it out while I was outside."

"Devon, what would you like to drink?" her mom asks on the way to the refrigerator.

"Water's fine," I reply and take a seat. Just as in Jillian and Raine's home, the family vibe here is strong and welcoming . . . enviable.

"Dad, here, take the salad and go sit. Mom and I will take care of the rest," Jenny says, handing him a big wooden bowl and a pair of tongs.

After everyone's seated and the plates are full, Jenny's dad leads us in saying grace. I'm ashamed to say that it's the first time in a long time for me.

I take a forkful of Jenny's baked salmon. Made with some dill butter and a side of green beans, it pleases my simple palate. "This is really good," I say to her.

Her face lights up next to me. "Thanks. I told you Raine was stretching the truth."

"I never doubted you." I wink.

Halfway through the meal and some small talk, Jenny's mom puts down her fork. She's wearing a deep frown. "Devon, honey, Jenny tells me you've asked her to go to the Memorial Hospital Gala with you on Saturday night."

"I have," I answer, wondering why she looks so worried.

"She also mentioned that you purchased her an outfit."

Her father's fork freezes in the middle of shearing off another piece of fish. "Huh? Pumpkin, why didn't you just ask your mom to take you shopping?" Then her father throws me a glance. "Devon, how much do we owe you, buddy?"

Jenny gives me a tight smile. "It's all you."

Crap.

I wipe my lips with the napkin and place it back on my lap. For emphasis, and to buy some time to formulate an answer, I push my plate forward, tent my hands in front of me, and clear my throat. Then I turn on my best CEO voice. "Mr. and Mrs. Lynch—"

"Kitty."

"Bob." Her parents blurt out simultaneously.

"All right, Kitty and Bob, then. There's a reason why I purchased Jenny's gala attire. I'm sorry, but I can't let you reimburse me."

"Oh?" Kitty's eyebrows rise with a look that tells me she's not ready to be swayed.

"I'll explain. This is an incredibly high-visibility event for my family and, this year, for me personally. I'm heir apparent to take over my father's conglomerate when I turn twenty-five this October. Being seen with Jenny by my side will go a long way in convincing the people that matter that I'm displaying the proper . . . stability."

"What does that have to do with Jenny's outfit?" her mother asks.

"The board members of my father's company, Kingsbridge Industries, will be there along with all the top local families in the social register. For Jenny to be on my arm at the gala, she needs to be dressed in the latest couture. I couldn't ask anyone without a clothing allowance, like the one my sister and I have, to pay for an outfit that expensive. I consider it a business expense."

Jenny's father gives me a puzzled look while her mother's eyes cut a swath right through me. "Devon, how much did Jenny's outfit cost?"

"I'm afraid I won't know that until my accountant gets the credit card bill. Honestly, even if I knew, I wouldn't tell you. Please just consider it a cost of doing business and a gift that will allow me to enjoy the pleasure of your daughter's company at the gala." I close with a pleasant smile and drain my water glass.

Kitty lets out an unhappy breath and digs back into her food.

"Kitty, would it make you feel better to know that my mother is thrilled that I'm bringing a date? She's really looking forward to meeting Jenny the night of the gala."

"So your mother will be there?" Kitty eyes light with interest.

I cringe as I think back to my argument with my mom earlier, and I shake my head. "No. My mom is bedridden with round-the-clock nursing care. Seeing Jenny in that dress before we go will put a smile on her face. Trust me."

Kitty's expression softens, and she gives me a sweet smile. "Lucas was right about you, Devon. You're a fine young man. Consider the matter closed."

"Glad that's settled," I say, hiding my surprise at the mention of Lucas and wondering what else he said about me.

I catch an approving glance from Bob and return to my food. Jenny gives my thigh a squeeze under the table, and I squeeze hers back.

The rest of dinner goes smoothly.

"Anyone ready for dessert?" Jenny asks, pushing back her chair. "I just need a few minutes to ice the cake."

Kitty chimes in. "Bob, why don't you take Devon out to the stable while Jenny and I clean up the kitchen and get dessert on the table?"

Bob's eyes sparkle eagerly as he scoots out his chair. "You sure you can manage without us?"

She gives him a knowing glance and a soft laugh. "Been doing it for years, sweetie. Enjoy yourselves."

"Ready, Devon?"

"Lead the way."

I follow him out the back door of their Victorian house and find myself staring at a large carriage house the size of a five-car detached garage.

"Wow. When you said stable, you weren't kidding," I say, betting it had seen a horse or two when it was originally built.

Bob smiles, slides open one of the doors, and flips on the lights to brighten the dusky interior.

My eyes pop open at his little showroom of classic cars. The carriage house has been completely gutted so that it's one large open space. One side has a lift and enough tools and equipment to build a car from scratch. The other side is like a showroom, with a polymer floor so clean you could eat off it.

There's an eclectic group of cars filling the interior: one in the lift and three on the showroom floor.

Rubbing my hands together, I say, "Show me what you've got."

Bob heads over to the red convertible Triumph with a soft top. "She's the youngest of the lot. A 1974 Triumph TR6. She's the closest thing I have to your little beauty out front," he says, giving it an admiring stare.

The car's British just like mine, but it's a two-seater while my Volante has a back seat.

He releases the hood and then secures it so we can get a look underneath. "The engine's been rebuilt to a SPEC Stage 2 with fuel injection, and she's been converted to unleaded fuel," Bob says.

"She's a stunner," I say.

"Jenny helped me with this one. I got her when Jenny was a freshman in high school. She'd come out back with me on Saturday mornings to help me rebuild her." Bob smiles. "Jenny's quite the little mechanic, you know."

The image of Jenny working on cars makes me smile, too.

"Was your father interested in cars?" Bob asks.

I shake my head as I take a look at the carburetor. "Not really."

"He had fine taste in cars based on what's sitting in my driveway."

"That was all me," I say, pressing my lips together. "He asked me what I wanted for graduation and I told him." My admission leaves a lonely hole in my middle.

"It was a nice gift either way. Were you close?"

"Not particularly," I say quietly. "I think he would've preferred that my sister and I came out of the womb as adults. He wasn't great with kids."

Bob clutches my arm and says warmly, "I'm sorry to hear that, son. Sounds like he missed a good opportunity." His arm falls away.

"I appreciate you saying that," I say, feeling suddenly exposed. Bob's warmth disarms me. His questions and his kind manner make me wonder just how much I've missed. If I'd had a father like him, what kind of relationship would we have had? Would I have felt loved?

He pulls down the hood and leads me to the next car, a 1957 Porsche.

Bob lovingly caresses the top. "356 C. 2100cc dual carbs. I

picked her up when Jenny was in grade school."

"Nice. How much work did she need?" I ask.

Bob wiggles his brows. "Not as much as you'd think." He goes into a full list of restorations that he has performed since he purchased her. I've done some work on cars but not nearly as much as Bob.

"Devon, you ever think about showing the Volante?" he asks suddenly.

"As in 'car show'?" I ask.

He nods. "Yeah. I'm hoping Jenny will be around for the Summit Classic Car Show in September. Do you think you'd be interested in joining us with your slinky little Aston Martin?"

I break into a smile despite myself until reality comes crashing down on top of me and I feel it wilt at the edges. "I'd like that, but I'll have to check my Kingsbridge commitments."

"No pressure, son. There's plenty of time to decide."

I nod. He has no idea how much I want to say yes, how much I want to stay in this garage and forget about life and just look at his cars.

His gaze meets mine, and now I realize where Jenny got her blue eyes. "Another thing before I forget," he says. "I want to thank you for helping my little girl when she was in trouble at the airport. I really appreciate it. You know, it kills me sometimes to think I can't protect her all day every day. I'm glad you were there."

"It was nothing, really," I say.

"You're wrong, Devon. It was something. You're a rare breed, I'm afraid. For a guy your age, you seem to have your head on straight, and there's a sense of honor in your heart that I admire. I wish I saw it in more people your age. But I don't. Value it."

"Thank you." I'm at a loss for anything else to say. What I would've done to hear those words from my own father.

Besides his eyes, now I know where Jenny inherited her powers of observation and directness.

"Come on, let's finish up. The girls are probably champing at the bit for us to get inside for some dessert. I'll give you a quick introduction to the last two ladies, but I'm hoping you'll be back for another visit," he says, catching my eye.

"I'd really like that," I say.

Bob claps my back. "Glad to hear it."

He shows me a 1954 Chevy Bel Air and a primo 1975 Ford Mustang GT.

By the time we head inside, I've come to two realizations: The first is that being with Jenny and her family makes me yearn for something I wish I had. The second is that the unbearable tightness of my shoes from my suddenly swollen feet will require a phone call to Lucas on my way out.

I'm hoping it'll be as simple as popping a diuretic and calling it a night . . .

Chapter 27

Jenny

"DEV," I GROWL before burying my nails into the smooth skin of his muscled ass as he slides his way home on top of me. I moan low in my throat and lose myself in his languorous rhythm. The feel of him filling and caressing the space inside me satisfies an ache I didn't know existed.

I've hated every second this week that we didn't touch. I wish we could skip the gala tonight and just stay here under the warmth of his covers and enjoy each other until we're too sore or too exhausted to move.

The last thing I want is to get off that plane in San Francisco tomorrow night. My life with Russ feels like ancient history, and the thought of returning to our apartment, even just to box up my stuff, turns my stomach. If I hadn't been concerned about the state in which my possessions would be returned, I would've taken him up on his offer to pack my things and send them back to me.

"Jen ...," Devon breathes into my neck, leaning on his elbow with one of his hips resting on mine as he rocks inside me. "I can't get enough of you."

He lifts his head, and our eyes connect a moment before his lips take mine. I run my fingers through his soft hair, savoring the feel of the fine strands against my fingertips, and hook my leg around his calf. I memorize the way he kisses me, every sensation of his tongue on mine and the patterns of our exploration. Tears burn underneath my eyelids as we kiss, and I arch up into him. My fingers press into the swell of his backside, encouraging him to bury himself as deep as he can go. I want that wicked-good sensation of him filling me to capacity with every thrust.

"Faster, Dev . . ."

I need to feel him come inside me. What I'd give to bottle the look that crosses his face in that moment.

I'm going to miss him so much, especially now. Try as I might, I couldn't stop myself . . . I've fallen in love with him.

I've spent the better part of the last two days guessing what he's not telling me and why on earth this can't continue. But that can wait until our six-hour flight tomorrow. For now I want to forget everything but being in the moment with Devon and convincing the Kingsbridge board that he's the best decision they've ever made.

The next time he glides over my core, he triggers a cataclysmic reaction, and a cry of ecstasy escapes from my throat. "Oh, Dev . . . ," I scream out. He presses me into his chest and I shatter around him, losing control of my limbs and turning boneless beneath him.

He hovers over me with his eyes closed. His dark-blond lashes lie in soft crescents on his cheeks. His breath comes in fits and starts until his whole body goes rigid, and his length pulses inside me. He lets out a satisfied groan as pleasure fills his features. I drink in the look of his release and store it for later.

Poised on his elbows, he drops his head and kisses the base of my neck. "Jen . . . baby, that was amazing . . . ," he whispers, and then he kisses a trail up from there to my lips with a small nibbling stop at my earlobe. He pushes back my hair and stares into my eyes as if he's memorizing me as much as I am him. Then, with a final look of yearning, he hugs me close before slipping himself out. Rolling over, he pulls me onto his chest.

I brush my fingers over the light covering of damp blond curls that I find there. "We have to get up soon and shower."

He squeezes me against him and whispers, "I know, but it feels so good here. I don't want to move. Five minutes . . . ten max."

His eyes slip shut. For a moment, there's a look of peace on his face so profound that he reminds me of an angel.

I relax into him and am ready to doze off when a loud knock sounds at the door. A couple of seconds later it swings inward, and Lettie stands in the open doorway.

Devon and I jolt upright in bed. "What the *fuck*, Lettie?" Devon screams as I grab for the covers to avoid flashing the room.

"Exactly!" she says, throwing up a hand before planting both of them on her hips. "I could hear the moaning halfway down the hallway. I'm surprised Mom couldn't hear you all the way up in the west wing!"

"Bloody effing hell! Get out!" he says as his face turns an interesting shade of crimson to match what must be fire-engine red burning its way up my neck to my cheeks.

A half smile touches her lips. "Fine. Honestly, I had to see for myself that you weren't in here alone. At least there'll be more than a little truth behind your performance at the gala this evening."

"Lettie . . . ," Devon growls menacingly. Glaring, he moves to get out of bed.

"Oh God, Dev," Lettie says and covers her eyes. "There are some visuals I can do without. You naked is one of them."

She turns back toward the door. "I actually came up here for a reason, you know. Jenny, Jean-Claude's here to do our hair and makeup. You have thirty minutes to shower and get downstairs." Lettie pulls the door shut on her way out with a resounding *bang*.

Devon throws himself backward on the bed with a look of mortification plastered on his face. "What the hell was she thinking?"

I lie down next to him and pull the covers over us. "Damned if I know. I'm sorry, Dev. I know she's your sister, but she's a little odd."

He snorts. "Only a little? And she's the one who wonders how we came from the same womb?" He blows out an exasperated breath and shakes his head. "I'm sorry, Jen. I should've locked the door."

I snuggle in close and inhale the scent of his skin mixed with our lovemaking. "Shower time? I'll wash your back . . ."

"Not yet. I want to hold you for a few more minutes," he whispers and kisses my hair. "I'm so tired . . . I wish we could ditch the gala."

Same here. The soothing warmth of his body next to mine overtakes me until I'm ready to doze again. I shake myself awake. "I've got to get up or I'm going to fall asleep."

I manage to get us both in Devon's shower after locking his bedroom door and saying a little prayer of thanks that he has an en suite bathroom.

We take turns washing each other. Devon helps with my hair. As tempting as it is to have another round in the shower, Lettie's visit signaled how little time we have to prepare and still take a trip upstairs to see his mother before we go. I have mixed feelings about meeting her. Not that I don't want to, because I do. It's just that meeting her might be setting up false expectations.

It's not until I'm drying Devon off that I notice his ankles look swollen and that there are circles cut under his eyes, making his skin look translucent.

"Dev, are you feeling all right?" I ask.

"Yeah. Why?" He avoids looking me in the eye.

I gently turn his chin toward me. "Babe? You sure?"

He gives me a wan smile. "Just nervous about tonight . . . and I think you wore me out."

"We could've waited, I guess," I say.

He pulls me close, our naked bodies pressing together until they're flush. "No way." His voice is soft, sexy gravel. "I don't care if I fall asleep in my soup. This afternoon was worth every second." His groin stirs next to me.

I chuckle. "You're insatiable."

"*Mmm*. Only when it comes to you." His lips are soft, firm, and all too briefly on mine. "Lettie's right, we need to get moving." He steps away and towels his hair dry.

Yeah. I only wish I didn't feel as if I were headed to the guillotine.

Chapter 28

Devon

THE MOMENT JENNY leaves to go downstairs, I collapse on the bed in my robe and rest my eyes. I've been dragging ass and retaining water since Thursday. It doesn't help that I haven't taken more than one piss so far today. I've been popping diuretics like candy.

Lucas wanted me to meet him at the office this afternoon, but there was no way I'd give up my last full day with Jenny. Instead I'll duck out of the gala at some point tonight, and we'll meet in my hotel room so he can check me out.

After Lettie barged in earlier, I'm glad that Jenny and I aren't coming back here. Between Lettie and the hired help, there's a general lack of privacy in this house. I have to say, I like the idea of a keyed lock between me and my sister.

In the meantime, the thought of crawling into a tuxedo makes me want to curl up in a fetal position. It'll take every ounce of energy I have tonight to dazzle the crowd and pass scrutiny. I can't say anything to Jenny, but the chances of my having enough energy to make love to her later are pretty low. Definitely a case of the spirit is willing but the flesh is weak. If I had my druthers, I'd spend the next week and a half lost inside her until either she threw me out or my dick fell

173

off.

Every time I think about our flight tomorrow, I want to retch. I've been kicking myself for making this two-week deal ever since I crossed the line last Saturday in my studio. If I'd only left well enough alone and let Lettie set me up with one of her vapid friends, I wouldn't be lying here facing the brutal reality of letting Jenny go. I might as well hand her a knife and ask her to carve my heart out. Why is it that we always yearn for the things we can't have?

Then again, who knew I'd fall in love with Jenny Lynch?

I let out a breath and try to refocus on the task at hand. If my eyes would only stay open. My mind drifts back to the afternoon Jenny and I spent in bed, and before I know it, my thoughts carry me under.

"DEV, WAKE UP," Jenny says, shaking my arm.

I pass a hand over my face and try to shake off the grogginess.

"What time is it?" I ask with a dry, pasty tongue. My vision clears and focuses on Jenny's elegant upswept hair. A smile tugs at my lips. "You look beautiful."

"It's a little after five o'clock." She kisses my forehead. "Can I get you coffee or something?"

I shake my head. "Just some water."

She runs over to the mini fridge by the television and pulls out a bottle.

After chugging half of it, I feel almost human.

"Hold up your arms," she says softly. I do as I'm told, and she hoists me onto my feet. "Come on." She leads me into the walk-in closet. It's more of a dressing room, with a mirror and a pair of chairs in the center. I plop down into the nearest chair and yawn as she makes a beeline for her dress bag.

She removes it from the rack and places it on a hook. "Where's your tux?"

I point and she retrieves it, placing it on the hook next to hers.

Her eyes light up. "I'll be right back."

"I'll be here," I say, trying to muster enough energy to stand.

She returns with a flat Victoria's Secret package, rips it open, and dumps out the contents. Two gossamer stockings fall into her waiting hand.

"Is there a garter belt that goes with those?" I ask, perking up a bit.

"They're thigh-highs. They stay up on their own," she says and smiles wickedly.

"*Mmm*, easier to take off," I mumble. "Or not . . ."

Jenny rolls them on, then drops her robe to reveal her lacy garments underneath. Unzipping the bag, she slides out the blue dress she selected at Neiman Marcus and shimmies into it.

She comes over and turns. "Zip me?"

I draw myself up onto my feet. The sight of her neck hits me below the belt with a rush of heat. Damn, even though I feel like crap, I can't go two seconds without wanting her.

She steps into her shoes and faces me. My lips part and I gape. "You look stunning, Jen. Really. Amazing." I shake my head to clear it. "Before I forget . . . I have something for you." I head to the other end of the closet, where I keep my watches, and pull out a jeweler's box.

She gives me a curious stare as I approach.

"Open it," I whisper. I bought it yesterday while she was waitressing.

Her eyes grow wide and she gasps when she opens the lid. "Oh, Dev." Her hand flies to her mouth. "It's gorgeous."

"Let me put it on you," I say, taking the diamond solitaire from the box and opening the clasp. I draw it around her neck and kiss her nape before securing it.

Tears fill her eyes when she faces me. "Why?"

"Stop, you'll ruin your makeup," I say, not wanting her to make a big deal out of it because if she does, I might not hold it together. "What's the matter? Can't I buy you a present?"

"Why?" she asks again.

I take her into my arms and press my eyes shut. "Because you make me happy. Isn't that enough?"

"I don't know if I can let you go," she cries softly into my shoulder.

I hug her tighter. "Please, Jen. Don't ... don't cry, baby. Please." The lump in my throat chokes me down to a harsh whisper. I want to hold her and never let her go. My heart squeezes painfully as if it's clenched inside an iron fist.

She sniffles and pushes away. "I'm sorry, you're right. I'm going to ruin my makeup." She blots at her eyes with the edge of a tissue she takes from the box I keep on the dresser and then blows her nose.

I stand frozen. I'm tempted to tell her, to say the words, but if I do, I can never take them back. I can't do that. I can't hurt her that way. Give her something and then take it away. It's better for her to have a reminder of our time together without the words that can change everything in the space of a second.

With a deep breath, I shuck my robe and put on the shirt that goes with the tux. Jenny does some last-minute facial repairs, effectively hiding any evidence of her breakdown a few seconds ago, while I finish dressing.

"I'm going to brush my teeth," I say and head to the bathroom, feeling a new sense of awkwardness at the unspoken words hanging between us. As much as I want to hear her say the words, too, I'm not sure I could handle them if she did.

Besides, we still have the gala to get through, and I need to be on my game and banish any distractions, regardless of how good they might be.

Jenny's sitting on the edge of my bed when I come out.

"You ready to meet my mom?" I ask softly, trying to smooth over our conversation.

She nods and then leads the way to the bedroom door. Tension buzzes between us, so I force myself to compromise. As her hand reaches for the knob, I clasp her shoulders lightly from behind and pull her into me.

"I don't know if I can let you go either . . . ," I whisper into her neck, wanting to give her more than I'm able.

"Let's go." She squeezes my hand and opens the door.

Chapter 29

Jenny

DEVON'S HAND IS warm in mine as we walk to the west wing. My thoughts attack me like a flock of angry blackbirds pecking at my soul. I couldn't form words right now if I had to.

Like a marionette I walk stiffly at his side, berating myself for losing it in his room. There's no doubt in my mind that he cares about me. My bigger worry is that I'm so addicted to his presence that the thought of losing him sends me straight into a fit of withdrawal.

But the last thing I want to do is let him down. I made a promise that I intend to keep, even if it means waking up tomorrow with a battered heart. He's doing this for his family, I remind myself. That much I know. If he can sacrifice what makes him happy to fulfill his obligation, then so can I . . . at least for one night.

I inhale deeply and force the tension from my shoulders.

We enter a part of the house where I've never been before. Partway down the hall, we stop in front of a set of double doors.

"You ready?" he asks quietly. There's sorrow and longing in his eyes, and those little creases that give away his burden are back.

I'm not the only one paying a price right now.

"Dev?"

"Yeah?"

My high heels put us at eye level, and I meet his gaze. I cup his cheek in my hand and touch my lips to his, taking strength from their firm warmth. He meets my kiss and pulls me against the hard muscles of his chest. I rest my forehead next to his when we part. "I'm ready now."

Devon knocks briefly, twists the knob, and pushes the door inward. We walk into the small living room on the other side.

A heavyset woman with Dolly Parton–like blonde hair, dressed in a nurse's uniform, greets us with a smile. "Devon, your mama's ready for you, darlin'. She put on her Sunday best to meet your lovely lady friend."

"Thanks, Becky," he says, his cheeks coloring with a faint blush.

A few butterflies stir in my stomach as I push down a feeling of discomfort. Devon prepared me earlier, giving me a brief description of his mother's appearance and the modified language he and Lettie have developed with her over the years.

Devon's fingertips touch the small of my back, guiding me through the inner door.

A hospital bed is situated in the center of the room, with the back elevated so his mother can sit upright. She's wearing a pale-blue satin robe, and her long gray hair has been brushed and styled to perfection. Underneath her half-frozen features lies what was once a beautiful woman. I notice the family resemblance immediately. Devon has her eyes.

"Mom, this is Jenny," he says.

A glimmer of a smile tugs at the good side of her mouth. She beckons us with her working hand while the other lies hidden beneath the blankets.

Reflexively I smile back, my feet carrying me forward alongside Devon.

"Have a seat." Devon leads me to the chair near the bed while he balances on the edge of the mattress between me and his mother.

She grabs Devon's hand and gives it a brief squeeze before pointing to me and then circling her face, repeating the gesture for Devon, and ending by placing her fist over her heart.

"She says we look nice," Devon says. His mother grabs his hand and raises her unfrozen brow. "Sorry, we look better than nice," he amends.

Then his mom tilts her head toward me, draws a wide circle around me, and points to Devon.

"You want Jenny to tell you how we met?"

She blinks once. Yes.

Devon glances at me and nods. "She'd like you to tell her." There no mistaking the blush that's rising over his cheekbones.

I wring my hands, wishing away the clamminess, and flash a glance at Devon with a nervous smile. "It's quite embarrassing, actually."

A twinkle shines in her good eye, and her lips tip up higher on one side in encouragement. At least I think it's encouragement. I tell her my story, and I leave out the part about Devon paying for my ticket since I don't want his mother doubting my motivations for being with him now. God knows the last thing I want him for is his money and what seem to be some heavy obligations. I'd rather be with the artist that lives inside him, the part that clearly makes him a happier person.

His mother presses her hand to her mouth and then reaches for Devon. She nods and squeezes his hand.

My heart swells. She's proud of him.

"It was nothing," he says softly.

She squeezes his hand again, frowns, and blinks twice.

"She disagrees," he says.

She bows her head to me with a quick tap to her chest.

"She says thank you," Devon says.

Then his mother waves her fingers from side to side, wiggles them downward like falling confetti, and nods.

"What's our plan tonight for the gala?" he asks her.

Yes, she blinks.

I'm amazed at Devon's ability to communicate with his mother. Surprisingly, I'm not having nearly as hard a time participating in the conversation as I imagined.

"Jenny, Lettie, and I are taking a car over. We'll meet Howard there, and he'll drive us back tomorrow," he says.

She points to Devon's midsection and spins her finger, giving him what I now realize is a questioning look. His shoulders stiffen, and I catch the faintest shake of his head.

Her eyes dart to me, then back to him, her smile fading. I'm at a loss; it looks as if she's asking him about his stomach, but that doesn't feel right. The only thing I'm certain of is that he doesn't want to discuss it in front of me . . . whatever it is.

His mother turns her attention my way and beckons me over. I crouch next to Devon. She takes my hand in hers. It's soft and warm against my skin. Then she places it on Devon's. He meets my eyes and twines his fingers through mine. She touches our joined hands, tilts her head, points back and forth between our eyes, and then touches her heart.

Devon swallows and says nothing. His lips press together, and he shares another private look with his mother. Her expression flits from one of worry to an empty smile. She taps our hands, dips her head, and blinks once.

"Thanks, Mom," he says. "We'll do our best to have a good time." He stands and pulls me to my feet, his face a smooth and unreadable mask.

"It was very nice to meet you," I say.

His mother lights up and motions to my free hand. She

clutches it and squeezes.

Devon leans in to kiss her. "I'll see you tomorrow."

On the way back to Devon's room to pick up our bags, I clear my throat and ask, "What was that all about?"

"What do you mean?" Devon asks, distracted.

"You know, the part of the conversation you haven't told me," I say, somewhat more sharply than I meant to.

Devon lets out a breath, shakes his head, and pulls me to a stop. "Listen, my mother sometimes thinks because she can't talk that it's okay to bring up certain topics in mixed company. Things she should only ask me privately."

My brows shoot up. "So I'm mixed company now? An hour ago you had an intimate piece of your anatomy buried inside of mine. I didn't feel like mixed company then."

He grits his teeth. "You know that's not what I mean, Jen. I've never asked you to tell me all your secrets, and I didn't promise to tell you all of mine."

I'm being irrational. I know it. But his words hit my overly sensitive heart with ice-pick precision. "I know." I turn away abruptly, not wanting him to see the tears welling in my eyes, ashamed to be acting so emotional. He's right; he hasn't done anything wrong.

I dated Russ for over six years, but since making this two-week arrangement with Devon, I've barely given him a second thought . . . even before I found out he cheated on me. Now, faced with the possibility of losing Devon, I want to curl up and die, as if our relationship has lasted for years.

No two ways about it, I feel like an idiot.

"Damn it, Jen." He grabs my arm and whirls me around. "Don't you know how much this is killing me? How I wish I could tell you everything?"

"Why can't you?" My jaw clenches and my nostrils flare.

"Because I'm trying to shelter you from all the bullshit I wish I didn't have to deal with. Stuff you might not be able to handle."

My ire rises, and I pull my arm free from his grasp. "How would you know what I can or can't handle? I don't want your protection, I want your trust!"

He reels back. "You think I don't trust you?"

"Obviously not. Either that or you think I'm weak. Which one is it, Devon?" I snap.

"Oh, for fuck's sake! Will you two just kiss and shut up?" Lettie says, storming down the hall in a full-length shimmery knit sheath and looking as ravishing as a runway model. "You're late for our briefing and I think you gave Becky enough of an earful for one night."

"Lettie . . . ," Devon growls and fists his hands at his sides.

"Don't 'Lettie' me, Devon," she snaps and then scowls at me and shakes her perfectly coiffed head. "Jenny, you silly girl, don't you recognize a man who's sick in love with you when you see one? God, you two truly deserve each other."

My mouth drops open, and Devon pales next to me.

"Now that we've gotten that settled, let's go. We only have forty-five minutes to prepare Jenny before the car arrives." Lettie turns on her stilettos and strides back down the hall. "Forget stopping at Devon's room, your bags are already downstairs."

Without a word Devon offers me his elbow, staring after Lettie with murder in his eyes. I hook an arm through his and we follow in silence.

My anger at Devon runs out of me like water down an unclogged drain.

Could it be true? Could Devon really be in love with me? If that's true, why hasn't he called off our deal? Then again, even though he didn't deny it . . . he didn't confirm it, either.

Chapter 30

Devon

BY THE TIME we've made it to the library, I've thought of fifteen ways to kill Lettie. I almost convince myself it would be worth the jail time. I couldn't have been more mortified if a picture of Mr. Happy and his lopsided friend showed up on Instagram tattooed with my name.

Damn her! My hands itch to wring her neck.

The words I've been careful to avoid saying have been spoken . . . by my meddling sister.

I note Jenny's stunned silence all the way downstairs, and I'm not sure what to make of it.

She's not the only one who's speechless. I'm hoping my ability to speak returns without the urge to lunge at Lettie's throat and throttle her. Tomorrow I'm going to have a serious "come to Jesus" discussion with my sister and remind her of the boundaries that I need her to respect. She, of all people, knows how difficult this whole situation is for me. She's intimately aware of my secrets and the reasons for the decisions I make. Wasn't it her encouragement to secure a convincing date that led me here? Or so I'd like to think.

Lettie dims the lights on the way in and parks herself at the desk. She turns on her laptop and the wireless projector. "I'll introduce you to the board members and then the most important guests in the room," Lettie says, her tone all business.

Good. I don't have to speak. This was Lettie's idea; she can run the show.

"But before that, Jenny, you should put this on," Lettie says and picks up a small box off the desk. My eyes pop wide when I see it. Lettie gives me a wicked smile and opens it. "Actually, why don't you let Dev put it on you?"

Jenny gives me a quizzical stare.

My molars grind together as I glare at Lettie. "What are you doing?"

She glares back. "You've come this far. Be convincing, damn it."

I jack up out of the chair and move toward her. "This is getting out of hand, Lettie. The least you can do is ask Jenny if she's willing to take this charade any further. Don't assume just because you want it that it's all right."

"What are you talking about?" Jenny cuts in.

I shake my head with my eyes glued on Lettie. "Lettie wants you to wear my mother's engagement ring and pretend we're engaged," I grit out.

"I—"

I cut Jenny off. "The answer is no, Lettie. Lucas knows Jenny's family. I won't have her lie and risk this filtering back to them. No. I'll tell people she's my girlfriend, and if asked, I'll hint that it's serious. But I won't lie," I say, realizing too late that I've given something away.

Even if I never I see her again after tomorrow, I'll always consider this relationship serious. In my wishing world, if I were ever to put my mother's ring on Jenny's finger, it would be because I meant to marry her.

Lettie's eyebrows flash up, and a smile touches her lips. "Have it your way, Brother dear. That'll do." She snaps the ring box shut.

Jenny sits silent, shifting her gaze between Lettie and me.

I stalk across the carpet, run my fingers through my hair, and blurt out, "Tell Jenny why we're doing this."

"Huh?"

"I trust her, Lettie. Tell her why this is so important."

Lettie crosses her arms over her cleavage, wearing a self-satisfied grin. "Isn't this where I walked in upstairs? You should be the one to tell her."

Then it dawns on me. Lettie's been playing me since she barged into my bedroom, manipulating me into exposing things — mostly my feelings — to Jenny.

The urge to throttle her resurges with a vengeance.

I come to a stop in front of Jenny and let out a defeated exhalation. Fine. I lower myself down next to her and gaze into her wide blue eyes. "Where do I begin?" I mumble and shift my concentration to my tented hands. "Here goes ... Three and a half years ago, our father died of a heart attack right after he changed the company bylaws. Kingsbridge Industries has been a privately held company for one hundred and fifty years, with the majority stake passing down to the oldest son on his twenty-fifth birthday in the event the father is deceased. As I mentioned to your parents at dinner the other night, I'm due to inherit the company this October ... with a few caveats. Originally our father's will and the bylaws of the company were clear. There was no question that I would be heir. But as I was undergoing cancer treatment, he modified them in case I died ... or ended up sterile and unable to produce the next heir. In the event that I couldn't fulfill the requirements, our younger half brother, Phillip, would take over when he comes of age a year from now."

Jenny's eyebrows draw together. "What about Lettie?"

"Thank you for noticing," she says sweetly.

I give Lettie a sour look and continue. "Our father was raised in an old parochial British family. He provided a small annual stipend for Lettie, but he didn't believe a woman could fill his shoes."

Jenny's head snaps back. "That's a little sexist, don't you think?"

"Amen, sister!" Lettie says.

I glare at Lettie. "Would you rather tell her?"

"No." She pouts.

"Then be quiet," I grit.

Jenny stares at me, a perplexed look etched across her brows. "But you're healthy now, right? So what's the problem?"

I rub my eyes and get up to pace in order to buy some time. What can I tell her without spilling my entire damn secret? There's no good place to take a conversation that starts with, "Well, I might die . . ." Taking a breath, I dance on the knife edge of truth.

"The chemo had some irreversible side effects," I say, weaving my tale as I tell it. So far, it's true.

A look of panic passes over Jenny's face, which was exactly what I was afraid of. "What kind of effects?"

"My kidneys, Jen. They damaged my kidneys. I've been on meds ever since," I say quietly. "That's why I don't drink and why I'm on a low-sodium diet."

Anguish fills her eyes. "But you're not going to die from it, right?"

How the hell do I answer that? The truth is that if they weren't degenerating, I wouldn't. But I'll need a new kidney to live or at least live longer. If I were willing—which I'm not—I could go on dialysis when the time comes. But I refuse to live my life that way. So I choose my answer carefully as Lettie's eyes bore into me.

"Not if I can help it," I say and take Jenny's quivering hand in mine. "But that's not the problem. It's our father's bitch of a mistress who's the problem. She wants her son Phillip to inherit, so she's been lobbying the board to look into my health. She's raised the question as to whether I'm fit to run the company. If she can prove that my longevity or my fertility is in jeopardy, she might be able to unseat me."

"But . . . what if that happens?" she asks.

"Everything Lettie, my mom, and I have will fall under the heir's control, including the house, leaving us with only a moderate annual stipend. But nothing's in jeopardy if I'm heir—it all works."

"Would Phillip really take your home?" Jenny asks, incredulous.

Lettie snorts.

"Without hesitation," I say. "He's a prick. He takes after our father." I brush a hand over my face. "We could live without the house, and mostly everything else, but what we can't do without is money to pay for my mother's care. Even if Lettie and I pooled our stipends and got jobs, it would be beyond tight, and I refuse to leave my mom in a Medicaid-paid facility." The thought creeps me out. I don't mention that my own medical condition will require some hefty expenses at some point.

"Your father didn't provide for your mother. What kind of husband was he anyway?" Jenny asks, indignant.

"Not a good one," I retort. "But up until a little over two years ago, it wasn't an issue. All her expenses were taken care of. She was in a Kingsbridge-owned luxury assisted living facility. But someone embezzled millions of dollars and it went under. She's been living here ever since."

Lettie cuts in, planting her hands on her small, shimmery hips. "Listen, our father was a paranoid jackass when it came to money. You've seen my mother. He was always afraid she would divorce him and clean him out. Then we found out why: he'd been cheating on her since she got pregnant with us. So he protected his assets inside his company to prevent us from getting a flipping dime. If he hadn't been such an asswipe, I'd be the one the board was scrutinizing, not Devon.

And that prick of a half brother wouldn't even be a consideration." Lettie throws her hands up. "At least dear old Dad was shrewd enough to stay married. That way, he protected himself from both our mother and his money-grubbing whore of a mistress. Hence our truly twisted situation. Any questions?"

Jenny sits with her mouth open, dumbstruck.

"So it's all on me, Jenny. I have to do this for my family," I say. "Does everything make more sense now?"

She tilts her head and narrows her eyes. "So that's what you didn't want me to know, isn't it? Your mother was asking about your condition ..." She covers her mouth and looks away, thinking about something. When the thought comes to her, her gaze swings back to me. "That's why your ankles were swollen earlier."

I nod. "That's right."

Well, half right. The other thing I didn't want Jenny to know? My mom congratulated us on being in love. She said that she could see it in our eyes. Although she had me pegged, I can't be sure about Jenny.

Part of me wishes she were wrong about both of us.

Chapter 31

Jenny

MY STOMACH KNOTS as the limo pulls up to the Grand Highland Regency, a private, members-only five-star resort and catering facility hidden in Morris Township, twenty minutes northwest of Summit. I used to read about this place in the society column of the weekend paper during high school, dreaming that Russ and I would get married here someday. Not that my parents could afford it, but his could.

Russ. It feels like a million years since we broke up.

Devon squeezes my hand. "You all right?"

I stare at the gold and brown flecks in his eyes and nod. "I'm fine." I really am. Whatever he needs me to do tonight, I'm here for him. I'm still processing everything that he and Lettie told me in the library back at their house. Wow. Makes me appreciate my straight-laced middle class upbringing even more; *twisted* doesn't seem to quite cover his. Now I understand those lines around his eyes a little better, and it renews my desire to pull Devon closer to the things that make him happy. I want to erase those lines forever, knowing full well I might not get that chance.

"Lettie, can I have my speech, please?" Devon asks, holding out his free hand.

She opens her bag and takes it out.

"Will you keep this in your purse?" Devon asks, handing me the pages.

I smile and tuck them away.

Lettie reviewed the night's schedule with us earlier. A posh—as well as long—evening lies ahead, starting with a cocktail reception. Afterward the attendees will gather in the main dining room, where Devon is scheduled to deliver a speech on behalf of the Soames Foundation, including recognition of the prior year's top financial contributors. After Devon's speech, the chairman will give a short presentation on the foundation's accomplishments over the past year, to segue into a discussion on upcoming projects.

All that should end by eight forty-five, with dinner and dancing to follow. The evening will wrap up with a closing ceremony in which they'll announce the night's top donors and the winner of the Mercedes-Benz sedan parked out front.

My feet ache just thinking about it.

The car door opens, and I give Devon one last look. A pang of loneliness hits my chest, marring the intimacy of the last two weeks, as I suddenly feel the widening divide between us. He'll soon be a powerful CEO in a world where I don't quite belong.

He squeezes my hand and brushes his lips over mine before ushering me out of the limo.

When Lettie emerges, Devon offers me his elbow, and I tuck my arm through his. We walk three abreast toward the entrance. The head valet bows and greets Lettie and Devon. "Ms. Soames, Mr. Soames."

Devon nods, Lettie smiles, and I try not to feel invisible.

The air-conditioning raises the hairs on my bare arms as we walk into the lobby. Too late I realize that my pashmina shawl is on its way to our hotel room with the bellman. Silently cursing my forgetfulness, I snuggle closer to Devon's side.

A large bear of a guy intercepts us as soon as we walk inside. People dressed in black-tie attire mingle around us, getting drawn into conversations on their way to the ballroom.

"Howie," Lettie says, giving him a chaste kiss on the lips followed by a look of hot promise.

His lips turn up in a roguish smile as he runs an appreciative and smoldering gaze over her before greeting us.

Somewhere in his early thirties, Howard's built like a linebacker, with intense blue eyes and a shock of dark hair that's a little shaggy around the edges. *So this is Howard.* For some reason, I had expected someone more corporate . . . with a neck. Hand him a football, and he looks like someone stole him from the lineup for the New York Jets and crammed him into a tux.

Howie tucks Lettie into his side. She looks positively petite hanging off his arm, like a blonde China doll.

"Hey, Devon." He shakes Devon's hand with his oversize mitt. His voice is deep, with a dash of sexy gravel. "I hear your sister's been giving you a hard time again." Howard smiles and eyes Lettie.

Devon chuckles. "What else is new?" Then he turns to me and meets my eyes. "I'd like to introduce you to my girlfriend, Jenny Lynch. Jenny, this is Howard Cato III, chief of operations, Cato Worldwide Shipping."

I'm taken off guard by Devon's introduction. I thought he'd be saving the "girlfriend" story for the board members.

Howard reaches his big paw out to take my hand.

"Lovely to meet you," I say as my fingers disappear inside his warm grasp. Even though he's not my type, I understand Lettie's attraction. In addition to his raw animal magnetism, there's a keen intelligence dancing behind his eyes. Hot and smart. *Go, Lettie.*

"The pleasure's all mine." Howard gives me a charming smile and kisses the back of my hand. "It's good to see that

Devon's taste in women has vastly improved."

"You've never seen my taste in women," Devon snorts. "All you've seen are Lettie's failed fix-ups with her gold-digging friends."

Lettie glares at Devon. "Hey! There's nothing wrong with the women I've fixed you up with. You're just picky."

Devon laughs. "Only if *picky* means that I expect them to have interests outside of shopping."

A deep chortle comes from Howard, and amusement fills his eyes. "I feel your pain. It wasn't until I met my sweet Lettie here that I found a good woman."

I'm tempted to smirk. *Sweet?* Not the first word that springs to mind when I think of Lettie.

Lettie flushes and squeezes closer to him. "Thanks, baby."

"Why don't we head in?" Howard says, extending his arm in the direction of the cocktail reception.

We don't get any more than a few steps into the room before Devon is bombarded by people who apparently know him. Lettie and Howard continue until her sparkly dress and his broad back disappear into the thick crowd. I paste on a friendly smile and nod my acknowledgment as people greet us.

My smile turns real when I spot a friendly face in the crowd. Lucas and his wife are several yards away, chatting with two other couples. "Lucas at ten o'clock. Do you want to stop?" I whisper to Devon.

"I'll talk to him later," Devon says, scanning the crowd. He pulls me tighter to his side as we walk deeper into the room. Lucas tips his chin at us as we walk past. Devon and I return the nod.

We don't make it much farther.

"Devon, my dear boy," says an older man with a British accent from behind us.

Devon stops, and his arm tenses next to mine. His face transforms into a polite mask as we turn. A tall man with shrewd eyes and Devon's nose stands beside a plump, rosy-cheeked woman encased in floor-length taffeta. They look exactly like the images on Lettie's slides.

I smile prettily and review their profiles briefly in my head: Gerald Soames, one of Devon's two uncles who sit on the board, and Gertrude, his wife; married twenty-two years; Gerald had a falling-out with Devon's father right before he died; dual residences in New York and London; no children but raise prize King Charles spaniels; family in name only.

"Uncle Gerald." Devon shakes his hand and then kisses the woman's proffered cheek. "You're looking lovely, Aunt Gert."

"Charmer. Just like your father," his aunt says, coupling the words with a hearty chuckle. "And who are you, my dear?"

"My girlfriend, Jennifer Lynch." Devon beams at me as the words roll naturally off his tongue.

"Pleased to meet you both," I say.

His uncle gives me a dismissive smile and turns his attention back to Devon. "Your Kingsbridge tour has been productive, I presume?" His snub strengthens my resolve to do whatever it takes to help Devon succeed tonight.

"Very."

He claps Devon on the shoulder. "Your father would've been proud of how far you've come, especially since your situation was quite bleak when he was alive. You're still doing well, I take it?"

Devon pulls me close. I feel the tension in his fingers. "Very well . . ." He glances at me and smiles. "On all fronts."

"Don't badger the young man, Gerald," his aunt says, squeezing her husband's arm. "Anyone with eyes can see they're in good form. You're looking quite dapper, Devon. And you, my dear, look radiant."

I tip my head and smile.

His uncle's lips press together, and he gives his wife a sour look that she ignores. "I look forward to your board presentation in September. Do let me know if I can be of assistance before your appointment in October."

"Thank you. I'll do that," Devon says. From the briefing, I know the chances of that happening are slim to none.

"Perhaps we'll see you later," his uncle says, taking his wife's arm and readying them for departure.

"Please join us one evening for dinner in Manhattan," his aunt chimes in. Despite her cheery voice, the offer doesn't seem to reach her eyes.

"That's most kind of you, Aunt Gert," Devon says as they walk past us and into the crowd. Now I realize why he and Lettie are so skilled at noncommittal answers. A hollow feeling hits my stomach as I watch his aunt and uncle leave. For the first time, I understand that the sadness Lettie and Devon carry contains a major dose of isolation.

The smile melts off Devon's face the moment they're gone. "And so it begins," he murmurs, and then he sighs. The cocktail party suddenly feels like a social minefield.

Two steps later, a man with white hair and a pinched look on his face walks up to take their place. I recognize him from Lettie's slide show: Jasper Parks, chief financial officer for Kingsbridge.

"Well, well, well," he says in an affected nasal tone as he grips Devon's hand in a firm handshake. "Not long now, is it, Devon?"

Devon stiffens next to me. "Sir?"

"Until you take your rightful place on the executive committee." He tilts his chin in my direction. "And who's the lovely young lady on your arm?" Despite the warmth in his words, there's something predatory in the way he looks at me that makes my palm itch to slap his face. Lecherous creep.

Devon either doesn't notice or chooses to ignore it. I vote for number two. Instead he introduces me as his girlfriend again. It sounds strange to my ears. A lie that I want to be true.

Jasper turns his slimy gaze back to Devon. "I hear you've impressed the Kingsbridge executives. Your knowledge of the businesses has been flawless, according to them. I understand your next stop is Nanotekx on Monday."

My heart lurches. Kingsbridge owns Nanotekx? Is that how Lettie found out about Russ? Did Devon know, too?

"Thank you. My father's legacy is important to me. And yes, I plan to fly out tomorrow."

Jasper's beady eyes take on a cunning shine. "I should give you fair warning that Ms. Cartwright's solicitor presented us with a petition this week to actively investigate claims regarding the viability of your health. I gather that she would like to see your brother Phillip replace you."

Devon stands rigidly next to me. "Thank you for the warning, but Ms. Cartwright is a desperate woman. She's grasping at straws," he says, wearing a pleasant smile and the appearance of nonchalance.

"Maybe. But certain people are listening," he says and gives Devon's arm a light squeeze. "I'm not one of them. But out of respect for your departed father, I felt obligated to tell you."

"I appreciate that," Devon says.

Jasper's gaze glides over me with appreciation one last time before shifting to Devon. "See you at dinner, Soames."

I mentally breathe a sigh of relief behind my pasted-on smile as the dreadful man departs.

Devon's brow furrows as he stares at Jasper's retreating back, and I catch the curious stares around us.

I clutch Devon's arm and draw his ear to my lips. "Smile and pretend I just said something provocative and sexy. People are staring," I whisper.

His eyes connect with mine. The furrow is still there, but his lips curl up into a smile and he dips in for kiss. He puts enough ardor into it to send a hot flash straight to my core.

That should give the crowd something to chew on.

"Bravo. Now back to business. I need to ask you something," I whisper. Before anyone else can approach, I lead Devon toward an alcove for a private chat. I glance over my shoulder to make sure no one is following. "Nanotekx? Russ works for Nanotekx." I drop his arm and filter my ire into a hushed tone. "Did you know Russ was cheating on me the night we kissed at the gallery opening?"

Devon clenches his hands and looks away. "Can we talk about this another time? I've got more important things going on tonight, Jen."

He hits my Irish square in the jaw. "Another time? This all ends tomorrow, remember? There *is* no other time," I hiss, knowing I'm not playing fair but unable to stop myself.

His head jerks around, hurt shining in his eyes. "Then I guess it doesn't matter." He stalks away. My heart free-falls and I berate myself for being selfish. If he knew . . . He's right, it probably doesn't matter. Then again, if he did know, he knew I was fair game even before I did. Russ had already dishonored our relationship by then.

"Dev, wait—"

Devon comes to a dead stop, but not because of me.

An average-looking guy with a narrow, aquiline nose and a beautiful dark-haired woman hanging from his arm stands in Devon's path. They're both wearing smug smiles with a tinge of evil glee.

My internal alarms sound when Devon's spine stiffens. Without thinking, I take my place next to him, thread my arm through his, and raise my chin higher. Whoever these people are, he won't face them alone. He doesn't fight me as I expect. Instead he pulls me closer.

"Phillip . . . ," he grits out, and then he glances at the woman. "Tessa."

A shiver slips over my skin as he says her name. I'm back in Devon's art studio. *"You're only my second . . . lover," I say.*

He squeezes me tight to his side. *"And you're mine."*
And then I know . . . she was Devon's first.

Chapter 32

Devon

WHAT THE HELL are they doing here? Subconsciously I pull Jenny closer and draw on her strength as I stare down my bastard half brother and the only other woman I ever fell in love with. The woman who abandoned me the moment I was diagnosed with cancer. The woman who broke my heart and shit on the pieces.

I kick myself for the wave of hurt and loss that courses through me, and replace it with anger over her betrayal and abandonment.

Of course, Phillip was there to ease Tessa's pain at Oxford when I returned home to the States for treatment.

He's dogged my every step since we met at the English boarding school my father sent us to, always ready to unseat me—in my father's heart and in all I've ever possessed. As much as he tried to bully me as the only "Yank" among "Brits" when we were kids, and then as a "eunuch in the making" to the girl I loved, he'll never keep me down or have my father's name.

Even so, my fists ache to connect with his jaw. It wouldn't be the first time we've drawn blood.

"Hullo, Devon," Tessa says, using the same silky tone that

used to melt my resistance. But absent is the warmth. In its place is a cool reserve. It's hard to believe almost four years have passed since I've seen her. I wish it had been as long for Phillip.

"Surprise, surprise," Phillip says in a cultured, Oxford-educated accent. "You look well, big brother."

I resist the urge to grind my teeth. "What are you doing here?"

Phillip tsks. "Seems Uncle Byron came down with a case of the stomach flu. As luck would have it, we were able to procure a pair of tickets . . . and his place at the table."

My gut tightens. Phillip and Tessa will be hosting a board table for dinner, along with me and Lettie. How in God's name did that happen? Last I heard, Uncle Byron wasn't a fan of Phillip's.

Phillip tucks Tessa into his side. "Timing couldn't be better, actually. Tessa and I are newly engaged," he says. An unmistakable gleam of satisfaction dances in his eyes. "I'm sure Father would've been pleased."

Pleased? Probably. My father had a penchant for conflict and bloodshed.

Glimpsing the dazzling diamond on her finger, I fight to control my expression and wonder where he got the money to afford something so grand. Last I heard, he didn't have any gainful employment beyond his stipend. He wouldn't have had time for it anyway, given that he's been doing his own visits to Kingsbridge holdings as my potential backup. "Congratulations," I say, keeping my face devoid of expression.

"I'm looking forward to introducing Tessa to the board," he says, drawing her closer. "Since I seem to be in serious consideration for the CEO chair."

Instead of lunging at his throat, I choose a pitying smile. "I can't imagine how you'd think that." My gaze turns to Jenny. "As a matter of fact, Phillip, Tessa, this is my girlfriend,

Jennifer Lynch."

"Lovely to meet you both," Jenny says. Without missing a beat, she bats her eyelashes and adds, "Dev, I think we should share our news."

I look into her eyes, open my mouth, and then close it, totally at a loss.

She chuckles, fingering the diamond at her neck that I gave her. "We're engaged, too." Then she pouts and leaves a chaste kiss on my stunned lips. "The jeweler's still sizing his mom's engagement ring to fit me."

I flush with pride and gratitude at her lie while Tessa blanches and Phillip's mouth tightens into a thin line. For that alone, it's worth it.

"Oh, really," Phillip says drily.

I play along. "Sweetheart, I thought we weren't going to say anything."

Jenny beams at them. "I'm just so thrilled, I couldn't contain myself. Isn't this so exciting? We're both getting married. When's your wedding? We're thinking about Christmas." She glances around. "I think my parents can pull some strings and get us in here, babe."

I blush for a moment and smile, wishing it were for real. "Whatever you want, *my love.*"

Vindication fills me as Tessa stiffens when I use the endearment I always reserved for her. Phillip stands dumbfounded for a moment and then rakes Jenny with a glare. "Slumming it with a Yank, I see. I guess she doesn't mind half a man. Does she know you can't father children?"

That lying son of a bitch! My blood pressure shoots through the top of my skull. Reflexively I draw back my fist, ready to strike. Before I can deliver a blow, Howard appears, and his meaty fist connects with Phillip's face. A loud crunch followed by a shooting stream of blood draws a scream from Tessa while Jenny and I jump backward to avoid the red spray.

Lettie stands glittering on the sidelines among the gawking, well-coiffed crowd, wearing a satisfied grin. "Wanker," she mutters.

"Mind your fucking manners, dickhead," Howard grinds out, as Phillip spins and groans, holding his broken beak. "Apologize to Devon and the lady."

"Get the police! Someone arrest this hoodlum!" Drusilla Cartwright screams as she pushes her way through the crowd to get to her bleeding son.

Great. That makes three tickets that have gone astray. I need to speak with Lettie when this is over about clamping down on the guest list and improving security for next year.

Tessa glowers at me with narrowed eyes. "You'll pay for this, Devon."

I snort and shake my head. "I already have." Twining my fingers through Jenny's, I turn on my heel and pull her through the maze of people until we're outside in the near-empty hallway.

A tremor passes through me as the last of the adrenaline drains out of my system. Before I realize it, I'm shaking and can't stop.

Panic rises in Jenny's eyes. "Dev, are you all right?"

My mouth is so dry I can't speak as my stomach and the rest of my limbs stage a revolt. Between the acute stress and the fact that I feel like shit, I'm one step away from melting down.

Jenny grabs my arm and scans the hall, then hauls me down to the check-in counter. She leaves me propped up against a wall and gets the room keys.

"Come on," she says, and I dissolve against her as she leads me to the elevator under the guise of a romantic walk.

I collapse on the bed the moment we get inside the room. "Water," I croak. She runs into the bathroom and returns with a cool, wet compress and a filled glass.

"Here. Drink this." She steadies my hand and helps me

empty the contents. Jenny's brow furrows as she lays me back on the pillow and applies the cold compress to my forehead. "Do you want me to get Lucas?"

"No," I say softly. "I'm just dehydrated. I've been careless with the diuretics. Get me another glass?"

Jenny refills the glass. I gulp it down. She glances at the clock beside the bed. "You're due on stage in less than twenty minutes. Are you going to make it?"

"I need a minute. I'll be fine," I say, not knowing whether that's true or not. I take her hand. "Thanks . . . for what you did down there. I appreciate it. I'm sorry you had to lie."

Her eyes soften, and she runs her fingers through my hair. "What did she do to you, Devon?"

Jenny's uncanny perception touches my exposed heart. I hate that Tessa damaged me. But it's Jenny who's been soothing my old wounds from devastating loss and insecurity. It's why her comment about Russ earlier hit a raw nerve, minimizing what we have back to a two-week arrangement.

I swallow. "She left. When she found out I had cancer, she left me," I say quietly. "I guess she figured I'd be left impotent or die before I was old enough to inherit. That's when I realized she didn't really love me. That there was no such thing as a happy ending . . ."

"I'm sorry, you deserve better that that," she whispers, taking my face in her hands and pressing her lips to mine. They linger there, flooding me with warmth, before she pulls away.

"I know that now," I say and shift up into a sitting position against the headboard and remove the compress. "Phillip's wrong, you know. I'm more than capable of fathering a child. My counts were almost nonexistent after treatment, but they've rebounded. What worries me is that someone may have hacked into my old medical records."

Jenny sits back and her eyes widen. "Do you think that's

possible?"

"Don't know, but what he said, plus Drusilla petitioning the board, makes me wonder." I swing my legs over the edge of the bed and fight back a wave of dizziness. "By the way, you're doing a great job so far. Given what's already happened, I really need you."

She pulls me onto unsteady feet. "You've got me, Dev. Whatever . . . Just ask."

I sniff and shake my head. "Just make sure I don't fall on my face anytime tonight. Deal?"

"Deal." She chews the inside of her cheek. "Dev?"

"Yeah?"

"Promise me that you'll let Lucas check you out tonight?" The worry in her eyes is back.

I'm relieved when I feel the pressure in my bladder. At least my kidneys are still working.

I nod. "We already planned on that."

Her shoulders relax. "Good."

After I take a quick trip to the bathroom and down a third glass of water, we head for the door.

"Dev?" Jenny says as we reach it.

"Yeah?"

She catches her lip between her teeth and shakes her head. "Nothing . . . It's nothing." I don't press her, even though I want to. It's not nothing. I'm dead certain of it, but I'm due on stage in ten minutes and there's still a long night ahead of us.

As I close the door, Lettie comes running down the hallway at full tilt. "That bitch had Howie arrested!"

Chapter 33

Jenny

"JUST TELL ME what happened," Devon says, clutching Lettie's shoulders and staring into her wild eyes.

"Security has him downstairs. The police are on their way," Lettie says, trying to catch her breath. "Phillip wants to press charges. It's all your fault." She shrugs out of his grasp.

"*My* fault? How is it my fault?" Devon snaps. The color is finally returning to his face although it's a shade redder than it should be. "And what the hell is he doing here anyway? The board was invited as a courtesy, but this is a family-sponsored event … by *legitimate* family. Who got them in here?"

"I don't know! I'm as surprised as you. Whatever. I couldn't let you hit that pompous ass in front of the entire board." Lettie glares at him. "What were you thinking?"

Devon sputters. "Me? What?" His brows furrow into an angry line. "Are you kidding? Did you hear what he said to us?"

"He was baiting you, and you fell for it hook, line, and sinker," Lettie says, throwing her hands up. "That's exactly what he wanted. Now I have to spend the night bailing Howie out of jail!"

"You should've let me punch him, then," Devon says in a low growl.

Lettie glares at him with her fists balled at her sides. "That's not what I meant. You should've walked away."

His lip twitches, and he glances at his watch. "I've gotta go. I'll deal with this after I give my speech."

"Lettie, I think I can help." I dig into my evening bag for my phone and pull out Devon's speech while I'm in there. "Here." I hand it to him. "Go. We'll meet you downstairs."

He frowns. "You sure?"

I nod. The thought of him collapsing again pulls at me, but in the scheme of things I think I can be of more use helping Lettie on his behalf.

"She's right." Lettie rolls her eyes and prods him. "Go. I'll finish yelling at you later." He reluctantly heads toward the elevator and gives us a last glance before he steps inside and disappears behind the closing doors.

"So? How can you help?" Lettie asks, a dubious look in her eye.

I ignore her and hit speed dial. John picks up on the second ring.

"Henshaw."

"Hi, Detective Henshaw. It's Jenny Lynch," I say, glancing at Lettie. Her eyes fill with interest.

"Hey, Jenny-girl, is everything all right?" John asks tentatively, his voice warm.

"I need your help . . ." It's been a long time since I've had to take advantage of our family's friendship to ask John for a favor. The last incident was my senior year in high school. A bunch of us had gotten caught on Mischief Night placing the realistic-looking sculptures of people sprinkled around town in provocative sexual positions.

"Anything for you, sweetheart. Tell me what you need." His manner shifts from relaxed to alert and coaxing. I recount the sequence of events.

"Let me make a few phone calls and see what I can do," John says.

"Thanks," I say.

"I'll be in touch." He hangs up.

"What did he say?" Lettie asks anxiously.

Before I can answer, her small purse *plings* with a text. She digs it out and glances at the tiny screen.

"Let's go." She grabs my hand, and we break into a high-heeled run toward the elevator.

The lobby is filled with red and blue spinning lights from the police car parked outside when we get there. We don't stop until we reach the security office. An officer in a wide-legged stance blocks the door.

"Sorry, ma'am. You'll have to wait out here."

Lettie throws her shoulders back. "The hell I will. This is my gala," she says with cool authority and pushes past him. The door shuts with a thunk behind her.

I'm torn between peeking in on Devon's speech and waiting for Lettie to come out. I move a little farther away to pace and clutch my phone in my palm, waiting for John to call back.

"So, Jennifer, is it?" Startled, I whip around at the sound of her voice.

My hackles instinctively rise as I face Devon's former girlfriend. I'm hit with a mixture of jealousy and fierce protectiveness. Looking at her, I can't deny that I feel out of my league despite the blue Armani dress I'm wearing. Another reminder that Devon's world and mine don't quite mesh. Dark, lush hair falls around her shoulders as she stares intently at me with long-lashed, slanted green eyes. Her creamy complexion and angular beauty could easily land her on the cover of some British fashion mag. Not to mention that she looks at home in her couture while I feel as if I'm playing dress-up.

I paste on a tight smile and raise a brow. "Tessa, is it?"

"Tell me, are you really marrying Devon, or was that just a ploy to anger Phillip?" she asks, her tone revealing a hint of jealousy.

My inner bitch awakens. "What's the matter? Regret your choice in brothers?" I snipe.

She looks away for a moment, and a blush travels up the side of her neck. Suppressed rage fills her features, flattening her lips into a thin line when she looks back. "Never."

"Oh, really? Then why are you asking me such a ridiculous question?"

She narrows her eyes and leans in. "I'm wondering why someone of Devon's stature would settle for a girl without a pedigree. Devon's father may have been CEO, but his two brothers are still board members. I know for a fact they'd prefer a more suitable match. They have the next heir to consider after Devon . . . or Phillip. If, of course, Devon can have children."

Heat burns a trail up to my cheeks, but unlike Devon, I refuse to take the bait. Instead I reach for my own ammunition. "Lucky for Devon there are twelve board members. I don't think two votes will do much to sway anything," I say coolly, seething inside. Then I lean closer and pour honey into my voice. "And do tell Phillip that he's heard wrong. Devon is fully capable of having children. He especially loves to . . . *practice.*"

A vein jumps in Tessa's neck, but she stays silent.

I glance at my watch. "Now, if you'll excuse me, I'd like to catch the end of my *fiancé's* speech."

So much for waiting on Lettie. I turn on my heel to leave as the door bursts open behind me. I step aside to make way for the oncoming crowd.

An officer marches Howard past me in handcuffs as a grim-faced Lettie follows behind him. Phillip steps out with another policeman. Thick white tape covers the bridge of his nose, and mottled red skin fans out under his eyes.

I can't resist. Casting a glance at Tessa, I smile wickedly and wink. "At least I picked the better man," I say low enough that only she can hear me, "and the better-looking brother."

As I leave, I wonder again why Devon can't commit beyond our two-week arrangement. My heart sinks. Could what Tessa said be true? Could Devon want to find a more suitable match? Someone English like Tessa?

Chapter 34

Devon

"ON BEHALF OF the Soames Family, thank you. Enjoy your evening," I say, closing the speech. I stare out into the audience, but the glare of the stage lights blinds me and obscures the faces in the darkened ballroom. I have no idea if Jenny or Lettie ever made it. I pass the microphone over to the foundation chairman as the audience applauds, and then I descend the stage stairs and head for the exit.

My limbs feel heavy, as if I'm trudging through mud. I spot Lucas across the room and make a mental note to see him as soon as dinner is over. I'm hoping it's just the stress of the evening. But honestly, I haven't felt right since my run-in with Phillip.

Jenny grasps my arm as I walk by.

I sigh with relief. "Follow me," I say and lead her to the board's private lounge off the dining room. It's empty. I lock the door behind us. "What happened with Howard?"

Jenny rubs her arms, looking uncomfortable. "The police took him downtown. Lettie texted me on the way out. She's taking his car and she's going to meet him and his lawyer at the station. She said to stay here and she'll be in touch."

Great. Just great, I think, feeling helpless.

"Lettie was right, you know. I should've never let Phillip get to me like that," I say, combing agitated fingers through my hair. "I'm convinced he wanted me to hit him just to gain points with the board. A desperate act to help his case."

Jenny's phone rings, and she fishes it out of the purse hanging on a thin strap over her shoulder. "Hi, Detective Henshaw," she answers.

I give her a curious stare. "Who—"

She holds up a finger to silence me, and her brow pinches in concentration as she listens. A gruff voice murmurs softly out of her phone, but I can't make out the conversation.

Her eyes close and her shoulders relax. "Thank you." She smiles. "Yes, I'll tell Mom you said hi."

I'm strung tight as piano wire by the time she hangs up. "Who was that? Was it about Howard?"

"John's a detective for Morris County and a friend of my family," she says, tucking the phone back inside her bag. "He pulled some strings to get Howard in front of a judge quickly. His bail has been set and they're processing the bond now. He and Lettie should be back here in less than an hour. Meanwhile Howard's lawyer is trying to get Phillip to drop the charges."

I reach for her hand to pull her closer. "Thanks for doing that."

"You're welcome." She twists out of my grasp and steps back, avoiding my gaze. "How are you feeling?"

Warning signals shoot through me like flares, stiffening my spine. "What's the matter?"

She raises her brow. "You didn't answer my question." There's a cool tone to her voice that suddenly makes me feel as if we're standing on opposite sides of a wide chasm.

"Better. Now tell me what's wrong." I frown, planting my hands on my hips. I feel like shit and I'm in no mood for games.

She chews the inside of her mouth.

"I ran into your ex-girlfriend, Tessa, outside the security office," she says.

"And?" I ask, not particularly alarmed, even though seeing Tessa earlier was a bit jarring. There's nothing recent between me and Tessa, so there's not much she can say that I'd keep from Jenny.

Jenny shifts her weight and rolls the thin strap of her purse between her fingers. "She suggested . . . that maybe . . ."

"What?" I say, growing impatient. "Just tell me. Whatever it is, it's probably complete bollocks anyway."

She stops fidgeting and gives me a hard stare. "She thought I was lying about the engagement because my social standing wasn't good enough for marriage or giving you heirs."

It takes me a moment of stunned silence to process what she's said. *"What?"* I stare, incredulous. "Don't tell me you believed her."

It's not until I see unshed tears glisten in her eyes that I know she did.

"Is that why you can't commit past our two-week arrangement? Because you need to start the hunt for someone more . . . *suitable?*" she asks.

Heat travels up my neck. "Do you really think so little of me? That I would give a shit about anything so ridiculous or even think it in the first place?" I grit out in a hushed whisper. Anger at Tessa for telling Jenny something so ludicrous, and at Jenny for believing her, elevates my blood pressure enough to create a dull ache behind my right eye.

A crystal tear cuts a path down Jenny's cheek. "Then why? Why can't you just tell me?"

I grab her shoulders and resist shaking some sense into her. "Jen. Stop. Just stop. Tessa is full of crap. What she said? It's not true. We'll get it sorted tomorrow. I promise. But tonight, I need you to stay focused." I point to the door. "I'm surrounded out there. Can I depend on you?"

I need her on more levels than I can count. But right now it's the one that's closest to the way a blind person needs a guide dog.

As if to prove my point, a wave of dizziness passes over me and my knees weaken for a second before I can lock them in place. Jenny seems too distracted to notice.

"Yes," she says and pulls away to wipe her eyes with her fingertips. "I'm sorry. I don't know what's wrong with me."

A knock sounds at the door. "One minute," I shout and look back at Jenny. "Just follow my lead tonight. That's all I ask. And whatever you do, steer clear of Tessa, Phillip, and Drusilla."

Weariness overtakes me, and this time when I pull Jenny into me, she doesn't resist. "Please." I kiss her forehead. "Trust me. I don't want tomorrow to be the end, either."

Another knock. This time louder. "Coming," I say and open the door.

Lucas is standing with his arms crossed, wearing a scowl. "Jenny, would you mind if I borrow Devon?"

"Sure," Jenny says, not giving any indication of her distress of a few moments before. She passes her fingers along my arm. "I'll meet you at the table?"

I nod, relieved at the unexpected sight of Lucas standing there like an irascible guardian angel.

Jenny heads to the ballroom while I give Lucas my room number and some time to get there before I head in the same direction.

On the way to the elevator, I'm hit with another bout of dizziness outside the men's room and use the wall to keep me upright. My ears prick up when I catch Drusilla's nasal London accent around the corner.

"I wish he had hit Phillip. A scandal would've been just what we needed," she says with frustration.

I hold my breath and listen.

"Dru, darling, we have more important things to worry

about. It won't be the end of the world if we can't unseat my nephew from the family throne. Either way, we'll bring Kingsbridge to its knees and solidify our own holdings in the process."

My heart hammers when I recognize the second voice as belonging to my Uncle Gerald.

"Shh! Keep your voice down," she says. "I'll see you upstairs later."

Not knowing if they are coming my way, I duck into the bathroom and grip the sink until the dizziness passes. I contemplate texting Lettie to give her a heads-up but reject the idea, thinking she's got enough on her plate at the moment. Instead I splash some water on my face before walking out into the now-empty hallway.

I make my way to the elevator without further incident as I mull over the overheard conversation. One thing's for certain: when it comes to forensic accounting and hacking, Lettie's skills are unmatched. No doubt they'll come in handy when I unleash her on this. Without Lettie by my side, I'm not sure I would've survived these last two years of preparatory work to take the helm of Kingsbridge. In truth, she would make a better CEO. God knows she would definitely enjoy it more.

Lucas is standing outside my hotel room with his medical bag when I step out of the elevator.

"Sorry for the delay," I say as I walk up and slip the card key into the lock.

Lucas gives me a hard stare through his glasses and settles the black bag on the desk across from the bed. He unzips it and pulls out his tools of the trade: blood pressure cuff, stethoscope, vials, syringe, specimen cup—the works. "You look terrible, Devon. Take off your jacket."

My lips turn up in a wry smile as I slide my arms out of the top half of my tux. "Gee, thanks." I drop down onto the edge of the bed and let him put on the blood pressure cuff.

The tight grip around my biceps loosens. "Your pressure's

on the low side. You feeling dizzy at all?" he asks.

I nod. "A bit, on and off."

"Tell me everything, and don't leave anything out."

I walk him through all the incidents I've experienced since Thursday as he taps a vein and draws several vials of blood.

Lucas's face is dark with worry by the time I finish. "Let's skip the ACE inhibitor tonight. If I didn't know how vital this gala is for you, I'd send you straight to the hospital."

I snort, rubbing my hands over my thighs. "The only way you're getting me out of here tonight is on a stretcher."

"That might not be out of the question," Lucas says and shoves a specimen cup at me. "Give me a few drops. Whatever you can manage."

I take it and suppress the sour look I'm tempted to give him because I know he's right.

"I'll get these couriered to the lab as soon as we're done," he says as I latch the bathroom door behind me.

A couple of minutes later, I emerge with what little I could squeeze out.

He writes my false identity on the cup in marker. "If I were you, I wouldn't make any plans for tomorrow. If your creatinine levels have dropped your GFR too low, we're going to have to do something to cleanse your blood."

A chill passes through me. That's not what I want to hear. Either way, I can't deal with it right now. The obligations of the evening bear down on me like a crushing weight. I'm just hoping to make it through the rest of the night unscathed. "Is there anything else you can give me?" I ask, grasping at straws.

Lucas shakes his head and zips his bag. "Not until I get the results of your tests." He passes a hand over his face, looking as tired as I feel. "Devon ... We need to start considering some ... *options*."

I pull on my tuxedo jacket. "Not tonight, Lucas."

He presses his lips together and nods. 'Tomorrow, then."

"Tomorrow." I concede but fail to mention my plans with Jenny. The last thing I want to do is send her back to San Francisco alone.

<h1 style="text-align:center">Chapter 35</h1>

Jenny

"WEARABLE TECHNOLOGY IS a major area of investment for Kingsbridge right now," Jasper says to Devon, holding an escargot shell tightly in tongs and dislodging the garlic-soaked snail with a tiny fork. "Devon, your visit to Nanotekx next week is quite timely. It's currently ranked the most promising start-up in Silicon Valley."

I flinch at the mention of Nanotekx and wrestle with an escargot of my own, praying I don't send it flying across the room like Julia Roberts did in *Pretty Woman*. Thankfully, at my prompting Devon explained all the odd silverware to me before we sat down with four of the twelve board members and their spouses. Escargot tongs. Who knew?

Lettie and Howard, back from downtown, sit at the table next to us with four more Kingsbridge board couples, while Phillip and Tessa sit in for Devon's uncle Byron and hold court at the table on our other side with the remaining three couples. Uninhibited by the bandages on his face, Phillip sits proudly and acts as if he and Tessa are the next Prince William and Duchess Kate.

"That's why we need to take Nanotekx public," says Sally Bennett, a stiff gray-haired woman who runs corporate

217

communications. Her husband takes a sip of Scotch, smiles politely, and pretends to listen as his gaze shifts to an attractive woman walking past our table. Her dress looks like the one I rejected because it made me look as if I'd been dipped naked in black paint. Maybe it's the same one.

Devon shakes his head. "Too soon. Maybe this time next year. That said, they'll need a substantial cash infusion to support their development schedule. But if we let in the venture capitalists who are courting them, we may lose our position as the majority stakeholder." Devon pushes aside his plate of uneaten snails. "Give me time to assess their operations and to review their products and financials more closely before any decisions—investment or otherwise—are made."

Sally's mouth turns down in a dour frown while Jasper's brows pop up, making him look suitably impressed. "Wise."

Lettie's table erupts into raucous laughter next to us. I glance over, wishing our discussion were nearly as entertaining.

"What are your thoughts about the competitive landscape?" asks another board member, a handsome man in his fifties wearing a dark-gray tux.

Devon leans back in his chair and answers with an air of confidence. "There are a few hot companies with attractive patents in complementary product lines. We may want to consider another acquisition." He takes a sip of the diet ginger ale that's masquerading as a mixed drink.

And so it goes for the next hour as board members grill Devon over dinner in what feels like a group interview under the guise of pleasant conversation. They seem very pleased by the time we've made it to dessert. They aren't the only ones. I'm more than "suitably impressed" with Devon's business acumen. It's obvious that Kingsbridge Industries will be in very capable hands come October.

Still, the ache in my back signals I'm reaching my limit for sitting prim and ramrod straight.

"So, Ms. Lynch, what it is that you do?" Sally asks, turning the spotlight from Devon to me. I swallow a bite of flourless chocolate cake and try not to act like a deer stuck in the middle of Route 287.

I dab at the corners of my mouth with my napkin, think fast, and clear my throat. "I've recently left publishing, and I'm in the process of securing a marketing role at an agency in Manhattan," I say, hoping for the right level of formality with my half lie. With a little luck and a good word from Raine, I might actually have a chance of being hired by Conrad Designs if I apply.

Her eyebrows rise. "Oh? What kind—"

Devon interrupts. "Jenny's being too modest." He squeezes my hand and looks a little too lovingly into my eyes, playing his part in our charade. "She's a talented photographer. I think she should entertain finding some *corporate* commissions." His gaze shifts to Sally, giving her a pointed look.

I beat down my surprise at his not-so-subtle hint. Honestly, I'd never thought of that. That's how Aunt Jill got started out of college—supplying her first husband's family's company with commissioned photography.

Sally gives me a tight smile. "I might have some contacts for you. I'm assuming you have a portfolio?"

"Of course." My original works are in San Francisco with the rest of my stuff, but I have digital images of most of my portfolio on my laptop.

As the waitstaff comes around to refresh the tea and coffee, the band starts its second set with a slow, romantic tune.

"Dance with me?" There's a sparkle in Devon's eye as he holds out his hand. This time, the look is genuine.

I clasp his long, tapered fingers, seizing the opportunity for escape. "Lead the way."

"If you'll excuse us," Devon says. His fingers entwine

tightly with mine, and he weaves us through the dancing couples until we're in the center of the floor, hidden from the view of anyone who counts.

I let out a deep sigh as Devon wraps me in his arms and pulls me in close until we're pressed hip to hip, swaying in a slow circle.

"Dev, that was brutal . . ."

He sniffs. "Glad I'm not the only who thought so. You're doing great." He leans in and places a kiss with warm lips where my neck meets my shoulder. "You look beautiful."

My insides warm and tingle. "Too bad we can't sneak out and go upstairs," I say, half-serious. *How do people do this regularly?* I wonder. I don't think I could handle more than one of these events a year, maybe two at most. It's like a bad prom that's gone political and slightly psychotic.

His lips brush mine on the way to my earlobe. He gives it a nibble, sending a chill down my arms that bristles the tiny hairs. "Mmm, I wish we could."

A drumbeat keeping time with my heart pulses in my core. I resist the urge to press more tightly against him.

"What did Lucas say?" I ask.

Devon's shoulders tense under my hands. "He wants to keep an eye on me."

Lettie breaks in before I can respond. "How's it going, you two?" she asks, sidling up next to us in Howard's embrace. She looks tiny engulfed in his arms.

"As well as can be expected. But given the choice between this and a root canal, I'd take the root canal," Devon says. "How'd it go downtown?"

Howard pipes up. "Thanks to your girl Jenny here, we got VIP treatment." He gives me a wink.

"Did Phillip drop the charges?" Devon asks.

Howard snorts. "You kidding me? I'll have to pay off the little shit to get rid of him."

Devon cringes and sighs. "I'm sorry. I shouldn't have

taken the bait. I'll pay you back, whatever it costs."

Howard breaks into a wide, toothy grin. "Not necessary. Just make sure you're not in a crowded room the next time you're tempted to throw a punch. Knowing him, you'll get another shot."

"No doubt." Devon scowls.

The music shifts to a pulsing dance beat. Devon drops his arms from my waist and finds my hand again. "Can you guys meet us at the bar in an hour? After I finish the rounds and check in with the pledge team?"

Howard shrugs and gives Lettie a look. "Sure."

Devon pulls Lettie in close and whispers something in her ear that I can't hear.

Her eyes widen, and her lips settle in a hard line. She glances at her watch. "Noted. See you in an hour."

"Rounds?" I ask as Devon leads me back to the table.

"We'll need to make a personal appearance at each table to thank everyone for attending, on behalf of the Soames Foundation. You up for it?" he asks.

I nod, but I'm not sure my feet agree. I'd like nothing more than to kick off my heels and go barefoot.

Most of the board members are still seated and chatting among themselves when we get to the table. Our drinks have been refreshed while we've been away.

Still standing, Devon eyes his glass eagerly. There's a slight tremor in his hand as he picks up the diet ginger ale and drinks it down. My concern over his health creeps back in.

Devon discards the glass and offers me his arm in preparation for departing. I take it, grateful to leave. "Ladies and gentlemen, thank you for the engaging dinner conversation, and enjoy the rest of your night. If you'll excuse us," he says, then leads me away to start the rounds.

"Let's get this one over with first," Devon whispers in my ear as we take a few steps over to Phillip and Tessa's table.

Devon stands strategically to the side of Phillip's chair,

giving Devon a full view of the seated guests while making it awkward for Phillip to turn and face him.

"Good evening, everyone," Devon says, smiling broadly. "I hope you're all having an enjoyable time. On behalf of my family's foundation, I'd like to thank you for attending."

Phillip sits up straighter at the sound of Devon's voice, while the other faces around the table smile politely back and nod. Standing at Devon's side, I get a good view of Phillip fighting for control over his facial expression. Tessa doesn't seem to have the same problem. She maintains her pasted-on smile with ease. Too bad it doesn't reach her eyes.

I surreptitiously size her up out of the corner of my eye. There's a duplicitousness about her that makes me wonder what Devon saw beyond her physical beauty, especially since he doesn't seem to be the shallow type when it comes to women. Then again, what do I know? Yet . . . my instincts tell me a sour center lies beneath all that exterior beauty.

"I do hope your table's discussion was as engaging as ours, Devon," Phillip says in an overly pleasant tone. "It sounds like there are a lot of exciting opportunities happening within the Kingsbridge holdings. The new CEO will have his hands full come October."

Devon claps Phillip on the back. "So I hear. I look forward to the challenges," he says, then addresses the table. "We'll see you at the closing ceremony. Thank you in advance for your support." With that we step away from the table. I catch the pale-pink flush on Phillip's neck and suppress a chuckle as we move to the next table.

I BREATHE A sigh of relief as we finish the rounds and walk away from the last table. My cheeks ache from all the smiling, and my feet are in a state of rebellion. We have ten minutes before we're due in the bar to meet Lettie and Howard.

As we reach the hallway, Devon wavers on his feet, taking

me off guard. I lunge for his arm to keep him upright. "Dev!"

"Thenny, I don'th feel so good," he says thickly, his speech slurring. "Thake me upthairs."

Alarm races through me as I hook Devon's arm around my neck and lead him to the elevator. I wonder if the waiter he tipped to help him with his little ruse forgot to tell the bartender to skip the alcohol this time. Even so, one drink isn't enough to have this kind of effect.

I prop up Devon in the corner of the elevator and hold him in place with my hip as I rummage around for my cell phone. I dial Lettie.

"We're on our way—" she says.

"Lettie! Get Lucas and bring him up to our room. Something's wrong with Devon," I say.

"Oh my God! Okay. I just saw him. We'll be right there."

I open the room door in time for Devon to struggle out of my arms and pitch himself into the bathroom. He drops to his knees in front of the toilet, barely making it there before losing his dinner.

The sound alone makes me want to join him, although it's the smell that really roils my stomach. Trying not to breathe, I snatch a washcloth and run it under water to a make a compress, then flush the toilet to kill the odor.

"Thenny, my thest hurts. Heart'ttack," he says in between gasps. He lets go of the bowl and slides onto the floor, unconscious.

All the breath leaves my body as panic tears a path through me.

"Oh God, oh God, oh God!" I rip off his tie and claw at his tux to unbutton it as I grasp for whatever basic first aid skills I can remember. I put my hand to his parted lips and feel his breath. I roll him onto his side in case he throws up again to prevent him from choking.

His skin is a sickly shade of gray.

The moment I hear a loud, insistent banging, I jump up

and race to the door. Lucas, Lettie, and Howard spill into the room.

"He passed out on the bathroom floor!" I say.

"What happened?" Lucas barks as he rips his way through the rest of Devon's clothes down to his waist. He dips down to place an ear on Devon's chest.

My whole body starts to shake until my teeth chatter so violently that I can't speak. Lettie grasps my arms and pulls me so close that I can practically taste her breath. "Get it together, Jenny!" she grits. "Talk to Lucas."

I shake my head and try to focus, fighting down the indescribable panic that's controlling me. "Okay-okay-okay." I gasp for air. "He threw up . . . then said his chest hurt."

"Calm down and take a deep breath," Lettie says, her eyes wild and on the edge of panic.

I glance at Devon and wonder for the first time if he could die. The specter of death that haunts me, complete with scythe and cape, suddenly fills the room and silently taunts me. My lungs collapse a second time, my voice dying in my throat.

Lettie shakes me. "Breathe!"

Blood rushes through my ears with a loud pulsing whoosh. In between shallow breaths I force out, "After the rounds . . . he had trouble walking . . . slurring my name like he was drunk. Got him up here . . ." I refill my lungs and go on. "Said his chest hurt. Heart attack . . . passed out."

Lucas doesn't wait for me to finish before making a call. "This is Dr. Lucas Wilson. I need an ambulance at the Grand Highland Regency, room 317, stat. Male, twenty-four, unconscious. Bring a dose of Antizol, and get an operating room prepped for an emergency pericardiocentesis."

He makes a second call. "John? It's Lucas. I have a situation and need your discretion. I'm at the gala . . . Someone just tried to poison one of my patients."

Chapter 36

Devon

BEEP. BEEP. BEEP.

My eyelids flutter but refuse to open as I crawl slowly toward consciousness. A moan escapes my throat before I can stop it. I feel as if I've been run over by a truck. Maybe I have. I don't remember. But whatever happened must've been bad. Why else would I be hearing the steady beat of a heart monitor?

"Devon?"

I squint and open one eye, giving myself a moment before opening the other. Lucas, dressed in scrubs, stands over me with a chart. I lick my parched lips. "What happened?"

He leans down to clutch my shoulder. "Technically? Acute renal failure."

"Why does my chest hurt?" I ask, drawing in an uncomfortable breath.

"You had emergency surgery to drain the fluid collecting around your heart."

Then it hits me, and my body tingles with an adrenaline rush. "The gala? Where's Jenny?" The beeping next to me picks up its pace.

"Calm down." He gives me a reassuring smile. "She's

outside with your sister and someone else who wants to talk to you. Do you feel up to some questions?"

I'm awake enough now to take in my surroundings. I'm hooked up to half a dozen machines. Tubes are running in and out of me. The most notable is the one carrying blood near my collarbone. Then the gravity of the situation sinks in, and I want to pound my fists in frustration.

"Dialysis?" I grit, my hands clenched at my sides. "How will I be able to hide this from the board?"

"It's not what you think." Lucas sighs and says softly, "Devon ... you were poisoned. Someone who knew about your condition may have tried to kill you last night."

The beats on the heart monitor double. "What? How?"

Lucas puts my chart on the tray next to my bed and rubs his eyes. "Let me ask everyone in so that I don't have to explain this twice," he says in a weary voice. It's then that I notice the dark circles cut deep into his skin and realize he hasn't slept.

"I'm glad you were there ... at the gala," I say, stricken but grateful.

A weak half smile flickers across his lips. "So am I."

Lucas goes to the door and calls everyone inside. Lettie and Jenny head toward me as soon as they pass through the door. Jeans have replaced the gowns they were wearing the last time I saw them.

Lettie gets to my side first. "You scared the bejesus out of me," she says, her eyes welling with tears. Last night's makeup now gone, she looks pale and as tired as Lucas.

"I'm sorry," I say. "Does Mom know?"

She sniffles and squeezes my arm. "She knows you're okay." Lettie's code for "I only shared the parts I needed to."

"Don't do anything like that again," she whispers and kisses me on the forehead before stepping back to make way for Jenny.

Jenny sits down on the bed and gently slips her hand into

mine despite the IVs. Fear lingers in her eyes. Without a word, I squeeze her fingers, and she squeezes back. Her gaze searches mine in silent question. Not exactly sure what she's asking and not caring, I have only one answer. I pull her fingertips to my lips and kiss them, ignoring that we have an audience.

A throat clears, interrupting our moment. A man I don't recognize takes out a notepad. He's in his fifties with a rugged face and salt-and-pepper hair cut tight to his head. He's got the solid, square build of someone who played contact sports back in the day.

"Devon, this is Detective John Henshaw," Lucas says by way of introduction. I recognize his name from my conversation with Jenny at the gala.

Jenny pats my hand and gives me a small smile. She still hasn't said a word. Then again, she doesn't need to. The haunted look in her eyes says enough.

He tilts his head in greeting, then motions to Lucas to begin.

Lucas pinches the bridge of his nose and lets out a breath. "All right. Near as I can figure, someone slipped ethylene glycol into Devon's drink sometime between the time we met in his hotel room and before dinner ended."

"Antifreeze?" Lettie asks, wrapping her arms around herself in a tight hug. "Why would someone use that?"

"It wasn't antifreeze but rather the chemical equivalent. It's odorless, colorless, and, most importantly … sweet. Easily ingested in a soft drink. Whoever poisoned Devon was counting on a couple of things."

"What's that?" Lettie asked.

Detective Henshaw scribbles a note on his pad and answers. "They knew your brother's kidneys were compromised, but they didn't know your brother doesn't drink alcohol."

"As soon as Jenny mentioned Devon was slurring his

words and had vomited, I knew it wasn't because Devon was drunk," Lucas says. "A second urine sample from Devon's catheter confirmed my suspicions."

"So, the question I have for you, Mr. Soames, is, who would want to harm you and why?" John asks.

I wince, thinking of at least three people and possibly a fourth. "How much lead do you have in that pencil?"

"Harm? Don't you mean murder?" Lettie asks.

John shakes his head and shrugs. "Maybe. Maybe not."

"They might've only wanted to unmask Devon's condition. Jeopardize his appointment," Lucas says.

"We can't let that happen," Lettie says, pacing. "We need to tell the board something else."

"We already did," John says matter-of-factly. "Lucas filled me in on the delicate nature of this situation. Either way, we're treating this as an attempted homicide. If the perp's intent was to expose Devon, they got exactly the opposite."

"I'm attributing Devon's condition to the poisoning. That should buy some time with the board," Lucas says and glances my way. "They want to assign a private security team to you until the person is caught."

"Are you serious?" I spout. "For all I know, it's one of them who tried to kill me."

"That's why I've picked the team," John says. "Men I know and trust."

"Why would you do that for me? Seems above and beyond the call of duty," I say.

John gives me a half smile. "Consider it a favor."

Lucas clasps my shoulder. "To me."

John nods. "And Jenny," he says and glances at her. "Any friend of hers . . . well, is like family."

Jenny gives him a warm smile and squeezes my hand.

"Thank you, Detective," Lettie says, wearing a look I don't see often—one of gratitude. "You too, Jenny. For everything. Howard, this . . . everything."

"Yes, thank you." I look at Lucas. "When can I go home?"

He sniffs and shakes his head. "You're here for at least a couple more days."

My shoulders sag. "I need to get Jenny back to San Francisco."

"Don't worry about that," she says. They're the first words she's spoken since she came into the room. "There's no rush. We can wait until you're better."

A wave of exhaustion washes over me, and my eyelids slide shut. "Why am I so tired all of a sudden?"

"It's probably the dialysis," Lucas says. "Rest. We can do this later."

I feel Jenny's lips lightly touch mine.

And then I'm out.

Chapter 37

Jenny

"DON'T LET ANYONE in who isn't on the list," John says, giving a hard stare to the hulking plainclothes guard standing outside Devon's door.

"I'm going to catch a few hours of sleep while Devon finishes dialysis," Lucas says to John. "Call if you need me. I'll do the same."

"You got it," he says, and they shake hands.

"Jenny, before I forget. My service confirmed that I had a cancellation first thing tomorrow morning," Lucas says.

"Thanks," I murmur. Now that I'm not going anywhere for a few days, I may as well get the physical my mom's been hounding me about and pick up a refill on the special brand of iron supplements I get from Lucas. I used the last one this morning, and over-the-counter vitamins don't pass muster according to him. Since Mom's paying, who am I to argue?

John turns to me and Lettie as Lucas disappears down the hallway. "I had hoped to get a little more out of your brother before he faded. How about we talk through a couple of things in the lounge?"

"Of course," Lettie says as she chews a nail, looking worried and distracted.

A television game show blares in the empty lounge. We take a seat in the far corner.

John digs his notepad back out of his pocket, licks his index finger, and flips a bunch of pages. "Let's start by reviewing the list you gave me last night and see if there's anyone else I should add."

Lettie sighs. "Sure."

"Drusilla Cartwright, your father's former mistress; her son and your half brother, Phillip Cartwright; his fiancée and Devon's ex-girlfriend, Tessa Morgan; and your uncle, Gerald Soames. Anyone else?"

Lettie shakes her head. "No one obvious. I'm not even sure I'd keep Tessa on that list, unless being a heartless bitch is a crime. Honestly, I don't think she has it in her. But who knows."

"She did threaten Devon," I say, remembering her parting words at the cocktail party after Howard punched Phillip. "She said he'll pay."

John takes notes as we talk.

"What have you found out so far?" I ask, still plagued by the surreal quality of the night. If it hadn't been for an old stash of Xanax I keep for anxiety emergencies, I don't think I would've slept at all . . . or kept my mind.

John stops writing and flips back through his pad. "The head of security is meeting me this afternoon at two p.m. He's got copies of all the surveillance footage, which will take some time to weed through. We haven't had any luck locating Devon's glass."

Lettie rests her head in her hands. "I never thought anyone would stoop to this level."

"Is there any other motive that you can think of beside envy over his inheritance?" John asks.

Lettie rocks her head from side to side between her palms. "Not yet." She looks up, wearing a look of determination. "But if there is, I'll find it."

"Let me know whatever you find out," John says and snaps his pad shut. "In the meantime, the board is sending a representative to meet with Devon at four. Will you be here?"

Lettie sniffs. "I wouldn't miss it for the world. Besides, Devon's in no shape to meet with anyone alone."

"He won't be alone. Lucas will be there, too." John rises. We rise with him. "I'm dropping Jenny off at home, you need a ride?"

"No. Thanks anyway. I have a car," she says, and her eyes shift to me. "Come back for the meeting later?"

I nod. "Of course."

Lettie flips her chin in the direction of Devon's room. "Everything okay with Lucas?" she asks, wearing a look of concern. I gave her a scare last night—not to mention myself—when I freaked out in the hotel room, but I have a different doctor for that.

"It's nothing ... really. Just a physical and a vitamin pickup," I say and give her shoulder a reassuring squeeze.

Her face relaxes. "See you later, then."

STARING OUT THE window at the passing houses and trees on our way back to Summit, I wonder what comes next. For Devon ... for me ... for us.

After I spent half the night curled up in one of the waiting room chairs, half-crazed with the thought that Devon wouldn't make it, it took Lucas a solid fifteen minutes to assure me that Devon would recover. I shiver when I think of last night and the absolute panic that nearly ate me alive. I was convinced Devon would be taken from me as the next installment payment for my original failure.

I keep thinking back to what Devon told me about his health before the gala, and I wonder if it's related to the two-week limit of his proposal. I believe him that it's not about what Tessa said ... about his finding someone more suitable. I was stupid to fall into her trap.

Then again, stupidity has been my flavor of the week. Make that two weeks. I should've never agreed to his proposal, but hindsight is always twenty-twenty, right? Who knew he'd steal my heart before this was over?

But now I'm too invested, and the mere thought of his dying squeezes the breath from my body and unlocks all my irrational fears.

Things I keep under lock and key threaten to break free: anxiety dreams and attacks; the pervasive feeling of death's stalking every person I love; feelings of helplessness coupled with the agonizing guilt and shame that I'm somehow responsible for all the deaths that have happened around me, starting with Brittany.

Maybe if I just step away from Devon per our agreement and force myself to let him go, he'll be safe and my death taint won't touch him.

The idea fades as quickly as it comes.

I hang my head and curse my weakness in wanting to stay despite the dread coiling thick in the air around me.

I'm afraid it's only a matter of time before I wake up screaming again.

Maybe a visit to Dr. Graham is in order, I think, giving it serious consideration. Before I can muse further, John interrupts my thoughts.

"You haven't said a word since we left. May I ask you something?"

"Sure," I say, still staring out the window at the passing landscape.

"How'd you get involved with these people?"

My head snaps around at his accusing tone. A chill slides down my spine. "What do you mean?"

He sighs and his brow furrows. "Do you have any idea who Howard Cato III *is*?"

My eyes narrow. "Other than the fact that he's some rich

guy Lettie is sleeping with and works for a shipping company? No."

"Damn it," he mutters and releases a long, patient breath. "I got a call this morning from my contacts at the FBI. About that shipping company? Turns out Howard Cato *II* is high on a list for suspected racketeering as part of an international crime ring. Bottom line? Chances are good that Lettie's friend Howard is tied to the mob."

Goosebumps assault my flesh, covering my arms and the back of my neck. "What does that have to do with Devon and Lettie?" I whisper, afraid of what he might say next.

"I don't know. Maybe nothing," he says.

"Then why are you helping us?"

He swipes a hand across his chin and shakes his head. "Because you asked . . ."

"Because of my mother, you mean," I say softly.

He swallows next to me and stays silent. I glance over. His cheek flexes, hiding his grinding teeth.

"You still love her, don't you?" I ask softly.

His nostrils flare, and a muscle twitches near his jaw. "Don't ever ask me that again . . .," he says in a harsh whisper.

I bite my lip. It's then that I realize I need to know if Devon really loves me as Lettie claims. And I need to tell him I love him, even if my feelings aren't returned and I never see him again. It kills me to watch my mother and John struggle with all the pain and love they've carried unresolved between them all these years. Each should at least know how the other one feels ... They deserve to know even if they can't be together. If I were one of them, I'd want to know.

We drive in silence, John sitting stoically beside me, until we reach my driveway.

"Thanks for everything." I lean over and give him a hug as he sits, unresponsive. The spicy scent of his cologne hits me. It's so different from the one my dad uses. Then again, they're nothing alike. John is a rough-and-tumble detective with a military background, and my dad is a corporate guy who loves cars. The only thing they have in common is my mother.

Slowly John reaches up and squeezes my arm.

"I care what happens to you," he says gruffly. "That's why I'm helping you."

"I know." Letting him go, I reach for the door handle and step outside. Before I lose my nerve, I peek back into the car. "She still loves you, John."

I shut the car door and walk to the house without looking back, feeling better. My message must've hit home. His car doesn't move for a full five minutes.

Chapter 38

Devon

"DEV? WAKE UP," Lettie whispers. The heat of her breath tickles my ear.

My eyes flutter open, and she comes into focus. No longer in jeans as she was this morning, she's wearing makeup and a business suit for the four o'clock meeting she called to tell me about earlier. She asked Jenny to come. I shouldn't be happy about that, but I am. I'd be even happier if I didn't feel like utter shit.

"*Mmm?*" A dull ache assaults my chest as I unstick my lips with my tongue and hit the button to elevate the back of the bed. "Water," I croak and glance at the clock. At least we have an hour before everyone arrives.

The heart monitor beeps softly in the background. Thankfully, fewer tubes are snaking their way in and out of me than when I fell asleep. I feel for my collarbone. The dialysis tube is gone, but the IV is still taped to my skin. A renewed sense of frustration latches on to me. I grind my molars, cursing my body's betrayal.

Lettie fumbles with her computer, abandoning it on the chair to fill a glass.

The cool liquid rushes down to my empty stomach, setting

off a chain reaction of hunger and nausea. "What's up?" I ask with a distinct rasp.

Her fingers dance excitedly on the keyboard. "What you whispered in my ear last night on the dance floor about Uncle Gerald and Drusilla? I've been working since this morning digging up what I can." Her mouth draws into a thin lipstick-covered line. "I think I found something."

Eager as I am to hear what Lettie has to say, the tinny taste in my mouth roils my stomach. What I'd give for the toothbrush in my shaving kit right now; I'm thankful that Lettie brought it earlier with a change of clothes. Still tethered to a catheter and a saline drip as I am, there's no way I'm getting up to get it, but if I don't do something soon my next move will be to heave into the bucket next to the bed. "Can you get me some mouthwash?"

She shoots me a look of disbelief. "I'm about to tell you something important, and all you can think about is your breath?"

In answer, my stomach revolts, and I heave up the water I drank into the bucket. Pressure pushes against the backs of my eyeballs as I choke out the bile that follows. Unpleasant memories of chemo rise up and batter me. Dying outright seems more appealing than living through the suffering that could happen before I do.

"Holy crap! I'll get Lucas," she says and breaks into a heel-clattering sprint toward the door.

"No," I say weakly, wiping the edge of the sheet across my mouth with an unsteady hand, and pull myself upright. My heart pounds from the effort. "I'm all right."

Lettie stops at the door, worry etching a path across her forehead. "Are you sure? Why did you . . . ?" She points to the wastebasket.

I shake my head. "I don't know. But I feel better. Mouthwash?" I need it now more than ever to kill the taste.

Lettie shifts directions, ducking into the bathroom for a

few seconds and coming out with a cup and a travel-size bottle filled with blue liquid.

After a quick gargle and rinse, I can tolerate the inside of my mouth again. Lettie takes the bucket and clears everything away, ditching it all in the bathroom.

Smoothing her skirt, she sits back down and repositions the computer on her lap. "Better now?"

I give her a half-hearted smile and nod.

Putting on her game face, she turns her attention back to the screen. "Okay . . . I pulled everything I could from the SEC filings on Uncle Gerald's trades since Dad died. Let's just say . . . he's been busy."

"Doesn't necessarily mean anything." I shrug.

"That's true, in and of itself. But here's what I found interesting. There's a bunch of small transactions for stock redemptions . . . the typical stuff. Then there's this one . . ."

Lettie swings her laptop around so I can see the screen and points to one in particular. It's a hefty sum, close to $20 million, which isn't a redemption but a purchase.

"Look at the date," she says.

It hits me with the force of a sledgehammer. The purchase coincides with the embezzlement from my mom's nursing home along with the amount. It equals the operating capital that disappeared from the Kingsbridge accounts and forced the facility into bankruptcy. "Holy . . . so Gerald's behind the embezzlement?"

"That's what I'm guessing," Lettie says, taking back her laptop.

"But he wasn't an officer there. He wasn't affiliated with the facility at all."

Lettie takes a deep breath and nods. "I know, but that doesn't mean he wasn't working with someone else. If what you heard in the hallway is true, his motivation is tied to us. He knew Mom was there . . . What better way to distract us than to force her care into our hands?"

I rub my brow to ease the ache behind my right eye. "What did he do with the money? The trail should tell us something."

"Yeeahhh … it does." Lettie drags her teeth across her lower lip and cringes. "And the news isn't good."

"Just tell me," I say, in no mood to play twenty questions.

"I'm glad you're sitting down," she mumbles and shifts in the chair. "He invested in a publicly traded technology company that was later taken private. They changed their name and reinvented themselves in the wearable tech market …"

Yeah, she's right. This isn't good. I have a feeling I know what's coming. "Go on."

"Looks like our Uncle Gerald is a major investor in Verotechx … the company Nanotekx wants to acquire."

Releasing a sigh, I shove down my annoyance and press a finger against the bridge of my nose. "And we didn't know this—*why*?"

Lettie huffs, her annoyance matching mine. "Because, little brother, his name wasn't attached to the incoming investment. The stake was purchased under the name of a generic-sounding holding company called V5 Tech Holdings. Not to mention, we're only halfway through that mess of paperwork from Nanotekx, and now that Verotechx has gone private, it's not like their financials are public record anymore."

"Now what?" I ask.

"I keep digging. Where there's smoke, there's fire."

There's a knock at the door, and a few seconds later it opens. Lucas pokes his head inside. "May I come in?"

Lettie snaps her laptop shut and stuffs it into her designer laptop bag.

"Yeah," I say, giving a small nod.

He comes in carrying a chart and latches the door behind him. The lack of sleep is still apparent in the shadows under his eyes. He pulls up the chair on the opposite side of the bed and passes a hand over his face. "Listen, I wanted to catch you two alone before the Kingsbridge meeting."

The grave tone of his voice trips my internal alarm.

He blows out a breath and flips past the first page of the chart. His gaze shifts to mine and locks on hard. "Devon . . . I'm sorry. I can't take you off dialysis."

"Lucas . . . ," I warn.

"That poison pushed you over the edge. We're here . . . where we didn't want to be. You need a kidney. Fast."

Lettie gasps.

I clamp my eyes shut and beat back the prickling behind my eyelids. "No. I can't. It's over if that happens." I grind my teeth. Not just Kingsbridge but Jenny. The hope I'd started to entertain is gone. For a brief moment, I thought maybe—just maybe—I could work something out . . . But I can't ask her to stay now. I couldn't bear the pity, or the rejection, that might come with this new development. Somehow I thought I'd have more time. But I don't, and I've lost even more than I anticipated. The unfairness of it all fills me with bitterness. A feeling I know well from my cancer years. Screw denial, I go straight to anger—the second of the five phases of grief.

Passing a wrist across my closed eyelids, I brush away any remaining evidence of my momentary lapse and open my eyes.

"Nothing's over," Lettie snaps and leans over to clutch my hand. "We'll get a kidney, Dev. What are the options, Lucas?"

"I've already enrolled you both in a paired kidney matching program," Lucas says, "it's just that Devon is a hard match."

"Can you test me again?" Lettie asks. There's a look of desperation in her eyes.

Lucas shakes his head and says quietly, "Lettie, we already know your markers are incompatible with Devon, even as his twin. But under the paired matching program, you can trade a kidney for someone else's who matches Devon . . . if we can find one."

Lettie squeezes my hand hard. "Ask Jenny."

"Ask Jenny what?" I rip my hand away and stare her down. "Are you out of your flipping mind?"

Her lip trembles, and her jaw tightens. "Why's that a crazy request? You love each other, don't you?"

My neck heats with a mixture of frustration and embarrassment, aware as I am of Lucas's relationship with Jenny's family. "Wha—what?" I sputter. "We barely know each other. I can't ask Jenny to do that for me. And I won't."

Anger infuses Lettie's cheeks and makes them pinker under her makeup. "Why are you being so damn stubborn? I love you, Dev . . . I'd give you a kidney. If she loves you, why wouldn't she?"

"She doesn't love me!" I fist the covers in my hands. She's never said that, and how could she now anyway? The heart monitor beats wildly next to the bed.

"What is it about testosterone that makes men so stupid?!" she snipes.

"Where do you get off being so presumptuous?" I fire back. "Jenny and I have only known each other a couple of weeks. How can you say that?"

Fury burns a hole in my chest. But it's not Lettie I'm furious with . . . it's myself. And Tessa. For leaving me, for breaking me, for the defeat that I'm feeling right this second. I can't ask Jenny to save me, and I can't ask her to stay. Like it or not, this is something I need to do alone. If she were to reject my love, I'm not sure I'd survive.

I have to let her go. The decision rolls around in my head as my heart withers in my chest, leaving me hollow and alone. Now I just have to figure out how to do it.

Lettie shakes her head as I melt down inside, and she whispers, "Sometimes a couple of weeks is all it takes . . ."

Lucas clears his throat and heads toward the door. "I'll

leave you two alone for a while." He stops just short of touching the handle and turns. "I agree with Lettie. I wouldn't count out Jenny Lynch." With that he's gone, and I'm left staring after him, wanting to claw my way out of my own skin.

Instead I hang my head into my hands. "I don't want Jenny here for the Kingsbridge meeting."

"*What?* Why?" Lettie asks, looking at me as if I've lost my mind.

"Because . . . it's best to end this now . . . before someone gets hurt," I mumble.

Lettie glares at me and plants her hands on her hips. "Someone? Someone! Don't you mean *you*? Why are you being such a coward? She's not that bitch Tessa . . . she won't do that to you! She won't abandon you when you need her most."

"How can you say that?" I seethe. "You don't know her any better than I do!"

"Maybe not. But there's one thing I do know. That girl loves you," she says with conviction.

I challenge back, "How do you know that?"

"Because I don't have a penis short-circuiting my brain! You're one of the most intelligent people I know, Dev, but one of the dumbest when it comes to women."

My lips tighten as I drag heavy breaths into my lungs, unable to respond. The thought of Jenny's loving me makes me ache with longing as the impossible weight of my situation crushes me.

The anger drains out of Lettie, and her shoulders relax. She takes my hand and says softly, "I've never seen you this happy. The way your eyes light up when you look at her. I know you love her, too. Why would you throw that away?" Tears creep down her cheeks, leaving me bewildered at her reaction.

"What's this about, Lettie?" I swallow, suspecting that this isn't about me.

She rips a tissue from the box and dabs at her runny mascara. "I want that, Dev. If I had it . . . I'd fight like hell to keep it for as long as I could."

Maybe things aren't as good with Howard as she's led me to believe.

Lettie is my strength, and to see her this way unwinds me. I do what I've done since we were little, and reach out my arms, careful not to dislodge my IVs. She throws herself into my embrace, and I pull her tight to my chest and stroke her hair. "We'll be okay, you and me."

Holding her like this serves as a lonely reminder that my heart yearns for Jenny to fill this space. If what Lettie says is true, there's even more of a reason to set Jenny free. Knowing that Jenny might love me strengthens my resolve to end things now. And it eases the tightness in my chest to know that it's out of love that I'll let her go, rather than my own selfish fear.

"Don't push Jenny away. Let her choose," Lettie whispers.

"I can't," I whisper back and fight back the lump in my throat. How can I explain to Lettie that not bringing death to Jenny's door is the best gift that I could ever give her? "She deserves a life with someone who can give her one." I squeeze Lettie tighter. "Promise me something, Lettie."

"What?" she asks softly.

"That you won't ask her to give me a kidney." I wouldn't be able to live with the guilt or the rejection.

Lettie slumps against me and stays silent for a moment. "All right," she concedes.

"One more thing?"

"Yeah?"

"Take her back to San Francisco for me."

Chapter 39

Jenny

"WHAT DO YOU mean I can't go in?" I ask, half wondering if I just stepped into the Twilight Zone. "I was asked to come here."

"I'm sorry, Ms. Lynch," the guard says, having the good grace to look abashed, "but the Kingsbridge representative asked that only members of the Soames family be included in the meeting. Ms. Soames will be in touch with you later."

My hackles rise at the suggestion that I'll be leaving. And why did he say "Ms." and not "Mr."? "I'll wait. I want to visit when they're done."

The guard shakes his head. "That won't be necessary. Mr. Soames has shut down visitation rights for anyone outside of his immediate family."

"What?" His words send a shock wave through me that nearly buckles my knees. "Why won't he see me?" The question is rhetorical, and I'm not really expecting an answer.

"He didn't say, ma'am."

Then it hits me—our two weeks are up. Was everything he told me, everything I thought was between us . . . Was it all a lie? Now that the gala is over, he no longer needs or wants me? Even as a friend?

Anger wells up behind my breastbone. I march over to the waiting area and text Devon:

What's going on? Why can't I visit you?

A message comes back that the text is undeliverable, and a shiver slips down my spine.

Lucas heads down the hall in my direction, and I breathe a sigh of relief. "Lucas!" I say, trapping his forearm in my grip. "What's going on? Devon told the guards not to let me in."

He gives me a weak smile and shifts uncomfortably on his feet. "I'm sorry, Jenny. I wish he hadn't done that. Leticia is planning to see you later. Hopefully she'll be able to explain."

I suddenly feel as if I've been left out in the cold to freeze while everyone I know is sitting around a blazing fire. "Can you tell me anything?"

Lucas blows out a breath. "You know I can't. For what it's worth, he's doing what he thinks is right." He squeezes my shoulder and then continues past the guard into Devon's room.

Tears of frustration well in my eyes, and I stumble in the direction of the elevator, now convinced that he's through with me. How could I have been such an idiot?

I make it to my mom's car before a sob breaks free. A scream of agony tears from my lungs like I've been wounded in battle, one that I won't survive. I sit with my head resting on the steering wheel, letting the drops fall freely onto my bare legs as I hiccup-cry.

I don't stop until all the moisture has fled my body through my tear ducts, leaving my eyes puffy and swollen. My sinuses are clogged to the point that I can only breathe through my mouth. I sit numb for a minute before scrambling for the tissues my mother keeps in the glove compartment. After clearing my sinuses, I'm overcome with a throbbing headache and a feeling of total despair. The physical ache in my chest constricts my breath.

So much for my romantic notion of telling Devon that I

love him. Loneliness washes over me until I feel empty inside.

My hand shakes as I pull up the flight schedule for San Francisco on my phone. Maybe I'll stay there for a while after I pack up my stuff. There are at least two friends who would take me in for a couple of weeks while I get my head straight.

Two weeks ago I was desperate to leave San Francisco, now I'm dying to get back . . . and away from Devon. Even the balm of seeing baby Rachel has lost its magic.

Great job, Lynch. Losing two men in the span of two weeks must be some kind of new record. Then I remind myself that they were never really mine to lose.

I blow my nose one last time and head for home.

"PUMPKIN, want to help your old man in the stable for a few minutes?" Dad asks, wiping grease off his hands onto a towel as I step out of the car.

He takes a step forward. His brow knits, and his voice fills with concern. "Are you all right, sweetheart?"

One look into his kind, bespectacled eyes and I burst into tears. He draws me into his arms, careful not to touch me with his hands.

"Did something happen to Devon?" he asks.

Something unintelligible comes out of my mouth through the blubbering. I'm not sure what.

"*Shhh.* Come inside and tell me all about it," he says softly, leading me inside the carriage house, the sanctuary of his well-loved beauties. The overhead fan gives off a nice breeze to keep the structure cool and prevent bugs from congregating.

He grabs a roll of paper towels, yanks off a piece, and hands it to me. "Sorry, sweetie. This is the cleanest thing I have."

I attempt to smile through my tears and dab at the overly sensitive skin around my eyes. "Thanks."

"Is Devon all right?"

I shrug and choke out a nasal reply. "He was doing better when I saw him this morning. Now he's refusing to see me." I fill my dad in on the details of the encounter with the guard and Lucas.

A puzzled look crosses my dad's face. *"Hmm."* Then his expression relaxes. "Maybe he feels odd about you seeing him like that."

"Like what?" Now I'm the one who's puzzled.

"Vulnerable, ill, not at his best." He squeezes my hand. "Devon strikes me as a proper kind of guy. He might not want the girl he cares about to see him in a position of weakness."

"But . . ."

"Did I ever tell you the story about when your mom and I were dating and I came down with the flu?" he asks, pulling me down onto the bench next to him.

"No." I snuffle.

"We'd been dating for about as long as you and Devon. Up to that point, everything had been perfect. Fresh. New. Then I was struck with this monster case of the flu. The last thing I wanted was for your mom to see me like that. But you know her—she likes to take care of everyone."

I laugh, but it comes out more like a snort. "Do I ever."

"The thought of her seeing me lose my guts into the toilet horrified me. Anyway . . . she showed up one night with a vat of chicken soup after I'd told her not to come."

"What happened?" I ask, wiping my nose with the rough paper.

"I didn't answer the door," he says. "When she called to check in the next day, I told her I'd been asleep and didn't hear the bell."

"Did she believe you?"

He gives me a sheepish look. "At first she thought I'd lied to her about being sick. She thought I was out running around and using the flu as an excuse not to see her."

"But you weren't . . . ," I say.

He bobs his head. "I know, but I should've been more up front. After I confessed that I'd felt too sick to see her and was too embarrassed to have her see me that way, she forgave me."

"So you think Devon just doesn't want me to see him vulnerable?"

"Possibly that, or maybe there's a security reason," he says and shrugs. "All I'm saying is give him the benefit of the doubt until you find out more."

"Then why did he let me see him this morning?" I ask, trying to make sense of it.

"Probably because he wanted you to know he's okay. By the way, I was right not to let your mom in that night," he says, breaking into a sheepish grin.

"How do you figure that?"

He chuckles. "When I caught a whiff of the soup she'd left outside my apartment door, I tossed my cookies right there in the hall. Boy, was I glad I didn't let her in. Otherwise she would've had vomit-covered shoes. My point is, sweetie, whatever it is Devon is doing—he's probably doing what he thinks is right."

I relax a little, feeling slightly better. "Lucas said the same thing."

"Don't worry." He drapes his arm around my shoulder. "I'm sure Devon's just retreating into his man cave until he feels well. He almost died last night . . . that does something to a person. Give him a little time." He lets me go and pushes up off the bench. "He'll come around, you'll see."

A smile tugs at my lips. I want to believe him. "I guess I'll wait to hear what Lettie has to say."

"That's my girl. So how about helping me with Betsy?" he asks, pointing at the GT. "I need an assist on the brakes—you game?"

I nod, happy for the distraction. "Let me change. I'll be back."

As I'm heading for the door, he says, "I'm counting on Devon doing the Summit Classic Car Show with us in September."

It's times like this that I catch a glimpse of why my mom must have chosen my dad over John. He's one of the most positive people I know.

Fingering the diamond at my neck, I sigh and wish I were optimistic like my dad. At this point I'd like to think that I'd settle for a proper goodbye . . . but in my heart I know I won't.

Chapter 40

Devon

"UNCLE BYRON?" I ask, giving a quizzical stare to my father's brother as he sweeps into the hospital room.

I'm surprised that he's the Kingsbridge representative. Even though Byron is the designated executor and standing head of the board, I expected them to send Jasper. Byron usually doesn't get his hands dirty. Between that and his seemingly acute illness, my suspicions flare. "I see you've recovered nicely."

He sniffs as he strolls over to Lettie. "I daresay you're not the only victim in this nonsense, my boy." He kisses the back of Lettie's hand. "You look lovely, my dear."

"Flatterer," Lettie says, flashing a coy smile.

Byron beams back at her. He has a reputation for being a ladies' man, which probably explains the five divorces and the new wife. Unlike his brother Gerald, who is the spitting image of my father, Byron Soames is balding, short, and squat with a pleasant-enough face. Personally, I'm not sure what women see in him beyond his bank account. He's the youngest of the three Soames brothers. Though arrogant like the rest of them, he's the least mercenary. The fact that he never got along with my father scores him points in my book.

But as a result he's had little to do with my immediate family over the years.

"So what's the purpose of this meeting?" I ask, putting on my future-CEO hat and kicking things off ... aware that I don't cut an imposing figure dressed in a hospital gown and attached to a heart monitor.

Uncle Byron takes the seat next to Lettie. The one she dragged over earlier from the other side of the bed. Part of an effort to ensure that she kept her body between me and whoever was sent.

He clasps his hands. "As you and Leticia are painfully aware, in order for you to inherit in October you need to be alive and in good health. Looks like someone would rather you be neither."

Not exactly a news flash. I release a breath. "Yes. Go on."

"Given what's transpired, the board has agreed to fund your security team until the offending party is apprehended."

"So I've been told," I reply, folding my arms over my chest, careful to avoid the IV tube taped to my skin.

"And once your personal physician clears you, a full physical will be conducted to determine your present condition," he says in a pinched tone.

Again, nothing to write home about. "Understood." I eye him with suspicion.

Our heads turn at the sound of the door latch releasing.

Lucas chimes in as he enters. "I wouldn't count on doing a physical anytime soon. It will be a couple of weeks before the toxins flush fully from Devon's system and he can submit to one."

"Be that as it may ... ," Byron says, standing to pace at the foot of the bed. "For good measure, and at the prompting of Drusilla Cartwright, we'll be putting young Phillip through the same rigors."

Anger sizzles in my gut, and my brow tightens. "A little premature, isn't it?"

Byron shakes his head, and the light catches his shiny pate. "It's not what you think. It's for pretense only, I assure you. I don't want your half brother running the company any more than you do." He turns to Lucas. "Do you have the results?"

Byron's on our side? Lettie and I exchange a glance. We figured the board's loyalties were tipped in our favor, but we've never had a firm grasp on my father's youngest brother. Especially with Phillip conveniently taking his place last night at the gala.

Lucas consults one of the two charts he's carrying and addresses Byron. "The lab results just came back. There were traces of a drug that can cause severe short-term intestinal reactions. Someone must have slipped it into your food within the last thirty-six hours."

Byron gives me a hard stare. "As I said, you're not the only victim here. You see, your aunt and I quite mysteriously fell ill yesterday afternoon. Enough to miss last night's festivities."

Lettie frowns. "Someone tried to poison you, too?"

He gives her a tight smile. "More like temporarily incapacitate."

"Why?" I ask.

"A question I plan to get to the bottom of ... with your help," he says, glancing between Lettie and me.

"Our help? How can we be of assistance?" Lettie asks, matching my best CEO tone. I admire her cool polish. Sometimes I forget how impressive she can be, especially when she's wearing a suit. Despite her accommodating tone, I pick up on her cue for good cop/bad cop.

"Why did you give your tickets to my half brother?" I stare Byron down and tighten my arms over my chest.

Byron frowns. "Are you daft? I didn't give my blasted tickets to Phillip. I gave them to your uncle Gerald," he says. "He rang me before the gala, frantic that his had gone missing. I'd already phoned him up to say we'd taken ill and wouldn't be attending. So he and your aunt Gert stopped by to fetch ours on their way to the gala. I thought nothing of it . . . until Jasper told me who hosted my table." The look on his face turns grave.

"Well, Phillip had to get his tickets from someone and so did Drusilla," I say and shift my gaze to Lettie. There are only two possibilities as far as I can figure, and they both involve Gerald. But I'm not sure I want to tip our hand to Byron about what I overheard in the hallway at the gala . . . at least not yet.

Lettie's lips tighten, and she taps her fingers on her knee. "True. Give me some time to figure out who else might've been involved in the swap."

I give Byron a pointed look. "Did you ask Gerald about Phillip?"

He waves me off. "Of course I did. He spouted some blather about Phillip having the right to get to know the board as your potential replacement."

Lettie cuts in calmly. "What would you like us to do?"

Byron folds his hands and lowers himself back into the chair next to Lettie. "It's obvious that my brother is building an opposing force inside the board. He also knows that I have a dissenting opinion. As much as I disagreed with your father's methods, my livelihood is as dependent on this company as yours. I've long suspected something amiss with some of our holdings, and I'm determined to get to the bottom of it . . . but I'll need help." He glances between us again. "From both of you."

"Why us, why now?" I ask, assessing his sincerity and leaning toward believing him.

"Because you have as much to lose as anyone . . . and I need allies. I'm not sure who I can trust on the board."

Again I contemplate telling him about the conversation I overheard at the gala between Gerald and Drusilla, and again I decide to hold back and let him continue.

"There's an emergency meeting regarding the merger of Nanotekx and Verotechx Tuesday afternoon in Silicon Valley.

I want Leticia to go as my proxy," he says.

I try not to look stunned. "Why?"

Byron blinks. "Which one? The emergency meeting or Leticia attending as my proxy?"

"Both."

"As for the meeting, Jasper thinks you spooked some of the board members last night at dinner on your position regarding the Verotechx merger, and news travels fast." His gaze swings to Lettie. "Regarding Leticia, according to Jasper and my security advisors, your sister has demonstrated both excellent business acumen working on your behalf and an uncanny knack for gathering intelligence," he says, fixing his gaze back on me. "And since you can't go in my stead, she's the next best thing."

"Why aren't you going yourself?" I ask, truly puzzled.

He shrugs. "I have a few other matters to attend to. One of which is cooperating with the police. There's still someone out there who wants to harm you, my boy. Plus, by sending Leticia, Gerald will think I have little interest in the merger and discount your sister as an inferior substitute." Then he smiles widely at Lettie. "He won't realize that I've just unleashed into their midst one of the most canny and competent spies I've ever had the pleasure of meeting." He pats her knee. "Careful not to run circles around them and tip your hand, Leticia."

Lettie beams back at him, pleased. "I think I can manage."

"As for you, Devon," he says, "Jasper was impressed with your take on Nanotekx, and, personally, the thought of Phillip stepping in for you makes my blood boil. Make no mistake. There was no love lost between myself and your father, but you are a fine man and by far the better choice." The look in his eyes holds something close to pride.

I can't stop my mouth from tipping up into a genuine smile. "Thank you." His words fill me with a surprising warmth. They're the words I craved to hear from my own father but never did. In the end I felt that he thought I was a disappointment. As if I chose to have cancer and ruin his grand plan.

I open my mouth to speak, but Lettie beats me to it. "We think Gerald is in cahoots with Drusilla."

Chapter 41

Jenny

"I'LL GET IT," I yell down the hallway to the kitchen on my way to answer the front door.

An hour in the stable with my dad, and a shower, only marginally improved my mood. For the first time since I've been home, I feel rudderless. Split between wanting to stay and wanting to leave. But I'm smart enough to know that running is never the answer. Besides going to Crystal's opening, it's not lost on me that I haven't made time to visit any of my friends while I've been home. Every spare moment—outside of baby duty and working a few shifts at the bar—has been spent with Devon.

I open the door to find Lettie standing on the porch. I'm surprised to see she's wearing a suit. With a Chanel bag slung over her shoulder and her pale-blonde hair twisted into a bun, she presents a convincing professional figure.

She raises her eyebrows. "Are you just going to gape at me or invite me in?"

Classic Lettie. I scowl and step outside to join her in the fading light, shutting the door behind me to discourage my mom from interrupting. There's a nice bite in the evening air that pierces through the humidity. "I didn't expect you in person."

She sizes me up. "Why not? Besides, I couldn't take the chance you'd say no."

"Say no to what?" I ask and plant my hands on my hips. "Wait. Before you answer that, why did Devon refuse to see me this afternoon?"

Lettie shakes her head and blows out an exasperated breath. "Because my little brother has a twisted sense of chivalry."

I look at her, deadpan. "You're twins."

"Yeah? You'd be surprised how much difference three minutes and a dose of estrogen make to a person's maturity level."

I fix her with a glare and use her as a proxy for Devon. "I'm not going to be dumped like yesterday's garbage, Lettie."

Lettie's face scrunches into a look of shocked disbelief. "Is that what you think? That Devon cast you aside because he doesn't *care*?"

I cross my arms over my chest like armor to protect my tender heart. "Why else won't he see me? Our arrangement ended last night after the gala."

She rolls her eyes and tugs on the fancy strap of her purse. "Between the two of you, I'm not sure who's more misguided. You have no idea how much I wish I could tell you . . . but he made me promise . . ." Her voice trails off, and she avoids my gaze. "You mean a lot to him . . . more than anyone has in a long time. He's not pushing you away to hurt you. There's just something he needs to do right now . . . alone." She shifts on her high heels and opens her mouth as if to speak. Instead she clamps her lips shut.

My heartbeat accelerates. The fact that I mean a lot to him just frustrates me more. "Why can't he just tell me?" I'm at a loss as to what that something could be.

Lettie huffs. "If it makes any difference, I told him he

should . . . tell you. In the meantime he asked me to take you back to San Francisco. So pack up. We leave tomorrow. I'll pick you up around three." She turns and heads down the stairs.

"Wait a minute!" I yell after her. The gall. I clench my fists and fight back the sudden urge to hit her with a flying tackle straight onto the lawn. There's a tie between which Soames twin I'm more pissed at — Lettie or Devon.

She stops on the walkway. Fireflies dance behind her in the dusky light. "What?" she asks, giving me a wide-doe-eyed look of innocence.

"Not a chance! I'm not leaving until I see Devon. Then we can discuss San Francisco." Besides that, I'm not mentally prepared for this. I canceled the movers and left Russ a message half an hour ago, thinking I'd put off leaving for a few days while I work some things out. Seeing Devon again is one of them. Seeing my therapist is another.

She gives me a cocky smile. "I've always liked your spunk. Fair warning, he won't be happy."

I bristle and narrow my eyes. "He'll get over it. He promised we'd talk, and I'm not going anywhere until that happens."

The front door opens, and my mom pops her head out, looking worried. "Is everything all right out here?"

"Fine. Lettie was just leaving," I say.

Lettie changes course and smiles brightly. "Mrs. Lynch. Hi, I'm Devon's sister, Leticia Soames," she says and extends her hand when she gets close enough. I'm amazed at the different faces she can trot out at a moment's notice, all without missing a beat. She's nothing if not versatile . . . and cunning. Despite her gift for manipulation, she loves Devon. That much I'm sure of, and that alone makes me like her a little bit. It's her delivery that I'm not a fan of.

My mom tucks the dish towel she's holding into an apron pocket, steps outside, and pulls Lettie into a hug. Leticia's eyes widen; the move disarms her. I suppress a smirk at her reaction to my mother's mom-ishness.

"Kitty, please. It's so nice to meet you. How's Devon doing, sweetheart?" she asks, releasing her.

"He's been better," she says, blushing. "But we're hoping he makes a speedy recovery." She shoots a glance my way. "I was just about to ask Jenny if she wanted to go back and visit him with me."

Liar. I give Lettie a knowing smile. "I'll get my purse while you fill my mom in on our plans," I say before she can backpedal.

Lettie's smile falters for only a second as I head inside. "Devon was so upset that he couldn't take Jenny back to San Francisco, so I'll be taking her on our corporate jet. It works out perfectly since I have a meeting in Silicon Valley on Tuesday . . ."

Now all I need to do is decide what I'm going to say to Devon when I get to the hospital. After that I'll tackle what I'm going to do once I get back to San Francisco.

<h1 style="text-align:center">Chapter 42</h1>

Devon

A COMMOTION IN the hallway jolts me awake. My tablet sits on my chest, where it must have slipped from my hands when I fell asleep watching a movie on Netflix. I brush a hand across my mouth to wipe away any drool, real or imagined, as I catch Jenny's raised voice on the other side of the door arguing with the guard.

Damn it. I sit up and lunge for my tablet as it tumbles off me. I catch it with my left hand. At least my reflexes still work, despite the fact that the rest of me is in dire shape.

"Take it up with him," Jenny snarls and shoves the door open. Lettie follows on her heels, rolling her eyes when she sees me—Lettie's nonverbal signal for "Don't blame me, it's not my fault." This time, I'm inclined to believe her.

I freeze for a second, then decide it's better to face Jenny head on. I meet her gaze, and the look in her eyes is a mixture of hurt and rage. I don't blame her. Part of me is glad she's mad enough to want to kick my ass, while the other part of me wants to drown in despair. Either way, it's time to man up and face her and to at least attempt to give her an explanation.

I stiffen my spine and take a deep breath. "Jenny." Thankfully, I muted the heart monitor earlier—the beeping was getting on my nerves — so she can't tell my heart rate just hiked up a few notches.

I'm not prepared for what happens next. If she'd clocked me square in the jaw, I would've taken it with grace. Instead she throws herself at me and bursts into tears. I would've preferred the punch. My arms instinctively pull her to my chest, and I bury my nose in her hair one last time. The sweet scent of jasmine fills my senses, and the next thing I know she's shaking against me, sobbing with such abandon it slices my heart open.

Lettie signals that she's going to wait outside and slips out the door. I'm glad for the privacy.

I draw Jenny in tighter, wanting to lose myself in the embrace . . . wanting my life back so I can give her everything she deserves.

Right now, she has my soul in her hands . . . she just doesn't know it.

"Why won't you see me? Why are you pushing me away?" she asks through her tears.

I don't trust myself to speak. My future, and my life, hang by a thread. She'll never understand just how much I need her to remember the best of me so I can do the hard part alone. The potentially undignified job of dying while I fight with my last breath to hide my condition and live long enough to be crowned CEO, change the bylaws, and turn it all over to Lettie. That's the plan I wove earlier, anyway. Worrying about hurting Jenny on top of that sends me straight into oblivion. No, I'm making the right decision.

But the feel of Jenny in my arms right this second? I hope I'm not wrong. What I'd give to freeze this moment and carry it forever.

My lips rest against her hair. I squeeze my eyes shut and kiss the silky, sweet-smelling strands. The looming specter of death has sharpened my appreciation for the smaller things in life while taunting me with their impending loss. "I'm sorry,"

I whisper. "What happened last night? It made things more . . . complicated."

She pulls out of my arms and wipes her eyes. "Why can't you just tell me?"

I release a breath and brush back a lock of her hair from her face, something I love to do. This isn't going to be easy. My hands drop to my sides. "Because . . . I need to . . . go. There are some things that I need to do . . . things that will require my full attention . . . without distractions."

"And I'm a distraction?" she asks softly as her lip quivers.

"The best kind, but yes," I reply just as softly.

"Why can't you just tell me?" The hopeful look in her eyes guts me.

"I can't say . . . I never could." Nothing I've told her was a lie.

Her gaze turns hard, and she spears me with an accusatory glance. "Didn't these two weeks mean anything to you? You said you didn't want this to end, either. That's what you said last night."

My chest clenches, and I ache to bridge the gap between us and touch her. But I don't. "I know what I said. These two weeks meant everything to me. It's the only reason I have the strength to move ahead and do what needs to be done."

She backs away from me and snaps, "That's it, then? Just like that? The end?"

I had known this wouldn't go well. "Come on, Jen. That's not fair. That's not what I meant. If I can work this out, I'll be back. You won't be able to keep me away," I say, this time more firmly. Yeah, if I find a new kidney and live, a whole new world of possibilities opens for me.

She shakes her head and gets to her feet. Her eyes glisten like bright-blue marbles. "I trusted you. I thought you trusted me, too."

I grind my teeth. "That's not what this is about." There's only one way out of this no-win situation, and a little piece of me dies inside as I do it. My stare turns icy. "Our time's up. It's over. You need to go. Now."

Her eyes widen and she gasps. She stands immobile for a moment and then slowly reaches around and unclasps the chain holding the diamond at her throat. She swallows and lays the necklace I gave her on the tray next to the bed.

My face drops into an expressionless mask. Behind it my breath seizes, and I fight with every fiber of my being to keep it together, preparing for her to walk out the door and out of my life. Maybe forever.

"Goodbye, Dev," she whispers and walks to the door. As she's on her way out, I hear what I think is a faint "I love you" before the door shuts behind her.

I bite my lip hard as my vision blurs. I'm powerless to stop the hot tears from burning paths down my cheeks. I sit and let them flow. If she only knew what this costs me.

Hopefully, someday she'll understand that I'm doing this because I love her, too. More than I love myself. I'm not foolish enough to believe there's a happy ending for me, but I hold out hope there's one for her.

MY FACE MAY be dry by the time Lucas shows up with John Henshaw when visiting hours are over, but I haven't fully recovered from Jenny's visit. I'm still wallowing in an ocean of self-pity.

"Devon, I'll stop back to talk about next steps when John is done," Lucas says.

"Sounds ominous," I retort, trying not to sound like a wiseass. I can't tell what I feel more: useless or frustrated. They could tell me the world is going to end, and I'm not sure I'd care right now, though I wouldn't mind getting rid of the damn catheter so that I could take a piss on my own. Or, even better, getting the hell out of here.

Lucas raises an eyebrow. He knows me well enough to

catch my tone. "See you in a bit." He tucks a chart under his arm and steps out.

John stands at the foot of the bed and shakes his head. "Nothing conclusive yet, and not sure what you consider ominous." He pulls a notepad out of his jacket. "I spent the afternoon at the Highland Regency reviewing surveillance tapes and verified the whereabouts of your uncle Gerald from the time you met Lucas in your hotel room to the time you were taken away in the ambulance. Based on what I saw, he isn't the one who poisoned you. At least not directly. I'm still working on the others — the tapes have some gaps. Interviews with the staff are still ongoing through tomorrow. We're also running down local suppliers of the chemical, and your uncle Byron's security team is checking Kingsbridge-owned labs."

I pass a hand over my face. "So where does that leave us?"

John gives me a hard stare. "Farther away than I want to be, which is why Luc and I talked about moving you someplace else. Where we can control the controllables."

"What's the matter? You think they'll try again?" I ask as a shiver rolls over me.

John presses his lips together. "I don't know." He takes a seat next to the bed and leans on his thighs. "I wanna ask you something, Devon. May I call you Devon?"

I frown. Something about his change in demeanor trips my alarms. "Sure. What do you want to know?"

"How'd your father die?"

My eyebrows pop up, and I shrug. "Heart attack. Why?"

John rubs his brow, takes a breath, and looks me straight in the eye. "Given the liberal and creative use of chemicals on you and your uncle Byron, it makes me wonder about the timing of your dad's death."

"You think . . . ?"

"Dunno, but hear me out." He wets his finger and flips through his notepad. "The terms of the inheritance in the corporate documents were changed by your father while you were undergoing treatment for testicular cancer." He looks up from his pad. "Let me ask another question?"

"Sure."

"Did you freeze any sperm before treatment?"

I gnash my teeth. "My father asked and I refused."

John narrows his eyes. "So you didn't freeze any, knowing it might be the only way you'd ever have kids?"

"Listen, back then, I had no intention of ever taking over Kingsbridge," I say, unable to contain my resentment. "I planned on pursuing a career in art. I told my father to take his company and stick it. And let's not forget I thought my number was up." I lock my arms over my chest, remembering the fight I had with my dad. It wasn't pretty. I'm convinced that's why he put the procreation stipulation in the amended document.

"So what changed your mind to take over as CEO?" John asks.

"When the Kingsbridge nursing home went bust after he died, all my mother's care landed on Lettie and me. No insurance. No financial help except very modest trust funds. I'm doing this for them. I've always done this for them," I say, clenching my jaw.

John nods and takes a note. "Since one of the suspects was your father's lover, I'm assuming she knew that, too. That you hadn't frozen any sperm."

"Safe bet." I snort and then smile with satisfaction. "But I never said I didn't freeze my sperm, only that I refused my father's request."

"Oh?" John's gaze locks on mine.

"Lettie arranged it. So, yeah, I have a few vials of frozen sperm under an assumed name. Safe and sound if I ever need them. Generally I'm not an idiot, but my sister's there to tell me when I'm being one."

"Good man." John gives me a crooked smile as he flips a page. "So your father filed the amended conditions less than three weeks before he died?"

I do the math in my head as best I can. "Sounds about right."

John rubs the side of his nose. "Would it surprise you to know he died the same day the amendment was ratified by the Kingsbridge legal team?"

Shit, I'd had no idea. "It would," I reply.

"That's what I thought." He reaches into his jacket to pull out an envelope. "I'd like permission to exhume your father's body. I think he was murdered."

Chapter 43

Jenny

"JENNY, GOOD TO see you," Dr. Graham says as she walks into her office, which is sleek and modern, and takes a seat behind her desk. In her late thirties, she's slender and attractive with long, dark hair and a nice demeanor. I can't help but smile. We've always connected well, which is why she's the only therapist I've ever seen. She opens what I assume is my file and picks up a pen. "It's been awhile."

I shrug and sink back into the small plush couch set up in front of her desk. It's the only piece of comfortable furniture in here. I'm almost sure that's by design. "Not really, only nine months." Last time I came was after Great-Aunt Vera died. "Thanks for seeing me on such short notice."

I figured I'd get all my medical needs covered this morning: first her, then Lucas.

"I'm glad I could squeeze you in." She tents her hands and gives me a pleasant smile. "How can I help?"

Great question. One I wish I could answer. I wring my hands. "Just having some slips lately."

"What kind of slips?"

"Typical stuff. Crying jags, crazy death thoughts, a few nightmares . . ."

Dr. Graham sits back in her chair. "What's changed?"

I tell her everything, starting at the airport and working my way through the breakup with Devon. "It almost feels like a death," I say, thinking about yesterday night and walking out of Devon's hospital room. The moment I left I couldn't breathe, as if all the light and oxygen had left my world. I fell into bed and woke up numb. The kind of numbness I usually feel after a funeral.

"It's obvious you love him, Jenny. And from what you've told me, I'd guess he feels the same. It sounds like he's protecting you from something."

"But I don't want to be protected," I say.

She clasps her hands, comes around to the front of the desk, and leans against the edge. "Jenny, your pattern is very simple. Your symptoms are greatest when you focus on what you can't control. You have to redirect your actions to the things you can. Does that make sense?"

I nod.

"There's no shame in letting go and feeling out of control. Whenever we take chances, the consequences and the outcomes are not always the ones we desire, but that doesn't mean we shouldn't take them. The question you need to ask yourself is, 'Knowing how it turned out, would you do it again?'"

I bite my lip and do my best to push back tears. "Yes," I say. "I would."

She touches my shoulder. "Then you made the right decision. A happy ending is never guaranteed."

"I know," I whisper, remembering what Lettie said about Devon's not believing in happy endings and how sad I'd found that. I'd just hoped ... stupidly... that it could be different. But maybe he's right after all.

She slaps her hands on her thighs. "So tell me the three things you're going to focus on when you leave."

Using my fingers, I count them off. "Moving back from

San Francisco, getting a new job, and my aunt Jill's wedding." Then silently I add a fourth: *And forgetting Devon.* If the Conrad Designs situation works out, maybe I'll get a roommate and move into the city. That should help.

"Good." She smiles.

"I'm going to focus on a new start and what I can control," I say with conviction, and for a second I even believe it.

WHEN I GET BACK to the house after seeing Lucas, it doesn't take me long to pack and set everything up with the movers for tomorrow. I text Russ to give him a heads-up. He doesn't reply, but my phone shows the text was delivered.

At least the scene with Devon has stopped looping continuously in my head after my visit to Dr. Graham.

I've only thought about it one more time by the time Lettie pulls into the driveway to pick me up for the airport. She's driving the Range Rover. A sharp pang hits the center of my chest, followed by the memories of Devon and me in his studio and the feel of his body our first time together. I'll miss him on more levels than one.

"Safe travels," my mom says and pulls me into a hug.

"I'll be home in a couple of days," I say and give her an extra squeeze. Tonight I'll share a hotel room with Lettie, at her insistence, though I'm not thrilled about it. Then, after I pack my stuff tomorrow, I'm staying with a friend overnight and returning home with Lettie on Wednesday afternoon.

I throw my bag in the back seat, and we head for Morristown Airport.

"Want a piece of gum?" Lettie asks, drawing my attention to her outstretched hand. Her hair is pulled back in a ponytail, and without makeup she looks like a teenager who stole her mother's car—even with the aviator sunglasses and sexy sundress.

"No, thanks," I mumble and turn away to stare out the

window. This is the first conversation we've had since I got in the car. As a matter of fact, it's our first conversation since we left Devon's hospital room last night. She drove me home, and we sat in silence the entire way. Other than confirming the pickup time for today, we didn't speak.

She pulls up by the hangar and parks.

As I reach for the door handle, she grasps my arm and clears her throat. "Listen. I know you're upset with Devon. I get it. And I'm not going to tell you it's undeserved or make excuses for him. But don't count him out yet. We're in a high-stakes game to take over this company, and we can't screw up."

I release a breath. "What does that have to do with me?"

Her hand drops away. "Nothing and everything," she whispers and shakes her head. "I've never seen my brother as happy as when he was with you. That was real."

I press my eyes shut for a second and then open them. "Then let me help. Somehow. Let me help."

Lettie nods. "I will. I promise."

As I reach for the handle a second time, she grabs me again.

"What?"

"John stopped by the house this morning with an exhumation order for my father's body. They think he was murdered."

My pulse quickens. "Oh my God, really?"

"Like I said, this is a high-stakes game," she says, fixing me with a hard stare. "So don't blame Devon for wanting to protect you, okay?"

I smile and jerk the door open. "Brava. Devon's right. You really are a master of manipulation." Shaking my head, I actually make it out of the car this time. Well played, Lettie. She succeeded. I forgave Devon just a little.

She snorts. "I'll take that as a compliment. If the two of you would ratchet down the pigheadedness just a bit, my job would be so much easier."

We grab our stuff and head to the jet.

I get to the top of the stairs first and stop short as soon as I enter the luxurious interior. Lettie crashes into me from behind.

"Hello, ladies," Phillip says, wearing a smug smile, from one of the luxury leather seats in the main cabin. The white tape is gone from his swollen nose, and the bruising under his eyes doesn't look as bad as it did on Saturday night.

"What is he doing here?" I murmur.

Lettie swings around me and gives him a predatory smile like a shark eyeing chum. "Great question. So, Phillip, to what do we owe this singular pleasure?"

He stretches his arms and laces his fingers behind his head. "Heard you were heading out west, Leticia. Figured I'd hitch a ride," he says, smiling broadly.

"You always were a freeloader, Phillip. Sure. Why not?" Lettie says and stows our bags. Rather than rows of seats, the plane has an open custom interior. In the main cabin are four pairs of first-class-type leather seats, a built-in entertainment center with a television, a bench sofa, and two areas for sleeping.

His gaze turns to me and his eyes narrow. "And why would Devon's fiancée—if she is his fiancée—be traveling with you on a business trip?"

My expression gives nothing away. Rather, I smile pleasantly at Phillip and shrug while Lettie raises her eyebrows at me before she turns to face him. I'm not sure if Lettie arrived in time to hear my little lie at the gala. Maybe, maybe not.

"I'm not the only one with business in San Francisco this week. Not that it's any of your concern, but we're planning to stay and spend an extra day shopping at Vera Wang in Union Square for a wedding dress," Lettie says without missing a beat. Sometimes I actually like her. "Maybe I should be asking you why you're here?"

He lets out a breath and looks around wide eyed. "Going to visit Nanotekx. Figured if I'm Devon's backup, I'd better get 'up to speed' as you Yanks like to say. And it just so happens that there's an emergency meeting tomorrow about the Verotechx merger. I thought it might be interesting."

"*Uh-huh.* Guess I'll see you there," Lettie says as we settle in across the aisle. "I'll be sitting in for Byron."

"So I heard," Phillip says, and then he plucks an issue of *Money* magazine from the pocket on the side of his seat.

"There is one thing I'm wondering, though," Lettie says, pressing a finger to her lip. "Why would they let a suspect in an attempted murder leave town?"

Phillip's nostrils flare, and he glares at her. "Leticia, I may be a lot of things, but a murderer is not one of them. It's no secret that I don't like our brother very much, but I most certainly would never try to kill him. If anything, I'll have legitimate means to snatch the company out from under him," he says, leaning back in his seat and regaining his composure. "As a matter of fact, I had my physical done this morning. And unlike our dear brother, I have nothing to hide."

I resist the urge to roll my eyes. Pompous jerk. For the umpteenth time since Saturday, I'm glad I'm an only child from a well-adjusted family.

A young, attractive flight attendant enters the cabin wearing a form-fitting dress featuring the company's logo. "I'm Marlene, and I'll be your hostess for the flight. Please prepare for takeoff by fastening your seat belts. Beverage service will begin once we're in the air. Thank you, and I hope you have a pleasant flight."

Long? Yes. Pleasant? Unlikely.

I'M DEEP INTO a new thriller novel, listening to Alicia Keys, when Marlene comes to take our dinner orders. Lettie and Phillip are both engrossed in whatever work they're doing on their laptops.

A few minutes after Marlene disappears into the galley, Lettie unbuckles her seat belt and taps me on the shoulder. I remove an earbud. "I'm going to get a refill on the way back from the bathroom. You want one?" She holds up her empty wineglass and points to my melting ice.

"Diet cola?" I say.

Lettie nods and heads to the front of the cabin with the empties.

"Since you're asking," Phillip yells after her, waving his glass, "I'll take another gin and tonic. Twist of lime, please."

Lettie stops and scowls at him. "Get your own . . . Oh, fuck it. Fine." She snatches his glass and slips behind the curtain.

I shake my head, replace my earbud, and turn back to my police procedural.

The hostess appears with our drinks. Before I even wonder where Lettie is, she comes back and sits down next to me. It's not until she flashes a secret smile that I suspect I may have missed something. Why am I not surprised? She has more tricks up her sleeve than magician David Blaine.

By the time Marlene has cleared our dinner plates, Phillip's snoring cuts through the cabin from across the aisle.

Lettie pops up from her seat. "You said you wanted to help? Here's your chance."

I glance at Phillip, put two and two together, and frown. "Lettie, what did you do?"

"Got creative." She grabs my hand and pulls me up. "Be the lookout. Make sure the oh-so-helpful Marlene doesn't come out here while I'm working."

"What if he wakes up?" I ask.

Lettie smirks. "Not likely. I put just enough Ambien in his food to knock him out for a couple of hours."

I plant my hands on my hips and glare at her. "What is it

with your family and pharmaceuticals?"

She waves me off and reaches for his computer. "It's just a little nap, it won't hurt him." She pulls a jump drive from her pocket and inserts it into the USB port.

"You have his password?" I ask.

She bunches her blonde brows. "Who needs a password? John convinced the Regency to let me place a little present for Phillip on their network. As long as he logged in before he and Tessa checked out this morning . . ." She pauses and keys something in. Her lips spread into a smile. "I can log in undetected as an administrator. *Annnd* . . . I'm in. Yowza!" She punches the air and smirks. "By the way. So far, you're a crappy lookout."

I give her the evil eye and station myself at the curtain. Marlene is in her seat reading a novel, from what I can see by peeking through the crack.

Fifteen minutes later, Lettie takes meticulous care in putting everything back as she found it. She fires up her computer and inserts the drive as I take my seat.

"So what did you do?" I ask.

"Copied all his files and downloaded a keystroke virus. That way, I'll be able to remotely monitor his PC if necessary," she says matter-of-factly, staring at her screen. "And let's hope he's been up to no good."

"Remind me never to get on your bad side," I mumble. At least now I know how she found out so much about me. It must've been child's play.

She gives me a blue-eyed look of mock innocence. "You won't, as long as you never hurt my brother . . ."

I shake my head. Like I'll ever get the chance. Guess I'm safe.

Chapter 44

Devon

THE MOMENT I walk through my front door, I feel like a prisoner under house arrest and tagged with an electronic ankle bracelet. Except mine is a portable dialysis machine, and I'm not wearing it around my ankle.

"I'll let you know what we find out after the coroner has a look at the body and runs some tests," John says, referring to my father's remains, which are being exhumed as we speak.

He doesn't follow me inside. Instead he points to the big burly guy holding my overnight bag in one hand and my medical equipment in the other. "Just tell Curt where you want this stuff. I'll have four men posted here at all times: one inside, one at the gate, one around back, and one outside your mother's suite."

I nod and scratch my forehead. "Thanks." I glance at Curt. "Up the stairs, second room on the right." He walks past me and keeps moving.

John removes a folded piece of paper from his jacket. "We have the list of approved visitors, which includes all of your mother's health-care workers. Let us know if there's anyone we need to add." He shifts on his feet for a second as if to leave. Then he opens his mouth to say something, blows out a breath, and looks me in the eye. "May I ask you something?"

Folding my arms over my chest, I lean against the jamb. "Ha! I'm not sure I could stop you. Though coming from you? That question precedes something either sensitive or shocking. Which is it this time, so I can prepare myself?"

John nods and gives me a crooked grin that transforms his rugged face into one that almost looks friendly. "Observant. Probably sensitive . . ."

"Go for it." I brace myself.

He locks eyes with me and asks quietly, "Why isn't Jenny Lynch on this list?"

Something inside me deflates. I release a breath and rub a hand across my chin. John's a friend of Jenny's family and a no-bullshit kind of guy. Given what he's done for me already, I decide to tell him the truth and hope like hell he follows the code of honor among men and keeps my secret. Before I can change my mind, I force the words from my mouth. "Because . . . I love her, and don't want her involved in this mess . . . And because . . ." I sigh and press on, feeling exposed. "I'm sicker than she thinks. I can barely take care of myself right now, much less her. What I can promise? If I make it out of all of this alive, with a future, I'll tell her everything. That's the truth . . . But for now I kindly request that you keep that between us."

John nods and we shake on it. "You have my word." There's a new glimmer of respect in his eyes.

"Thanks."

"She's good people, Jenny."

"No doubt." A pang of regret hits my chest. Regardless of my decision, I still can't help wishing I, not Lettie, were taking her back to San Francisco. I wish that I could've made a better exit.

"Get some rest before Luc comes." He claps me on the shoulder. "We still have a long road ahead of us."

"Do you think this will work?" I ask about the plan we

hatched to flush out my would-be killer.

John's mouth flattens into a grim line. "I'm not sure, kid. But I'd say the chances are good." He points to my chest and the microsurveillance device hidden underneath my shirt. "Keep that turned on." Developed by John's Fed friends, complete with an embedded GPS and a voice-activated recorder, the device is connected to the strap holding the Holter heart monitor I agreed to wear for Lucas. Kind of a two-for-one deal. Modern technology at its finest.

I give him a wry smile. "Even in the bathroom?"

He gives me a hard look. "Even then."

I snort. "Great." It won't be the first time I've had to sacrifice my dignity.

After I close the door, I'm hit by a wave of exhaustion. Lucas would've liked to keep me another day at Memorial. He agreed to John's plan under duress and only with the agreement that I wear the monitor and follow his long list of rules: plenty of rest, take my meds, eat the meals sent over by his nutritionist, yada yada yada. But a nap will have to wait—there are a few things I need to do first.

MY MOM IS watching her afternoon shows, when I walk in. Her eyes light up, and she presses the button to turn down the sound. I break into a smile, glad to see her, too. She holds out her good arm and beckons me over. A look of relief grips the half of her face that works.

As soon as I'm within reach, she sinks her fingers into my upper arm, and I let her pull me into her chest. Guttural sounds rise from her throat, and a teardrop hits my hair, soaking through to my scalp.

"I'm all right, Mom. Really." I pull away and sit facing her on the bed.

She draws an angry X over her chest and frowns.

"I know. I almost died. But I'm alive, and I plan to stay that way. Lettie told you about the added security, right?" Too bad I don't feel nearly as confident as I sound. All the guards on the planet couldn't protect me from what I'm afraid of.

She blinks yes and wipes her eyes with the back of her good hand. Then she points to my middle and shakes her finger from side to side.

"Yeah. Lucas is working on getting me a kidney," I say. "But Lettie already told you that, too, didn't she? And she told you I'm on dialysis until I get one?"

Lucas agreed that I could do it overnight while I slept. On the days I need it, he'll stop by to set up the machine before I go to bed and come in the morning to disconnect it.

She pauses and then blinks once. Yes, Lettie already told her. Why am I not surprised? My sister conveys news faster than TMZ.

I glance at my watch. "I have a delivery coming, but I'll come back later with a surprise. I just wanted you to know that I was home."

Half her face rises in a smile, and she fists her heart.

"I love you, too," I say and leave her with a kiss on the cheek.

DING-DONG.

Curt taps his earpiece outside my bedroom door as I return from the west wing. "Checkpoint verified your visitor. Want me to get it?"

"Nope. I got it. Can you duck out of sight somewhere?" I ask as I stride past him on my way to the stairs, feeling like a prisoner again.

I pass the library, which doubles as my home office, giving it a sour look on my way to answer the doorbell. At least all the prep for Nanotekx will serve Lettie well and wasn't for nothing.

A quick check through the peephole confirms my visitor

before I swing the door open. My friend James is waiting outside with a large draped canvas.

"Good to see you, man. I appreciate this," I say and give him a fist bump.

James grins and tucks a shaggy clump of dark hair behind his ear. He's tall and on the gangly side but looks well. We did our treatments together, and he's been in remission as long as I have. "You kidding me? You made me an offer I couldn't refuse. I have the other two canvases, your easel, and a box with all your supplies in the van." He slides the painting inside, then turns to go get more.

"Wait. I'll give you a hand," I say and follow him out before Curt can step in and stop me. I grab the unfinished paintings from the back of the van, and James gets the box.

"I'll leave the easel on my way out," he says.

"Cool. Follow me," I say, leading the way back inside and up to my room, where I plan to set up. If I'm careful, I shouldn't wreck the place.

"Hey, we miss you at the studio. Am I to assume, based on this delivery, you won't be back for a while?" James asks.

"I'm housebound for a few weeks," I say.

He comes to a halt at the top of the stairs. "You sick again, man? Is the cancer back?"

"Nah, nothing like that. More of a security issue than anything else. Work related. Crackpot threats," I say, providing an acceptable half truth.

"Shit. That sucks," he replies, and we continue on our way. "So . . . uh. . . who's the girl?"

"What?"

"In the painting. Who's the girl? We've been speculating since she showed up on your easel last Saturday," he says, following me into the bedroom.

I shrug and lie. "Just a friend." I prop up the canvases against the wall.

James sets down the box next to them. "She's pretty hot.

The painting … it's good. Think any more about entering a piece in the SOLO show for next spring?"

I look at him blankly. "Huh?" A vague memory of our discussing it comes to mind—PJ—pre-Jenny. To say I haven't given it any further thought is an understatement. It's a juried show for independent artists and would give me a chance at international exposure. Before I was diagnosed, I would've jumped at the chance—without a doubt. But now my life doesn't have any room for that part of me. The part that makes me happiest. Besides, I might not live long enough to see my work exhibited. The thought wrenches my guts.

He looks at me as if I had two heads. "The SOLO show, man. The one the rest of us have been preparing for since winter?"

I shrug again. In truth, I was so wrapped up in Kingsbridge that I didn't pay much attention to or care about what anyone else was doing.

James claps me on the shoulder. "That painting of the girl? You should enter it. She's shaping up to be something pretty special."

I swallow and nod. "I'll think about it. What do you say we grab the easel?" James means well, but I just want to be alone and lose myself in my work—the kind I actually love. My fingers itch to hold a brush.

James retrieves the easel and leans it by the front door.

I dig three hundred-dollar bills out of my front pocket and hand them over. "Thanks, man," I say. "Tell everyone I said hello."

He pockets the money and grins. "Will do. Take care. I'll see you when I see you." He stops halfway down the path. "I'm serious about that painting."

With a final wave, I shut the door and breathe a sigh of relief.

"Let me get those." I flinch at Curt's voice behind me.

He lifts the easel in one hand and the covered canvas of

Jenny in the other. "Dr. Wilson doesn't want you straining yourself. You should've let me carry the other stuff, too," he says. We're about the same age, but he's built like Lettie's Howard. Linebacker strong.

I open my mouth to argue but think better of it. The last thing I want is Lucas chewing my ass out for not following his damn rules. Plus I'm starting to feel shitty again. Like I'm slogging through mud.

We make our way upstairs, and I close my door once he's gone. My hands tremble with excitement, anxious to unveil the unfinished picture of Jenny. But if I do that, I'll get distracted and won't be able to put the finishing touches on my mom's birthday present. An oil painting inspired by Georgia O'Keeffe, her favorite artist. Thirty minutes of my time is all it really needs. It's not lost on me that I'd nearly forgotten about it and wouldn't have had this opportunity if I'd gone to San Francisco.

I set up my station with the abstract pastel oil and prepare my paints. I finish my mom's present, all the while aware of the draped canvas next to me. By the time I've cleaned up and set the painting to dry in the corner of the room, my hands tremble with anticipation. I undrape Jenny's painting and suck in a breath. James is right. It's good, and not just because it's Jenny.

A pang of desire hits me as my eyes settle on the curve of her neck. Memories of our afternoon in my studio come rushing back. Mr. Happy inappropriately stirs in response. Quite frankly, I didn't think he had it in him. Nice to know that nothing can keep a good man down. The alarm on my phone shatters my reverie and any stray amorous thoughts.

Damn it. Time for meds. I cover the painting and move it to a safer location, leaning it against the far wall.

I head into my bathroom and spot the extra toothbrush on the sink. Jenny's toothbrush. She must've left it here the night of the gala. Without warning the pain of the loss crushes me, and I grip the sink with both hands.

Not for the first time, I feel as if I can't breathe without her.

"Mr. Soames?"

I spin around and glare at Curt. "You have to stop sneaking up on me like that, man."

"Sorry," he says. "There's someone at the gate who wants to see you. Someone not on the list."

"Who is it?" I ask, totally at a loss.

"A woman."

I stare at him, palms in the air. "Um . . . Can you be a little more specific? Does she have a name?"

He shifts on his feet, looking uncomfortable. "It's Tessa Morgan."

My heartbeat accelerates for more reasons than I can list. Most of them bad. I grit my teeth. "Let her in." Curt ducks out.

I say loud enough for John to hear me, "This could be our chance."

Chapter 45

Jenny

IT'S EIGHT O'CLOCK by the time we crack open the hotel room door at the InterContinental. Why am I not surprised we're staying in SoMa—South of Market—at one of the nicest hotels in town? Oh, yeah, because I'm staying with a crazy-rich person; heavy emphasis on *crazy*.

"I'm exhausted," I say, relieved there are two queen-size beds in the room and that I won't have to share a bed with Lettie. The time change always crushes me on the first night when I come west.

Lettie moves past me with her bags. "Hope you don't mind, but I have some work to do."

I shake my head. "I still don't get why you wouldn't look at Phillip's files while we were on the plane. God knows you knocked him out for long enough."

She unzips her suitcase in front of the closet and grabs a hanger. "Because I'm not sure I could've restrained myself from strangling him in his sleep if I found something inflammatory. Trust me, it was enough just to take a quick look and confirm the transfer worked."

I grin. "I thought he was going to have a cow when he woke up."

We lock eyes and break into laughter.

Phillip's snoring comes to a shuddering halt. He mumbles something and sits up. Out of the corner of my eye, I see him wipe the drool from his mouth and take in his surroundings as I flip a page in my book and pretend to read. Lettie feigns sleep in the seat next me. The moment he stirred, she closed her laptop and winked at me.

He looks over at us. I'm sitting on the aisle, my body partially blocking Lettie from view. Ignoring him, I feel the heat of his gaze practically burn a hole in my cheek. Then he mumbles something else and reaches for his laptop.

I bite my lip and wait. It takes somewhere in the neighborhood of three seconds before he notices our prank and screams, "Fucking hell! Leticiaaaa!"

He's out of his seat and looming over us, his face in full flush within the space of a heartbeat. "You miserable bitches," he seethes. "How do I get this off?" He waves his hands at us with his fingers splayed apart. Fire-engine-red polish gleams on each of his nails.

Lettie pretends to wipe sleep from her eyes and glances at his hands. "I'd stay out of the Castro if I were you," she says, naming a popular gay section of San Francisco.

He grits his teeth and shoves his hands in her face. "How. Do. I. Get. This. Off?"

She bats his hands away and scowls. "You can get a two-dollar bottle of polish remover at any drugstore, loser. San Francisco is filled with them. Personally, I think you should wear it. You might get lucky."

Phillip's eyes bulge, and his face takes on a shade of red between cherry and crimson. It goes nicely with his new nails. He opens his mouth to say something . . .

"Is there a problem?" Marlene asks, wearing a look of alarm as she walks swiftly toward us.

Phillip snarls at Lettie and gives her a murderous glare as he jams his hands in his pockets. "Everything's fine," he says to

Marlene, and then he glowers at us one more time.

I'm glad there are no sharp objects within reach.

He returns to his seat, cursing under his breath.

Lettie wrinkles her nose and pulls me close enough to whisper in my ear. "I think we should've gone with the hot pink."

Lettie wipes her eyes as we finish laughing and hangs a suit in the hotel closet. "It was enough of a distraction to keep him from suspecting that I hacked into his laptop. Then again, he usually underestimates me . . . the conceited fool."

I hate to admit it, but I had some fun moments on the flight with Lettie—except for the times I'd randomly catch a glimpse of her resemblance to Devon and my chest would tighten. Turns out they share the same dimpled smile and slightly pointy chin.

I point to the bed by the window since it's farthest from the desk area. "Okay if I take that one?"

"Sure," she says and continues to unpack. I'm only staying tonight, so there's no reason for me to do the same. I pluck out my toiletry bag and a long Victoria's Secret nightshirt.

"I'm going to get some room service. You hungry?" Lettie asks.

"Nope. I'm good," I say, wanting nothing more than to clean my teeth and have my head hit the pillow.

"Mind if I call Devon?" she asks.

I snatch my stuff and head for the bathroom. "Go ahead." I get that feeling of freezing to death in the cold while everyone I know is sitting inside around a warm fire. I pull the bathroom door shut behind me and turn on the faucet.

There's silence on the other side of the door by the time I'm finished. I open it a crack. Lettie's typing away on her computer.

"Hey," she says, still staring at her screen. "Weird. His phone is going to voice mail."

I shrug. "Maybe he's asleep. It's way past eleven back home."

There's a knock at the door. Lettie pops up to get it. A guy wearing a uniform rolls into the room a cart with a silver dome on top, a bottle of white wine, and two glasses.

"Expecting company?" I ask after the waiter is gone.

She wiggles her eyebrows and removes the dome; there's a pizza underneath. "I'm hoping to change your mind. Besides, I don't like drinking alone." She breaks into a pout that makes her look about sixteen. I can see where that might work on a guy.

I chuckle and shake my head. "You're a piece of work, you know that?"

"No argument there. Pull up a chair," she says, opening the bottle of wine. She pours two glasses and dishes out a couple of slices of pizza.

I sit next to her.

"Toast?" She holds up her glass.

Is she serious? The last thing I feel like doing is toasting anything. Begrudgingly I lift mine. "What are we toasting to?"

"Girl power ... and happier tomorrows," she says and taps my glass. There's that look of Soames sadness at the outer corners of her eyes. Another glimpse of her resemblance to Devon. This time it hits me harder, like a punch in the face.

I bite my lip and curse the tears gathering in my eyes. I chug the wine without thinking about it, put the glass down, and push out of the chair. "I'm going to go to bed," I say softly.

Lettie grabs my arm. "I'm sorry. I didn't mean to upset you." There's a look of vulnerability in her eyes that I'm not used to seeing. A loneliness that unexpectedly touches me. Then I realize I'm as much of a substitute for Devon to her as she is for me. He is our link. Whatever is going on with him, it's affecting her, too. If there's one thing I understand about Devon's family, it's that his bond with Lettie is deep. They make each other stronger, and there's nothing one wouldn't do for the other. Maybe it's a twin thing, or maybe it's just out of necessity.

"You didn't," I say. "I'm just tired." Before I think too deeply, I reach down and hug her. As much as I tease my mom about all her hugging, the truth is that my family is a pretty physical bunch.

Lettie's shoulders feel fragile inside my arms. I've forgotten how small she is since her personality takes up at least twice as much space. The tension eases from her shoulders, and she hugs me back. I say, "Thanks for bringing me here. I know this has been hard on you, too."

"Don't give up on him," she whispers.

A tear breaks free and rolls down my cheek. I can't speak. Instead I give her another squeeze and then head over to the bed.

"HOLY SHIT! WAKE up." Lettie shakes me the rest of the way into consciousness.

My head feels like someone stuffed it with cotton. "What?" I mumble, looking at her through half-cracked eyelids. I glance at the clock next to the bed. It's 2:15 a.m.

"I've got to show you this . . ."

"Huh?" I mumble without lifting my cheek from the pillow.

Lettie grabs my arm and pulls me upright. "Come on, Jenny. I mean it. Wake up!" Her face is flushed, and there's a look of wild excitement in her eyes. She changed into pajamas at some point while I was sleeping.

I let her drag me over to the desk. The computer screen is the only light in the room besides the twinkling lights of the city shining through the sheer drapes.

A collection of empty beverage containers crowds the space next to her laptop. She picks up a can of Red Bull, takes a sip, and then unleashes her fingers on the keyboard.

I yawn. "What did you find that's so important?"

She shakes her head. "More incriminating evidence than you could shake a stick at."

"Do tell," I say, stifling a second yawn with the back of my hand.

Lettie shoves her Red Bull over to me. "Drink."

"You're the bossiest person I've ever met." I take a large swallow.

"Thanks," she says.

I roll my eyes and put the can down. "It wasn't a compliment."

She ignores me, and her gaze stays glued to the screen as she pulls up a document. "Devon was right. Phillip has a copy of his medical records. The old ones before Lucas started filing them under an assumed name."

A caffeine rush hits my bloodstream and my brain snaps awake. This is why I try not to drink coffee at night. "Why would he keep his records under an assumed name?"

Lettie waves her hand. "A long story and not important to this discussion . . . But I suspect that's why Drusilla thought she had a leg to stand on petitioning the board. This also explains Phillip's sudden engagement to that gold-digging bitch Tessa. And third, I'm assuming your little white engagement lie was why Phillip egged on Devon at the gala."

"What? None of what you just said made any sense to me," I say.

Lettie frowns at me. "You're a terrible Dr. Watson to my Sherlock Holmes. Step up your game, sister."

I shrug and look to the heavens.

Lettie takes an exasperated breath and points to the screen. "Let's try this again . . . There are two germane pieces of information in Devon's medical records. First, his fertility was compromised after he completed treatment. In the new bylaws, if he can't produce an heir, the company could pass to

Phillip as long as he could prove he's fertile. Second, Devon suffered kidney damage as a result of his cancer treatment. Anyone who knew that would also know that the poison put in Devon's drink would 'out' his condition, or worse, kill him." Lettie clutches my arm, and her expression softens. "You probably saved his life that night by telling Lucas that he slurred . . . I won't ever forget that."

My lips part as I take in a breath. The night of the gala is such a blur in my head. I never stopped to think that something I did was of value.

"So . . . you think Phillip was the one who poisoned . . . ?" I ask.

Lettie shakes her head. "Not certain. It still could be any one of those four lunatics. Having access to this document isn't conclusive. But I think your little lie cleared up questions around Devon's fertility, and it may have forced someone's hand."

"Are you going to give this to John?"

"Eventually. What I found next is even better," she says and hands me the Red Bull. "Have some more. You'll need it for this one . . . On second thought . . ." She takes the can out of my hand and goes to the refrigerator. She pulls out a small bottle of liquor and mixes it in a glass with the Red Bull, then hands me the glass.

"Drink up. I'm not kidding, you're going to need this," she says, taking a seat. "Before we left, I found out that our uncle Gerald bought a large stake in Verotechx while it was public. The company bought back all the shares and took it private. Very unusual. Meanwhile, Kingsbridge funds the majority of Nanotekx. Can you say *conflict of interest*?"

I didn't grow up with parents who are finance professionals and not pick up a thing or two. "I'm following, go on." I put down the drink, not needing it yet.

"A few things. Phillip is running a shell company with his mother and Gerald named as partners. There are a ton of trades that terminate into their account in the Cayman Islands. I need a little more time to analyze the activity and companies involved to get the full story. But I've found enough other illegal activity to bury them all without that or a pesky murder charge." Lettie wiggles her brows and points to my glass. "Get ready to drink that."

I eye the glass and frown. "I'll wait."

She cracks her knuckles, then starts to type. "Have it your way. A little background before we start. Nanotekx is thinking of acquiring Verotechx with their next round of funding so that they can go head-to-head with the next-largest competitor, who happens to be publicly held. Theoretically, this move could solidify Nanotekx's market leadership in wearable technology. We already know Gerald is a major investor in Verotechx and wants to see Nanotekx go down in flames. That alone helped me untangle this web of crap on Phillip's hard drive."

"I'm assuming the meeting tomorrow is about the acquisition? Devon didn't seem in favor of doing this yet, based on the discussion he had with the board at the gala," I say.

She gives me a smug smile. "Correct. And he would've been right to wait ... because by the time the purchase happened, Verotechx would've been worthless."

"How so?"

Lettie pulls a slew of documents up on her screen so that they appear side by side. "It appears as if the Verotechx technology that Nanotekx wants to acquire them for is being secretly siphoned off to a Nanotekx project manager, who in turn is passing it along to the competitor. The competitor is filing the patents prior to Verotechx."

My eyebrows pop up. "Corporate espionage?"

"That and much more, sista."

"But how does draining Verotechx help Gerald and Phillip?" I ask.

Lettie laughs. "Think about it. If Kingsbridge approves the Nanotekx-Verotechx deal, Gerald collects a nice return on his investment before they find out what's going on. And to sweeten the pot? Phillip's company in the Caymans? They have a huge margin trade pending based on the competitor's stock rising. So when the truth comes out, they're all sitting pretty. Still, last I heard, that's called insider trading. So, between those two little ditties, I think I have Phillip by the short and curlies." Lettie tents her hands and leans in. "That said, I need your help."

I gape. "My help? What could I possibly do to help?"

Lettie takes a deep breath and meets my gaze. "You can help me save Devon's life."

A tingle travels along my scalp. I'm not sure if it's the Red Bull or the chill that just passed over me. "What do you mean?"

She swallows and looks away. "Phillip has something Devon desperately needs, and I need him to agree to give it to me before we breathe a word of what I just told you to anyone."

My mouth dries out, and I clench my hands into fists until my nails bite into my palms. "Lettie . . . what does Phillip have?"

She rubs her eyes, and when her hands fall away there's a look of weariness that cuts deep into the skin under her eyes. "A kidney, Jenny. Devon needs a kidney to live . . . and he needs it soon."

"What?" I whisper as my brain tries to process Lettie's words. Then it all makes sense. Devon thinks he's going to die . . . That's what he didn't want me to know . . . That's what he has to do alone.

The breath leaves my body and I slump forward, dropping my face into my hands. I choke back the bile rising in my throat as my pulse thrums against my eardrums. Feelings of helplessness threaten to pull me under, followed by the familiar bitter guilt because I'm responsible for another person I love being taken from me. My curse coming back to haunt me one more time. I rock back and forth in the chair, sitting on the edge of panic with my heart pounding in a relentless staccato rhythm against my ribs.

Breathe in, breathe out.

Lettie shakes me. "Jenny?" She shakes me again, this time with more vigor. "Jenny!"

Just when I think I'm going to spiral downward into the place of darkness, I feel something change inside me. Dr. Graham said to focus on what I can control. *Focus on what you can control . . . focus. . . focus. . . focus.* I repeat my new mantra a few more times until I'm able to speak.

"I'm fine," I whisper. Then something strikes me. "Why can't you give him one of your kidneys?"

She sighs and looks at her hands. "For some reason, I carry too many rejection markers. Devon's chances are best with family—just not me. Like it or not, Phillip is our only other sibling."

The weight of the situation settles in a knotted mass in the pit of my stomach. But maybe, for once, I can actually save someone's life rather than watch it slip through my fingers. Then the mass begins to unknot, and I know with sudden clarity that this could be my chance to find some redemption. "How can I help?"

Lettie's hand quivers as she holds out the forgotten glass of Red Bull mixed with some unknown alcohol. "It's time to drink this," she says. There's a look of kindness in her eyes.

I decide to trust her and drain the contents of the glass in two giant gulps to avoid tasting it.

She chews the inside of her cheek. "The project manager at Nanotekx?"

My stomach drops to my knees. "It's Russ, isn't it?"

She nods. "We need him to help us blackmail Phillip."

Chapter 46

Devon

"STAY OUT OF sight," I tell Curt and head to answer the doorbell for the second time today. My heart pounds and I break into a sweat as I reach for the handle. I curse the small piece of my soul that hopes Tessa is here because in her heart she still cares.

Taking a deep breath, I feign a look of disinterest and open the door. I'm not a half-bad actor when I put my mind to it.

"Hullo, Devon," she says softly, looking shy and self-conscious. Like the day we met when I was eighteen. The iciness from the gala is gone from her voice, replaced with warmth and silk. For a split second, I forget how long it's been since she said goodbye.

It takes me a moment to speak. Tessa's hair is up, the way I always liked it, and she's dressed casually in jeans and a top that clings to her curves. She stands twirling a loose tendril of hair around her finger, a nervous habit I used to find endearing.

I swallow, trying to get rid of the sudden dryness in my throat. "What are you doing here?" My tone is less biting than I intend.

"May I come in?" she asks, wearing a demure smile.

I hesitate and then step aside for her to pass. The hallway feels smaller as the door shuts behind her, but maybe that's just an effect of my shallow breathing. It feels weird having her in my home and out of context. As if she's stepped out of one of my lives and into another. It's only now, seeing her again, that I realize how far I've traveled.

"Devon . . . I've wanted to come ever since I heard what happened at the gala," she says, her brow furrowing. "But I figured it was best to wait until Phillip left town."

I eye her with renewed suspicion and lock my arms across my chest. "Why do you care?" As much as I'd like to think she's had a change of heart about my welfare, I don't buy it. "Help me out here. You made it clear you wanted no part of me and my illness four years ago. Yet now—when I'm almost due to inherit—you care about what happens to me? I'm sorry, why are you here?"

A tear appears in her eye and falls. She brushes it away. "I deserved that. There's a lot that happened back then that you didn't know about, Devon. A lot of things . . ." She trails off and hangs her head.

I wish I could believe it was all a mistake. A bad dream. Part of me wishes she could tell me something that would allow me to forgive her just a bit. The other part of me is way past that. She chose my half brother over me, and that can never be forgiven for any reason.

"Like what?" I press my lips together, glad she can't hear my heart's hammering rhythm.

She looks around the entry hall. "Can we sit and talk somewhere?"

I point to the living room on the left. It has the perfect level of cool formality and lack of personal warmth. When I was young, before Mom was disabled, she used to say you could tell how much she liked someone by how far they made it into our house.

I take one of the wing chairs near the grand piano, forcing

Tessa onto the sofa by herself. She perches on the edge.

"For the last time, why are you here?" I ask over my tented hands.

"It's just … I couldn't let you marry that girl without knowing …" She hunches over and stares at her hands. I realize that she's not wearing her engagement ring.

"Without knowing what?" I ask, holding my breath.

"That day you came back from the oncologist's office with the final diagnosis … ?"

My jaw tightens and I frown. "You mean the day you told me you weren't like me? The type of person I could count on when shit got bad? That I should grow up and stop expecting the best from people, and that I should face the fact I might die and that you had no desire to be there to watch? Or when you told me you didn't want to be with someone who may never be able to have children or normal sex again? You mean that day?" I bite out, clamping the arms of the chair so hard my knuckles turn white.

Sniffling, she nods and blots under her eyes with a tissue she retrieved from her purse. "I'd been in the hospital that morning as a patient."

My fingers turn cold as a sense of foreboding grips me hard.

"I had a miscarriage …"

My eyes press shut for a second as I absorb the news like a blow to the ribs.

"I didn't even know I was pregnant. I was afraid to tell you after our fight … so I called Phillip," she says, wringing her hands.

A wave of dizziness passes over me. I lock my jaw in place so it doesn't drop open. "You're only telling me this now?" I grind out.

"I couldn't manage it all then," she says, wincing and rubbing her arms. "And then it was too late."

As staggering as her story is, her actions tell me everything

I need to know and reignite my feelings of betrayal. "So rather than calling me about a private matter between us, you called my *bastard brother*?" I whisper and narrow my eyes. "Am I supposed to forgive you for lying to me? Or is it for sparing my feelings?" An ache develops in the center of my chest despite my only half believing her.

She stays silent as I glare at her.

With a mirthless laugh, I say, "You were right about one thing, Tessa. Thanks to you I did grow up, and I see the world more clearly. What we had ..." I shake my head. "Wasn't enough, wasn't real. Me saving you from your troubled past? I couldn't fix you, and I never should've tried. But a woman like Jenny? What we have? Now that's real."

As I say the words, I feel the closure I've needed taking root. A shift occurs inside me as a door closes on that painful part of my life, and a new door opens. I discover I don't want to live whatever time I have left alone ... without Jenny.

Tessa's eyes widen and her lips part as shock replaces her sorrow. "But—"

"Thank you, though, for helping me put our past to rest." I rise out of the chair, feeling renewed. "It's time for you to leave."

"Devon ..." The forlorn look on her face is Oscar-worthy.

I hold up a hand and shake my head. "Don't."

She nods and dabs at her eyes. "I ... uh... would you mind if I use the loo before I go?"

I hesitate, wanting to refuse and be rid of her, but instead allow manners to dictate. "Second door on the right, next to the stairs." I sink back down onto the cushion.

She pushes up onto shaky legs and fumbles with her purse, avoiding my gaze. "I'll be right back." She disappears through the doorway.

Five minutes pass before I'm up and out of my chair, wondering where she is. The hairs rise on the back of my neck as I head down the hall toward the bathroom. I knock lightly on the door. "Tessa?" The door creaks open . . . It's empty.

"Shit," I mutter under my breath and take the stairs two at a time.

My bedroom door is ajar, and Tessa's staring at my sword collection with her back to me. I fling the door the rest of the way open.

"Still a dreamer, I see," she says, emotionless.

"What are you doing in here?" I snarl.

She turns to face me. Gone is the Tessa from downstairs, and in her place stands an assassin with hard green eyes and lips twisted into a cruel line. A high-powered dart gun points straight at my chest.

My pulse jumps off the scales as my gaze flickers to the weaponry behind her.

"You'll never make it," she says with a hint of malice. "Close the door."

I chastise myself for being so naive. Just goes to show that you never really know a person. I kick the door shut with my foot and sneer at her, raising my hands for effect and projecting bravado I don't remotely feel. "A gun? Really? So you came here to kill me? You hate me that much?"

Tessa snorts and compresses her eyelids into a harsh squint. "When are you going to figure out that you were just a means to an end? Bloody annoying and tiresome with all your 'I want to be a painter' rubbish, but no, I've never hated you. I'd actually have to *care* about you in order to hate you."

As much as I don't want to admit it, her words strike a nerve. "Nice performance downstairs. That story . . . ?"

"The miscarriage? True," she says, staring down her nose at me. "But I was glad to be rid of that mistake."

Her admission twists my gut. My jaw tenses, and I tip my chin at the gun. "So you're going to shoot me and get out of here how, exactly?" I ask to keep her talking and buy some time.

She narrows her eyes and smiles. "Easily. When I run out

sobbing and screaming for an ambulance, saying that you've just collapsed. You see, what's in this dart? It's nearly undetectable. No one will question a blood clot that gets stuck in the heart. Especially in someone who just had surgery . . . or someone like your father, the old letch."

I clap slowly. "Let me guess. The ethylene glycol was your idea? Was it you who dropped it in my drink?"

"Picking the poison, yes. As for who did the deed? Not me. Drusilla. But she didn't need much convincing."

I shake my head. "Figures. But you were the one who killed my father?"

Her smile is angry and smug. "Right again."

"You're one sick bitch," I say, throwing up my hands.

"Perhaps. But one with a plan." She adjusts the gun's aim. "And you're next on the hit list, *my love*, leaving me the very wealthy wife of the next CEO."

Sweat trickles down my sides.

The door bursts open as Tessa fires. The dart hits my chest with such force I'm knocked off my feet. Curt, John, and two other officers charge into the room with their guns drawn.

Tessa screams as one of the guys tackles her to the ground and handcuffs her.

Curt stands over me, wide eyed. "You okay, Mr. Soames?"

"Yeah," I say. "What took you so damned long?" He gives me a sheepish shrug and pulls me onto my feet. The dart is embedded in the heart monitor under my shirt. I tug it out and hand it over. "Careful with that."

"Good shot," I say to Tessa as John reads her the Miranda rights.

I lift my shirt and touch the tender skin under the rectangular box, which is now fried. "That's going to leave a bruise," I mumble. Hopefully, the device captured enough of Tessa's confession.

"John, you get all that?" I ask, looking at Tessa and wearing a cocky smile.

Tessa's eyes widen.

John breaks into a broad grin. "You betcha. Nice job, Devon. And you, missy? Hope you like orange. You're going away for a nice long time."

Tessa growls at him and stamps her foot.

I shake my head and gloat. "One thing you forgot, Tessa."

"Piss off," she bites.

"That dart? They would've found the hole during the autopsy."

But my triumph is short lived. Yeah, just like that, my knees buckle underneath me and everything turns upside down before it all goes black.

Chapter 47

Jenny

THE MOVERS TOOK my last box thirty minutes ago. The apartment looks the same without my stuff since I have no intention of fighting over the crappy furniture. Russ can have it all. This place always felt more like his than mine anyway.

The only things I'm taking with me are the things I came with—my clothes, photography, and keepsakes. Well, that's not entirely true. There is one other thing I'm leaving behind: my fragile, oxygen-starved existence.

I sit, waiting, in the stark white-walled living room on an old leather club chair. It's one of a pair that Russ and I bought at a Sunday flea market back in March.

I'm checking e-mail on my phone when the key turns in the lock and Russ walks in, out of breath, his briefcase slung across his body. "Jen? What the hell's the emergency?"

His familiar halo of reddish-brown curls entering a room no longer holds any appeal. It's hard to believe that just a little over two weeks ago we were engaged. So much has happened since then that I feel five years older. I thought it would be hard seeing him again, but it's not. What was difficult to recognize before is crystal clear to me now. Just like everything else in our relationship, I was the afterthought

. . . the puzzle piece to complete his vision of coupledom after I forced his hand. There's no denying I'm just as much to blame as he is for where we are now . . . if not more.

A new distance exists between us. My heart has moved on and so has my soul. I no longer want to burst into tears at the mere mention of death. All that changed last night. The Vault of Black Doom that has snapped at my heels for years has gone silent. I feel stronger somehow, more centered. I plan on updating my résumé as soon as I get home, and I'll talk to Raine about getting an interview at Conrad. Most importantly? I'll do whatever it takes to save Devon. Because if I can save him, I know I can save myself.

I look up from my device and smile. "I wasn't the one who texted you."

His brow pinches. "Then who did?"

Lettie steps into the room still dressed in the Chanel suit she wore at the Kingsbridge meeting. She looks impressive, I'll give her that.

"Me," she says. "Might I say how lovely it was meeting you earlier today?" Her smile is cold and calculating.

She can be scary when she wants to be. In my opinion, it works for her.

Russ jumps back and his eye twitches. "How do you two know each other?"

I tap away on my phone, posting one of the photographs from my portfolio on Instagram, and chuckle at the irony. "Yeah, about that? Remember that guy in the picture with me on Instagram? It's her brother. He's my boyfriend," I say matter-of-factly, still staring at my cell. Okay, so technically Devon and are no longer dating, but I truly hope to rectify that situation once I return.

"You're sleeping with Devon Soames?" he says and gives me an incredulous stare. "The incoming CEO of Kingsbridge Industries?"

I run my tongue over my teeth and tip my chin. "Yup,

that's the one. What's the matter? Jealous?" Baiting Russ feels good, even though it shouldn't. The collapse of our relationship is as much my fault as his.

Red faced, he mutters under his breath, "Bitch."

Lettie cuts in. "As scintillating as it is discussing my brother and Jenny's sex life, I requested this meeting for a reason . . . and that's not it."

He shakes his head as if to clear it and plants his hands on his hips. "Then why *are* you here? And what does this have to do with Jenny?"

"Jenny's just along for the ride," Lettie says, then lifts an eyebrow and waves a folder in her hand. "I'm here, Russell, because you've been a very naughty boy. Lucky for you, I'm going to make you an offer you can't refuse."

Russ stares at the folder. His Adam's apple rises and falls as he swallows. "What's that?"

A new smile touches Lettie's lips. She glances at the manila file stuffed with paper and weighs it in her hand. "I'd guess about fifteen to twenty in a California penitentiary."

All the color drains from his face. "What are you talking about?"

Lettie wrinkles her nose. "All that Verotechx intellectual property you've been laundering through Nanotekx to our largest competitor? Did you think no one would find out?"

A small bead of sweat rolls down the side of Russ's face, and he shifts on his feet, looking like a scared rabbit ready to bolt.

"No way . . ." Russ blinks fast and licks his lips.

"Oh, yes way," Lettie gloats. "Do I throw you to the wolves, or do you want door number two?"

"Jen?" he pleads.

The desperation in Russ's eyes leaves me with a pang of regret, and I feel genuinely bad as I reply, "I'm sorry . . ."

His jaw tightens, and he swings his gaze to Lettie. "What's door number two?"

"A plea deal," she says.

There's a momentary pause. "What kind of plea deal?" he asks, tension riding his shoulders.

She taps the folder. "Testify against Phillip Cartwright if he doesn't agree to his deal."

Russ's cheek twitches, but he says nothing. Then he shakes his head and swears under his breath. "And if he agrees?"

"Then you both testify against the remaining players and walk away. What do you say?"

Adrenaline pumps through me as I bear witness and play along with Lettie. Regardless of how things ended with Russ, the last thing I want is for him to end up in prison. Now it all makes sense—the big bonus he talked about. Never in a million years did I think it would be from stealing corporate secrets.

He swipes a wrist across his forehead, displacing an errant curl. "Wait. What if Phillip doesn't agree?"

Lettie shrugs. "Then I guess you'll both need good lawyers."

The doorbell rings and Russ flinches.

"I'll get it," I say, popping out of the chair to answer it. "You might want to pack a bag," I yell back at Russ and swing the door open.

Wearing his Kingsbridge attire, Phillip looks almost as impressive as Lettie in a brooding, slightly-bruised-around-the-eyes kind of way. His expression darkens when he sees my bright smile there to greet him.

"You? What are you doing here?" he sputters.

I scratch my head. "Up until an hour ago, I used to live here. Come in. We're expecting you."

Phillip gives me a puzzled look and steps inside. He freezes when he spots Lettie.

"Hello, brother dear," she says, rocking her Chanel in a power stance.

Phillip's eyes dart between her and Russ as he mutters

something under his breath that sounds like "Bloody hell." Then, "What's this about?"

"A charitable donation," she says, smiling pleasantly. "Not that you have a charitable bone in your miserable body. But once I provide the proper incentive, I'm sure you'll at least consider it."

He squints at her. "You duped me into coming here to ask me for a donation? You could've just sent me an e-mail, Leticia."

She shakes her head. "It's not that kind of donation."

The doorbell rings again. This time, I'm at a loss. I glance at Lettie.

She shrugs and gives me a wide-eyed stare. "You didn't think we'd get them to the airport by ourselves, did you? Howie sent over a couple of . . . *helpers*."

"What?" Phillip spouts, looking indignant. "I'm not going anywhere with you. One plane flight was enough, thank you very much."

I let her deal with them and trek back to answer the door yet again. Two guys with no necks who look a lot like Howard stand in the hall. The only difference is that they're wearing more gold and look as if they stepped out of *The Sopranos*. I step aside to let them in. They tip their heads respectfully and crack their knuckles as they walk by.

My discussion with John after the gala comes rushing back, and suddenly this seems more dangerous than it did before.

Lettie is pacing when I return while Phillip and Russ look jumpier than when I left. The no-neck brothers station themselves next to the wall and stay silent. "As I was saying, Phillip . . . about that donation." Lettie hands him a sheet from the folder.

Phillip's lips move as he reads, and then his eyes bulge. "Are you *mad*? I'm not giving Devon a kidney!"

She taps a finger to her lip. "You might want to reconsider.

Especially since I've found ample evidence tracing your company in the Cayman Islands to some very shady deals that both the SEC and the FBI might just be interested in." Lettie glances at Russ. "He gets a plea deal if he testifies against you."

Phillip blanches and wavers on his feet. "What are you talking about?"

She shakes her head and tsks. "Since I'm in a generous mood, I'll give you the same deal if you sign that paper . . ."

Phillip recovers his composure and snarls. "You've got nothing."

With a raised brow and pitying smile, Lettie recites the number of his Cayman bank account.

Phillip opens his mouth, then snaps it shut a moment later. "Give me a bloody pen," he grits.

Nice. Lettie was right about him. He'd sell out his own mother.

Lettie hands him the Montblanc she had ready on the coffee table and claps her hands with delight. "Fabulous! Let's get going, shall we? We have a surgery to make . . ." Then she glances at the no-neck brothers. "Escort these gentlemen down to the car, please?"

"Wait. I can't pack?" Russ sulks.

"Bruno, take Russell to pack a bag?" Lettie says. One of the thugs peels away to follow Russ into the bedroom as the other escorts Phillip out.

"Who are these guys?" I whisper.

"Howie's cousins." She giggles and covers her mouth. "They're actors. Good, aren't they? They drove up from LA for the gig."

I breathe a sigh of relief and work up the courage to ask the one question that's been bothering me all day. "Are you sure Phillip is a match?"

She clucks her tongue. "O ye of little faith. I asked Uncle Byron to order the test. He confirmed Phillip's suitability this morning."

A second wave of relief hits me as Russ trudges past, followed by the *Sopranos* look-alike.

"I'll lock up," I say. He shoots me a glare that I return with a sweet smile before he passes over the threshold. "Don't worry. I'll give you back my key when we're in the car," I shout after him.

"Hey, I'm sorry we have to go back early," Lettie says as I grab my purse.

"Are you kidding me? We have a life to save." I grin and clasp her shoulder, pleased that we've made it this far. With a little planning, I had time to tie up all my loose ends before the movers came.

I take one last glance around the apartment and silently say goodbye to this chapter of my life.

Lettie's cell rings in her purse. She fishes it out as I lock up.

"What?" She goes pale next to me. "What do you mean he's in surgery?"

My stomach clenches as panic rises up to grab me by the throat. I stare at Lettie's pained expression and hold my breath.

"We're on our way. Yes, Phillip's with us." Lettie checks her watch. "We'll be there by five a.m. Thanks for letting me know."

Lettie grabs my hand and her voice comes out breathless. "That was Byron. It's Devon. We have to get home."

I squeeze her hand in mine, and we run to the elevator. We don't let each other go until we're in the car. I say a prayer for Devon and barely breathe for the next seven hours until we get home.

The one saving grace? This time, Lettie and I have each other.

Chapter 48

Devon

"WE HAVE TO stop meeting like this," I say, as Lucas's face comes into focus and my eyes adjust to the artificial overhead light. He looks tired, but he's wearing a smile. I take that as a good sign. A heart monitor beeps in a soft rhythm close by. It doesn't take a genius to figure out that I'm back in the hospital.

"You're one lucky guy," Lucas says, resting his hand on my shoulder and giving it a brief squeeze.

My mouth tastes like tin. "What happened this time? The last thing I remember is collapsing."

His grin grows wider. "Which do you want first? The good news or the bad news?"

I croak out a chuckle. "You suck, man. For once, can't you give me only good news?"

"The bad is minor compared to the good. You might want that first," he says.

I roll my eyes and brace myself. "Hit me with it."

"How do you feel about scars?" he asks.

"Just one more for the collection," I reply. Assuming he doesn't mean the emotional ones, I take a mental inventory of the physical ones I've already acquired: from an appendectomy, getting clocked on the head with an oar during crew practice, a mishap with one of my swords, and let's not forget the tiny knotted scar on an intimate part of my anatomy. Granted, you'd have to be feeling around for the last one to find it.

He nods. "Well, you have a new one on your chest. Small, about three inches, won't be too noticeable."

"Is that why I feel like an elephant is parked on top of me?"

"Probably. You should feel better in a couple of days. Turns out you had a small heart valve defect. A little microsurgery and you're as good as new. I missed it on the scan for the pericardiocentesis due to fluid obscuring the image. You'll have to take it easy for a while." He sits on the edge of the bed and raises his eyebrows. "Want the good news now?"

I try not to wish for anything too big for fear of disappointment. "Shit, after that, I could use some. Go for it."

"You have a new kidney."

A thrill shoots through me, but I'm quick to tamp it down. "You found one?"

Lucas pats my arm. "More than found one. It's already inside you and doing its job. So make that *two* new scars for your collection."

The heart monitor picks up steam. "Are you freaking serious?"

He tilts his head toward the wheelchair. "You up for meeting the donor for a few minutes?"

I hesitate and pass my fingers over my lips. "Will that be weird?" I'm flooded with gratitude, but the idea makes the skin on my arms prickle with discomfort. Besides that, I feel a little like dog meat, even though the painkillers seem to be doing their job.

"Some people you love went through a lot of trouble to make this happen," Lucas says softly. "I think it would mean a lot to both of you."

I nod. "Okay." I'm not entirely sure what he means, but who could say no to that?

The move to the wheelchair is less than pleasant, but once I'm sitting in it and all the stuff tethered to me is in place, I'm good. "Lettie should be here soon," he says as he wheels me down the hall. "She'll fill you in when she gets here."

Part of me is afraid to hear what she has to say. I just hope she didn't do something illegal or immoral to secure me an organ.

He stops in front of a door halfway down the corridor and opens it with his back. We reverse inside and do a one-eighty. I'm facing a white curtain. "Lucas—" I hiss over my pounding heart, not sure I can go through with it.

He ignores me and pulls back the fabric partition.

I inhale sharply and blink. Then blink again.

How is this possible?

Jenny's eyes flutter open, and a dreamy smile comes to her lips. "Dev? Is that you?" A wave of raw emotion flows through me as my brain strains to process what I'm seeing.

Lucas rolls me over to her bedside. I pass a wrist across my eyes to beat back the tide that's forming behind my eyelids.

"I'll be back in a few minutes," Lucas says. The door closes softly behind me.

"Jen?" I say, hardly believing she's lying in front of me. "What are you doing here?"

"I came to save you," she says in a slow murmur still groggy with sleep. "Phillip's kidney's not viable . . . failed the second blood test."

My brain short-circuits and my mouth drops open. "What?" *Phillip?* What the heck did I miss while I was sleeping? Then it hits me, and my elation dampens. "Did Lettie ask you to do this?" I ask and brace myself for her answer.

Jen shakes her head and reaches for my hand. "No. It was

my idea. Long story for later, okay?"

Dumbstruck, I just stare at her. I've been handed the third-best day of my life by the woman I love, and because of her, I'm going to live. The full impact seeps into my brain, and like an eagle released from a cage, my spirit soars.

I press the back of Jenny's hand to my face. "I love you, Jen."

Her breath catches and her eyes glisten. "I love you, too, Dev," she whispers.

This time I do nothing to stop the inevitable. Hot tears escape and sear their way down my cheeks. "I'm sorry I pushed you away."

She smiles wider. "Let's not do this again, all right?"

I nod.

"The drugs are good, though." She chuckles.

I laugh with her, sniff, and desperately wish for a tissue so I can blow my nose. Any pain I feel is overridden by an unbridled sense of happiness.

She squeezes my hand. "Will you be my date for Aunt Jill and Uncle Raine's wedding?"

A smile forms on my lips. "Of course."

"I'll buy my own dress this time," she says.

"You do that, baby," I whisper.

Her eyelids slide shut. "And the car show ... My dad wants you to do the car show with us," she says as she drifts off to sleep.

"Consider it done." I kiss her hand, take a deep breath, and—for the first time in years—I let myself dream.

Chapter 49

Jenny

"FASTER, DEV," I say, panting, and brush my nails lightly down his back, careful to avoid the newly healed scar over his kidney while enjoying every delicious thrust of the man I love.

God, I've missed him. Lucas mandated that Devon wait six weeks to have sex due to both of his surgeries. Not that either of us was in the mood for the first couple of weeks anyway. We both still suffer from fatigue on and off, but it's much better than it was. I'm still amazed that there's a piece of me living permanently inside him.

A side benefit of all the waiting? The break gave me enough time to go on the Pill, and now that we're in the safe zone, we're in full celebration mode.

I grip the top of his backside and sink my fingers into his warm muscled flesh. Flashbacks to the last time we made love, the afternoon of the gala, come rushing back. But a couple of things are different now. For one, joy and promise replace the heaviness I felt then, thinking we were savoring our last moments together. For another, this time, Devon locked his bedroom door.

Devon places a featherlight kiss on the sensitive skin of my neck and says in a low growl, "Your wish is my command." He tucks his head next to mine and picks up his pace to my liking.

I release a satisfied moan from deep in my throat as he rests his hips on mine and rocks deep to fill the aching need inside me. I press my pelvis up to meet him, unable to get enough.

He breathes hard next to my ear.

Curling my hand around his neck, I force out a breathless whisper: "Look at me?" He rises on his elbows and hovers overhead without slowing. I want to see his face as he takes me to the point of shattering.

"Better?" he asks, wearing a faint smile and catching his lip between his teeth as his gaze locks on mine in a look that's both sensual and hungry. Hooking a leg around his thigh, I arch up into him until he's as deep as he can go.

"Dev . . . ," I gasp. The sensation of him sliding against my core sweeps me away until my body surrenders to the involuntary shock waves overtaking me.

Devon's lips part, and his eyes close. His body goes rigid as he lets go to join me. Our bodies mesh in a harmony I've never experienced before. I drink him in through half-closed eyelids and promise myself I'll never tire of this view.

I embrace him body and soul.

He drops down next to me, breathing hard, and pulls me close. I run my fingers through the damp blond curls on his chest and enjoy the feel of his slick skin pressed next to mine. "Was it worth the wait?" I ask through shallow breaths.

"Hell yeah." Resting a hand on his midsection, he chuckles and coughs. "But man, I'm out of shape. Back to the gym this week."

I pinch his nonexistent fat. "Yeah, you're just falling apart," I joke.

He flinches and rolls onto his side, then reels me back in so that our eyes meet and I'm staring into the blue depths of his.

"Hey," he says softly and pushes back a piece of my hair. "Thank you."

"For what?" I ask.

"For saving my life," he says.

I run my fingers lightly over his collarbone and melt my lips onto his to hide the fact that I have no retort. I'm not sure how to explain that in saving him I made up for Brittany's death and found my own redemption. It sounds weird even to me, but I'm finally at peace with death in a way that I never imagined.

Devon's lips ease away from mine, and he collapses back onto the mattress.

"If it wasn't for Lettie, I might not have gotten the chance," I say between heavy breaths, giving credit where credit is due. The air-conditioning kicks on and dances over the moisture on my skin, giving me a chill. I pull up the sheet to cover us. When I think back to the brilliance of Lettie's plan and what turned out to be a sting operation, I can't help being impressed.

Devon snuggles me back to his side and clears his throat. "I know it was your idea to be my donor, but there's something that's been bugging me ever since I saw you lying in that hospital bed."

The tone of his voice tells me that whatever it is, it's weighing heavily on his mind. "What is it?" I ask, absently tracing a random pattern on his chest with my fingertip.

"How did they know you were a match? When were you tested? From what Lucas said, you were rolled into surgery within an hour of landing."

I feel the muscles in his arm clench under my neck as he waits for my answer. I keep tracing. "Just because Lettie never came out and asked me to give you a kidney doesn't mean she wasn't involved."

True to her word, she never even hinted at my being a donor. She didn't need to. As always, she was one step ahead.

She took a bet that I'd at least wonder about my own compatibility before the surgery. What we hadn't counted on was the second test Lucas had to perform unexpectedly when he spotted an elevated level of red blood cells in Phillip's urine—information Lettie procured after the fact.

Devon pushes back to lean on his elbow and stares into my eyes, frowning. "What do you mean?"

"Before we left for San Francisco, she overheard me talking to Lucas about getting a physical, so she used her powers of persuasion to have him test me. I didn't really give it a second thought when he requested a spare vial of blood during my appointment for some personal research he claimed he was conducting." Not really a lie, rather a stretching of the truth. Something I can forgive him.

"*What?*" he snaps. His jaw tightens. "Without your knowledge? I can't believe he agreed. That's unethical."

Chuckling, I reach over and tickle his exposed abs to wipe the indignant look off his face. "Have a little faith, will you?"

A laugh slips out as he bats my hand away. "Hey, stop! This is serious."

"She didn't ask Lucas to reveal the results to her, just to have them handy in case I asked to be tested," I say as he recovers. "Which I did after we landed, and we found out about the second blood panel they conducted on Phillip while we were in the air. Even though his kidneys were a match, the panel indicated he had an autoimmune disorder, which made his kidneys unviable for the transplant. It saved us critical time.

"So before we even left San Francisco, Lucas knew that I was a match for you—as crazy as that turned out to be." I brush a finger lightly over his bottom lip. "I guess we're just made for each other."

He takes my finger and gives it a playful nip. "Lucky for me."

"And give Lettie some credit," I say. "She believed I would

save you given the chance."

"So when did you decide? You never told me," he says, fixing me in his gaze.

Now that I think about it, he's right. We never did talk about it. Rather, we skimmed over it, wanting to get past the whole mess. At the time, I was just thankful Devon would live and that we were back together.

Phillip's health issues were the least of his worries that day. Poor guy hadn't even known he was ill. For that part I truly felt sorry, but for the next part I didn't feel one iota of remorse.

"It happened right after Byron dropped the bombshell."

Devon's eyes brighten, and his lips twist into a smile. "What I would've given to be there for that."

I chuckle. "The look on Phillip's face was priceless," I say, thinking back to our arrival at the hospital on the day of the surgery. Rising up onto my elbow, I recount the blow-by-blow for Devon. His eyes stay riveted to my face as I talk.

John Henshaw and Byron Soames were there to greet us when we arrived. Devon was still unconscious from the first surgery. Little did we know the surprises they had in store for us.

Byron had one doozy in particular to share. After what Lettie and Devon had told him about Drusilla's involvement with Gerald, his suspicions had flared. In addition to Lettie's secret request for a donor match test on Phillip, Byron slipped in a paternity test as part of Phillip's Kingsbridge physical. As fate would have it, between the exhumation of Devon's father's remains and some ill-gotten strands of Gerald's hair, they had enough DNA to draw conclusive results . . .

Phillip wasn't Devon and Lettie's half brother.

Nope. He was their cousin — *Gerald's* son.

"I don't think I've ever seen anyone turn that shade of white before." I giggle. "Lettie made Byron repeat himself twice more, and then she laughed so hard that tears rolled down her face. Phillip went absolutely nuts, spewing all sorts of conspiracy theories, demanding to have the results sent to his lawyer. I thought John might have to Taser him, but instead he threatened to put him under house arrest for disturbing the peace."

Devon's face splits into a wide grin, and he slaps the mattress. "I can't believe I had to miss that."

"Anyway, as soon as I found out that Phillip wasn't your brother, it hit me that maybe I could be a donor. That's when I decided to find Lucas and ask. I didn't have to look far. He was on his way down the hall to deliver the next surprise."

Devon's grin wilts at the edges. "The news about Phillip's kidneys?"

I give a somber nod. Any smugness I feel flees.

"He may be a dick but I'm not happy he's sick. That part sucks," Devon says before his melancholy passes, and the gleam in his eyes changes to quiet mirth. "So what happened after that?"

I skip to the next part of the story. "John told us about Tessa, her attempt on your life, and your father's murder," I relay. "John and his FBI contacts kept Tessa in questioning long enough to prevent her from contacting her co-conspirators. In the meantime, Byron made the executive decision to withhold information on your attack from Lettie while we were in San Francisco, not wanting to disrupt her progress on getting Phillip's consent to donate a kidney and not yet knowing the results of the second test. Which reminds me . . ."

"What?" Devon gives me a questioning look.

"Tessa?"

His expression darkens and he looks away. "What about her?"

"Why did you let her in that day?"

He shakes his head. "I thought she might give something away to help us . . . I never thought she'd turn out to be a murderer." He chews his lip. "There's one thing I can thank her for, though."

My brow shoots up. "What's that?"

A smile flickers across his lips. "I realized I couldn't let you go. I had to be with you whether I lived or died."

Warmth fills my chest, and I lean over and tenderly kiss his lips.

When we separate, he comes back for a second kiss and lingers there. Rather than pulling away, he rests his forehead against mine. "I'm just glad they'll all be brought to justice," he says.

The whole lot of them—Phillip, Tessa, Gerald, and Drusilla—await trial on charges ranging from first-degree murder to insider trading. Happily, Russ will walk away since he took the plea deal Lettie offered him to testify against them.

Then he draws back and narrows his eyes. "So finish your story. What happened with Lucas?"

I shrug. "After all the news, I asked to be tested. He told me that I was a match, and we jumped into action. All I had to do was sign some paperwork and a waiver to pass on all the psych evaluations and counseling," I say. "Meanwhile, Phillip was handed over to the Feds with his computer and a corroborating flash drive with incriminating evidence, compliments of Lettie."

Devon nods.

I kiss the tip of his nose. "So ... that's the scoop. You thought Lettie broke her promise, didn't you?"

Devon blushes and has the good sense to look embarrassed. "Not that so much. I just didn't want you to feel obligated."

I stare at the sexy gold and brown flecks in his eyes and cup his cheek in my palm. "Nothing could've stopped me that day. Nothing," I say in earnest. Which is why I didn't call my mother until the moment before they rolled me into surgery.

I'll never tell Devon about the firestorm that followed between me and my parents. It's one for the history books, and won't be soon forgotten. But in the end, they agreed the ends had justified the means. There's even a glint of pride in their eyes whenever we tell our story.

He kisses my palm, then falls back onto the bed and groans. "We need to hit the shower or we're never going to make it."

I pull away and pick up my cell from the bedside table to check the time. Crap. He's right. Jill and Raine's wedding is in a few hours. My dress supplied by me, thank you very much. I toss the phone down and snuggle back into Devon's arms.

"Five minutes," I murmur, wanting a little more cuddle time after all that talking.

Before I can get too comfortable, he kisses my forehead. "Wait here." There's a mischievous glint in his eye as he rolls out of bed and pads naked to his closet. I roll onto my stomach and enjoy the view before he disappears inside.

He emerges a couple of minutes later, carrying my finished portrait in front of his body like a rectangular piece of clothing. I draw myself up and gasp. "Dev, it's amazing," I say, my eyes darting over the canvas, taking it all in. "What? Wait—" I don't remember resting my hand on the windowsill. My gaze homes in on my fingers, and my lips part in surprise.

I'm wearing an engagement ring in the painting. The one Lettie flashed the night of the gala.

He rests the canvas against the wall and climbs back into bed. "Will you wear my ring?" he whispers. "Be mine for real?"

My heart swells to the point that I'm not sure my chest can contain it. I bite my lip and nod. "Yes."

He props himself on his elbow and passes his finger lightly down my neck and along my shoulder, sending a shiver over my skin. "I don't know where my life is going to end up, Jen.

All I know is that I want you in it. Are you all right with that?"

I know he's still afraid my kidney won't last forever inside him and someday he may need another one. But at least with Phillip out of the picture, his place at Kingsbridge is secure. He has a plan to change the bylaws. If he succeeds, he'll have a chance at the life he wants. The one that will make him the happiest ... though I'm willing to share whatever life he is dealt.

"More than all right." I wave my ring finger at him. "*Ahem.*"

He pulls me into his arms. "It's being sized ... really."

I crane my neck up to meet his gaze. "Should I even ask how you know my ring size?"

He gives me a crooked smile and raises his eyebrows.

"Lettie." I shake my head and snort. "I don't even want to know."

He chuckles and dips in for a kiss, his groin stirring next to my belly. "*Mmm*, stay in bed another couple of minutes?" he growls softly. My core tightens in response. I do a realistic calculation of how much time we need to make it to the wedding and give my answer by running my palm over his swelling length. He moans softly next to my ear.

A smile touches my lips, and I realize that I no longer envy what my aunt found with Raine.

I don't need to, because I found it with Devon.

Epilogue

Two years later...

Jenny

"JENNY?" IT'S LUCAS. My heart rate accelerates. I'd stopped by his office yesterday for a blood test—I'm a month late.

"Hi," I reply into my cell and glance at Devon, who's standing in front of a large canvas on the other side of the studio that used to be Aunt Jill's, contemplating his next brushstroke.

"Good news, sweetheart. You're pregnant," Lucas says through the phone.

I suppress a squeal but can't keep the smile off my face as I rest my hand on my abdomen. "Awesome," I whisper, hardly believing it happened on our first try.

"Jen?"

"Yeah?"

"Based on your HCG levels, it looks like twins, honey. Congratulations."

My smile falters. Okaayyy . . . I can handle that . . . I think.

"Come in tomorrow, we'll talk more," Lucas says. "See you at ten?"

"Yup," I reply and hang up.

"Hey, babe, who was that?" Devon asks, his eyes glued to his canvas. We bought the house from Jill and Raine a couple of months ago, in September, when their new home was finished in Morris Township. Raine worked side by side with an architect to design it. A dream come true for him, and a place they could finally call their own.

I've always loved this house, and between Devon's role on the board of Kingsbridge, his position as the chief art curator, and the project commissions we received—thanks to a ten-year contract from Lettie after she stepped in as CEO—we had more than enough of a down payment to take it off their hands.

Aunt Jill was thrilled to keep it in the family. So was Raine. A lot of good memories were made here, and we're hoping to add some more.

"It was Lucas," I say and glance at my favorite piece of photography on the wall—a Christmas present from my aunt. It's a view of Devon and me from behind, standing next to each other, holding hands. We're both wearing jeans. Our backs are bare except for the string from my bikini top. I have my hair in an upswept do, exposing my neck and shoulders, just the way Devon likes it. The photograph captures our matching script tattoos—our love letters to each other written forever on our skins. We got them on Devon's twenty-fifth birthday. His idea. Well, kind of mine really, but I let him think it was his.

Mine is written just above the scar over my missing kidney. It's to him and reads, "To Dev. I love you. —Jen." His is above the scar from the kidney he received from me. His message back to me reads, "From Jen. I love you more. — Dev."

Surrounding that portrait are the pictures I took of Devon in Central Park the day he painted me in his studio. They're some of my best work, but then again, I have to give credit to the subject.

I smile and walk over to where he's working. He's letting his hair grow—it's not quite as long as Raine's but just enough for him. He has a beard now, too; it's a beautiful sandy blond. Who knew that kissing his supple lips surrounded by all those soft whiskers would make my toes curl?

I throw my arms around his neck and stare into the gold and brown flecks in his blue eyes and wonder if at least one of our children will have them. "I have some news," I say, and I trap my lip between my teeth.

He circles my waist with an arm, careful not to touch me with the paint on his hands, and smiles. The dimple in his cheek dents his beard. "You going to tell me, or do I have to guess?" he asks. There's an unmistakable twinkle in his eyes. The sadness that used to live in the creases is gone.

"You're going to be a father," I whisper and bite my lip harder, waiting for his reaction.

He freezes, and my breath catches in my throat. My gaze never leaves his, and I watch as his eyes glisten. "Really?" he asks. "It worked the first time?"

I nod, and before I know it, my vision blurs and my mouth twists into a smile. "We're having twins."

He stares for a moment, and then hugs me tight. "I love you." His lips take mine and I say a prayer of thanks for this chance with Devon. For being able to save him, and for a chance at living our best lives.

I think about calling my mom and then realize there's someone we owe these lives to who deserves to know before anyone else.

"Let's call Lettie," I say. "I want her to know she's going to be an aunt . . . twice."

Devon

"That'll make her day," I say, squeezing the woman I love tighter in my arms. Twins. Holy crap. I mean, wow.

Jen smiles and kisses me as I've never been kissed. Mr. Happy stirs and decides to throw a party. I try to remind him that I have a painting due for a location opening. He ignores me.

What can I say? I'm living the dream. A life I thought I'd never get. And Lettie has the one she always dreamed of . . . at least professionally. The least I could do was pay her back and give her the company she so desperately wanted to run. God knows I never wanted it. I can't help her in the romance department—not that she'd take my help anyway—but I have to thank her for all the meddling she did in mine. If she hadn't, things would've turned out differently, and not for the better. Man, Lettie can be a pain, but she's loyal to the bone and has always had my back. I can only hope my own kids will have the kind of relationship I've had with Lettie.

I'm exactly where I want to be. Making my art with my wife at my side, and having a chance at a family. Lettie was also right to have me freeze my sperm. Turns out what was left had signs of genetic damage from the cancer treatment, so when we decided to try, we went straight for the good stuff. Another case of sister knows best.

I'm looking forward to telling my mom that she's going to be a grandmother. Lettie found all my father's private holdings and reverted them back my mom, so her care is no longer in question. We combined two of the guest rooms upstairs and moved her here since Lettie travels most of the time as CEO of Kingsbridge. Seemed lonely leaving Mom there by herself. Plus, she and Kitty have become good friends. I've never seen my mom happier. She finally broke down and let us buy her a tablet. We taught her how to use this software package for people without speech. We can actually talk now by way of technology that verbalizes what she types. Even one-handed, Mom's a whiz and not afraid to share her opinions.

I brush a strand of Jenny's hair back behind her ear. Sometimes I think she keeps a few strands loose just so I can do that. "We need to tell Lettie something else, too."

She looks at me with wide blue eyes. "What's that?"

I give her a crooked smile and say a silent prayer of thanks. "That I believe in happy endings again."

Dear Readers,

Thank you so much for reading *SHELTER MY HEART*! I hope you enjoyed Jenny & Devon's story. It's not over! See them again with Jillian & Raine in *SURRENDER MY HEART,* and finally get Kitty & John's full story in a dual timeline that shares both past & present in an emotional story you won't want to miss. If you haven't read it yet, the *CAUGHT UP IN RAINE* Collection is Jillian and Raine's complete story.

For Jenny & Devon's FREE prequel novella, *ONE SUMMER DAY*, visit my website and click on the cover to download: https://lgoconnor.com/library/

Before you go, please consider leaving a review on Amazon, Goodreads, or sharing on Instagram or TikTok (#BookTok). Please and thank you! Truly, word of mouth is what helps authors sell books. Request these books from your local library, or read it with your Book Club (questions to follow)! Did you know that you can request this series from your local library? Stay in touch!

Warmest Regards,

LG O'Connor

L.G. O'Connor

Want more?

Get Caught Up again and again…in the *Caught Up in Love* series. Missed the full story? Get caught up in Jillian and Raine's story from the beginning…

CAUGHT UP IN RAINE (Novel)
Two hearts. One soul-shattering decision. Plagued by loss, bestselling romance author, Jillian Grant, enlists a young landscaper with an uncanny resemblance to the boyfriend she lost at eighteen—and the male lead in her next novel—as her cover model. When Raine ends up in the hospital with no place to go, Jillian offers him a place to stay until sparks ignite, giving Jillian more than she bargained for and forcing her to confront the past that she has tried to forget.

REDISCOVERING RAINE (A Caught Up in Raine Novelette)
Two Hearts. One Magical Night. Pick up where we left off in CAUGHT UP IN RAINE from Raine's point-of-view and experience his magical night with Jillian. But putting a ring on Jillian's finger doesn't mean all is easily forgiven.

CAUGHT UP IN RACHEL (A Caught Up In Raine Novelette)
Two Hearts. One Small Miracle. Giving birth at an "advanced maternal age" isn't without peril, as Jillian discovers when she develops a condition that threatens mother and child.

SHELTER MY HEART (Novel)
Two Weeks. One Life-Changing Proposal. Devon, an ailing young CEO, persuades Jenny, an engaged young woman with a crippling secret that he meets on an airplane, to attend a society gala with him so he can convince the board of

directors he's healthy and going to marry to fulfill the terms of his inheritance and save his family. Two weeks are all Devon needs, and two weeks are all Jenny can give--until the stakes rise, forcing Jenny to face her traumatic past and ally with Devon's twin sister to save his life.

SURRENDER MY HEART (Novel)
Two old flames. One new destiny. Kitty McNally knows sometimes you need to make the best of the worst choices for the ones you love. Ever since their high school breakup, Kitty McNally has secretly loved Detective John Henshaw. The hardest thing she'd ever done was leave him behind—not once, but twice. Decades later, a hint of what they had still shines in his eyes. But only the dead know the secrets she still keeps. At their 35th High School reunion, Kitty has one last chance to confront the past and rekindle their love—if John can forgive her once he learns the truth.

Acknowledgments

I want to say thank you to my tremendous team for all your love and support. Thank you to my critique partner, Joan Sorensen, for her critical feedback early on; the "cross-stitch" beta reading crew (Marilyn, Pat, and Lesley); Wendy Rossi & Rachel MacAulay; my editors, Ray Rhamey, for his guidance and for making me laugh with his editing comments, and Sadie K., for making the manuscript shine; Beth Cone Kramer for answering my questions about kidney matching programs and the procedure she experienced as a donor; and fellow author Kristen Harnisch for offering her very welcome opinion on the ending.

Thank you, my wonderful support team; without you this book wouldn't have reached its full potential.

About the Author

L.G. O'Connor writes romantic women's fiction, paranormal, and suspense that touches the heart with themes of family, redemption, forgiveness, and most of all, hope. She's the author of the multi-award-winning romantic women's fiction trilogy: *Caught Up in Raine, Shelter My Heart,* and *Surrender My Heart*, which follows a family of three New Jersey women who must confront the past to find redemption and second chances. She is also the author of the epic angel & demon fantasy, *The Angelorum Chronicles*. Besides writing, L.G. is a Mayo Clinic & Board-Certified Wellness Coach. She's passionate about connecting with readers and loves food, antiques, and excellent coffee. Find her books or stay in touch:

Photo credit: Oak & Ivy Photography

Looking for something different?

Try The Angelorum Twelve Books

DOWNLOAD EXCERPTS from the DOWNLOADS page on my website, LGOCONNOR.COM

From L.G. O'Connor, award-winning author of **Caught Up in Raine***, comes a 4-book epic angel & demon fantasy series with forbidden and fated love, enemies-to-lovers, found family, and sizzling romance that will leave you wanting more.*

Science and spirit meet in The Angelorum Twelve, an epic angel & demon fantasy. For 2,000 years, the Angelorum—the next generation of angelic Watchers—has maintained the balance of good and evil between humanity and Lucifer's Dark Ones. Both sides have played by the rules…until now. Lucifer has a score to settle and a celestial loophole to seize to restore his rightful place in the final battle of good and evil. Twelve souls will stretch the limits of Heaven and Earth to stop him…

TRINITY STONES, Book One.

There are no coincidences, only destinies to be fulfilled.

Cara Collins is questioning her choices. Between a back-stabbing boss, a non-existent social life, and lingering feelings for Dr. Kai Solomon, a man she can never have, things need to change. After discovering she has the power to restore the gift of youth the same day she receives an unexpected $50 million windfall, it seems Fate agrees.

Learning she is part of a Trinity, Cara is shaken to discover she can become the angelic weapon needed to defeat Lucifer and his Dark Ones in their quest to conquer Heaven and enslave humanity. Torn between her duty to save the world and the promise of a new love, the timing couldn't be worse.

Cara's unseen Nephilim Guardian, Chamuel, knows he has a problem the moment he sees his new charge. His heart stirs for the first time in over a century for the one female on earth forbidden to him under Angelorum Law. After a chance encounter under his human identity, he's powerless to resist her — regardless of the devastating price he will pay if anyone, including Cara, discovers the truth.

When dark forces kidnap Kai and his daughter, forbidden love, betrayal, and destiny collide, forcing Cara to make an impossible choice to save the people she loves without sacrificing the future of humanity, and playing right into Lucifer's hands.

WANDERER'S CHILDREN, Book Two.

Los Angeles. San Francisco. Chicago. New York. The Wanderer's mission three decades ago: secretly sire children to hide his bloodline, and protect them until their destinies unite to fight the final battle between good and evil.

Duty will call soon to gather the rest of the Angelorum Twelve and prepare them for battle. Before that happens, Cara Collins wants one peaceful weekend with her bridesmaids before her wedding to her former Trinity Guardian. But we don't always get what we want …

Life has changed. Cara's newly acquired Nephilim DNA is wreaking havoc on her body, with an overabundance of pheromones triggering a mortifying outbreak of "insta-love" among her friends that would make Cupid proud. If only she could point her arrow at her Trinity Messenger, Michael Swift, who has been running from his attraction to Cara's brazen best friend, Sienna, the only woman ever to skirt his defenses. Even if he wants a future with her, first, he must confront his tormented past, or risk threatening the future of the Angelorum.

After a chance encounter, runaway rock star Brett King is harboring a crush on Cara, but, infatuation aside, Brett is more than he appears. One of the Wanderer's children he and his siblings are the key to gathering the rest of the Twelve souls destined to fight in the final battle of good and evil. With the growing threat of Lucifer's fallen angels, Cara has more to worry about than petty jealousy, drunken debauchery, and a bridal shower. An enemy within the Angelorum is determined to see them fail, if a traitor in Cara's inner circle doesn't destroy them all.

HOPE'S PRELUDE, Prequel Novella, Book 2.5.

Save the *One* who will save them all.

Enter the world of the Angelorum for a glimpse into its origins as destinies entwine to deliver us one step closer to battle …

Stolen as an infant by Achanelech, the Archdemon of Fire, Samuel has lived in his kidnapper's dungeons for over a century. Unaware of his angelic origins, he is persuaded to help capture his Nephilim brethren in exchange for a longer leash and a chance to plot his own escape.

While dealing with visions of her death, Dr. Sandra Wilson races against the clock with research partner, Dr. Tom Peyton and her Nephilim mate, Isa, to develop a vaccine that will save the One.

With Isa ensnared in Achanelech's trap, and the Archdemon closing in on Sandra, it is Samuel who must risk his freedom to ensure the future of the Angelorum … and the mother he has never met.